Strangers in the Forest

By Carol Ryrie Brink

Buffalo Coat★
Harps in the Wind
Stopover
The Headland
The Twin Cities
Château Saint Barnabé
Snow in the River★
The Bellini Look
Four Girls on a Homestead★★
A Chain of Hands★

★Published by and available from the Washington State University Press.
★★Published by and available from the Latah County Historical Society, Moscow, Idaho.

Strangers in the Forest

Carol Ryrie Brink

With a Foreword by Mary E. Reed

Washington State University Press
Pullman, Washington

Published in collaboration with the
Latah County Historical Society
Moscow, Idaho

Washington State University Press, Pullman, Washington 99164-5910

Copyright © by Carol Brink, 1959

This edition is reprinted by arrangement with Macmillan Publishing Company, a division of Macmillan, Inc.

Foreword and cover copyright © by the Board of Regents of Washington State University

Cover photo courtesy of the Latah County Historical Society, Moscow, Idaho

Library of Congress Cataloging-in-Publication Data
Brink, Carol Ryrie, 1895-
     Strangers in the forest / Carol Ryrie Brink ; with a foreword by Mary E. Reed.
       p. cm.
     "Published in collaboration with the Latah County Historical Society, Moscow, Idaho."
     ISBN 0-87422-096-3
     1. Government investigators—Idaho—Fiction. 2. Forests and forestry—Idaho—Fiction. I. Title.
PS3503.R5614S7 1993
813'.52—dc20
                                 93-12731
                                     CIP

Author's Biography

CAROL RYRIE BRINK was born in Moscow, Idaho, in 1895 and spent most of her life there until her junior year in college. Her youthful years spanned the settlement period of rustic one-story, wood-frame buildings lining Main Street to an era of paved roads and automobiles. At a young age her father died of consumption; a crazed gunman murdered her grandfather, one of the town's builders; and her mother committed suicide after an unfortunate second marriage. Carol's maternal grandmother and aunt raised her in their Moscow home.

Brink wrote more than thirty books for both adults and children. Her most acclaimed work, *Caddie Woodlawn,* won the Newbery Medal as the outstanding contribution to children's literature in 1936. It details and synthesizes in fictionalized form the stories her grandmother told her about growing up in Wisconsin. In addition to the Newbery Medal, Brink was honored with the Friends of American Writers Award in 1955, the 1966 National League of American Pen Women's award for fiction, and an honorary degree of Doctor of Letters from the University of Idaho in 1965.

Brink wrote three stories for children based upon her experiences growing up in Moscow. She also wrote an adult series of novels about her family in and around Moscow: *Buffalo Coat* (1944); *Strangers in the Forest* (1959);

and *Snow in the River* (1964). In 1993 the Washington State University Press, in collaboration with the Latah County Historical Society in Moscow, Idaho, reprinted the latter three novels, along with Brink's previously unpublished reminiscences about characters she knew in Moscow, *A Chain of Hands*.

Carol Ryrie Brink died in 1981 in San Diego. Her home town recognized her posthumously with the naming of a building on the University of Idaho campus in her honor and with the naming of the children's wing of the Moscow-Latah County Public Library after her.

Among Brink's contributions to Western American literature are her works about her native state of Idaho. In view of the relatively few Idaho writers of this period, that is of interest in itself. But there are more important considerations for recognizing Brink, especially her portrayal of a West between two eras.

Although many writers concentrate on a colorful pioneer period and the heroic feats of those who plowed virgin ground, opened the first mines, and platted towns, the chronicle of those who followed is certainly equally or more important. These were the people who established the libraries, invested their lives and fortunes in the new communities, and generally created civic life as we recognize it today. Brink's portrayal of the lives and experiences of men and women in an Idaho town during this crucial period of growth and maturing serve as an antidote to numerous works about the wild American frontier. In her three Idaho novels and *A Chain of Hands* she shows us a small town whose citizens had to weigh justice with empathy, who had to learn that the resources of the West were not entirely at their personal disposal, and who discovered that the promise of these new lands was at times ephemeral.

Acknowledgments

I N 1987 THE Washington State University Press and the Latah County
Historical Society collaborated in the publication of two books, Richard
Waldbauer's *Grubstaking the Palouse* and Keith Petersen's *Company Town*.
The recognition those two works received, including awards from the American Association for State and Local History, the Idaho Library Association,
and the Council for the Advancement of Secondary Education, greatly
pleased both institutions and led the two to seek ways in which to collaborate
again. This reprint of *Strangers in the Forest* represents another such venture.

Carol Ryrie Brink wrote more than thirty books for children and adults.
Idahoans frequently point out that Ezra Pound was born in the state, although he left as an infant, and that Ernest Hemingway lived here for a
while. Both writers were obviously accomplished, but neither wrote about
Idaho. In seeking true regional writers—writers who knew the state and wrote
about it—Idahoans have virtually ignored Brink.

In the late 1970s and early 1980s the Latah County Historical Society
undertook several projects, including giving presentations about Brink
throughout the state, with the goal of bringing recognition to this talented
writer. Those efforts have largely been rewarded with renewed recognition
for Brink in regional anthologies, with the recent publication of a biography of the author in Boise State University's Western Writers Series, and
with the posthumous naming of two significant buildings in Moscow in
Brink's honor.

In 1992 the Historical Society and WSU Press agreed to collaborate
on a major publication venture that would bring back into print Brink's
three adult novels about Idaho, *Buffalo Coat* (originally published in 1944),
Strangers in the Forest (1959), and *Snow in the River* (1964). In addition,
the two collaborated in the publication of Brink's previously unpublished
reminiscences about characters she knew growing up in Moscow, *A Chain
of Hands.*

This publication venture would not have been possible without the kind
assistance of the Brink family, and we are indebted to Carol's son David
and daughter Nora Brink Hunter for their encouragement and help.

The Latah County Historical Society has gained a national reputation
for its publications program. Special thanks are due to its publications committee and board of trustees for their foresight in recognizing the importance

of regional publishing in general and Carol Brink's work specifically. I would especially like to thank our two longtime friends, Carolyn Gravelle and Kathleen Probasco, who maintained unswerving faith in this publication venture for almost a decade. I have greatly profited from their encouragement and affection for our native author. I also wish to thank Bert Cross, who supported this project when others became discouraged.

At the WSU Press, I would like to thank my colleagues and friends director Thomas Sanders; assistant director, Mary Read; editors Keith Petersen, Jean Taylor, Glen Lindeman, and John Sutherland; designer Dave Hoyt; and promotions coordinator Vida Hatley. All of them proved not only receptive but also enthusiastic when approached about a possible Brink publication project. We at the Historical Society want them to know how much we have appreciated their support and collaboration over the years.

Mary E. Reed
Latah County Historical Society
Moscow, Idaho

Foreword to the Second Edition

WHEN CAROL BRINK was 15 years old, her aunt, Elsie Watkins, invited her and three friends to spend the summer at her homestead cabin in the Idaho wilderness. The cabin was 28 miles by packhorse after a train ride on the Washington, Idaho & Montana Railroad to Bovill and a horse-drawn-stage ride to Clarkia. Brink remembered being "wild to spend the summer there" after growing up hearing stories of Aunt Elsie's adventures. Years later, Brink came across the letters she had written to her grandmother from that cabin, and was surprised to find "how little they add to the wealth of detail which I remember." Indeed, it is this richness of her memories of that summer in 1911 that surrounds our senses with the presence of great white pine forests. Here under the lofty green canopy she brings to life an assortment of characters to whom we so avidly listen.[1]

Strangers in the Forest is the most complicated of Brink's trilogy of novels set in north Idaho. The other two, *Buffalo Coat* and *Snow in the River,* have also been reprinted in a collaborative publishing venture between the Washington State University Press and the Latah County Historical Society. Along with recreating the personalities and motives of the strangers who hoped to claim tracts of valuable timber land, the novel also chronicles the fruition of the conservation movement in setting aside wilderness areas and the beginning of a national forest service. Although Brink was normally a writer of memory, imagination, and emotion, this novel demanded considerable research into the establishment of forest reserves in the West under the leadership of the forest service's first director, Gifford Pinchot. She attempted to make the book as accurate as she could. When the *Reader's Digest* selected the novel for condensation, it received a note from the chief forester of the United States corroborating the facts and recommending the book. Brink was pleased with the official endorsement, as well as having her novel included in the *Reader's Digest Condensed Books* series. However, she remarked that at first she was afraid to look at the condensation: "They cut out most of the factual part of it, but kept all the romance."[2]

The premise for the plot of *Strangers* begins with the 1906 act of Congress that created a forest reserve system, passed in response to a rampant destruction and exploitation of natural resources. However, the act contained a great loophole. It permitted homesteading of lands within national forests if the homesteaders could prove that these lands were more suitable for agriculture than as forest reserves. The lumber companies hurried to take advantage of this provision by helping to locate homesteaders on sections containing valuable timber. One such region was in north Idaho where the Weyerhaeuser conglomerate had decided to build a logging empire around its new town of Potlatch. Here the Forest Service under Pinchot decided to do battle, to investigate the homesteads, and then hold hearings.

The book's interpretation of the historical struggle between speculators and the government, through Pinchot and his men, was not entirely a product of research. Brink had personal experience with all types of speculators. Her stepfather, Nat Brown, dealt in timber lands. He was the son of C. O. Brown, whose interest in Idaho white pine had led him to convince Frederick Weyerhaeuser to purchase vast tracts of land in northern Idaho. Brink's mother, Henrietta, and Nat Brown had entertained Weyerhaeuser and his sons at dinner.[3]

Brink was also well acquainted with smaller timber speculators, because they included many Moscow women like her aunt Elsie. Elsie's father, Dr. William Watkins, had refused his daughter's request to become a nurse. She had no livelihood and continued to live with her mother after her father's death. The homestead was an opportunity to make money, but just as important it was "a chance to get out and do something and have some adventures."[4] These women and others laid claims to homesteads under the pretext of turning them into agricultural enterprises; upon receiving ownership, they could then sell them to the timber companies. The scheme was not as calculating as it might appear. In a time when most women could not make their own living, a homestead claim could be a means to financial security. The homesteads were not entirely free. The claimant had to prove up on the claim, which meant living there during the summer and spending some time on the land during the winter. This was not an easy task, for homesteaders on snowshoes followed a trail over a high pass that even horses could not navigate. In addition, the homesteaders had to build a cabin and barn, plant a garden, and in other ways carry out the pretense of making a self-sufficient home. For many, if not most, the connection to their claims was emotional as well. Although the homesteaders built cabins and barns, traveled back and forth to their claims, and tended their struggling gardens in this region of poor soil and short growing seasons, the government investigators concluded that the purpose of the claims was for speculation and not settlement. The homesteaders, including Elsie Watkins, lost their homesteads and their investments.

In *Strangers in the Forest*, Bundy Jones, a young forest ranger in the guise of a botanist, has the task of investigating the settlers' true intentions.

Indeed, Brink had met just such a young man that summer of 1911, and she carried with her the suspicion that he was really working as an agent for the Forest Service. In the tension between the homesteaders and Bundy, Brink is able to present with understanding and empathy the interests of both. After all, she knew her aunt's great disappointment when the government disallowed the homesteaders' claim and put the land into forest reserve. As Brink recalled, "Aunt had put a good deal of time and money into the place and we loved the homestead dearly. Yet it was never really intended as a home, and it is a pleasure now to know that it remains unspoiled, virgin forest, part of Idaho's rich heritage."[5]

Brink portrayed Bundy Jones as the one person who belonged in the forest; the others were strangers who did not. Yet in the process of living in the wilderness, they learn much about themselves. The character least prepared for the tasks of creating a homestead, Meg Carney, learns the most from her experiences. She is modeled on Elsie Watkins, who, as Brink remembers, went into the forest as a "sickly, green, inexperienced girl," but by the end had matured and was "ready to cope with anything. She felt that she'd grown up."[6] Through Meg's character, Brink explores the thoughts and experiences of town women learning to live in rustic, isolated conditions. In fact, when Brink herself returned the summer of 1912 to her aunt's cabin, this time without her friends, she experienced "the most lonely summer I'd ever spent, and I wasn't very happy about it."[7]

Like Elsie, Meg discovered she could be brave, resourceful, and independent. At the government hearing to decide whether homesteaders would be allowed to take possession of their claims, Eye MacGillicuddy, the old-time forest ranger, defends Meg. His assessment of her reveals the changes Brink witnessed in her aunt: "She started out a wee bit of a lass that every misfortune happened to, but she's toughened up now. I seen her grow up...on that homestead...she walks trail the way a man does.... She's got her a sourdough bucket and she rustles her own wood. One winter they was lost in the snow, trying to get in there. She froze her feet and had to stay alone in her cabin whilst the cougars yelled outside.... Seems like she's earned her right to that homestead if any woman has."[8]

Meg's antithesis is another woman in the forest, Lorena Carney, who married Meg's brother. Lorena is a familiar character in many of Brink's novels, particularly *Snow in the River* and *Stopover*. She is the beautiful, restless woman who cannot be satisfied with her lot in life. Lorena wants the homestead for the money it will bring, and she despises her weak husband who has brought her to this crude cabin. Although Brink maintained that her restless women were fictional creations, most probably she modeled them after her other aunt, Winnifred Watkins. The youngest of the three Watkins daughters, Winnifred was high-spirited, self-centered, talented, and adventurous. Like Winnifred, Lorena is full of ambition, and she disdains the mundane responsibilities of making a home and raising children. Of all the strangers, she is the most ambitious and the most articulate. Yet even here, Brink is able to show another side of a type of woman for whom she had little affection. Although her youthful poverty had taught Lorena not to depend on others, the birth of her child in the forest brings a tenderness. In one of the most poignant passages of the novel, Lorena holds the helpless, sickly baby, tears running down her cheeks, "not in anger, but in sorrow and pity for another life, for something outside herself."[9]

The character of Jeff Carney, Meg's brother and the nephew of the great timber speculator Ralph, is clearly fictional. Yet the link between him and Brink's stepfather, Nat Brown, raises interesting contrasts. Brink never admitted the true harm Brown caused her mother and herself, but it must have been a traumatic experience to exchange the kind and gentle Alexander Ryrie for this man who brought loud and frequent arguments, dissension, and finally her mother's suicide into her young life. In the novel, Jeff is almost the opposite, dominated by his wife and crippled by his lack of resolution and strength. Even though Jeff fails, the author reveals another side of his character, perhaps to soften what could have been her own judgment of her stepfather. Jeff Carney finally realizes that the only right course of action was "to pull out now and leave the forest as they had found it. He thought only that they had all been wrong to come here in the first place.... He remembered how the forest had first moved and delighted him when he came here as a boy. Yes, I am on the wrong side, he thought. I have sold my soul for a mess of pottage."[10]

Many of the characters in *Strangers* are based on people the 15-year-old Brink met that summer at her aunt's cabin, a testament to her keen powers of observation and recall, even at a young age. One of the central figures is the French Canadian lumberjack, Charlie Duporte. During that summer in the forest, Brink, her young companions, and her aunt had met a strange man suspected of murder. The unwritten law of the forest demanded that strangers be given a meal, and on their part, the strangers were required to fire a couple of shots about a quarter of a mile up the trail, signaling their arrival. "Silenced for once," Brink writes, "we girls sat in a solemn row on one of the bunks and watched the dark little French Canadian with the unsavory reputation putting away Aunt's homemade bread and dried-apple sauce with an honest man's relish."[11] From that brief but strong impression, Brink created in Duporte a resourceful man of the woods: strong, masculine, and handsome. True to her ability to see both sides of a person, Brink gives him a tenderness as well, and he is the one character who truly knows how to meet a crisis, whether childbirth or a fire storm. Other minor characters in the novel bring to life the history of the Idaho forests, like the lumberjacks who build Meg's cabin and barn and then quarrel over her in a rowdy fight, and the old forest ranger, MacGillicuddy, tight-lipped but devoted to his mongrel dog. The proprietress of the saloon in Cold Spring (Clarkia), Madame Pontarlier, is an intriguing portrait of the real French woman, Madame Pierre, the four high school friends had met on their way in to Aunt Elsie's cabin. When Elsie announced that she was taking them to call on the saloon keeper's wife, the girls were shocked and amazed. "But it seemed that Madame Pierre was a very proper person, and, as one of the few women in town, one to be reckoned with." What they found in the back of the saloon was "a little round French woman with expressive white hands and wings of black hair laid smoothly back on either side of her tranquil brow. . . . Madame was a genuine personality. In this tiny room behind a saloon on the edge of a rough Western frontier, she had managed to create an atmosphere of charm, respectability, and middle-class propriety. I am sure that the Saturday night revels of the men from the timber must always have been tempered by Madame's lace curtains and pink bows and her elegant sobriety."[12] Madame Pontarlier's room in the Cold Springs saloon follows the original model, but it also becomes the scene in which the strangers unknowingly reveal their own strengths and weaknesses.

Beyond the interplay of the characters and plot, the great western white pine forest of northern Idaho dominates the story. Brink advised young readers and writers to use all of their five senses in learning about the world. The young girl who listened so avidly to her aunt's stories about the cabin and then lived there for two summers was able to recreate this special landscape and open all of our senses to it. She takes us, as strangers, into a world of smell, sight, sound, taste, and touch. The novel begins as the stage travels through a meadow approaching Cold Spring. The young botanist, Bundy Jones, is drawn into this place, where the "thimbleberries, like miniature wild roses, bloomed, and there were some late-blossoming syringa and sweetberry honeysuckle to add heavy and lighter perfumes to the bracing odor of pine. The air was still and, beside the liquid odors of pine and syringa, there was a dry smell of dust and of horses. The stage seemed to be moving between green walls in a close opacity of summer."[13] When the homesteaders reach the heart of the forest on horseback, they enter another world of beauty. "The path was soft and deep in brown needles, and a palpable stillness was only intensified by the snorting and blowing of the horses and the alien tinkle of pack bells. . . . The white pine grows straight and strong with a sturdy masculine upthrust that is suddenly crowned by a feminine delicacy of foliage. . . . Beneath interlocking boughs the sun is filtered away in an unseen sky, leaving a cathedral dimness under high groined arches."[14]

Like other western novels, the landscape of trees, water, and mountains dominates the characters and events in this one. Brink's time in Idaho encompassed an era of unusual opportunity for exploiting and experiencing a wilderness close at hand. The journey to Clarkia and then to the homestead was in reality a short distance, but it meant a transition from a town with all the accoutrements of western civilized life to a single-room cabin where neighbors were miles apart and a deep snow might mean starvation. This type of frontier was short-lived, and by the time Carol Brink had matured into a young woman, highways, logging roads, and hiking trails made this wilderness accessible to most travelers. Through *Strangers in the Forest* Brink offers us a penetrating insight into this brief period of time. The time was not always marked by pioneer courage or a restorative experience. Living alone in the forest could also exact a high price on the human psyche, and Brink was able to suggest what could happen to people living in isolation.

On their way to their claims the homesteaders come into a valley. The packer, McSweeney, fires a shot into the air to announce their arrival to the family living up the trail. As they approach they see a man and woman standing in the doorway. A small boy runs toward the pack train, shouting an excited greeting. "His arms were spread in an unconscious gesture of welcome. About his thin legs flapped a man's old overalls which had been tailored unskillfully to his size. He ran along beside the horses, leaping and shrieking with joy. The man and woman stood somber in long-held silence, like sleepers disturbed in a dream. . . . It was only when McSweeney held up a packet of mail for them that they came out of their sullen dream and began to smile and talk." Their paralyzing sense of lonely detachment then dissolves.[15] Brink's perspective as a woman from a period of rapid change shows us that the western landscape could be defeating as well as restorative. Through her skill as an author she creates this interlocking world of wilderness and human frailty that is firmly rooted in the history of north Idaho.

MARY E. REED
Latah County Historical Society
Moscow, Idaho
May 1993

Notes

1. Carol Ryrie Brink, *Four Girls on a Homestead* (Moscow, Id.: Latah County Historical Society, 1977), p. 5. The book is illustrated with Brink's sketches and photographs of that summer in 1911.
2. Transcript of taped responses to questions from Sam Schrager, June 1975. Available at Latah County Historical Society library, Moscow, Idaho.
3. Interview with Carol Ryrie Brink by Mary E. Reed, July 1981, San Diego, California, transcript of tape 4, p. 6. The tapes and transcripts of a series of interviews with Brink in July 1981 are in the collection of the Latah County Historical Society library, Moscow, Idaho.
4. Brink oral history transcript of tape 4, p. 5.
5. *Four Girls on a Homestead,* p. 33.
6. Brink oral history transcript of tape 4, p. 3.
7. June 1975 Brink transcript, p. 23.
8. *Strangers in the Forest,* p. 304.
9. *Strangers in the Forest,* p. 30.
10. *Strangers in the Forest,* pp. 256, 257.
11. *Four Girls on a Homestead,* p. 16.
12. *Four Girls on a Homestead,* pp. 8-9.
13. *Strangers in the Forest,* p. 2.
14. *Strangers in the Forest,* p. 68.
15. *Strangers in the Forest,* pp. 68-69.

Foreword to the First Edition

In the Panhandle of northern Idaho, there is a green and silent wilderness which few people know. The Clearwater River with its many branches and tributaries flows through it, drawing down turbulent waters from the snows that fall in the Bitterroot Mountains.

Much of the region is covered with Western white pine trees which stand straight, tall and close together. This seems a virgin forest in which a man-made history has no place. Yet Lewis and Clark journeyed through here in 1805 and returned by the same trail in 1806. The Lolo Trail was already worn deep in many places by moccasined feet before Lewis and Clark encountered its hardships. In 1832 John Work of the Hudson's Bay Company passed through the region with a large company of trappers and Indians. In 1854 Captain Mullan used the Lolo Trail while seeking a pass for a transcontinental road. In 1860 Captain Pierce discovered gold in the region, and for a time a surge of hopeful miners fanned out and prospected every major stream in the forest. In 1877 Chief Joseph led his people, two hundred and fifty Nez Percé warriors and nearly twice as many women and children, along the Lolo Trail in his attempt to escape General Howard and the United States soldiers.

But all these travelers were transients in the forest. They suffered hardships or defeat. Lewis and Clark found this one of the most arduous parts of their journey. Later, when Captain Mullan built a wagon road from the east, he chose a more northerly route that presented less difficulty. The gold rush was short lived and the prospectors soon sought other streams. Sometimes old mine shafts were left yawning emptily among the trees, but, for the most part, mining had been confined to streams, and the floods of spring obliterated traces of abandoned hopes. Even the Indians were finally overtaken and defeated.

The mountain forest put up a strong resistance to change. It remained virgin and silent. So we see it today, although there are many complicated reasons why it remains so. During the early years of the century when the lumberman's slogan was still "cut out and get out," Gifford Pinchot, head forester of the United States, made himself the leader of the effort to conserve the nation's forests, streams and grazing lands. It would be an oversimplification of the facts to say that Secretary of the Interior Ballinger was the leader of the Special Interests. He was a politician with wealthy friends interested in lumber and coal, and if he became a symbol of undeserving privilege, it was Pinchot who made him so. Their battle was like the single combat of medieval times in which two men on horseback jousted against each other to resolve the quarrel of opposing masses of silent people.

The simile of chivalric jousting is not accidental. Gifford Pinchot, or G.P. as his friends liked to call him, was a kind of modern Don Quixote. A long thin man with high nose and drooping moustaches, he had not only the aristocratic bearing but the fanatic single-mindedness of the mad Don. He had been warring against land graft and special privilege for twenty years. With his friend Teddy Roosevelt behind him, he charged the windmills of long-entrenched greed for the people's good. "The greatest good for the greatest number" was the slogan he put up against the cry to "cut out and get out."

Pinchot had had his training as a young man in the forests of France. He admired the ordered beauty of the French forests, and he saw how cutting and clearing could be practiced in the forest without total destruction; how new trees could be planted to replace the old; how underbrush and slashings could be cleared out to prevent fire, and the whole could be made beautiful and productive with intelligent planning. It was this ideal, a sort of "age of reason" in nature, that Pinchot brought from France to America.

In the first years when the new Forest Reserves had been under the supervision of the Land Office and the Department of the Interior, rangers were stationed here and there throughout the region, but they were untrained men. The Land Office was unprepared to deal with the sudden accession of so much public land. Fires raged unchecked on some parts of it, in other places private and monopolistic enterprises entered unhampered and cut or stole what timber they wished. The railroads took their cut. The Land Office had had a long history of careless selling and giving away of land to settlers and private enterprises.

In 1905 the Forest Service, re-established under the Department of Agriculture, began the herculean task of policing the western reserves. Yet the job was so enormous that many regions continued under the old system for a long time.

Meantime, an even tougher problem had to be faced in the rush of homesteaders into the newly opened regions. For an Act of Congress, passed in June, 1906, left one great loophole in the forest reserve system. It permitted the homesteading of lands within the national forests, if examination showed these lands to be more suitable for farming than for forest purposes. Many people looked on this law as a means of acquiring valuable timberland. The Forest Service refused to list lands which did not give reasonable assurance of supporting a home; but here was the doubtful ground of battle. How could the Forest Service know its newly acquired millions of acres well enough to say "This plot is farming land, and this is forest"? And in the meantime the lumber companies, seeing with apprehension the ending of their national favors, were rushing homesteaders into the disputed forest regions with the hope of grasping what they could before the Forest Service became strong enough to protect its holdings.

Between them, Pinchot and President Roosevelt decided on the word "conservation" to express their belief that all natural resources should be considered together for the good of man.

Conservation was not a particularly good name, since it connoted saving, whereas they meant intelligent usage; it suggested cautious, old line policies, whereas they were almost radically socialistic in their intention of giving back to the people what was being taken from them by the monopolies and special interests. Yet the name persisted. The conservation issue was fundamentally a moral issue, and T.R. took it up enthusiastically and laid about him with his Big Stick to see that it was accepted.

Under Roosevelt, Pinchot appeared to be on the way to a successful demolition of the windmills of graft. Later, however, under Taft, all sorts of hard-won land rights began to slide quietly back into the grasp of corporate ownership and big business. A final struggle was inevitable. If the waste lands of the East and Midwest were beyond help, still there was virgin country in Alaska, Washington, Oregon, Montana, and Idaho worth saving.

Here was a battleground for the young crusaders with whom Pinchot had surrounded himself. His fanaticism inspired loyalty, and he was training a group of young men whose enthusiasm for the public good was equal to his own. It was a time for idealistic young men. The musical comedy war with Spain had only whetted the young men's appetite for high adventure. They had not yet been disillusioned by scientific slaughter on a world-wide scale.

Bundy Jones was one of G.P.'s young men, and he was on his way, for the first time, into the white pine country of the Idaho Panhandle with idealism and determination written all over him. Yet this is only incidentally the story of the struggle between conservation and the lumber interests. Primarily it is the story of a small group of civilized individuals who returned to primitive living, and of what the forest did to each of them.

I

THE STAGE

1.

The stage road between Bolster and Cold Spring in the Idaho Panhandle was newly made. Rutted, narrow, and uneven with rocks and stretches of corduroy, it wound between walls of heavy vegetation. In earlier years the trappers, the homesteaders, the adventurers had gone on horseback to Cold Spring, following blazed trees at first and then a pack trail. Other trails led from Cold Spring into the wilderness, sometimes traversing a section of the old Lolo Trail that was worn deep by many feet. Most things in this country, however, were as raw and new as this road, which linked the logging train at Bolster with the pack trails of Cold Spring.

The stage was a large open wagon with five cross seats and a place for luggage in the back. Four horses pulled it. The afternoon was hot, and most of the incongruously assorted passengers had been jolted and thrown about long enough to have become thoroughly insensible to the scenery.

Only Bundy Jones sat bolt upright, looking about him with the unflagging interest of curious and dedicated youth. He had pored over imperfect and newly platted maps in Pinchot's house during the previous winter, and he had the happy conviction that whatever he observed now, keenly and truthfully, would be important to the sum of knowledge which they were trying to amass in Washington about the Western forests.

He felt responsible and important, away on a man's errand, and fit to accomplish it. His quick eye noted where the slashings and devastation of the lumbering invasions began to give way to un-

1

molested country. Trained primarily as a botanist, it was as a botanist that he expected to present himself at Cold Spring where horses would be waiting to take him into the virgin white pine country. It was part of the plan made for him in Washington that he should not identify himself in any way with the Forest Service or the Department of Agriculture. They already had a ranger of sorts in here, and there were other things they wanted of Bundy, things that were better accomplished unofficially.

Nevertheless, his training as a botanist made him name every plant he saw along the wayside, either consciously or unconsciously, much as a musician may hear music at the fringe of his consciousness while conducting the ordinary affairs of his daily life. After the cutover land came scrub and lodgepole pine as the raw, new road wound gradually upward. A heavy underbrush closed in on either side of the road, and Bundy said to himself: serviceberry, huckleberry, elder. Deeper in the woods thimbleberries, like miniature wild roses, bloomed, and there were some late-blossoming syringa and sweetberry honeysuckle to add heavy and lighter perfumes to the bracing odor of pine. The air was still and, beside the liquid odors of pine and syringa, there was a dry smell of dust and of horses. The stage seemed to be moving between green walls in a close opacity of summer.

Besides being an enthusiastic botanist, Bundy was also a rather impressionable young man. While he noted *Sambucus melanocarpa*, kinnikinick and pipsissiwa along the wayside, he saw also that there were two very pretty girls in the seat ahead of him.

He knew much less about women than he knew about plants, but he was not averse to learning more. A certain reticence had held him back, but he could not help looking at these young women, partly because they were handsome, and partly because they were utterly incongruous on a frontier stage. One of them was blonde; the other and handsomer of the two was dark. They were dressed fashionably in light-colored summer dresses, and securely pinned to their upswept hair by ornamental hatpins, they wore the large and fantastic hats that were in fashion.

Above the noise of horse's hoofs and hard-rimmed wheels on a raw road, Bundy could not help overhearing snatches of their chatter.

"So I said to him, 'No, I haven't got another dance left on

my card,'" the blonde and younger-looking girl was saying, "and it was perfectly true, I was all filled up. And you know what he said, Lorena?"

"Well, what?" the dark girl asked. She seemed indulgent and slightly bored by the other girl's naïveté.

"He said, 'Let's throw away the card then.' Really, that's what he said. Wasn't it amusing of him?"

"And did you?" Lorena asked.

"Did I what?" inquired the younger girl.

"Why, throw away the card."

"Of course not," said the blonde girl, shocked by the idea. "But when they put in the extra dance I looked all around for him, but he wasn't there."

"Dancing with someone else?" said the older girl lazily.

"Well, I s'pose so," said the younger one ruefully. "Still, I'd vow he preferred me. I did look nice, didn't I, Lorena? Even in the old blue dress?"

The dark girl yawned and stretched. "Oh, yes, you did, Meggie," she said carelessly.

"What a little fool!" Bundy said to himself of the younger girl. His inexperience with women made him scorn some and idealize others. Without understanding them as well as he understood flowers, he was accustomed to looking at them in the same way, viewing them almost academically. The rarer types gave him the esthetic pleasure which he derived from arbutus at the edge of snow or a field of blooming squaw grass on a mountainside. The common variety of girls he classified with the yarrow and chickweed that gather dust along every roadside.

Now he looked at the older girl, the one called Lorena, with his arbutus-and-snow admiration. She was certainly an unusually fine specimen. The smooth dark hair. The mysterious dark eyes with straight black brows, and the full red lips, gave her a richness of coloring that immediately attracted attention. Her features were neither regular nor particularly distinguished, yet they combined well to produce an opulent effect. There was petulance in the girl's face, and also enigma, a hint of unseen depths that were immediately disturbing and might in the long run be rewarding.

As she talked to the other girl, her face was half turned toward him, and Bundy found that he could not take his eyes away from her. Apparently she was not insensible to admiration. She must have felt his gaze like a stirring of air on the side of her face, for she turned slowly with a graceful movement of the neck and shoulders and looked at him. The full mouth curved at the corners into a half smile, but the eyes were wide and serious. Those eyes, dark and lustrous, held his without embarrassment in a long look. Gradually it seemed to Bundy that the eyes began to smile with the mouth, bathing him in unexpected intimacy and approbation. Surprised and disconcerted, Bundy found himself blushing. In the end it was the girl who lowered her eyes and turned back to her companion.

The stage rattled on, the horses sneezing and blowing, the driver occasionally cracking his whip, or shouting a direction.

A lumberjack, probably a French Canadian to judge from his swarthiness and smart new Hudson's Bay jacket, sat on the seat with the driver. He kept looking around at the two girls on the seat behind him, as if he, too, were attracted by that exotic beauty. He talked very volubly to the driver, but his sly glances backward showed which audience he wished to reach.

The young blonde girl, wrapped up in her own recent past, paid no attention to him. But Bundy noted fretfully that the dark girl accepted with calm appreciation this indirect homage as she had accepted his own admiring stare.

The stage was not crowded and Bundy had one of the cross seats to himself. Behind him sat another woman, middle-aged, and wearing a flamboyantly feminine hat over a high-arched masculine nose. He had noticed her briefly as they climbed aboard and then had forgotten her. Now she leaned forward so that one of her feathers tickled his ear, and said to him in a low voice, "Do you know them?"

"No," Bundy said, half turning around to look at the woman who had spoken.

"They're the Carney girls, real nice ladies, they are. Of course, you know Jeff, don't you? I s'pose he's locating you."

"No," Bundy said a trifle irritably.

"Aren't you taking up a homestead?" the woman asked.

"No," said Bundy for the third time, but now his interest was somewhat aroused. "Are you?" he asked.

"Sure," said the woman. "I'll try anything if it'll earn an extra nickel."

Bundy looked her over and he thought that she might be almost anything except a homesteader. Women's hats in 1908 were architectural achievements and Bundy was used to them. He had merely noticed the hats worn by the girls in the seat ahead of him. But the older woman's hat was so large and overflowing with bird and blossom that it was overwhelming. Yet the woman beneath the hat looked respectable, even virginal, and at the same time competent and self-assured. She saw that he was looking at her hat, and she said, "Don't you like it?"

"Ma'am," Bundy said, "I'm a botanist and I don't like blue roses. Pink ones or yellow ones or red ones, all right. But I object to blue ones. And the feathers are green. What kind of bird has green feathers?"

"All right," she said, "so you think my hat's loud. That's just what I want you to think. I'm a milliner, and I say, if you've got a talent for creation, you might as well show it. A shop window stays in one spot and maybe people look in it, maybe they don't. But, if you wear your own hats, you can circulate them and people look and see them."

"That seems reasonable," Bundy said.

"I made the Carney girls' hats too," she added in a confidential voice not intended to reach the Carney girls' ears. "But they've got pretty faces, they don't need loud hats. However, you take an old maid like me—"

"Old maid?"

"Yes," the woman said with a gleam of humor in her eye. "My name is Nan O'Rourke and it's just plain Miss. I'm one of those that missed it. You know the story about the old maid praying in the woods at night for the Lord to send her a husband? An owl in a tree overhead said 'Who-o? Who-o?'

" 'Oh, anybody, Lord. Any man will do,' the old maid said. That's me all over." Miss O'Rourke laughed.

Bundy saw that he was in for it. Since he preferred traveling with his own silent thoughts instead of with this kind of running chatter, he laughed perfunctorily and was about to turn away. But

Miss O'Rourke said, "I told you mine. It's only fair you tell me yours."

"My name is Bundy Jones," he said.

"Bundy is a funny name," she said.

"I think so too," Bundy said. "It's a family name. Don't think I haven't had to suffer for it."

"And you're a botanist," Miss O'Rourke pursued. "Is that a man's job?"

"I believe so," Bundy replied shortly, and this time he definitely turned away. He thought that the woman had a talent for saying the uncomfortable thing, but probably he had started it with his aversion to blue roses. Anyway, he refused to be chivied into further comment.

Carney, he thought to himself, so their name is Carney. The name was somehow familiar to him, but his mind did not make a connection. And so Blue Roses made their hats? She could probably tell me a lot more about them if I wanted to listen. And they're going to homestead? all of them, I expect, with city stamped all over them. Well, they'll bear watching along with the others.

The horses slowed to a walk, climbing laboriously upward in the heavy heat. The passengers fell silent. The blonde girl took off her hat and put her head on the dark girl's shoulder and went to sleep.

Stirred by his encounter with Lorena Carney's eyes, Bundy kept thinking about her and watching her. Could he make her turn around again if he stared long enough? He saw how neatly her head was poised on the graceful neck and how a mist of dark hair clustered at the nape. The line of her jaw was sharp and clean, and high on her cheek there was a dusky rose of summer heat. He coughed experimentally, but she did not look around. The blonde girl slept heavily with gently parted lips. Perhaps Lorena was asleep too. How could he know when he could not see her amazing eyes? She was very still, and he fancied that she would have a talent for indolence, a gift for idling away hours. He could almost see her, lying relaxed and fresh among colored pillows, and smiling her half smile while the eyes remained grave.

Finally she shifted the heavy weight of the younger girl a little farther forward on her shoulder.

"Wake up, Meg," she said. "You're giving me a crick."

The younger girl woke with a start and sat up staring around her.

"Oh, it's hot and tiresome," she said. "I wish we were there."

"We will be soon," Lorena said. As she spoke she lifted her left hand to push up the stray hairs at the nape of her neck. The fingers were long and delicately formed, and suddenly Bundy saw that there was a wedding ring on her third finger. The realization of it came to him as a shock. He had not had any idea where the look she had given him was leading, until suddenly the ring brought him to an abrupt halt.

Well! he said to himself, and again, *well!* Not that it mattered, of course. Here were two strange girls in a stage on a wilderness road, and one of them was married! Only it seemed a pity that the more attractive one should be the one with the plain gold band on the third finger of the left hand. Bundy began to name the plants along the way again: saskatoon, huckleberry, mountain ash, black chokecherry, thimbleberry—

2.

It was a relief when the long shadows slanted across the road. The dust that followed the stage like a cloud began to turn golden. To Bundy there was a wistful quality in the closing of a summer day, almost a sadness. He was quickly sensitive to changes of time, of weather, of light and dark. He felt everything keenly without always understanding or analyzing his feelings.

Suddenly the green walls fell away, and they came out of the woods into natural meadows where the sun lay low on deep lush grass.

The tired horses began to trot again, knowing themselves near the end of the road, and eager to be knee-deep in cool grass and free to fill their stomachs or roll and stretch or hang their heads in sleep when the darkness came.

The road ran straight across the valley between the meadows to the little town of Cold Spring. Behind the town the first beginnings of larger timber could be seen. The town itself consisted of one long street with two outfitting stores, a blacksmith's shop, three saloons, a hotel, the packer's house and corral and a few small log houses where the other residents lived.

It was very still here in this upland valley, and the air was fresh, almost chilly. Because the road was soft instead of rocky, the stage seemed suddenly to enter a tangible silence, a silence broken only by a distant tinkle of bells. These were the bells of the pack horses grazing in the open meadows.

Men began coming out of the buildings as the stage progressed down the street. They called out greetings and facetious remarks. The fact that there were women on the stage quickened the interest which naturally attached to the daily arrival of mail and news from the outside.

By the time the stage reached the hotel, most of the town's population was converging upon it. The horses stopped here, as their custom was, and the driver stuck the whip into its holder, wound the reins around the whipstock, and climbed down over the wheel.

Among the faces of the men who surged up around the stage was one which struck Bundy Jones as very like the face of the younger of the two women on the seat ahead of him. There was the same blonde naïveté, as well as turn of nose and chin. The mouths were not the same; the girl's mouth had the firmer outline of the two; yet the resemblance was unmistakable.

They began to call greetings back and forth, and Meggie Carney said, "Hey, Jeff, get us out of here. I'm joggled to the marrow of my bones!"

Lorena only smiled her mysterious smile and said nothing.

There was an immediate confusion of descending and of unloading baggage. In the midst of this Mrs. Pulver came onto the porch that ran across the front and around two sides of the hotel, and stood there looking down at them and counting noses, her hands folded under her apron. The Cold Spring Hotel was a transition point, the point where the traveler made his adjustment between civilization and the wilderness, and Mrs. Pulver was its custodian.

Standing just above the confusion of arrival, her tight little colorless face showed no emotion. She regarded the new arrivals with calm appraisal, figuring how she would fit them into the unoccupied space in the hotel and how many extra potatoes she had better peel.

There were only six bedrooms in the hotel, but, when they got this far out, Mrs. Pulver found that people weren't too fussy about bunking up together. If there were women she usually put them in the big front room, regardless of whether or not they had husbands. Nobody stayed long anyway, and the couples could endure a night or two of celibacy and keep everything neat and proper. Mrs. Pulver was a very respectable widow, and had a keen head for business.

Her brother, Sam Carlson, was cut from a different piece entirely. He was talkative and open-fisted, and always came at the stranger with a loud noise of welcome. He was in the crowd around the stage now, shaking hands, helping the ladies, shouting hearty and well meant directions.

He could be taken at cards or almost any confidence game, and he was somewhat too fond of drink. Yet they made an excellent pair to run a frontier hotel, Sam to come out with the glad hand of welcome and to spin the intriguing yarn; Mrs. Pulver to see that the bills were paid and everything kept aboveboard and regular.

It was because of Mrs. Pulver and Mrs. McSweeney, the packer's wife, and Madame Pontarlier, wife of the owner of the chief saloon, that Cold Spring had been kept entirely respectable. It could have been the dirty, brawling place that many frontier stations were, but it was clean, orderly and not given to vice or disorder. If the two lesser saloons got out of line, Pontarlier had his ways of dealing with them. Pontarlier ruled the town with a mild benevolence, tempered by the fact that he, in turn, was ruled by Madame Pontarlier. Mrs. Pulver and Madame Pontarlier were fast friends.

The two ladies saw to it that there were no "girls" in Cold Spring. When the men came out of the woods, they got good hot food at the hotel, and there were the three saloons to drink in; but they had to go on as far as Bolster to get female society. Few of the men complained. Cold Spring gave them a chance to shave and even to bathe in a washtub in the hotel kitchen after the evening dishes were cleaned up, if they were that fastidious; and, if they wanted to go crazy drunk after being a long time without liquor, they could do that, too, and not risk losing their wallets to predatory women.

But all this Bundy learned later. Now he climbed down stiffly, brushing the dust from his shoulders and realizing that his spine had taken a terrific jolting. What had the little Carney girl said? "Joggled to the marrow of her bones"? It was a fact. He always preferred a saddle horse to a wagon on raw roads. In his opinion a horse could become so much a part of a man that the two were really one—and that one a better animal than either horse or man alone.

As he climbed down, he saw the young man called Jeff reaching up his arms to help Lorena. There was a look on Jeff Carney's face that told Bundy he was her husband. It was a look of wistful, almost helpless, adoration. He held up his arms, and Lorena hesitated a moment, as if she liked to choose rather than surrender blindly, then she put her hands on his shoulders and let him lift her. When she was on the ground she turned a cool cheek for his kiss, and her fingers strayed over his hair as a woman touches the hair of a child.

Bundy saw that another person beside himself was watching this meeting. The French Canadian, who had ridden beside the driver, also looked at Mr. and Mrs. Carney, and his bright dark eyes were interested and full of speculation.

Suddenly Mrs. Pulver spoke from the railing of the porch above them.

"Charlie Duporte," she said in a severe voice, "I thought you went up to the mines."

The French Canadian looked up at her, and bared his even white teeth in an attractive grin. He was darkly handsome in his white wool jacket with its broad bands of pure color, a man who liked to make a good appearance.

"Sure, Mis' Pulver," he said easily. "Sure I go up to mines. Sure I come back again. Ain't you glad to see me?"

"Not particularly," said Mrs. Pulver.

"I tell you what," he said to her with what appeared to be habitual volubility. "I got no love to crawl around underground in mines. By gar, we all die and get bury underground soon enough, no? I t'ink we got more money in lumber now as we got in silver, lead, anyway. What you t'ink?"

Mrs. Pulver did not tell him what she thought. The interest

which had momentarily lit her eyes vanished; her hands were quiet under her apron.

"Well, behave yourself," she said.

"Sure, Mis' Pulver," Charlie said, grinning all around at anyone who happened to be listening. "Sure, I always behave myself. You never catch me into no trouble, do you now? No, by gar, you don't."

Mrs. Pulver only sniffed.

Sam was helping the driver hand down luggage and at the same time making a running commentary on everything for the benefit of his saloon cronies. They stood by ready with appreciative laughter while they waited for their mail.

A large flowered hatbox caused considerable mirth among them.

"That's mine," the old maid milliner said, "and I'll thank you not to laugh. It's got a pair of pants and a flannel shirt in it." They got a laugh out of Bundy's vasculum, the rounded tin box he used for collecting and carrying botanical specimens.

"What's this?" Sam asked.

Bundy knew the laugh was coming, but after all he wanted to be set down as a botanist right from the start.

"It's a vasculum," he said. "That's a box I use to collect plants and mosses and keep them fresh until I can classify and sketch them."

"You don't say!" Sam said heartily. "Plants and mosses to classify and sketch! You don't say!" The astonishment in his voice was tinged with comedy, and it produced the desired guffaws.

"You ain't taking up a homestead?" someone said.

"No," Bundy said, "I'm a botanist. I'm here to study the mosses and lichens."

They regarded him with incredulity and amusement.

"You make much money doing that?" inquired Sam.

"Not much," Bundy admitted.

"Better take up a homestead," they advised.

"Maybe I will," said Bundy, smiling to himself.

"Here, Mr. Carney," Sam called, "you got another prospect. Carney, he's built himself quite a business locating homesteaders, ain't you, Mr. Carney? Making a pretty good thing out of it, I guess, ain't you, Mr. Carney? I don't know why some of us fellas here in Cold Spring wasn't smart enough to go into that business before Mr. Carney come up here and beat us to it."

There was raillery in Sam's voice, but a certain asperity, too, that indicated something less than cordial feeling for the city interloper.

Jeff Carney, his left arm still around his wife, held out his hand to Bundy.

"Glad to be useful," he said, "if there's anything I can do. I'm Carney. You're—"

"Bundy Jones," Bundy replied, "and I'll bear you in mind, Mr. Carney." They shook hands, and Carney said:

"This is my wife, Mr. Jones."

"We met on the stage," Mrs. Carney said. "Do get the bags down, Jeff. I'm tired to death." But she softened her words with a look from her great dark eyes.

Now Sam held up his last exhibit for the inspection of his cronies. It was an oddly shaped canvas and leather case with a long neck and a round little belly like a melon.

"Here's another contraption," Sam said. "What the devil? Another vascularium? Something to keep the butter fresh in?"

Miss Meggie Carney stepped up quickly and cried, "Oh, be careful! Handle it gently. Don't drop it. It's my mandolin."

"Mandolin?" said Sam. "What in hell do you do with a mandolin, Ma'am?"

Miss Carney flushed, but Bundy saw that although she was easily embarrassed by rough language, she did not take offense.

"Why, you play it," she said, "to make music."

"Good gar!" said Sam. "What won't they think of next? You ain't going to pack that over Freezout with you, are you, Ma'am?"

"Yes, I am," said Miss Carney with a show of spirit. The men all began to laugh.

"See what the packer says to that," one said, and another one said, "I knew a fellow packed a banjo in onct. But a mule stepped on it the first night out. An accordeen carries a whole lot better than one of these here."

Miss Carney took the mandolin case and held it in her arms

like a baby. Her beautiful sister-in-law looked at her with indolent amusement.

"Jeff and I told her to leave it to home, didn't we, Jeff?" Lorena said.

Jeff was unloading a box from the back of the wagon. But he lifted his head and looked at the two girls with the level gray eyes so like his sister's.

"Yes," he said, "we told her."

"It won't do anybody any harm," Meggie defended. "I'll see to it. I haven't got so many things to pack in, except food and supplies."

"Let the leetle lady have it," said Charlie Duporte. "By gar, she sit all summer listen to the birdies sing, she need a little plinky-plink to play on, don't she?" His dark face sparkled when he smiled. It was an effect of white teeth and liquidly bright eyes and mobile facial muscles that suddenly transformed him.

Just then Miss Nan O'Rourke, with her hands full of luggage, inquired plaintively, "How about a cup of tea? A good strong cup of tea. I'm dead on my feet."

"Come on up," Mrs. Pulver said. "We're just going to sound the supper bell. There's a pump and a roller towel on the back porch if you want to wash first, or I'll show you to your room if you want to wash more private."

"I'll take the tea before the privacy," Miss O'Rourke said.

3.

When the dinner bell rang, twelve people gathered around Mrs. Pulver's long dining table. She could seat fifteen or sixteen if necessary and, if there were more, as sometimes happened when the deer hunting was good or on a Fourth of July when lumberjacks and settlers came out of the woods to celebrate, Mrs. Pulver set a second table.

Besides the stage driver and his five passengers at the table this evening, there were Jeff Carney and three lumberjacks called Spike, Rudy and Dynamite. They had been engaged to go in with the homesteaders to help them clear land and build cabins. Spike was a middle-aged man and Rudy and Dynamite were young ones. Nobody bothered to distinguish them by last names, and although they differed in age, they did not differ greatly in appearance. All three had black hair combed wetly back, in what was apparently an unaccustomed neatness, since between the hairline and the fine, ruddy mahogany color of the lower face, there was a strip of pale, unburned forehead.

The last person to come to the table was the forest ranger. Bundy looked at the man curiously, alert to the fact that his confidential opinion of Ian MacGillicuddy was one of the objects of his mission from Washington. The ranger was not young and he was neither impressive nor prepossessing—a stringy old man with a gnarled look that suggested many winters in the open. While the weather had given the younger men a color of warm mahogany, it had turned the ranger's face into rough-grained, grayish oak, broken by the swath of a yellow-white moustache and two very light blue eyes. Either the startling effect of the keen blue eyes in the weathered face or the unfamiliarity of the name Ian had given the old man the nickname "Eye." Eye MacGillicuddy, Bundy knew, was a Scotsman by birth, but, after years in the Western United States, trapping and hunting and leading the nomadic life of a "timber willie," he seemed to have lost any characteristics that were not pure American woodsman, except for the fine Scots brogue.

MacGillicuddy had come into the ranger service by way of the Land Office in the Department of the Interior, before the nation's forest lands had been transferred to the Department of Agriculture. How much of the former Land Office readiness to exploit and hand out public plums still clung to the old ranger, Bundy did not know; but he was here to find out. He did know that MacGillicuddy had managed to fill out his required reports but that it was probably a triumph of industry over illiteracy. Generally, such rangers were ignorant pioneers. Their pay was sixty dollars a month; it did not attract educated idealists.

Eye brought with him to table a small mongrel bitch with a bellyful of undropped pups. He kept the little animal beside him and fed her morsels from his plate. Bundy had already seen enough of Mrs. Pulver to be surprised that she would tolerate this, but the ranger seemed to be a privileged character.

"Where'd your bitch get them there puppies, Eye?" one of the lumberjacks inquired.

"Danged if I know," the old man replied. "Jessie, she gets around. Some high-tailed son of a coyotee done the trick, I guess."

The Carney ladies curled their noses in disgust, whether because of the crudity of this exchange or because of the strong aroma of smoke and horse and old leather that came in with Eye and joined them at the table, Bundy could not tell.

Sam sat at one end of the table and Mrs. Pulver at the other—the end nearest the kitchen. They had a Chinese cook and a boy, but still Mrs. Pulver did a lot of the hopping herself. The oilcloth-covered table was always loaded with good, substantial food in large serving dishes that went the rounds.

Mrs. Pulver's cuisine enjoyed a great reputation among the lumberjacks and homesteaders. Appetite seasons the food, and it is true that, after a summer of boiled beans and sourdough biscuit, anything will be tasty to a woodsman. But Bundy came to Mrs. Pulver's table fresh from the gustatory propriety of civilization, and still he was impressed. There was a great profusion of plain food, but, for all its plainness, each dish had its own integrity of flavor. There was a platter of cold ham and deviled eggs; a dish of hot pot roast with plenty of mashed potatoes and gravy; a big bowl of boiled cabbage and another of baked sauerkraut; there was beef and potato hash from last night's pot roast; and a jug of home-baked beans. There were canned tomatoes, cold slaw and potato salad. The baking powder biscuits were as big as teacups. On the sideboard were canned pears and spicecake and blancmange pudding. And there were lemon meringue and dried apple pies. If the pies were not consumed at supper, they usually appeared again at breakfast, making a nice accompaniment to fried mush and ham and eggs.

Mrs. Pulver's one gesture toward elegance was the big silver and cut glass cruet in the center of the table. But this was largely for show, and she did not encourage the heavy-handed lumberjacks to use it.

"You don't need no condiments on *my* food, gentlemen," she used to say reprovingly if she saw a large red hand groping for the cruet. The hand was usually withdrawn.

Mrs. Pulver's coffee could stand by itself, and, even before the dinner bell was sounded, it had wafted its own unsubtle message abroad to whet the appetites. It was served in big white crockery cups without saucers. Once a hunter, fresh from town, remarked that the cups reminded him of chamber pots. But Mrs. Pulver gave him such a glance of reprimand and disdain that nobody dared to laugh. She tolerated her brother's jokes as part of a genial atmosphere which was good for the digestion of the guests, but the free-lance humorist received little encouragement.

Sam's humor was never subtle. When the well seasoned beef was passed to him, he used to cry out in mock dismay, "What's this? burro?" and everybody would laugh except Mrs. Pulver who pressed her lips together in a little acid smile of toleration.

The small windows of the dining room faced east, and even in June the room lost its brightness early. The serving boy came in to light the ornate coal oil lamp which was suspended above the table. Suddenly the whole complexion of the room was changed. The high center of illumination cast a pale, cadaverous light on the faces of the diners. It brought out the shadows of approaching age and pointed up unsuspected weaknesses of character.

Looking about him with surprise, Bundy saw that the artificial light had waved a Circe wand over the other diners; that Jeff Carney's open, friendly face appeared weak and sullen, that Charlie Duporte's laughing one looked sly. He saw that Miss O'Rourke's belligerent competence and well-being had become tired and uncertain. Meggie Carney looked immature and impressionable, possibly a little silly. Bundy judged that she had reached the age of twenty with most of her adolescence still intact. Her responses seemed to be simple and direct. She had made a long journey into a strange environment and she was hungry and tired. She was eating well and she would probably sleep well, not thinking about tomorrow until it came. She reminded him of a young sister he had left at home.

The only person who came off well in the baleful lamplight was Lorena Carney. Nothing seemed to dim her beauty. She looked across the table at Bundy and gave him one of her pensive smiles with gently curving mouth and wide eyes. Even in this light there was something unusual about her eyes. They were dark and yet the iris seemed to be flecked with gold. Bundy thought that he had seen

the same somber sparkle in a woods pool where the sun falls sparsely
through the interlocking branches and flecks the deep brown surface
of the water with bits of light; and all is very still, almost sad, waiting for the breeze which never penetrates this silent place to break
the dark surface into gaiety or rejoicing.

If Bundy could easily classify Meggie Carney as like his little
sister, he found no easy category for the older woman. She was out
of his limited experience and this made her seem to him mysterious.
He was susceptible to mystery. The unknown had a challenge and
a fascination for him, whether it lay in virgin forest or in a woman's
beauty. Still he was well brought up and he did not intend to lose
his head over a married woman, no, nor over a homesteader either.

Mrs. Carney rarely joined in the desultory conversation about
the table. Yet Bundy saw that other men were conscious of her besides himself. After they had spoken, they glanced at her to see if
she had taken note.

Sam was in a fine humor and brought out an assortment of his
yarns. Repetition never seemed to bore him, and Bundy was to become terribly familiar with all of the yarns as the years went on.
Now he heard for the first time about the old maid hugged from
behind by a bear, who cried out, "Hug me as hard as you want to,
honey, but I wish you'd shave your beard."

Eye MacGillicuddy entered the conversation at this point to
remark in a nasal voice that he'd spent last night in Echo Canyon
where you shouted "Time to get up!" just as you bedded down,
and the echo finally came back and woke you up at five-thirty the
next morning. From there he went on to relate an anecdote about the
lady homesteader who was lamenting that she forgot to bring her
toothbrush. "I told her, 'Ma'am,' s' I, 'if I was in the habit of usin'
one, I'd sure as hell fire lend you mine.' You think that lady was
pleased?" Eye demanded. "Not on your life! These homesteadin'
females is verra ungrateful critters."

Bundy saw that the ranger was not averse to mixing fantasy
with fact; and he also suspected that both he and Sam had a livelier
line of anecdotes when they stood along the bar with a glass in hand
and a purely masculine audience.

However, some of the ladies had begun to grow restive.

"It seems to me," Miss O'Rourke said sharply, "that you're

rather hard on the lady homesteaders. What's so funny about a woman alone taking up a homestead? We've got to live like the rest of you."

"No," Sam said, "we ain't hard on you. If a nice pretty lady can turn over a quick dollar on a piece of timberland, I'm not agin it. It's the homesteading that's getting harder though. Not so long ago a feller use to could go in overnight with a timber locator, build a little brush shack that wouldn't stand up under the first winter's snow, dig a hole and throw in a sack of potatoes. The next day when he pulled out, he could leave the potatoes to rot, or he could dig 'em up again and carry 'em back with him, as he saw fit; but, when it came to proving up on his homestead, the son of a bitch could honestly swear he'd built him a house and planted potatoes. An hour after the government give him his land for a dollar and a half an acre the lumber company would pay him ten to thirty times as much, and he was all set up. But you can't get by that easy now, Eye can tell you that. He's the ranger."

"We're doin' our durnedest to make it harder," said Eye Mac-Gillicuddy, his gray face still knotted with something like humor. "A man got to work a wee bit these days for what he gets."

Jeff Carney moved uneasily in his chair.

"We know that," he said mildly. "We're going to build good cabins, clear land and make good gardens. We aren't trying to cheat anybody."

"Of course, with you folks," Eye said, his face still contorted with some inner amusement, "and all the folks you're locating— you're permanent. You're makin' homes here, are ye no?"

"Of course," Jeff Carney said, "naturally."

"It sure will make the winters nicer," Eye remarked, "havin' you folks for neighbors all year round."

Bundy Jones said nothing, but he looked intently from the face of one man to the other. Here was a turn of conversation that touched him keenly. He saw that Jeff was slightly discomfited.

"Well, certainly," Jeff said. "But I guess we'll hardly get things in running order this first winter. We'll fulfill the six-month residence requirement and that's probably the best we can do the first year. That's all the government requires, isn't it?"

"Aye," the ranger said, "Gov'ment will give you anything you want, if you can prove the place is fit an' proper for a permanent home."

"But permanent," Jeff said. "What do you mean permanent? If a man gets a piece of property in town, he doesn't have to agree to spend the rest of his life on it, does he? Has the government any right to attach more strings to its land?"

"Likely not," Sam said. "Only what Eye means, land is gettin' scarcer. It used to be they was honing to give it out and get rid of it. Now they're beginning to wonder."

"They ought to begin to wonder," said the stage driver, entering the conversation for the first time. "Driving around, I sure seen enough cutover land. Them loggers run through fine timber and leave the land as waste and dead as if a forest fire had gone by. It's a God-damned shame."

"I had my free land back in Wisconsin," Sam said, "a right pretty bit with good water and a fine stand of timber. I sold out for two thousand dollars and the lumber interests made, I s'pose twenty times that much off it. Somebody got rich, not me, and they left the place a shambles, stumps and rocks and brush piles for the rabbits. The stream's dried up, I spent my two thousand, the timber's gone. Sometimes I remember back and think how pretty it was."

"So you got your cut, Sam, you don't want no one else to, is that it?" one of the lumberjacks asked.

"No it ain't quite that," Sam said without anger. "It's pretty country here, and, by gosh, I kind of hate to see the same thing happen here that happened back East."

"This here ain't plowland," said the stage driver. "You can't grow corn. All the lumber companies want is cut fine trees and let the dirt underneath go plumb to waste."

"We're lookin' out to stop it now," said Eye mildly. The humorous twist had finally left his face.

He sounds all right, Bundy thought. The old man sounds all right, but I wonder how he performs.

Mrs. Pulver, mindful of the homesteaders and the occasional representatives of the lumber companies who were her best paying and tipping guests, stirred restlessly on her chair. "You men just tend to your eating," she said. "There's plenty more in the kitchen.

Send round the bowl of pot roast again, and don't hold back, folks."

"But the land has to be cleared, doesn't it?" asked Meggie Carney, looking around with her naïve gray eyes. "What would happen if nobody cut any timber or cleared any land? We'd be right back in the wilderness with the Indians wouldn't we?"

"We need the lumber to build," Jeff said. "Do you know that last year the lumber consumption in the United States was forty-five billion feet? That's the highest peak it's ever reached. We're building a great nation, we have to have wood. There'd be no progress without lumber and wood."

"So pretty soon the wood's all gone," said the driver. "What then?"

"Yes, what's the solution then?" demanded Miss O'Rourke.

"Well, there's no use to lay waste," Eye said cautiously.

"It's a Scotchman talking," said Charlie Duporte, laughing.

"Aye, it's a Scotchman," said the old man more warmly, "and not ashamed neither. We ought to take a little and leave a little, and we ought to replant. It took a long time for them trees to grow. Folks got to be a little slower about sawin' them up."

The conversation had begun to bore Charlie Duporte. He looked at the young ladies and surmised that they were bored too. Leaning toward Meggie Carney, but with an eye for Lorena, he asked: "When you going to play that mandolin, Mees Carney?"

"Oh, I don't know," Meggie said. "I hadn't thought."

"You like to sing, eh?"

"Yes. I haven't much of a voice."

"I bet you have," said Charlie.

"No really. Jeff's the singer. Lorena, too."

"Leave me out of it," said Jeff. "I've given up singing, as you well know."

"Don't be tiresome, Jeff," said Lorena softly.

"I tell you what we do," said Charlie. "After supper you bring the mandolin, we all go call on Madame Pontarlier and have some music, eh?"

"Madame Pontarlier?" asked Meggie. "Who is she?"

"She's the saloonkeeper's wife," said Sam, beginning to raise a laugh from the depths of his belly. It always gave him pleasure to astound the innocent little ladies from the outer world.

"*Oh!*" said Meggie Carney, as shocked as he had expected.

But Mrs. Pulver intervened in her dry, respectable voice. "Madame Pontarlier is a very fine lady," she said. "Everyone calls on her. She'll be offended if you don't. You won't find a nicer lady anywhere around here. You had better go."

"It's all right," said Charlie Duporte eagerly. "Like Mrs. Pulver says, Madame Pontarlier is a great fine lady, *une grande dame*. She expect you."

"Not me," said Miss O'Rourke. "I'll be darned if I call on anyone tonight. I've got to have my beauty sleep."

Eye MacGillicuddy threw her one of his keen blue looks. "Beauty!" he snorted.

"That's what I said," asserted Miss O'Rourke.

"All right," Meggie said. "I'll go, if everybody's sure it's proper. Will you come, Lorena?"

"I don't care if it's *proper* or not," Lorena said, smiling around the table at the faces turned toward her. "Will it be *interesting?*"

"Yes, interesting, I promise you," said Charlie, beaming at her.

"Then we'll all go," she said, "Jeff and Mr. Jones and Meggie and me."

Bundy was surprised to be included. He had notes to write up and, like Miss O'Rourke, he wanted to get to bed early. He had no wish to go calling on the local gentry, and Madame Pontarlier and her offended sensibilities were nothing to him.

"I'm sorry," he said. "I'm afraid you'll have to leave me out of this. I have some notes to write up."

But the young Carneys, after swallowing the first shock of making a respectable social call at the back door of the saloon, seemed bent upon turning it into a lark. They were equally determined that Bundy should go with them.

"Mr. Jones," said Meggie archly, "you haven't said a word all through dinner. You need the social experience."

Bundy laughed. "I'm just chock full of social experience," he said, "any more would ruin me."

"Come on, Jones," said Jeff. "I understand Mrs. Pulver has put us in the same bed tonight. If you went to sleep early, I'd wake you up when I came in late. You might as well make a night of it."

"Sure! Sure!" said Charlie Duporte. "You come along, Mister, we all have a mighty fine time."

Bundy hesitated, wondering how to refuse without causing ill feeling, and then Lorena's deep, languid voice said softly, "Leave the poor man out of this. Can't you see he wants to be alone with his flowers and his mosses? Don't torment him."

"I'll go," said Bundy, laughing. "That's the clinching argument."

"Fine!" said Meggie heartily. "I'll get my mandolin, and you can carry it for me, Mr. Jones."

Bundy looked at Mrs. Carney, and the mysterious eyes approved of him, so he was content to take Meggie's arm and carry the mandolin case, and let the notes go hang for the present.

4.

So the five young people went laughing and talking up the street and around to the back of Pontarlier's saloon. Behind the main building was a small log wing where the Pontarliers lived. It had a neat door, painted white, and the window sills were painted white too.

Charlie knocked at the door, and almost immediately his knock was answered by the strident barking of a small dog. Then the calm, deep voice of a woman called to them to enter.

Probably none of the four newcomers had formed any clear notion of what they would find inside the Pontarlier's house; certainly, however, they were unprepared for the ornate propriety with which Madame Pontarlier had surrounded herself.

The single room which they entered had three windows shrouded in white lace curtains. The rough-hewn logs of the interior had been whitewashed, and were hung with enlarged photographs and steel engravings in black frames, so that the whole effect was starkly black and white.

In one corner of the room was a large white enameled iron bedstead, high and rotund with a feather mattress which was covered with a white crocheted spread. Folded at the foot was a crimson feather comforter that raised the whole impressive mass well up toward the low-raftered ceiling.

A monumental white washbowl and pitcher occupied a small rustic table, draped in ruffled white cloth; and there was a little blue Madonna on a shelf by the bed with a crimson lamp burning before it.

The other end of the room was given over to daytime living, having an oilcloth covered table, a small kerosene stove on a side shelf, and an attractive array of copper pots and dishes on open shelves. A tray of glasses on the table seemed to anticipate hospitality.

The central part of the room was occupied by a large, black iron stove which Madame had shrouded now, it being summer, in a petticoat of white lace curtain, tastefully draped and adorned with a crimson satin bowknot. There were easy chairs about, two of them platform rockers, which must, Bundy thought, have been devilishly hard to bring in here by stage or pack horse over the rough roads.

Madame Pontarlier sat in the largest of the platform rockers and gave them a calm smile. She did not exert herself to rise after the initial exertion of calling to them to enter.

A miniature poodle, white except for a black nose and teary black eyes which seemed to have spilled over and dyed his hair in a melancholy blur, sat on her lap and yapped angrily at the intruders. Madame allowed him to bark for a few moments; then she boxed his ears and he was silent.

Charlie Duporte went up to Madame Pontarlier at once and kissed her hand. He introduced the others with considerably more skill and grace than Bundy had expected to find in him. One by one they went up and shook Madame's proffered hand, Bundy and Jeff lacking the Gallic audacity to kiss it. The hand was plump and white, very smooth and shiny, and it was adorned with rings.

Madame Pontarlier wore a plain white dress, and, with her smooth black hair and heavy black brows, she seemed an integral part of her black and white room. Even the touch of crimson was repeated on her lips. *Rouged,* Bundy thought in surprise. Nice women rarely rouged their lips in 1908. Yet this was obviously no barroom hussy.

She had a gracious word for each of them, like a queen at a levee. At first only she and Charlie Duporte were at ease. The others had come with an expectation of light-hearted slumming, only to find themselves in the presence of an austere nobility. Their devil-may-care spirits were considerably dashed.

Madame looked from one to another with interest and a shrewd appraisal. To Jeff Carney she said, "It is about time you come to see me, Mr. Carney. I hear you have been in town two, three times, yet you do not honor me by calling. Your uncle always comes to see me. It is a long time I know your uncle Ralph."

Ralph Carney! Bundy thought, Good Lord! Why didn't I connect the names before? So this is the nephew of the lumber baron! But I should have known all that, only it's strange to find him here. Still I've got to be a little sharper if I'm going to be any good at this job. He sat thinking, feeling a trifle chastened and abashed.

"Well, I'm sorry, Madame," Jeff Carney was saying, awkwardly it seemed. "Accept my apologies, please. You see—"

He was fumbling for a reason, and Lorena said easily: "You see, Madame Pontarlier, he was waiting for his wife to join him before he called on you. I have only arrived today."

"Ah, yes," the Frenchwoman said, turning her sharp, appraising eyes upon Lorena.

Lorena said, "So you know Jeff's uncle Ralph?" There had been a quickening of interest in her mobile face, Bundy thought, at the mention of Ralph Carney.

"Yes," said Madame Pontarlier. "He is one of my very great and valued friends."

The two women looked at each other, and curiosity, understanding, almost hostility, seemed to vibrate between them for an instant.

Then the Frenchwoman turned to the others and said slowly and graciously,

"Be seated, please. This is so pleasant that you come to see me. We shall have a drink together."

"Oh, no," Miss Meggie Carney said in a panic. "I don't drink anything intoxicating."

Madame Pontarlier smiled a tolerant smile. "We do not intoxicate you, little miss."

"But really, really, I don't," Meggie said.

"For Heaven's sake, Meggie," Lorena said sharply, "be civilized for once, can't you?" She seemed to be irritated now and discontented, as if the name of Jeff's uncle had somehow changed the color of her evening.

"You see," said Madame Pontarlier, "the intoxicating—that is only for the front room. Here it is not. No, not even for the poor gentlemen who may be so very thirsty. This is only for the little ladies, and to make a pleasantness among us all. Adolph!" she called.

From the doorway which led to the saloon, M. Pontarlier came smiling and bearing bottles on a tray. He was a large, sleek man with a ruddy face. Meeting him on the street one might have taken him for the local butcher.

The bottles he had brought contained a sweet, unfermented juice of the white grape, something Bundy had never tasted before. It was a rather thick liquid, yellowish clear, an inoffensive drink, yet distinctive and pleasantly palatable.

With a wink and a nod to the three men, he indicated that there was better to be had in the front room when they were at leisure.

Having drunk together, even thus innocuously, they were, in a few moments, all mysteriously at ease and having a good time. Even Lorena smiled again. The mandolin was brought out of its case and Miss Meggie favored them with several carefully practiced tunes.

Bundy was tired and he had some difficulty in stifling his yawns. He did not share the mania of the times; and, heretic that he was, the mandolin seemed to him the least promising of instruments, a little plinking, twittering voice that lacked the solid substance of either guitar or banjo. Nearly every little town, certainly every little college, had its mandolin club, and its serenaders and troubadours who spent long hours perfecting the trill and the tremolo with a small tortoise-shell pick on metal strings. They hung their mandolins about their necks with colored ribbons and plinked their hearts out. He had heard much better performers than Miss Meggie Carney and had not been greatly moved.

But Charlie Duporte watched her with a gleam in his restless eyes which appeared to Bundy to be impatience. It was no surprise to him therefore, when, Meggie having exhausted her repertoire, Charlie took the instrument from her hands and began to experiment with it.

"You know how to play it?" Meggie asked.

"Oh, no," Charlie said, shaking his head and showing his white teeth in a flash of laughter, "but I watch you do. Maybe I learn a little how to play, no?"

Bundy had no way of knowing whether the French Canadian had ever played a mandolin before or not, but he suspected that Charlie had one of those natural gifts for music which put the laborious efforts of ordinary performers to shame. Suddenly there was authority, sparkle and gaiety in the sounds which the mandolin gave out.

"My goodness, Mr. Duporte!" Meggie exclaimed. "You certainly can play. Don't tell me you never had any lessons!"

"Never!" Charlie said. "I only got a little music, here in my fingers. What you want me play—organ? flute? Maybe you got a saw you want me play a tune on, eh? I play on anyt'ing."

"Charlie," Madame Pontarlier said, "Give us a French song for my pleasure. It is only from you I hear my native tongue."

Feeling his way at first but with accelerating confidence, Charlie began to play and sing the old French Canadian voyageur songs, and some which Bundy took to be love songs, although he knew little of the French language. Madame Pontarlier closed her eyes and beat time on the chair arm with her finger. "Ah! Ah! Ah!" she said in a kind of ecstatic lament.

But Charlie's bright eyes wandered to the faces of the younger ladies also, and he did not wish to lose their interest by catering too long to the nostalgia of his hostess.

"Enough of France," he said. "We all sing now. You know 'The Old Mill Stream'? Poor 'Clementine'? Come now, everybody!"

The two girls joined in with alacrity. Meggie had a fragile high soprano, and Lorena a rich contralto. They seemed to take delight in singing. Bundy had a rusty baritone of which he was not proud, but he had often enough been coerced into glee clubs and quartets, and he knew most of the popular songs and the baritone parts in them.

Only Jeff sat silent, his expression indrawn and sullen.

"Come, Mr. Carney," Madame said to him.

"No, I don't sing any more—not at all," Jeff said.

Lorena looked at him with an expression of exasperation. Then she went up to him and took his hand.

"Come on, Jeff," she said. "Take the chip off your shoulder. Sing, for God's sake, sing!"

He looked up at her with the vulnerable face he had shown when he lifted her from the stage that afternoon.

"You want me to, Rena?" he asked.

"Of course I do," she said. "Would I ask you otherwise?"

After that he sang with them as they ranged through the popular songs of the day, and his tenor voice was sweet and true. Bundy was no musician, but he thought that this was an exceptional voice. What pique or hurt or fancy kept him from wishing to use it? Bundy wondered.

The singing went on for some time and it was evident that Madame Pontarlier, although she did not sing, was enjoying herself very much. Bundy thought that she must often have been lonely in this frontier place. How she had managed to build up the convention that strangers in town were obliged to call on her, he did not know, but it served her purpose and doubtless kept her from dying of ennui.

After they had sung most of the things they knew, they began to talk.

"You know what it is to go in homesteading?" Madame Pontarlier asked. "You ladies are so young, so little, with your pretty dresses. You know that you must cross over a mountain on horseback? They tell me the winter's snow is not all melted up there yet. And there are no houses waiting for you in that place. You must clear land first before you build. Are you not afraid?"

"Yes," Meggie said, "I *am* a little scared. But I've made up my mind to do it, and it's going to be fun, I think—a lark."

"All singing and dancing, eh?" Madame asked. "So you think it will be fun?"

"Well," Meggie said, "there are different ways of having fun. Of course I adore singing and dancing, but I think it will be fun to build a house in the wilderness too. It's the Strenuous Life that counts, isn't it?"

President Teddy Roosevelt's magnificent clichés were on everybody's tongue in those days. The lure of the Strenuous Life had certainly shaped Bundy's career, and doubtless because of it the three young Carneys were in this strange environment tonight. But, if Madame Pontarlier had heard of the Strenuous Life, she remained unimpressed.

"Ah, *that!*" she said contemptuously, and turning to Lorena she continued, "And you, Madame, you are going to hide your beauty among these dark forest trees where nobody will see?"

"At least it will be something new," Lorena said. In the rich voice there was a wealth of boredom that struck to Bundy's heart. She is unhappy, he thought. Her life is intolerable to her. Against his better reason, he was moved.

Charlie Duporte also looked at her, and smiled a slow smile.

"If I am in these woods, Madame Pontarlier," he said, "her beauty is not lost. Charlie Duporte can see."

Jeff moved impatiently. He must always be meeting this extravagant gallantry of other men for his wife. He spoke brusquely. "Lorena will be all right," he said. "Meggie's the one who'll make a poor homesteader. If she sees a mouse, she jumps on a chair and screams. Spiders give her fits."

"And snakes," said Meggie complaisantly, "I scream for those too."

"I never see no poison snakes in here," Charlie said. "I think the only snakes we got is garter snakes."

"It doesn't matter at all," Meggie said. "I can scream just as loudly for a garter snake as a rattler. It's the way I am."

"And you, Madame Carney," pursued the old Frenchwoman, "do you scream too?"

Lorena shook her head, and Jeff said seriously, "No, she doesn't. I've never heard Lorena scream. Never."

"Perhaps that is a pity," Madame Pontarlier said, and Charlie Duporte burst out laughing.

"My gar!" he said, "What kind of husband is it who has never heard his wife scream? This is a thing you should put right, Mr. Carney. No?"

Jeff missed the Gallic lightness of tone. He replied heavily and perhaps a trifle resentfully, "Why should I wish to make my wife scream? I want to see her happy."

Lorena was growing restive under all this talk about herself. She liked to be looked at but not discussed. She glanced across at

Bundy, who was as usual silent, and cast him a warmly conspiratorial glance asking him not to think hardly of her.

Madame Pontarlier took up Jeff's last word as a player catches a ball.

"Happy?" said Madame. "Who is happy? So few, I think. But we can learn patience and perseverance and finally content. Perhaps this beautiful little Madame is learning patience and perseverance. Perhaps she has content."

Lorena did not reply, but she shrugged her shoulders lightly and turned her head aside.

"Rena isn't either patient or persevering," Meggie said, "and neither am I. But I'm sure we're both happy, aren't we, Rena?"

"You've talked me over enough," Lorena said sharply. "How tiresome such talk is! Really I've had too much of it."

"We didn't mean to hurt you, Rena," Jeff said humbly.

"Oh, hurt? Of course, I'm not hurt," Lorena said. "Why in the world should I be? But it's certainly past bedtime, and tomorrow we have to brace ourselves for this homesteading thing. Can we thank Madame Pontarlier for a very pleasant evening, and get along?"

"Yes, yes," Jeff said. "We have certainly stayed too long."

"But it was so much fun," Meggie said. "I hope you'll let us come again."

So the party broke up with polite remarks all around, and the visitors went out into the crisp clear night. There was a chill in the air that had come down from snowy mountains, and above the placid meadows the millions of stars and planets sparkled with a brilliance never seen near a city.

Jeff and Lorena went ahead, Jeff holding her close to his side with a kind of possessive aggression. Between the other two men Meggie bounced and chattered, like a small gay toy, freshly wound, not minding their unresponsiveness.

Bundy couldn't help remembering with sardonic amusement that Mrs. Pulver had put the three women to sleep in the large front room, and that Jeff Carney would have to sleep that night in a double bed with him. He'll hate it worse than I do, Bundy thought.

In the bright crystalline silence, a bell on a grazing pack horse in the meadow sounded a plaintive note of loneliness.

5.

The room that Bundy and Jeff entered already reeked and re-sounded with the heavy slumber of two of the lumberjacks who had turned in early under the relaxing effects of some of Pontarlier's stronger beverages. Jeff brought a coal oil lamp with them and set it on the plank table while they undressed.

"I'm afraid this is hard luck for you, Mr. Carney," Bundy said.

"It's Mrs. Pulver's way," said Jeff shortly.

"I noticed Madame Pontarlier spoke of your uncle Ralph Carney," Bundy said. "I hadn't made the connection before. I should have known at once, I suppose."

"Why should you?" said Jeff. "You wouldn't expect the old man's nephew to be locating homesteaders, would you?"

"Well, I don't know," Bundy said. "It's all to do with lumbering and the woods, I suppose."

"That's a way of looking at it," Jeff said.

"Wasn't there a senator from this state named Carney too?"

"That was my father," Jeff said. "He died last year."

"I'm sorry," Bundy said. "I didn't mean to probe."

"I'm sorry, too," Jeff said shortly. Then he added, "He left things in a hell of a mess."

Bundy was silent, thinking that he had already said too much; but Jeff seemed willing to keep the conversation open.

"You know Uncle Ralph?" Jeff asked.

"Not personally," Bundy said. "I guess most Westerners know who he is."

"Yes, he's a big man," Jeff said, "a great big hell of a man who's got everything he wanted out of the West. The trouble is he began at the bottom and he thinks everybody else should."

"I suppose that's natural," Bundy said.

"No," Jeff said violently, "every generation is different. He and my father started with nothing and that was all right, but I started on a different plane. Why should I be set back where they were?"

Bundy took refuge in the silence which never embarrassed him. But Jeff Carney was on the defensive. He repeated, "I expect you think it's funny that I'm in here locating people on homesteads; that my wife and sister are in on it too. Well, it *is* funny. It's darned funny, and I won't be the last to say so."

"I didn't say a thing," said Bundy. "I hadn't even got around to thinking so."

"You will," Jeff Carney said. "Most people do. I expected to be at Yale getting a degree in law this year. I expected to be singing, to be using my voice for something besides amateur quartets in a backwoods saloon parlor." He looked at Bundy angrily as if he dared him to contradict. At the same time there was a kind of helpless appeal in his look. Bundy saw that this was a young man who wanted people to think well of him so that he might think well of himself. Somehow the discovery surprised him. Hadn't being the son of a senator, the nephew of a lumber baron, the husband of an exceedingly beautiful woman given him sufficient confidence in life to meet any setback? It seemed not.

Jeff went on quickly, as if he were repeating an oft-told tale. "My father died of a heart attack, very suddenly. His affairs were all in a mess—unbelievable, really a mess! And do you think the great Ralph came through with anything handsome? He did not. This is the extent of his munificence—to give me a job as a timber locator. Well, I spent my summers in the woods working for him as a kid. He couldn't do any less than give me a woods job somewhere. But it's a sell really, really a sell. So I don't mind telling people. They look at me and think I own the earth and why am I doing a pindling job like this? And I tell them. I don't mind their knowing, because I haven't had a square deal. I was brought up to expect more."

"Yes, I can see that," Bundy said. "Sometimes it's better if a kid does not have expectations, I suppose."

"You're damned right," Jeff Carney said.

"Still," said Bundy reasonably, "you've had a lot of privileges. You must have the best part of a handsome education. Perhaps you can swing the rest of it in a few years."

"Maybe I can," Jeff said, "but I'm married, I've got a sister who's as helpless as I am. I was always led to expect more. My wife was led to expect more. It's not easy to take."

One of the lumberjacks in the next bed turned over restlessly.

"We'd better get to sleep," Bundy said.

"What about you?" Jeff asked. "Do you like being a plant cataloguer? Is that what you expected to be?"

"Yes, I like it," Bundy said. "I never expected much, and I've enjoyed what I got."

"Then you're damned lucky," said Jeff.

They lay down on the lumpy mattress.

Bundy thought. Good Lord! Imagine me sleeping in the same bed with Ralph Carney's nephew! The idea appealed to his sense of humor.

6.

Bundy Jones was twenty-four years old, although being tall and solidly built, he appeared to be older. He looked pleasant and wholesome in a nondescript way, but he was far from handsome. He was the second of six children and the only one so far who had shown any aptitude for higher learning. His brother Arnold, who was the eldest in the family, worked in a bank, was as yet unmarried, and had loaned Bundy the money to get an M.A. degree from the University of Oregon. Bundy had been earning a little money of his own ever since he was ten, and now, a year after graduation, he had almost paid his brother back.

Bundy's family had come to Oregon from Kansas before he was born, and he considered himself a complete Westerner, as indeed he was. He had carried newspapers and raised chickens and rabbits, and tended the family garden, sometimes selling the surplus of beans or onions or potatoes that his mother did not need to feed the family. He could never remember a time in his life when he had not been engaged in some project to make pocket money or to acquire knowledge or to get himself along in the world.

Bundy's father was the photographer for the small town in which they lived. The photographic studio occupied the front part of their house, and a glass-enclosed box set up on the front lawn displayed the latest wedding and commencement pictures for the interest and enticement of passers-by. The business made a decent living for the family, but it allowed no margin for frivolities.

Bundy was fond of his father, but he hated the smell of chemicals that clung to him and in fact permeated all of their family life. Possibly that was what sent him off to the surrounding woods whenever he had time to go. His younger brother, Harold, was handier than he was around the studio, and liked to shift the painted backgrounds for his father, to help arrange the brides' trains or shake the rattle for unhappy babies. Harold apparently enjoyed the darkroom with its damp and awful odors, and everyone was pleased to see that he was going to help his father carry on the business when he finished high school.

Bundy realized his good fortune in having a self-supporting and helpful older brother on the one side and a younger brother who enjoyed the family business on the other. It left Bundy free to pursue his own interests which at first included the whole of the natural world. Animals, insects, trees, flowers, plants—everything was grist to his mill. Even before he went to college, the vastness of nature impressed on him the fact that a man with a finite span of living must specialize in order to get below the surface. Gradually he discarded the animals, the insects, even to some extent the trees; and now, in the final stages of his scientific enthusiasm, he was sharpening his special knowledge of plants to the fine point of hoping to learn everything there was to learn about mosses and lichens.

This interest seemed bizarre to his literal-minded family. But it was a good-natured family, full of toleration for its members' foibles, and nobody tried to dissuade Bundy from his peculiar yen to be a botanist. He was the queer one, but they were all proud of him and loved him anyway.

In college, Bundy stumbled onto the books of John Muir, and they fitted him like a glove. Here was a man after his own heart who knew how to live in the wilderness and put its meaning into words for other people. To live like that, wandering and observing, independent of other people, and his own man, became Bundy's great ambition.

After graduation he managed to get a summer job watching for grazing infringements in the forest reserves of the California Sierras. He might have stayed on at the University to assist in the laboratory that summer, but a job in the Sierras sounded to him like the opportunity he wanted; and so, after his father had photographed him in his cap and gown and his mother had packed him a box of cookies and kissed him goodbye, he was on his way.

That summer in the Sierras, Bundy worked under a forest ranger named Matt Hinson. There was not much difference in their ages or enthusiasms, although they had different backgrounds. Hinson was an Easterner, a forester rather than a botanist, and freshly turned out of the new training program for rangers. He was one of Gifford Pinchot's smart young men who formed the spearhead for what had lately become the Forest Service under the Department of Agriculture.

This was before the days of lookout towers and telephones, azimuth boards and airplanes; it was before the days of a settled conservation policy that everyone accepted. The idea of the conservation of natural resources was so new in the rich and prodigal United States that it was practically limited to a small group of young men who made it an enthusiasm and a crusade. The sun about which these young men revolved was Gifford Pinchot, head of the Forest Service. Pinchot had, almost alone, built up the service and started the fight for conservation. He had a gift for leadership, and he aroused an almost fanatical loyalty in his young men.

Much of Bundy's knowledge of the growth of the Forest Service came to him informally at this time through his talks with Matt. Matt had the whole story on the tip of his tongue. He could take his listener through all the Acts of Congress, from the Homestead Act which Lincoln signed in 1862 and which turned over five hundred million acres of the public domain to private ownership, through the Desert Land Act of 1877 and the Timber and Stone Act of 1878, all giving away valuable resources with the prodigality of a careless and rich young nation whose only desire was to see its wilderness settled and its frontiers pushed forward.

"And now," Matt would cry, his face hot with impersonal anger, "all this land, or at least a lot of it, around fifty million acres they say, is coming back to us. It's been wrecked and exploited, and now it's reverting to public ownership. There'll be more millions of acres coming in, creating the new public domain of denuded lands, robbed of natural wealth, a national liability instead of an asset. And who has benefited? Not you or me or any of the little people—not the people this land was intended for. It's the lumber interests, the railroads, the big concerns. By God! it's the biggest crime and scandal of our times!"

Bundy too had seen wasteland, slashed and cut, its waters dried and its soil eroded. The memory of this moved him more powerfully than Matt's abstract figures did.

"But what can you do?" Bundy asked. "How are you going to stop it?"

Matt had the answers to that too, and his answers all began in the same way. Pinchot, he said, Pinchot and President Teddy Roosevelt, working together, they were the men who were saving what was left. If enough people backed them, they could put a stop to waste and save the unspoiled West for the greatest good of the greatest number of people.

"It's a crusade," Matt said. "It goes beyond the mere care for public lands, and becomes a struggle for political liberty."

That summer Pinchot came through the Sierras on one of his Western trips, and Matt saw to it that Bundy met him. In spite of a certain will to resist the man's influence, which came perhaps from his feeling that Matt's admiration was excessive, Bundy was impressed.

Pinchot had a courtly manner and looked like an Old World aristocrat; yet he could outdo the younger men in endurance on the trail. This was an almost irresistible combination. What finally won Bundy's complete loyalty was, in fact, a small incident that had nothing to do with conservation or democracy.

One day on the trail he saw Pinchot, mounted on a nervous, dancing horse, blow the head off a rattlesnake with a first shot from a small pearl-handled pistol. Bundy admired good shooting; he liked a cool head and a steady hand. Beyond the cool head and the steady hand he sensed the intensity and singleness of purpose that set a leader apart from men with ephemeral enthusiasms.

So, when Pinchot interested himself in Bundy's work and asked him to spend the next winter in the nation's capital learning more about the conservation of natural resources, Bundy agreed to go. For a time he was even persuaded that he might abandon botany for forestry in the name of a great democratic cause. But Pinchot had immediate use for a botanist and in the long run there was too little difference of direction to warrant quibbling.

Bundy enjoyed his first winter in Washington. He had never been East before, and although he loved and was loyal to the West, he had a touch of that inferiority which often afflicts young Westerners. It is a feeling that Western life, while good, is only a peripheral life, that the center is in the East. Bundy had not yet learned that each man's center is the spot where he stands.

The public shrines, the sights, the sounds, the smells of the nation's capital filled him with satisfaction; and being one of the chosen young men of G.P., gave him a feeling of belonging there—made him a national figure in his own small way.

With his mother as hostess, Pinchot held fortnightly suppers at the big family house on Rhode Island Avenue. Here, over gingerbread and baked apples, the young foresters transferred the business of the day into a realm of social comradeship which cemented interests and enthusiasm even more closely.

Everything G.P. did was planned with conservation in mind. On these recurring social evenings, it was possibly not so much the conservation of trees as of young men's minds and social habits in which G.P. was interested. However, if, as Bundy suspected, the master was pruning away their dead wood and uncouth underbrush, they were never made to feel the curator's hand. They simply put forth leaf and limb in a congenial atmosphere, as plants develop chlorophyll from the sun.

Bundy remembered one evening when they pored over a new map of the Idaho Panhandle, and someone said: "That's the best and one of the last of the Western white pine stands. If we can keep fire and the lumber companies out of it, we'll put it under a sane and ordered economy. We'll make it thrive and produce."

"The ranger?" someone asked.

"An old man named Ian MacGillicuddy. We don't know much about him, except that he was a Land Office man before forestry went over to the Department of Agriculture. That fact alone inclines one to suspect him. What we need is a trained observer to go in there quietly and get some bearings for us."

"A spy?" Bundy asked.

"Observer is a more agreeable name," Pinchot said, "but spy, if you like. Perhaps it amounts to the same thing in the long run."

His observant eyes rested on Bundy briefly and speculatively. "You don't like spying?"

"No," Bundy said.

"But trained observing?"

"That has a different sound to me. I can't agree that they amount to the same thing."

"Perhaps you are right," G.P. said.

Senators, visitors from abroad, figures of note around Washington often came to these meetings to speak or argue, or merely to listen. The most impressive visitor and one of the most frequent was the President himself. The cartoonists had given the President a familiar façade of glasses, teeth and Big Stick. The glasses and the teeth were there, and it was easy to imagine the Big Stick, but there was also an informal warmth and vitality in Roosevelt's manner which reached out and touched those who came in personal contact with him.

Altogether it was an illuminating winter for Bundy. When G.P. asked him to be the trained observer in the Clearwater forest that summer, his loyalties and enthusiasms had prepared him to give an affirmative answer.

Now, as he lay awake beside Jeff Carney, Bundy looked forward to putting all he had learned in Washington to some useful purpose.

7.

Lorena Carney, too, lay awake for a long time that night entertaining thoughts which were far different from the thoughts of Bundy Jones. She lay flat on her back, rigid and tense, beside Meggie who slept softly in a fetal curl of security.

The name of Ralph Carney, which had started Bundy's train of thought in one direction, had set Lorena's thoughts to racing in another.

Sometimes Lorena's mind was like the Japanese wind bell that used to hang on Grandma Wilson's front porch. Lorena had always hated the meaningless contrivance of glass that hung where one might strike one's head against it in the dark and set it to ringing when one most wished to be silent. In the daytime it would hang quiet and unnoticed until a breeze came in at the right angle and transformed it into an agitated mass of tinkling, clanking glass. So now all the brittle bits and pieces of her mind had been set ajangle by a man's name. There was an almost unbearable tinkling and clashing together of unyielding surfaces. The many bright, sharp parts struck together and made a meaningless, hard sound of fretfulness and frustration.

She thought of Ralph Carney in the many ways she had known him, the good and the bad, the trivial and the momentous. She thought of Madame Pontarlier, and the possibilities of her relationship with Ralph. The thoughts were all brittle and quick and badly tangled. They were little hard, clear scenes shifting and mingling without regard to chronology.

She was standing again in the employment office, fresh from a course in Gregg shorthand and speed typing, and Ralph Carney was looking at her. There were other girls there with more experience, but he had looked at her and she had known that she would be the one. That was a good moment, one of the moments of triumph and elation. His eyes were dark and decisive. They were eyes which appreciated beauty as well as utility. She hadn't minded that he was twice her age, because he had that virile something which she admired in men and which seemed to her ageless.

Her thoughts shifted again and she remembered a time when she had looked into a mirror and thought that since she was uncommonly beautiful, she could, perhaps, make something of it. She was a very young girl and she had been having a scene with Grandma Wilson about some trivial thing she had neglected to do. She was angry. But already she had learned to suppress her anger, because to strike back at Grandma Wilson did no good and only made more trouble. She turned and walked quickly out of the room where Mrs. Wilson was talking. In the hall she passed a mirror, and there she saw reflected a pair of flashing eyes in a wonderfully vital face. She paused, surprised, and, as if regarding a stranger, she sized herself up and compared herself to the girls she knew. Yes, she said to herself, I've got nothing else, but I've got *this*. Maybe it could be everything. The eyes, the rich color, even the breasts that had caused her anxiety and shame as they pushed out and tightened the little-girl dress she still wore—these were things she had that no one could take away from her. Not Grandma Wilson, or anybody else.

Mrs. Wilson was not really her Grandma. If she had been, perhaps they might have been closer and understood each other better. Mrs. Wilson had married Lorena's grandfather late in life, and her entry into the family had coincided almost perfectly with the return home of a stepdaughter who had no wedding ring but was about to present the family with a child. If Lorena's mother did not seem to feel her shame sufficiently, Mrs. Wilson felt it for her.

Mrs. Wilson very soon survived both Lorena's mother and grandfather, and, against her inclination, found herself in charge of a child born out of wedlock, and the only person with the responsibility of remembering that a sin had been committed. She guarded herself against forgetfulness.

Because Lorena's mother had been beautiful, Grandma Wilson always warned Lorena against beauty. Lorena could not remember her mother, and the old photographs were not very helpful. But it is wrong, Lorena thought, to blame a child for her mother. There is more sense to blaming a mother for the child. Yet she would not do that either. Lorena was an individualist, and, while she was afraid of loneliness, she saw with fatalistic clarity that in the long run every soul is alone and must act for itself. She feared loneliness because it had been the bugbear of her childhood, loneliness and austerity. Mrs. Wilson had thought to correct and control a child predestined to wildness and disorder by keeping her at work and out of mischief. The house had been very quiet, so quiet on summer afternoons that one heard the bees humming in the clover; so quiet on winter evenings that one heard the dripping of the leaky faucet in the kitchen sink.

She might have learned to love me a little bit, Lorena thought, but Mrs. Wilson had never ceased to be resentful and scandalized. She had adopted the role of patient martyr in the face of her world's commiseration and she had tried to do her duty by instilling moral principles in the child and keeping her out of harm's way.

Lorena looked back at Grandma Wilson without love and without resentment. It was the way the older woman saw things,

Lorena thought; maybe she couldn't help it. But, if she had thought to subdue Lorena's appetite for life and comfort and pleasure, she had completely failed. Lorena's bare and hungry childhood had filled her with the resolution to have warmth and admiration and luxury and love at all costs before she died.

And she had almost had it—almost. She could still feel Ralph Carney's hard, strong arms as they folded the coat about her shoulders. "You shouldn't go cold in that threadbare little coat."

"But this is so wonderful—too expensive, Ralph."

"Dark fur becomes you, Beauty."

He had always called her Beauty. She wondered if it was because he saw himself in the role of Beast? But no, he didn't plan these things. He took what came. He was old for her, but he had everything that she admired in a man, and in addition his wealth and success cast a kind of halo of glamour about him. At the time she took the coat she had hoped—yes, really hoped very much that she was going to share the wealth and the success with him. Yet when he gave her the ring, it had been an emerald and for the little finger.

"It cost as much as a diamond, Beauty," he had said, laughing, and he had kissed her. She should have known then—really she did, without letting herself admit the knowledge.

Yet Grandma Wilson's disparagement of her mother's weakness had taught Lorena one thing—and that was not to give too much. She gave a great deal because Ralph gave a great deal. But she never completely surrendered her pride or her sense of her own importance. If he had given more, she would have surrendered everything, because she had loved him. But Lorena was a bargainer. She had suffered too much isolation and heartache not to have learned the value of making a bargain and of keeping something for herself in reserve in case the deal fell through.

By the time Jeff came, she had known in her heart that there was no real future for her with his uncle. She had seen Jeff standing there in the office with his hat in his hand, the raw light from the unshaded electric bulb shining on his crisp blond hair. There had been that look of wondering admiration for her in his eyes, to which she had become accustomed by now. Jeff was her own age and he looked to her as much the man as his uncle was. Perhaps she had even thought at first that by encouraging Jeff she might make Ralph jealous. But now sometimes she wondered if this was what Ralph had wanted or planned all along. Ralph managed everyone and everything, dexterously and without ostentation. He soon tired of people, but he let them down easily without impairing a devotion which might yet be important to him at some later time. Jeff was young and good looking and he was a Carney with all the Carney wealth and privilege.

It was only after they were married that she saw the lacks in him, the lack of force, the lack of resolution. These were the particular qualities, she realized then, which she had admired in the uncle. It was the positive force and resolution that had made Ralph seem ageless and desirable. She was angry with herself for being deceived, she was angry with Jeff, but most of all she was angry with Ralph. He still smiled at her and called her Beauty when he saw her. But in the ruin of Jeff's father's financial affairs he gave them no help but this—to homestead and locate homesteaders.

If she found it impossible to endure this kind of life, she would have to start again to plan and work and lift herself. But it would be harder a second time because of the entanglements she was involved in, and because she had learned how easily one could be disillusioned and undone. Her initial confidence in her beauty and power had been shaken.

It was almost a certainty, however, she told herself, that they could sell the homestead soon and get on their feet financially again. Ralph wouldn't have abandoned them like this unless it was a sure solution to their problem. Yet she did not sleep for a long time. The facts of her life had never bred blind hope.

II

THE TRAIL

1.

The homesteaders took two days to prepare for their departure. The Cold Spring outfitters furnished all the staple homesteading supplies: flour, beans, salt pork, nails, sugar, canvas, dried peas, rice, canned milk, blankets, hominy, saws and planes. They had candles and lanterns, needles and pins, washtubs and pocket combs. What could a horse carry on its back into the wilderness? Within reason the Cold Spring stores had it.

But the Carney girls had brought some of the unreasonable luxuries with them from the larger town. They spread these treasures out on a blanket and solicited admiration and advice. They had extract of beef, olives and caviar, raisins and chocolate, little tins of potted ham and dried fruits. Bundy had never seen powdered eggs before or dehydrated vegetable soup, but the Carney ladies had them and were proud of their resourcefulness. They even had glass jars filled with butter which they meant to bury in the interior of their sacks of flour, so the butter would keep fresh and cool and the jars remain unbroken. Sam Carlson and Bundy stood in the group of interested spectators.

"You going to live pretty high, ain't you?" Sam inquired. "Where you going to keep all this until you get your houses built?"

"Under a pine tree," Meggie said, laughing, "and pray it doesn't rain."

"We're going to try to live like human beings," Lorena said—"civilized ones."

42

"They brought everything but their ball gowns," said Jeff. "I set my foot down at that."

Watching their preparations, Bundy tried to keep aloof. But they were full of gaiety and anticipation which they were determined to share with him.

"Doesn't it make your mouth water, Mr. Jones?" Meggie Carney cried. "I'll bet you'll be stopping by for dinner with us after you've seen all this."

"Maybe I will," Bundy said.

He had just come back from an interview with McSweeney, the packer. His horses were ready and his wants were simple. One day would have been enough to prepare him for the trail. There was nothing McSweeney needed to show him about packing a horse or throwing a diamond hitch. But McSweeney had been reluctant to let him start alone.

"You won't gain anything that way," McSweeney said. "There's still snow on Freezeout and sometimes the trail's hard to find. You better stay around until the pack train's complete, and hit the trail along with the rest of us."

"But I haven't any definite destination," Bundy said. "If I wander around a couple of days on the mountain, who's to care?"

"Have it how you like it," the packer said, "but folks out here take company when they can get it. Even the ranger joins the train instead of striking out alone. It's lonesome enough most of the time in there anyhow."

Some of Bundy's stubborn will to go it alone was lacking today. He was easily persuaded. He told himself that, after all, the homesteaders and the ranger were his job this summer, and where could he get to know them better than by riding the trail with them? Because he could so easily rationalize it, he felt no surprise at his own sudden preference for society instead of solitude.

Meggie Carney was looking at him archly now, and she said, "That's a promise, Mr. Jones. I'll expect you for dinner as soon as I've got a house built."

"Be careful, Bundy," Jeff said. "She doesn't know a thing about cooking. I don't think she can even light a fire."

"Now, Jeff," Meggie said, "I can make Welsh rabbit and fudge, and a fire is easy as long as there are matches."

Everybody laughed, and Bundy thought that Jeff and Meggie were playing the accustomed roles of indulgent big brother and addleheaded but charming little sister to perfection. Perhaps their parents had set them the pattern when they were children; perhaps they had originated it themselves. In any case it was a pleasant skit in which Jeff played the straight man and Meggie the amusing brat.

"I brought a cookbook, too," Meggie said, "and I know how to boil water. It's going to be a treat to attend my dinner parties, I can tell you."

"But where's your sourdough bucket, lady?" Eye McGillicuddy asked. Bundy saw that the ranger had joined the group of spectators and was ready to contribute to the laughter.

"Sourdough?" repeated Meggie. "What's that? It sounds horrid."

"You ain't no homesteader," the old man said, "until you get you a sourdough bucket."

"Never mind," Bundy said, "I'm coming around for one of your dinners before you get down to the sourdough bucket. I'll bring along some fresh trout, and if you can't cook it, I can."

"Fresh trout!" Lorena said, looking at Bundy with her slow and intimate smile. "I love fresh trout, and I can't cook either—at least not very much."

Bundy felt the smile strike through him, but he said lightly, "Your husband looks hale and hearty, Mrs. Carney. I don't believe you starve him."

"He's healthy," Lorena said lightly. "You can't kill him."

"Rena's all right," Jeff said seriously. "She cooks very nicely— plain food, that is." Lorena made up a little face that expressed amused distaste. Bundy wondered if Jeff cast everyone close to him in a theatrical role: Meggie, the funny little sister; himself, the thwarted hero; Lorena, the perfect wife. Someday Jeff was in for a rude awakening, Bundy thought, someday the curtain would go down and the homemade masks would fall, and Jeff would have to see the world as it was. Or would he? Didn't some people go through life rejecting reality in favor of the scene they preferred to enact? To misjudge and be misjudged, wasn't that the final role some people liked to play?

"Well," Bundy said, "I'd like to sample both of the ladies' cooking. How soon are those cabins going to be built?"

"About ten days, we figure," Jeff said. "Maybe two weeks. The season's short. We aren't going to waste any more time than we have to."

2.

On the morning of departure, everyone was up before daybreak. Lanterns bobbed in the predawn chill and the eyes of the horses gleamed in the moving light. McSweeney did some solid cussing before all of the Carney ladies' luxuries were stowed on the backs of their pack horses. Finally the mandolin and the last folding camp chair went on top of the last load.

"Damn the mandolin!" McSweeney said, but he said it to himself for he was invariably polite to ladies.

Mrs. Pulver had a big hot breakfast ready to serve at their convenience, and people came in and ate as they found time.

It was light by the time the horses were packed and lined up for departure.

The Carney girls appeared that morning in appropriate costume. The big hats, pretty dresses and high heels had been left in storage with Mrs. Pulver. They wore neat khaki divided skirts, men's tan flannel shirts and broad-brimmed felt hats, and on their feet, high laced boots with calked soles. In spite of her informal outfit Lorena was serene and reserved, and, as always, beautiful.

Meggie was excited and busy playing the clown. She had a big, old-fashioned pistol strapped around her waist in a leather holster, and it was evident that this was more of a comic property than a serious asset. It produced the desired effect. The packer, the lumberjacks, the other men who stood around in the half light of early morning to watch the departure, all twitted her about it.

"Is your gun loaded, lady?" they asked.

"I won't tell that," Meggie said. "It looks enough to scare anyone, doesn't it?"

"Maybe you can scare some *man*, Ma'am. But there ain't no bear going to step aside for it unless you're prepared to shoot it."

"Well then, it's loaded," Meggie said, "really and truly."

"It's more dangerous to *her* than to anything else," Jeff said. "She couldn't hit a red barn door."

"I could do pretty well by myself," Meggie said, "if I didn't always have a big brother around to tell on me. It isn't fair."

Jeff put his arm affectionately around her shoulder. "She's a good little fool," he said, "one of the best."

Miss O'Rourke had gone a step further than the Carney girls in her costume. She wore the flannel shirt and the calked boots, but instead of the riding skirt she wore an old pair of man's trousers which she had rolled up from the bottom to make the right length. "A relic of my late lamented third husband," she told everybody with a grin. "He was the one that robbed the First National Bank and got hanged for shooting the cashier."

"So you're a widow, eh?" said Eye MacGillicuddy, looking her over. "I placed you as one of them wisht-he'd-ast-me girls."

"I'll thank you to leave my private life alone, MacGillicuddy," Miss O'Rourke said good-naturedly. "It's nobody's business but my own how many husbands I've run through. Nobody needs to know that the first one used to horsewhip the butcher, and that the second was a kleptomaniac—"

"A which?" said Eye.

"A maniac to you," Miss O'Rourke said. Having had two good nights' rest and being mildly drunk on tea, she was in fine fettle this morning. She sat her horse like a jaunty Irish squire, and she was going on to relate the exploits of an imaginary fourth husband, when the tinkle of pack bells up ahead warned that the first section of the train was beginning to move.

"Here, Jessie," Eye called to his little dog. She had been keeping close to the heels of his horse, her eyes fixed on the old man's face, eager for departure and waiting for the sign. Now she gathered her haunches for a leap onto the horse's back. With her unaccustomed weight, she barely made it, clinging and clawing on the saddle blanket to draw herself up. The horse stood patiently as if used to this procedure, and in a moment the little bitch gained the summit of Eye's bedroll which was strapped behind his saddle. She stood precariously on top of it, wagging her tail and ready to go.

"Good lass," Eye said. "Hang on tight, and hang onto them

pups, too, till we get home. Ain't no use droppin' them along the way for the wildcats to feed on. Dogs is valuable out here." He turned to Bundy and said, "You ought to get you a dog, man."

"Well," Bundy said, "how about one of Jessie's pups?"

"We'll see how many she brings forth," Eye said. "Some is already spoken for."

"I'd like a puppy too," Meggie Carney said. "I'm going to be all alone on my place when we've built our cabins."

"Is the gun not enough protection for ye, Ma'am?" asked Eye grinning.

"It'll be fine when I learn to shoot it," Meggie said, "but it won't keep me from getting lonesome."

"It sure won't," Eye said. "Out here a lady who's handy with a gun is the lonesomest critter there is."

"I'd even pay you something for a nice little dog," Meggie coaxed.

"I'll take your offers under consideration," Eye said. "To be honest with ye, I'm more interested in good homes for the lassie's pups than I am in pay. I'll look you up later and see what kind of place you got."

"That's something to aim for," Meggie said. "I'll make my place so nice that even one of Jessie's pups will like it. How's that? Is that ambitious enough, do you think?"

"We'll see," Eye said. "We'll see."

The horses were all moving now, and the bells tinkling through the dewy woods. Sunlight was yellow on the tops of the trees, the shadows still deep and chill below. Somewhere a wood thrush sang. It was a fine morning and Bundy was glad to be going.

The trail led right away from the meadows and almost immediately Cold Spring was lost behind trees. They moved slowly, single file, eleven people on horseback and eighteen pack animals. They made a caravan. Besides the Carneys, Miss O'Rourke, Bundy, Eye and the packer, Charlie Duporte was riding along and there were the three timber willies who had been hired to help the homesteaders clear and build.

Just beyond the village the trail became more primitive and ill-tended. Winter storms had brought trees down across the path in several places, and no one had been public-spirited enough as yet to saw a way through them. It was as if, Bundy thought, the end of the wagon road marked the end of any public responsibility. Whoever went beyond that point was bound to take things as they came. It was every man for himself.

At the first fallen tree, a temporary trail led around the log that blocked the path; at another, the horses jumped and scrambled over it, their bells clanging. They were sturdy and patient animals, schooled to follow and to bear burdens. Yet the wilderness had also taught them a certain resourcefulness. If a tree barred their path they had their ways of getting over it.

Bundy was well enough pleased with his own horses. McSweeney had furnished him with a little sorrel mare for riding and a shaggy chestnut gelding with a white star on his forehead to bear the pack. The pack horses were assembled head to tail in the front part of the train. McSweeney, Charlie Duporte and the lumberjacks rode at intervals among them. The other riders followed along behind.

Bundy saw the tail of Eye MacGillicuddy's Jessie waving like a flag as Eye's horse lifted man and dog jerkily over the second log. Lorena came next, sitting lightly and firmly and taking the jump with grace. Meggie bobbed and shrieked, but all in the best of humor and agog for adventure. Jeff Carney and Bundy brought up the rear of the procession.

The trail went gradually downward for awhile, although most of their journey that day was to be upward into the mountains.

For a long time before they reached the bottom of the downgrade, Bundy could hear the sound of running water, and he remembered that there was a stream to ford. People in Cold Spring had made light of the ford, "shallow and a good hard bottom," they had said. But Eye MacGillicuddy had added mildly, "Snow's coming out now. Happen we'll have to swim it."

The ranger was right, Bundy thought, as he heard the increasing noise of the water.

The horses ahead went more and more slowly, and presently Charlie Duporte came riding back along the narrow trail, looking for the ladies. He was bearing bad tidings, but with zest. Charlie's lively curiosity made anything unforeseen enjoyable to him. Now he was wholly preoccupied with the pleasure of shocking the ladies by news of high water.

"By gar! The horse she have to swim!" he cried joyously. "River boiling. Ain't no ford today. By gar! You ladies going to take a bath, I t'ink!" His white teeth gleamed with laughter.

"Swim?" cried the Carney girls, and Miss O'Rourke cried, "*Swim?*" There was a flutter of consternation, and Charlie was rewarded for his efforts.

"I take care of you," he said. "I see you safe across. You bet!"

McSweeney halted the pack horses on the bank of the stream and rode back to the others to give instructions. He was calm and matter-of-fact.

"She's up several inches since I come by last week," he said. "But there's no danger. We'll make it easy enough. It's the snow coming out of the hills this hot weather. All you ladies got to remember is keep your feet up out of the water and hang on. The horse'll know what to do. He'll get you across all right."

"You mean there's no other way to get across?" Miss O'Rourke asked.

"Not unless you want to walk across," the packer said. He said it grimly. He kept his wife quiet and safe in a log house in Cold Spring. As many times as he had made the trip over Freezeout Mountain into the white pine country, he had never taken her with him. He had a certain opinion of homesteading females and it was not flattering. "Women belong in town," he said among the men. "They belong in houses with pots and kettles around them and babes in the cradle. I hate like the devil to have 'em in my train." To the gallivanting women he was infallibly courteous and considerate. He did the best he could for them, and only an occasional flash of grim irony betrayed his feelings. He was in command now, like the captain of a ship or a general on campaign. He gave orders and he expected the others to obey. His concern at the moment was not so much with his inexperienced townsfolk as with their pack horses. He told Eye MacGillicuddy to lead off, followed by the pack animals. The three lumberjacks and Charlie were to go along beside the pack horses, keeping them in line, and, if possible, out of trouble. Mrs. Carney was to come after the pack horses with her husband behind her to look out for her. Next he ordered Miss O'Rourke in line, then Meggie, and finally Bundy.

Bundy began to understand that he had been urged to join the train as much to give McSweeney an extra hand with the ladies as for his own comfort and protection. McSweeney himself, on a sturdy horse, crossed over and back several times, shouting instructions and encouragement. He wanted no stragglers, no soaked packs, no horses carried downstream by the current.

Bundy sat on his little mare on the bank of the swollen stream and awaited his turn. He would have preferred to look after pack horses rather than women. His own pack horse meant a lot to him. He had invested every cent he had in his summer's supplies and they were all on the back of one horse. His wages for this summer wouldn't come in until fall. He hoped that the shaggy chestnut pony with the white star was sure-footed and a good swimmer, because he wanted to eat during the next two months.

The stream made a sound which drowned everything but the men's shouts. It gave Bundy a half-paralyzed feeling of having lost one of his senses. Ears choked with the meaningless roar of moving water, he felt suspended in unreality. The sensation was not new to him. It had often come over him when he was fishing or waiting to ford or swim in mountain water. Wading in cold water to his thighs in a rushing mountain stream, he had sometimes doubted his own identity, until suddenly the fierce tug of a trout on the end of his line brought him back to the land of the living once again.

Feeling this numbness of mind and spirit, he watched Eye, his dog in his arms, lead off the line of waiting horses. One by one the reluctant beasts began plunging in after him. Each horse gathered its quivering haunches into a knot of desperation and resolution, and then made the plunge from slippery bank into swirling water. Their eyes rolled wildly as they began to struggle with the cold flood. At first they were turned by the current and momentarily pulled downstream; then they thrust their necks forward and strained upstream and toward the opposite shore as their legs found the stride of swimming. It was a short crossing but a stiff one.

Lost in his own preoccupation, Bundy felt rather than heard the nudge of a horse close to his. Looking around he saw Meggie Carney beside him. She too was watching the plunging horses, and she was not clowning any more. Her mouth moved in speech, but, with the noise of river and shouting, Bundy did not know what she said.

The packer had given her a poor-spirited little horse, probably because it was old and not too mettlesome for an inexperienced rider. But Bundy saw that it must have seen livelier days, for both of its ears had been cropped. This was a way the woodsmen had of marking an outlaw horse, one that had killed a man or been stubborn to break or had somehow run counter to the law which man lays down for helpless brutes to follow. Nobody had told Meggie that the horse she was riding had been an outlaw, or she would have made a comedy out of it, along with her antiquated pistol. But the comedy and the bravado of an hour ago were suddenly gone out of her. She looked like a scared child.

Bundy was sorry for her, yet involuntarily his eyes went beyond her to Lorena, and his sympathy for one girl was lost in admiration for the other. Lorena was pale but she sat quiet and straight on her waiting horse. She isn't afraid, he thought. Suddenly he wanted an opportunity to show Lorena the best that was in him, to be heroic for her sake. He had never before had the urge to exhibit his strength for a woman. A kind of happiness accompanied the wish.

When the pack animals were all across, the line of riders moved forward. Lorena's horse hesitated for an instant and then plunged in and began to swim. Jeff followed her. Miss O'Rourke, with a loud "Here goes" and "God help us," came next.

Now it was Meggie's turn, but her little outlaw stood stubborn and balky at the edge of the stream, refusing to go. Meggie cast a baleful glance over her shoulder, and Bundy could see her mouth working as if she were going to cry.

McSweeney rode up then and gave her horse a smart slap on the haunch that made him leap off suddenly into the swirling water. As Bundy moved his horse into place, ready for the plunge, he saw that Meggie was in trouble. Her horse was frightened and felt his rider's fright, for Meggie had lost hold of her reins and clung helplessly to the high pommel of her Western saddle, "pulling leather" as ranchers say. The outlaw turned half round as if to return to the bank he had just left, and the current caught him and began to carry him downstream.

Unreasoning joy flooded Bundy's mind. Before McSweeney could take action, Bundy urged his horse into the stream after them. Cold spray flew up all around him; he felt the tug and pull of the water. His horse was steady and would have gone for the other bank, but Bundy turned her downstream after the outlaw. Lacking the authority of a taut rein, Meggie's animal was floundering helplessly, swept along by the water. Bundy's horse gained on the other one easily, and soon he was close enough to catch the slack rein and steer the bewildered outlaw to safety. They reached the other shore some distance downstream, where the landing was more difficult than at the open ford, but they were able to scramble up the bank and return to join the others.

It was a small incident, but it had a certain effect on all of them. It was their first taste of the grim reality of wilderness living, and as such it was sobering. Further than that, it subtly altered all their relationships in one way or another. McSweeney and the lumberjacks looked at the botanist with more interest and respect. Jeff, although he was loud with thanks and praise, began ever so slightly to dislike this quiet young man. Charlie Duporte, who enjoyed being the hero of every occasion, was envious. Bundy was happy because he saw admiration and approval in Lorena's eyes. He scarcely looked at tearful Meggie who was the cause of it all. But Meggie looked at him, and, whether he wished it or not, she was prepared to give him gratitude and devotion.

Meggie was soaked to the knees and shivering, but she did not complain as much as she might have. She had left some of her volubility on the other bank of the stream.

After that they began to climb slowly, and the sun grew warm. The horse's shaggy legs steamed in the sun; the women regained their color. Miss O'Rourke, having surprised herself by crossing without mishap, began to sing an Irish ditty full of the sorrows and misfortunes of the world but so sentimentally set forth that the tears it evoked were purely agreeable ones.

As Bundy's glow of personal satisfaction began to cool, he had an impulse of friendliness toward unfortunate Meggie. He rode up beside her, and asked kindly, "Well, are you drying out?"

"Yes," she said.

"Let me show you how to hold your reins," Bundy said. "You must keep them firm. Let them pass through your fingers in this way. I'm new enough at this business myself to appreciate the little tricks that McSweeney and the others take for granted."

Meggie let him place the reins more easily and firmly through her fingers.

"You see," he said, "you've got to hold onto a horse as if you mean it. Otherwise he gets the idea that nobody's in control. You see?"

"Thank you," Meggie said meekly. "I hope I'll learn."

"Of course you'll learn," said Bundy cheerily. "You're doing fine." He drew his horse back into line behind her, and he felt satisfied with himself and the upward trail and the sunny morning and the clear, rare air.

They stopped for lunch at Cloudy Camp. There was a spring here and good grazing for the horses, but the wind was chilly, and old snow lay in the northern folds of the slopes above them.

Bundy was pleased to find that their morning's ride had brought them from summer back into springtime. The fresh, lush grass was full of early flowers. Climbing up the slope a short distance, Bundy found trilliums and glacier lilies. He made a little nosegay of them and took it down to Lorena Carney who was standing below watching him. To see the delicate yellow and white lilies in her hands gave him a fresh appreciation of their beauty.

"How do they bloom so near the snow?" she marveled.

"The prettiest flowers bloom at the edge of the snow," Bundy said enthusiastically. "That's the wonderful thing. In the Alps it's like that—almost at the edge of the snow there are the tiny cyclamens, the edelweiss, the gentians and alpine roses."

"But have you been in the Alps?" she asked.

"Oh, no," said Bundy, laughing, "only in books, of course. You can go anywhere in books."

"You're very funny, Mr. Jones," she said, but she looked at him kindly. She stuck the little bunch of flowers into her belt.

"Come and get it!" Charlie Duporte shouted to them.

They went to the fire where McSweeney and Eye MacGillicuddy had been busy cooking the lunch.

The ranger might have been camp cook or general roustabout, Bundy noted. The old man seemed to have no particular pride in his position, or desire to assume authority. A good ranger, Bundy thought, should invariably be neat and competent, reserved and in authority. Eye was untidy and garrulous, and his position as ranger evidently did nothing to elevate him above the other woodsmen.

Still Bundy's feeling of uneasiness was somewhat tempered by his hunger. From the campfire came a fine aroma of coffee and of frying bacon. In the top of a sack of flour the ranger had stirred up water and salt to make bannock which he fried in the bacon grease. It was crisp and tasty. Their appetites made a fine thing of it.

"Where have you been, Rena?" Jeff said to his wife.

"Nowhere," she said. "Look, Mr. Jones gave me flowers. They bloom near the snow. Aren't they nice?"

Meggie and Nan O'Rourke were already drinking their coffee, their hands around the tin cups to get all the warmth they could. They all stood up to eat, glad of the change from sitting in the saddle.

3.

After lunch they continued to climb up a winding rocky trail, now in deep woods, now out on a bare slope of the mountain.

Homesteading country? Bundy thought. My God, no! What are these women doing here? Do they themselves know? And Jefferson Carney and his precious Uncle Ralph, do they think they can fool the Government into giving them its best white pine? And I am the one who will have to see that they don't get it. Would Eye Mac-Gillicuddy really put up any opposition? I don't think so. If I weren't here, who would know or care? It would be simple for them. If I weren't here to make a report—

Soon they were in the remnants of last winter's snow. The trail was hard packed, but the drifts which lay on either side of it were rotted with age. They had been so deep that in this high altitude, summer had as yet only gnawed and fretted at them. A few weeks more of roaring streams and swollen rivers, and the snow would be gone. Now it was another hazard to the travelers.

"Keep away from the big trees," McSweeney cautioned. "The

snow's rotten around their roots. It looks all right on top, but it won't bear weight. It's gone underneath."

It was Meggie's little outlaw that went astray and broke through the surface crust near one of the trees. His hind quarters sank in the gutted snow, and he floundered and thrashed about in frightened efforts to extricate himself. McSweeney and one of the timber willies worked to pull and help him out.

This time Bundy sat and watched. Lorena drew her horse in beside him. "Poor Meg," she said coolly. "She draws trouble."

Jeff rode up and down, concerned but ineffectual. Bundy saw Lorena's lip curl with a certain scorn as she watched him.

Meggie managed to keep her seat, and, when she was back on the trail again, Bundy noted that she was holding the reins as he had shown her. She looked peaked and on the verge of tears, but she didn't cry.

Later, when they came out on the open shoulder of the mountain where the icy trail seemed to hang between open sky and the ravine below, it happened to be the horse carrying Meggie's pack that lost its footing and rolled over and over down the slope. She didn't cry then either, but her pale lips twitched and trembled as she watched the men working to get the animal back on the trail.

The pack horse had a precarious footing among some twisted alpine firs halfway down. McSweeney and old Eye scrambled down after the horse, unloaded the battered pack, and got the animal back on the trail.

"My mandolin," Meggie said, when they were up on the trail. "What happened to my mandolin?"

"God damn your mandolin," McSweeney said. "If the horse had broke a leg, we'd have shot him, and your mandolin could have laid down there and rotted."

They brought up the various sections of the pack, and the mandolin, by some miracle or freak of fortune, was only slightly cracked along one of the back ribs.

It was later discovered that the paper bags of rice, split peas and lentils had burst and the contents run together inside the flour sack which held them all, so that Miss Meggie could never cook one without the others that summer. By the time she had acquired a place to cook, however, she had rallied her good humor, and she took a facetious pride in what she called her "packhorse special mixture."

After this they climbed on uneventfully and doggedly to the summit of a pass, and just beyond it reached the shelter of a cabin where the travelers of this trail always spent the night.

No one had ever lived in the cabin. It had been put up as a convenience to travelers on the Freezeout trail, and anybody was welcome to use it. Bundy was to know it well before the summer was over, but he saw now for the first time its rough-hewn, smoky walls with dates and initials scrawled or carved by many passers who felt that they had reached a point of experience and endurance which must be recorded. Literary efforts accompanied some of the names.

> *A fool there was.*
> *Here his name, Chuck Harger*
> *Lewiston, Ida., '01*

> *God helps them that helps thereselves*
> *but only old Devil on this here Mt.*

> *O. D. D., '06*

And the romantic note,

> *Ada, for you I pine*
> *for you I balsam.*
> *Billy B. '03*

Some were obscene and blasphemous, some were illegible. Mostly however, the inscriptions were only names and addresses and dates.

This cabin was a monument which immortalized the transient man. Chuck and Billy, O. D. D. and all of the others had registered here on their way from one hard day to another. There were no faces, no histories, only the ghostly names penciled and carved into the blackened logs for later travelers to read and ponder on.

The pack train was out of the snow on this side of the pass, but it was still high and cold. The men unpacked and hobbled the horses and throughout the night the pack bells tinkled and clanged about the cabin as the horses sought the sparse feed.

Indoors the lumberjacks built up a roaring fire in the stone fireplace. The builder of the cabin had done pretty well except with his chimney. If the breeze was not right it smoked abominably, but it was tolerable that first night, and they relished the hot coffee, the bacon and flapjacks it helped to provide. The cabin had a couple of rough bunks, like wide shelves pegged into the wall.

"Where are we going to sleep?" Nan O'Rourke asked belligerently. "The ladies, I mean."

"Ma'am," said McSweeney, "we generally hang up a blanket in the middle of the room, and the females choose the best side."

For awhile after eating they sat around the fire. The women were silent, but this was the time of day in which the men delighted. The trail behind them, food in the belly, companions brought together for a time between the long periods of loneliness that frontier men know too well, it was a good time.

Eye McGillicuddy led off the talk in his nasal drawling voice. He was full of yarns about bears and wildcats, horses, dogs, and his own prowess. The lumberjacks and McSweeney contributed their tales and Charlie Duporte, his.

The name of Paul Bunyan slid into the yarning and gave it a fresh impetus. Paul Bunyan was still alive in 1908. He had not yet become a character of literature, and he was at his best among the yarning groups around the iron stove in the lumber camp or by the open fire in a mountain cabin. He was half joke, half real to the woodsmen.

Eye told about a Swede who attended a sky pilot's meeting in one of the camps and heard the preacher talking about John Bunyan's *Pilgrim's Progress*. The Swede got up in the back of the audience and shouted, "Say, mister, vas Yon a brudder to Paul?" Yes, the woodsmen believed in Paul Bunyan, as children believe in Santa Claus, with a mind half convinced and a will to hold off doubt.

After a while the air in the cabin reeked with the close relaxation of men who had spent an active day in the open. Bundy yearned for air, and, catching Jeff Carney's eye, he swallowed the distaste he had felt for Jeff on the trail, and grinned at him. They both arose and went outside.

The mountain air was like a dash of cold water in the face, but, after the first sharp gasp, it was invigorating.

The three women followed them out, and for a moment they

stood silently looking up at the stars above the low wall of twisted
mountain firs. All about them were the tinkling bells of the hobbled
horses.

"Old Eye was talking about bears and wildcats," Meggie said.
"Are we—are we going to see any?"

"Not tonight, I guess," Jeff said, "with all these bells to scare
them off."

"They carry on about women being such talkers," said Miss
O'Rourke. "That old ranger takes the cake for shooting off his
mouth. No woman has a chance when he's around."

"I like to listen to them talking," Meggie said. "I wish I could
put it all down to remember."

"You'll get enough before the summer's over," said Lorena. "I
think maybe I've got enough already."

"You're tired," Jeff said. "It's been an awful day for you girls.
Tomorrow it's all downhill and back into summer. We'll be there
by noon. And you never saw prettier white pine."

"I can't seem to care a whole lot whether it's going to be pretty
or not," Lorena said. She put her hand very lightly on Bundy's arm
and added, "The only pretty thing I've seen so far was the bunch
of flowers Mr. Jones picked for me this noon."

A voice behind them said, "You like wild flowers, lady? I pick
you lots of them." Charlie Duporte had come out and joined the
others so quietly that no one had noticed him.

"That will be nice," Lorena said. She turned to him and her
hand left Bundy's arm as lightly as it had come.

"I sing you songs too," Charlie said, "if you got time to listen."

"Time is about all we will have, isn't it?" Lorena said.

Bundy could imagine how her mouth smiled in the darkness.

Miss O'Rourke yawned loudly with a crackling of her jaws.
"Let's get them to hang up that blanket and let's turn in," she
said.

McSweeney had hung up the promised blanket across the middle
of the cabin when they went indoors. They spread bedrolls and
blankets on the rough floor, removed their boots, and made themselves as comfortable as possible. The men's side of the cabin floor
was crowded, and Bundy thought, Thank God, I'll be out on the
trail by myself tomorrow night. He liked clean air and his own
society.

After everybody was bedded down Eye McGillicuddy continued to talk. "Yon deer I shot, when I went to pick up the carcass, had a hole as big as your two hands right through the guts of it. Aye, and when I come to dress her out, the liver was missing. The liver's a tasty bit, an' I went back down trail to see what had become of it. Danged if I didna find it, lying there in the trail, a hundred yards or so back. I'd shot the liver clean out of her, I had."

Miss O'Rourke's voice came shrill and testy from the other side of the blanket. "You're a mighty man, McGillicuddy. Think what you'll be tomorrow, after you've kept your mouth shut for a couple of hours."

"Well, Ma'am, good night to you," Eye said, "and sweet dreams."

There was a ripple of laughter from behind the women's curtain, then silence. Bundy lay awhile letting his thoughts roam. They took an unaccustomed path, away from trees and plants and the questions of morality and justice that often seriously occupied them. With surprise he found himself conscious of the fact that he lay in the same room with the beautiful Mrs. Carney. He wondered if this thought was plaguing each of the other seven men who lay in the insurmountable safety of numbers all about him. But soon their heavy breathing rose like a palpable hum of innocence and mingled with the sound of wind in the trees outside the cabin. Bundy reproached himself for his own unguarded fancies, turned over and went to sleep.

It was not a completely restful night. The floor was hard and cold, and there was a good deal of snoring in various keys and rhythms. Toward morning Eye's little bitch, Jessie, started to have her pups.

At first light the men began to stir, and one by one they arose, stiff and blear-eyed, to face the new day. McSweeney and Charlie built up the fire. The rest of the men pulled on their boots and cleared out of the cabin with the tactful idea of giving the ladies some privacy. Grumbling or in silence, they splashed the icy spring water on their hands and faces, and began to round up the hobbled horses.

Smoke from the cabin chimney hung in the misty air, carrying with it a fragrance of pitchy wood, coffee and bacon that revived their interest in the coming day. When they returned to the cabin it was hazy with smoke, but it was warm. The women had set out tin plates and cups on the trestle table, and Charlie and the packer were dishing out the inevitable bannock and bacon.

Bundy had resolved not to look at Mrs. Carney this morning, but there she was, standing near the fireplace twisting her long dark hair into a coil at the back of her neck. Her cheeks were pink in the firelight, her face still beautiful and serene. The uncomfortable night seemed not to have touched her at all.

As he was standing by the table looking at her, lost to all his resolutions, Meggie Carney came and pulled at his sleeve.

"Look here a minute," she said.

"What is it?" Bundy asked, still watching Lorena twist her hair into a soft dark coil.

"It's the puppies," Meggie said. "Look at them. If he lets you have one, which are you going to choose?"

Eye had installed his bitch on an old blanket in a corner of the cabin where she lay, proud and watchful. Three small, blind, living creatures, no bigger than moles, nuzzled and bumped her. Bundy allowed Meggie to propel him to the corner of the room, and they stood together looking down at Jessie and her pups. Jessie returned their regard with bright eyes, but warily, and her tail thumped a propitiatory tattoo on the floor.

"There are only three," Bundy said. "How many did he say were spoken for?"

"We'll get around him some way," Meggie said. "I've taken a fancy to the runty one with the white tip on its tail. You don't want that one, do you?"

"I wouldn't have the runt," Bundy said. "I'll take the fat one with the yellow ruffle. They're real pure-quill mongrel, aren't they?"

"I think that's why I like them," Meggie said.

Lorena came and joined them. Her lovely hair was pinned now; her eyes and voice were lazily mocking. "Our little four-footed friends," she said. "Are you really interested in them?"

"Why not?" Bundy said. "They added their bit to the horrors of the night, didn't they?"

"That should be more than enough for you. You aren't thinking of possessing one?"

"Why, Rena, a dog is just what we need!" Meggie said seriously. "Whoever heard of a homesteader without a dog?"

"You hear of one now," Lorena said. As she looked at the squirming puppies, her face changed. A kind of loathing disgust spread over it. "I believe they're blind," she said. "How horrible! What would you do with a blind dog?"

"They're only just born, Rena," Meggie said. "They'll open their eyes later. They aren't really blind."

But Lorena said stubbornly, "Blind. How horrible."

Eye MacGillicuddy had been watching them, as nervously, Bundy suspected, as Jessie did.

"I'll bide here a few days," the ranger said, "until the wee things are fit to travel."

Bundy looked at the old man curiously. "Your duties don't sit very heavily, do they, Ranger?"

"I been up to the lookout the morn. There ain't no smoke. I got no cause to fash mysel'. My dog is more important to me than time is to another feller."

"Mr. MacGillicuddy," Meggie said, "what in the world are you going to do with so many dogs? Don't tell me they're all spoken for?"

"Three," said Nan O'Rourke, looking over their shoulders. "That's one apiece for the ladies, eh, MacGillicuddy?"

"Not for me," cried Lorena. "I don't want any little helpless thing depending on me."

"But me," Meggie said. "How about me, Mr. MacGillicuddy?"

"Aye," the ranger said. "You had all the bad luck yesterday. Today I give you first pick of Jessie's pups."

"Oh, thank you!" Meggie beamed. "But how shall I get it? Will you bring it to me?"

"You get your house built," said the ranger, "and then in three, four weeks, I come along by your place to see how you're a-farin'. Then I bring you your dog." He looked around at Nan O'Rourke. "You want one, too? You've a cranky tongue in your head, but that oft betokens a soft heart."

"Leave my tongue and my heart out of it," Nan O'Rourke said, "but I'll take a dog to look after my virtue."

"Ye've no' done badly lookin' after that yoursel'," remarked the ranger, "but I'll give ye a pup anyway."

"You told me the other day your pups were all spoken for," Bundy said.

"Man," the ranger said, "I'd never lie for nobody but my bitch. But she deserves the best. I wanted to travel along with you folks for a day before I seen whether you was fit to look out for a dog. So now I come to the conclusion you'll do as well as the next feller, Mr. Jones."

"You know I'm not a homesteader," Bundy said. "I'll be roaming around."

"I'll find you," said the ranger. "Don't nobody roam these woods I canna locate. A small dog rides fine behind the saddle, and a friendly face is more important to a dog than a shake roof. Don't think I'd give my pup to anybody neither. I'm a true judge of character, Mr. Jones, and I like your face fine."

It was an accolade in its way, but one which Bundy was unable at the moment to return. He was beginning to feel a certain human warmth toward the ranger, but respect was lacking. Bundy's unqualified approval must always have respect mixed up in it, as well as human warmth.

Lorena took up the ranger's words. "You see, Mr. Jones," she said. "We all like your face just fine." Her horror of the blind puppies was suddenly dissolved in the splendor of her smile—the personal and intimate smile that he had first encountered on the stage between Bolster and Cold Spring. With irritation Bundy felt himself blushing again.

He heard Meggie's voice saying plaintively, "Well why don't we eat?"

"Why not?" he said. "A man shouldn't even accept a dog on an empty stomach."

Over his tin plate he saw that Lorena was still smiling, but to herself now, with a certain satisfaction.

4.

After breakfast they left the ranger, his two horses and his four dogs at the halfway cabin; and the rest of the pack train took the downward trail toward the Floodwood Valley.

Bundy had intended to talk seriously with Eye MacGillicuddy about forest problems, but there had been no opportunity. Their talk had been of the most casual nature and had consisted in anecdotes of Eye's prowess as hunter or trapper or had been concerned with dogs and horses. How much the old man knew besides remained a mystery.

Bundy's own destination on this initial journey was unfixed. He wanted first to see the white pine country. Later he could devote his time to mosses and lichens and to the serious intentions of homesteaders and ranger. After he left the homesteaders, he expected to establish some sort of camp from which he could move freely, and perhaps he would do a little fishing while he figured out his next steps.

It was a morning to remember, golden and green, and full of the sound of pack bells and the distant song of the thrush, bell-like, too, in its way.

Soon after leaving the halfway cabin their trail joined a section of the old Lolo Trail, and became wider and easier than it had been the day before. Nothing of history remained here. The forest was unchanged by the transient feet of explorers and Indians. Few people remembered that the Nez Percés had trekked through here on their last futile attempt to find freedom. There were no Indians in the forest now. The surviving Nez Percés were restricted to their reservation in the cous and cammas country. At Lapwai the Macbeth sisters and their nieces, following the Spaldings, were at work, with considerable success, in turning the Nez Percé braves into Presbyterian ministers and deacons.

For a long time the forest had been given up to the birds and animals and the migrant trappers. Now the homesteaders were on the march, fanning out into seemingly impossible areas of wilderness with the avowed intention of establishing farms. Behind them, as Bundy saw it, followed the predatory shadow of the lumber companies.

Yet on a beautiful morning such as this, Bundy found it difficult to organize the thoughts and plans which had been so clean-cut and important in distant Washington. Here on the spot, which had previously been only part of a dotted line on a blueprint, sun poured through green branches, mica sparkled like diamonds in brightly colored rocks, spring flowers thrust their delicate freshness through the brown layer of last year's needles. It was impossible not to surrender oneself to this moment, leaving the philosophical or economic cogitations to men in swivel chairs in upper offices.

Only one facet of his multiple duty continued to wink at Bundy in his present sense of content with the day, the weather and the place. He felt urgently that he should warn these people against hoping too much. He had not yet seen their homesteads, but he was sure that they would be unsuited to agricultural purposes. If Eye MacGillicuddy would not fight their claims, he would be bound to do so himself. Let Jeff Carney, backed by his uncle, take the risk, Bundy thought, but alone. Don't let him drag a lot of helpless women into it. He could not tell them openly that he would fight their claims; but he could drop a word of warning.

He had thought that he would speak to Meggie or Nan O'Rourke rather than to Lorena. But, as the trail widened, Bundy found himself riding directly behind Lorena; and then, as her horse paused to snatch a mouthful of grass from a green bank, he was riding beside her.

"Are you happy?" she said to him. "We've crossed the mountain and the river, and now we're going down into a warm, green valley."

"Yes," he said, "I'm happy. But I remember, too, that there will always be the mountain and the river to cross before we reach the valley. Doesn't that alarm you? To make a home in such an inaccessible place?"

"When we go out again, the snow will be gone on the mountain. The river will be a little stream. A person has to look forward to something, doesn't he?"

"Yes, yes," he said, "but to make a home here! Do you think you can?"

"A home is hard to make in any place," she said.

"But you have one in town," Bundy said.

"We have a house," she said. "What is a home? Sometimes I wonder."

"Usually it starts with a house, I suppose. And here you have nothing. You'll be starting from scratch. To make walls and beds, you'll first have to cut trees. You'll have to clear a little space. You know all that, don't you?"

"I haven't seen the place yet," Lorena said. "Jeff says it's all right."

"I haven't seen it either," Bundy said, "but I believe it is forest land, not land for building homes."

"How you do harp on homes," she said. "Somewhere you must have had a happy one."

"Why, yes," he said. "And didn't you?"

"No," Lorena said. "I have never had a happy home. Don't begrudge me the opportunity to make one now."

Bundy was contrite and embarrassed.

"I meant nothing unpleasant," he said formally. "I am sorry if you have been unhappy. Sincerely I am. Only I hate to see you people waste your efforts on an impossible venture."

"Impossible?" she said. "You'd make a poor pioneer, Mr. Jones. Lots of folks in the West went farther and fared worse than we aim to do." She looked at Bundy curiously, conscious of her ability to move him.

"But that was forty or fifty years ago," Bundy said doggedly. "The whole setup is different now. There's not so much land being given out."

"Well," Lorena said, with one of her quick changes of mood, "don't think I didn't try persuading Jeff against this thing. I really didn't want to come. But obstinacy is one of his virtues."

"Obstinacy or determination?" Bundy asked.

"Obstinacy," she repeated coldly. "Determination is another matter. Judgment, stanchness, all those things he lacks. But he has obstinacy, whether right or wrong."

"Your husband was disappointed in his expectations," Bundy said mildly.

"So he has told you?" she asked. "But of course he would. He is obstinate there, too, as you can see. Most men would forget their grievances and go on to pull themselves up out of the hole. But Jeff prefers to stay in the hole and cry out for the sympathy of everybody who goes by."

Bundy could see Jeff Carney riding some way ahead of them,

engaged in conversation with McSweeney. He was talking rapidly, using his hands in vague gesticulations. Bundy could almost hear him explaining, giving reasons, defending himself. What Lorena said was true, yet her quiet words chilled him. He felt a sudden stab of pity for Jeff whom his wife so coolly failed to defend.

"But surely this homesteading is an effort to get himself out of the hole," he said.

"Oh, yes," said Lorena, and now there was a touch of scorn in her voice. "But this is the least he could do, isn't it? A man should take a chance, a gamble on something better. Almost any man has the opportunity to make his future. A man should be able to do anything. That's not true for the woman, of course. It's harder for a woman."

"I'm sure it is," Bundy said, looking at her curiously. He did not quite enjoy the turn the conversation had taken. Yet he could not look at Lorena without feeling sympathy for her.

"A woman may think she has planned her life in a smart and intelligent way," she said. "Then suddenly maybe she finds she's only managed to turn her future over to someone who doesn't plan very well, who makes a botch of everything. What is she to do then? A man can walk out and try some other way. But what is a woman to do? Society tells her she's got to stick with her bargain. A woman never gets a second chance."

Bundy did not know how to answer her. For a moment they stared at each other openly, and he saw with surprise that behind the lovely, languid eyes flashed unsuspected purpose. Suddenly her face was brilliant with rebellion.

"I thought I had what I wanted," she said with an intensity that was almost terrifying. "I didn't ask to be poor all over again."

"All over again?" Bundy repeated stupidly.

"Yes," she said. "I was born poor, but, Lord knows, I didn't intend to stay so. This is the trick I didn't bargain for. It's what I mean about a woman's intelligent planning being all lost unless there's a man to put it across."

"And so you think that homesteading will be a way out?"

"For the moment," she said, "I do what I have to do."

They continued to look at each other, and, to Bundy's bewilderment, the great dark eyes seemed sardonic and calculating. Her horse had paused again to snatch a mouthful of grass from the trail-side. Lorena pulled him up sharply, looking away from Bundy as she did so. When she looked back again, the hardness was gone from her face. For the first time he saw that her perfect poise was broken by some sort of embarrassment.

She smiled at him in one of her engaging transformations, the eyes warm, the smile intimate.

"Forget it," she said. "I was babbling. A woman never ought to let herself think out loud, should she? Don't you ever get blue, Mr. Jones?"

"Yes," he said, "I guess I do."

"No," she said. "You're only agreeing with me to be polite. I think you're always cheerful, always positive you know what's right. Isn't that so?"

"Perhaps," said Bundy. "I've never had time to enjoy my regrets."

"That's nice!" she said. "I like that way of putting it. Jeff enjoys his regrets, and I'm as bad as he is. I enjoy mine too. And as for you, I don't believe you have any regrets to plague you at all."

Bundy was busily trying to put his hand on some regrets to edify her, when she went on archly, "There is only one thing that really frightens me about the homesteading."

"What is that?" he said.

"I hoped you'd ask me," she said. "The thing I really fear is being bored. Not seeing people, living so silently, all shut in by trees, I dread that awfully. Don't let me be bored, will you, Mr. Jones? Don't let that happen to me."

Her tone was gentle and imploring.

Bundy wanted to tell her that he would never let her be bored if he could help it, that he would eagerly turn himself inside out to amuse her. But some shred of his habitual reserve bound up his lips and kept him silent. Only he looked at her quietly and smiled.

Now he saw that Jeff was riding back along the trail looking for Lorena. He let his horse draw back into single file, so that Jeff could ride beside his wife.

"We're getting down now," Jeff said. "We'll be among the big trees soon. Nice country, isn't it, Jones?"

"Beautiful," Bundy said. He dropped back farther, and found himself riding beside the lumberjack called Spike.

"Hot!" the man said. "First you freeze an' then you sweat in this here neck of woods."

"Um," said Bundy thoughtfuly.

5.

In the valley the trail became very narrow again. Here the white pines stood so close together that a wide trail was impossible without cutting and clearing. The path was soft and deep in brown needles, and a palpable stillness was only intensified by the snorting and blowing of the horses and the alien tinkle of pack bells.

The white pine grows straight and strong with a sturdy masculine upthrust that is suddenly crowned by a feminine delicacy of foliage. The clusters of five needles, instead of the two- or three-needle groups of most other pines, give an appearance of feathery lightness to the upper branches. Beneath interlocking boughs the sun is filtered away in an unseen sky, leaving a cathedral dimness under high, groined arches. Gracefully curved small cones hang green in summer, and, when they ripen and drop in autumn, they are tipped with white resin as if already touched by frost.

When the pack train had gone some distance among the trees, McSweeney took his pistol and fired a shot into the air. The sound reverberated up and down the valley. Some of the riders were startled, but the horses did not flinch, for this was the usual way of announcing an arrival in the woods. It said to the isolated homesteaders, "You're not alone any longer. If you have a secret, hide it. Put on the pot for company."

Presently the pack train came alongside a rough clearing full of enormous stumps. The felled trees had been used to build a small cabin and a kind of barn or outhouse. A woodpile was curing near the barn, and doubtless there was hand-hewn furniture inside the cabin.

A man and woman stood in the doorway of the cabin, and a small boy ran toward the pack train, shouting an excited greeting. His arms were spread in an unconscious gesture of welcome. About his thin legs flapped a man's old overalls which had been tailored unskillfully to his size. He ran along beside the horses, leaping and shrieking with joy.

The man and woman stood somber in long-held silence, like sleepers disturbed in a dream. These were the first of the valley homesteaders, a man and wife named Klein and a little boy named Jimmy.

It was only when McSweeney held up a packet of mail for them that they came out of their sullen dream and began to smile and talk. McSweeney knew from experience that the sight of a letter addressed with a man's own name would do more than anything else to dissolve the homesteader's paralyzing sense of lonely detachment. With a letter from the outside in hand, a man could laugh and josh again and ask for news of the world. He could place an order for coffee or prunes or carbolic acid to be brought out next time, or tell how a falling tree had pinned him against another until his wife had managed to saw the trunk through and roll the log back. Half reluctant as they had been to see the pack train come, the homesteaders were even more reluctant to see it go. They found a dozen excuses to prolong the pause, and keep the travelers from going on.

But Jeff was in a hurry now, his face flushed and his eyes bright.

"Come along," he said to McSweeney, "we're nearly there, let's push on and noon on our own place."

There were three more homesteads to pass after they said goodbye to the Kleins. The tiny, stump-filled clearings were far apart, each on its quarter section of land. Mrs. Klein was the first and only woman in the valley.

Taggart's place came next, and they found him planting potatoes in crooked rows between the big stumps. He straightened himself and wiped the sweat out of his eyes with his sleeve, staring at them sullenly, without surprise.

The soil about his feet was brown and loamy. Big green brakes uncurled their fiddle necks at the edge of the potato rows, thriving in the man-made light and opportunity of the clearing. Green and golden, the forest watched in vegetable patience as a man tried to plant civilization for the first time in ancient soil.

The morning was almost gone before they reached Smith's

homestead, yet they found him still in bed. He appeared shirtless, buttoning his pants as he came. Time often came to mean nothing to a man alone in the woods. The sense of time was in himself, and if it ran down there was no one to care. Smith frequently escaped the overwhelming magnitude of the job he had undertaken by a lonely session with one of the bottles which he had packed in for consolation.

Beyond Smith's there was an empty cabin. A tree had fallen across the roof and caved in one end of it. The brakes pushed up unchallenged around the stumps in the clearing.

"That feller couldn't stand it," McSweeney said. "Feller name of Peters. 'To hell with homesteading,' Peters says, when he come out last fall. He stuck it till winter set in. Froze his feet trying to get out on snowshoes. He hadn't never used snowshoes before and there's a trick to it. Anyway, he ain't back yet this year, and I don't s'pose he'll come."

"We'll repair the roof and use it for shelter until we get our own places going," Jeff Carney said.

The Carney girls looked at it dubiously.

"But our cabins will be better, won't they, Jeff?" Meggie asked. "This will only be until we get our *better* cabins built, won't it?"

"Sure," Jeff said. "Of course."

"It's a good solid cabin," McSweeney said. "You get the roof fixed up, I don't know how you going to build a better one."

The new homesteaders were all anxious to see their own places now.

"How far is mine?" Nan O'Rourke wanted to know.

"It's on beyond Meggie's," Jeff said. "We'll get there this after-noon."

"I never saw my stone and timber claim," Nan said. "Oh, they showed me something that was s'posed to be mine, but half a dozen others saw the same piece of land. I got the money all right, but this time it'll be good to see what I'm getting."

"You'll see this one fair enough," Jeff said. "This won't be as easy as the stone and timber claims were."

"Where you going to put *me*, Mr. Carney?" Charlie asked. "I make a good neighbor. Don't stick me off in some place by myself."

He winked genially at Meggie. "I got to help Mees Carney play her mandolin some times, eh?"

Jeff looked at Charlie's handsome, smiling face with distaste. "You're on the north quarter," he said. "We'll get to you tomorrow. It will be near enough."

"And aren't you going to change your mind about a homestead, now, Mr. Jones?" Meggie asked. "Look at all these nice woods going to waste."

"No," Bundy said. "I wouldn't take the risk."

"What risk?" asked Nan O'Rourke. "You could build a cabin and go out looking for plants from there. Then you'd have something besides dried weeds when you got through."

"Listen," Bundy said. "I don't think any one of you will ever get this land. Does it look to you like homestead land? It's forest, it's not farm country."

There was a moment of silence and Bundy saw that the faces of the women were clouded with uncertainty. Then Jeff said roughly. "Everything in life is a gamble, Jones. You know that, don't you? Why try to spoil our fun?"

"*Fun?*" said Lorena derisively. "That's just the word for it! *Fun!*" She burst out laughing.

"We're moving," called McSweeney. "Save your talk for the long winter evenings, folks. We'll noon at Mr. Carney's place."

6.

After the deserted cabin the trail turned to cross a little stream on a narrow log bridge, and for some distance the stream leaped and bubbled beside them. The trail grew less distinct as they went on, and, when they left the stream, they sometimes had to refer to blazes on the trees to find their way through the luxuriantly growing brakes and sword ferns. The trail made another turn to avoid a giant cedar that hung its gray-green branches like a lacy curtain, barring their way. Beyond this they saw the beginning of a clearing. A few trees had been cut, and a rough lean-to of boughs had been thrown up. In front of this half shelter, a circle of blackened stones showed where cooking had been done.

The trail stopped and Jeff dismounted with a certain air of triumph. "Well, here we are," he said. "Here's the Carney mansion, girls. Get off your horses and look around. And don't go telling me you don't like it, until McSweeney's cooked us some lunch."

"Oh, God!" Lorena said. "So this is it?"

"Look at the trees," said Jeff exultantly. "Look at the trees."

Bundy had already seen the trees. He was impressed.

Soon there was a fire in the circle of stones, and the coffeepot and skillets were out and the bacon and bannock cooking. Jeff and the lumberjacks were at work unpacking the Carney horses and piling the supplies under the shelter. Jeff would keep one saddle horse for himself, but the other horses would go back to Cold Spring with the packer.

The three women stood together by the fire, looking slightly appalled. Over his pan of crisping bannock, McSweeney smiled reassuringly at Lorena. "Don't worry, Ma'am," he said. "Them timber willies 'll have you a decent cabin in a couple of days or a week. You'll be living in style pretty soon."

Lorena did not reply, but Meggie and Miss O'Rourke began asking questions about their places which lay beyond.

"They're just like this, ladies." McSweeney said, "only without the improvements. You got a hundred and sixty acres of fine white pine, and, Lord knows, that's about all."

"*About all?*" Charlie Duporte cried. "By gar! That's what you want, ain't it? *White pine!* You never see no finer white pine—not in Wisconsin or Michigan or Montana. That's what I come in here for, to get my share. You go dig in a mine—maybe you find silver, copper, gold—maybe not. But here you got it all on top of ground. Money, money, money, growing like hell."

"It's for them as likes it," McSweeney said.

"Ain't you never took a claim yourself?" Charlie asked. "Man, are you crazy?"

"I'm making a heap of money packing in the homesteaders," McSweeney said, "and that don't cut down any trees."

After lunch most of the pack train moved again. Leaving Spike and Rudy to start work on Jeff's clearing, the others pushed ahead to find Meggie's claim. Later Jeff and Dynamite would go on to locate Nan O'Rourke's.

Bundy intended to ride as far as the homesteaders went, and on beyond them to the North Fork of the Clearwater River which he hoped to reach before dark.

"I been there," Charlie said. "You find good camping spot and plenty trout for supper. Maybe I go with you, if Jeff don't show me to my homestead till tomorrow. I got enough of bacon, bannock for a while. Some trout taste pretty good, I t'ink."

Bundy thought so, too. Yet he had no particular desire for more of Charlie's company. He was eager now to go on alone.

Stakes had been set and trees blazed to indicate the site of Meggie's clearing. At sight of them she was suddenly jubilant.

"Look, everybody, look!" she cried. "It's my place. Something all my own at last!"

"Don't count your chickens till they're hatched, sister," Nan O'Rourke cautioned, but it was all in fun and she was jubilant too in her own way.

"Don't worry," Meggie cried confidently. "The Great White Father's going to give it to me."

"You've got the stream in front here," Jeff said, "and there's a spring out back. You're well off for water."

"Oh, Lorena," Meggie said. "It's beautiful, isn't it? Just beautiful!" She caught Lorena about the waist and hugged her. Lorena smiled, and the two young women stood together with their arms linked for a few moments, knee-deep in ferns under the tall trees. From high above them a shaft of light came down and touched them in the sea-deep shadow of the forest.

Bundy looked at them and felt a tug of reluctance at parting. Before he rode on he fixed a romantic picture in his mind. It was a picture of two girls standing bright-eyed and expectant in a ray of filtered sunlight under the great calm trees.

"Remember you're coming to dinner," Meggie called to him.

"I'll remember."

"And bring some trout."

"Sure enough."

Lorena only said, "Goodbye, Mr. Jones," but she looked at Bundy and her eyes said, "Don't let me be bored, will you? Will you?"

Or was it only at Bundy that she looked? Lorena had a way of making everything she did seem very personal. Bundy wondered about it later, for it appeared that Charlie Duporte had received some message from her also.

Charlie went on with the diminished pack train as far as Nan's claimstakes. Then he said, "I'm going back, help them Carney ladies build. Four men better than three to clear and put up cabins."

"How about your own?" McSweeney asked.

"Oh, by gar, I got me lots of time before winter. I don't care if I sleep *aux belles étoiles,* so long the summer lasts. But them poor ladies. They better get their cabins built."

"How about your trout supper?" Bundy asked. For a man who had recently been eager to be rid of Charlie's company, he was unreasonably annoyed.

"Fish always swimming in them streams," said Charlie with a happy grin. "But pretty ladies only need a little help one time."

"Pretty ladies!" Nan O'Rourke sniffed, "and their *four* men! It's sure nice to be young and have a pretty face. But me—at least I'm *safe.* Come on now, Dynamite, let's see if you can live up to your name. We got to get two tents up before dark."

Dynamite looked at Bundy with a wink and a grin. "Yes, *Ma'am!*" he said.

7.

Bundy rode on down the trail alone. He had settled up with McSweeney the night before. He was the only one except Jeff Carney who would keep his horses. Tomorrow McSweeney would start back to Cold Spring with the train of unloaded horses and the homesteaders would be left with only "shank's mare" for transportation.

Bundy rode on slowly toward the bottom of the valley. The trail was wider again as it neared the river, and there was a wonderful sense of peace and relaxation in the declining afternoon. The lowering sun slatted shafts of light in golden bands between the trees.

Bundy never felt lonely in the woods. There was always a sense of quiet movement as he walked or rode among trees. The nearby trees remained steadfast, but, as he shifted his own position, the farther trees seemed to be shifting and changing their positions also. Like the sailing moon which seems to accompany a person as he rides near fixed scenery, this is a trick of perspective that is not difficult to understand. Yet for Bundy the illusion never lost its uneasy mystery. The trees seemed to be silent stalkers who spied upon him for unspoken reasons. He felt that there was no hostility in this, only the shy curiosity of an innocent wilderness which breathed and lived about him.

From the stream in the depth of the shallow valley came a wild and lonely music. A dampness and coolness also rose from it and this was welcome to Bundy after his long day in the saddle.

He chose a cleared spot on the bank of the stream that had been camped on before but not too frequently. All the freshness of a clean place was there, and yet he inherited someone's ring of stones and dry bough bed. He set up his pup tent over the boughs and spread his blankets. There was ample grazing for the horses.

Before dusk he wet his line in the clear cold water that rushed and hurried around scattered boulders, and, in a matter of minutes, he had two very pretty trout. As they sizzled in the pan, he went back for water cress which he had noticed in a spring that oozed from nearby turf. This was a land of trees and water, and, for a resourceful man, the living could be choice and plentiful.

His hunger satisfied, Bundy sat in the deepening evening and looked around him at the forest. It was more beautiful and impressive than he had been able to imagine as he sat at a desk in the security of Washington.

He drew a long breath of contentment. To be here in the wilderness was all that he wanted at the moment. People and causes became as insubstantial as the thin blue smoke that spiraled from his fire and lost itself among the trees. This was enough.

III

THE MANDOLIN

1.

With Jeff, Charlie, Rudy and Spike working together, Jeff's trees came down and his cabin went up quickly. As soon as the roof was on the cabin, the two lumberjacks moved over to Meggie's place and began to work there while Charlie and Jeff continued clearing, gardening and making furniture at the first cabin.

Charlie had temporarily abandoned his own homesteading to work for the Carneys. Jeff was paying him the same wage he paid the other two, and Charlie, singing and laughing about his work, his white teeth gleaming in his dark face, was doing a good job.

Meggie had stayed with Jeff and Lorena until her cabin roof was finished. Then she moved into her own place, in spite of the mosquitoes that swarmed through the gaping chinks between the logs.

The two workmen had a bough shelter nearby in the clearing, but Meggie was not disturbed by their proximity. She trusted everyone, and expected everyone to trust her. If Jeff was not going to worry about her, she certainly did not intend to worry about her own situation. There was plenty of work to keep everybody busy.

Chinking the cabin was the first thing to be done, and Meggie worked along beside the men with considerable satisfaction.

Her hands were black with mud and her face streaked with it. Occasionally she stood back to survey her new home and speak her mind about it. "Looks like it would last forever, now doesn't it?

Logs are so solid. It isn't fancy, but I think it's beautiful. Really I do. You men have done a wonderful piece of work on it. Just wonderful!"

The two lumberjacks stood beside her and looked at their handiwork through her eyes. It appeared very good to them, and the novelty of feminine praise elevated the whole project to a plane of distinction. She was a good little wench and they worked hard for her. She was a new experience for them, and they were baffled as well as intrigued. Mrs. Carney they could understand. She was a beautiful and desirable woman whose glance said: "but I'm not for you. Look, if you like, but don't touch."

Miss Meggie, however, was full of democratic friendliness. Her glance was arch and provocative; her praise was lavish, and her gratitude outspoken. She called on them to admire wild flowers and listen to birds. She asked them about their mothers, and laughed at their jokes. They were puzzled to know exactly what she meant and how far she was prepared to go. They circled about her warily, and each one tried to outdo the other in soliciting her admiration.

When the chinking was finished, Meggie hung mosquito netting over windows and door, and began to wrestle with the problems of indoor living, while Rudy and Spike went on to construct the barn. Barn was an odd name for it, since Meggie had neither horse, cow nor fowl, but a second building was essential in making the place appear self-sufficient. As soon as the barn was habitable, the men moved their bedrolls into it, and destroyed the bough shelter.

However, the barn progressed more slowly than the house had done, because Meggie needed a great deal of help to get her house in running order. The sheet iron stove, that had been taken apart for packing on horseback, baffled her completely, and Spike had to come up and help her put it together and get the stovepipe into place.

Rudy watched these proceedings out of the corner of his eye as he continued notching logs for the upper walls of the barn. That evening he started to build a chair and table for her.

Part of the equipment of the cabin had been a bunk bed built against the wall and a wide shelf near the chimney which served as cooking table and temporary eating place.

It was a good cabin, and Meggie had reason to be proud, although some homesteaders who could not rid themselves of the memory of city conveniences, never did appreciate a good cabin. But Meggie was easily pleased, and, when McSweeney, on his next trip, packed in real panes of glass for her two windows, she was filled with proud enthusiasm.

Jeff and Lorena had windows, too, but they remembered how much the glass and the packing in of it had cost, and that these were only half the size of ordinary town windows. They did not share all of Meg's easy enthusiasms. Lorena's stove smoked and she hated the constant smell of smoke in her hair. She spent as little time in the cabin as she could. It was pleasanter to sit on a log in the sun and dream of other places. When Charlie saw her sitting thus, he sometimes stopped his chopping or spading, and came to sit on the other end of the log, wiping his brow and smiling at her. If he sang something under his breath in French, she did not mind that it sounded like a love song. She couldn't understand the words anyway.

When Meggie came over and sniffed their smoky cabin, she was insufferably triumphant.

"*My* stove doesn't smoke!" Meggie boasted happily.

"Well," Jeff said, "those timber willies profited by the mistakes they made in our chimney to build yours straight. All around they've done a better job on your place than they did on ours, and Charlie and I worked with them all the time here, too."

Meggie wanted to give her place a name, and she began to think what would be nice. She thought of "Trail's End," and "My Castle," and "Ever So Humble," but none of these quite suited her. Then she remembered that she had once seen a house called "Bide a Wee," and something about this name delighted her.

She went out and got a hand-split shingle from the men and printed the name out large and clear with some of her precious ink that had survived the fall of her pack horse down the mountain. In her happiest mood she tacked the shingle up over her door.

Next Meggie had to have a shelf built beside her bunk for books.

"Of course, I've only got two books," she said to Rudy, who put up the shelf, "but I'm going to have lots more. Next time I come I won't have to bring a stove or a washtub or my mandolin. There'll be room on the horse for books."

"How many books a person got to have to read?" Rudy asked her in a teasing voice. "Ain't one book enough?"

"Good heavens, no!" said Meggie. "I aim to have a library. I s'pose I ought to have started with the Bible and Shakespeare like the people who choose what they'd take with them to a desert island. But I've got Myrtle Reed's best one and *The Trail of the Lonesome Pine*. I couldn't resist the Lonesome Pine one because of the title if nothing else. Doesn't it fit this spot to perfection?"

"It sure does," Rudy said.

"There's only one little tiny thing wrong with this beautiful cabin of mine," Meggie said. "I wish it had a little front porch where I could sit out."

The next two days the men spent in building her a porch, and Spike made a railing for it and then took crooked branches and nailed them around to make a rustic trimming. It was really beautiful. Meggie herself nailed up small wooden boxes, that had contained some of her supplies, to make porch boxes. Then she went into the woods and dug and transplanted ferns to fill the boxes. All three of them were proud of the result.

"Now, if only I had a little rocking chair," said Meggie. "Next time I come in I'll have to put one on a pack horse."

The two men scoured the woods after that for branches with the right curve to make rockers. They went separately and with haste, each hoping to be the first to produce the little rocking chair. In a short time Meggie had two rocking chairs, rather clumsy and somewhat halting in their rhythm, but much nicer than one because they suggested hospitality and company.

In the evening now she sat on her porch and rocked. Sometimes she played her mandolin. The men built a smudge fire to discourage mosquitoes, and sat below her on the steps of her porch.

When she did not play or sing they took over the entertainment, recounting their adventures and bragging of their exploits. Their tales grew wilder and more lurid as the evenings passed. They looked at each other with hard eyes, prodding their brains to produce better and taller stories, but stories curiously deficient in the blasphemies and obscenities that spiced their ordinary conversation. It was a strain, but nevertheless they enjoyed it. They had never found themselves in such a novel situation.

Meggie rocked back and forth, and cried, "No! You never did!" or "What a terrible experience! How did you live through it?"

Later, when she complained that she had read her two books over twice, Spike came bringing her three dog-eared copies of *The Wide World Magazine,* which had been his companion for some months. Reading them to help pass the time, Meggie came across some of the same adventures in far lands that had befallen Spike. Meggie was not particularly shocked to find that Spike was a liar. She had suspected both of them all along, and instead of being angry she was amused.

One thing bothered Meggie a little. She knew that the men had a bottle, maybe more than one, hidden away in the barn they were building. Sometimes when they came in to supper she smelled liquor on their breath. She knew the smell because Papa had always liked his toddy or his nightcap, and the odor was associated with his goodnight kiss. But Papa had always been a perfect gentleman, and so far Spike and Rudy, in spite of their rough clothes, had always been gentlemen too. Still she realized that she was a girl alone here, and sometimes she wondered— She had them make a bar of wood that could be lowered across the door from the inside to lock intruders out. The two men laughed at her.

"Most folks puts locks on the outside, Ma'am," they said. "Looks like you don't want visitors."

Meggie laughed with them. "I just want to control my visitors, that's all. I want to keep independent."

Meggie had never felt so independent and so happy as she felt this summer. It was strange, too, because Mama's long illness and Papa's sudden death, with the blowing up of all their plans and expectations, should have made her sad. When she remembered, she did feel very sorry for Jeff who was losing so much in the way of a future. But money had never meant very much to her, and Papa had certainly never planned a career for her unless it lay in a good marriage. Money helped with a good marriage, she knew, of course— still she had read a lot of romantic books, and she always hoped that her marriage would be more of a love match than a money arrangement. Now, she thought ingenuously, without the money, it would have to be for love, like Lorena's and Jeff's marriage which had disturbed Papa so much, but which seemed to Meggie a lovely thing.

Jeff had not married for money or position or any of the things Papa had hoped for him. Lorena had been as beautiful and as poor as Cinderella. Of course the marriage had not turned out to be a properous one because of the difficulties Papa was in at the time of his death. But that made the whole thing the more perfect. Since they had married for love, money could not really matter to them.

Meggie loved to think about Lorena and Jeff and their romantic marriage, yet somehow she did not always feel comfortable when she was with them. She realized this more now that she was alone on her own place. She could expand here, and be something more than what they seemed to think her.

At home Meggie's life had fallen easily into an accepted pattern. She had never needed to rebel against her life because she had been so happy in it. So happy? Well, of course! Her family had decided everything for her.

She remembered the time when she was five and she had tried to break the pattern, not realizing that it was already set. She had brought home a stray cat with the idea of making it a permanent member of the household. The cat was willing to cooperate. It lapped milk eagerly and later submitted to being dressed in her doll's clothes and pushed in a doll carriage.

When her father came home he had laughed at her and been delighted, such a taking little girl she was! But, of course, the cat had to go. The smell of the fur or something made her mother's head ache, and Papa never wanted pets around the house. She had been serious about the cat, and it was somehow baffling to have them all so pleasantly amused by her exploit, yet so resolutely set against letting her have her way.

Meggie had never learned to throw a tantrum in order to get her way. Life was too pleasant to spoil it by futile rebellion. She was too good-natured. So she went along with Papa's idea that she was a little fool, a dear and funny little fool like Mama whom he loved so much.

It was easy to accept Papa's appraisal. If one did not look the character too fully in the face, there were advantages in it. There were fond indulgences, allowances made, merriment created, and she was surrounded by a genial atmosphere of good-tempered amusement. The role of little clown was usually to her liking. If at moments she felt other impulses stirring, Meggie pushed them resolutely aside. Papa was an important man and he knew best. Who was she to imagine herself bigger than the character which he in his wisdom had created for her?

Now it appeared, after his death, that he had not always been so wise in his financial dealings, but Meggie was too loyal to question his wisdom in family matters. It was too soon and his memory was too green in her heart. Perhaps she was even more resolutely his little clown than she would have been if he had gone on living to enforce his opinions with his presence.

Meggie worked hard around the homestead. She learned to cook salt pork and make bannock and get food on the table reasonably near mealtime. Spike showed her how to start a sourdough bucket. He came into the cabin and showed her how to mix condensed milk and water and flour into a batter which was allowed to stand for three or four days on the back of the stove or in the sun until it was sour. Soda and a little salt were added just before frying, and the hot cakes it made were very good. She could make sourdough muffins too.

"But why not just make it up fresh every day and use baking powder instead of soda?" Meggie wanted to know.

The men laughed at her.

"Look here," Rudy said. It was after breakfast and there were a couple of pancakes left that had not been eaten. He took them up in his hairy-backed and not-too-clean hands, broke them into pieces and dropped them back into the bucket of sourdough.

The two men were delighted by her cries of protest. They were having a circus with this little greenhorn.

"You don't waste nothing when you got a sourdough bucket," Rudy said seriously. "Tomorrow it all comes out fine again, and you always got something ready to eat when you come in from work."

"If'n it don't sour quick enough in the woods, where you got so much shade," Spike said, "you climb up an' put your bucket on the roof where you got sun."

Meggie couldn't believe her eyes and ears. Still she was elated to have a sourdough bucket started. "Old Mr. MacGillicuddy will think I'm a real homesteader," she said, "when he comes to bring me my dog and I fry him some sourdough pancakes."

Before the barn was finished the two men began to dynamite stumps so that she could make a garden. There was no question of trying to clear all the stumps this year, but, in order to make any sort of garden it was necessary to blow out a few of them.

Meggie had become accustomed to the crash of falling trees, but dynamite terrified her. She ran indoors and covered her head with a blanket when the fuse was lighted. The blast, when it came, seemed to go all through her. Her few precious dishes rattled on the shelves; even the logs of the cabin seemed to tremble.

The men laughed at her. "You sure scare easy, Miss Carney."

"I sure do," Meggie said, happy once more.

There were wonderful bonfires of slashings and blasted roots.

"You ever see them Injuns dance around one of these here?" Rudy asked. He began to whoop and dance around the edge of the fire. Meggie stuck a fern in her hair and danced, too.

"Yippy-ki-yi!" she shouted, throwing up her arms. But then she saw that Spike was regarding them with a look of disapproval, and she remembered that a grown-up homesteader ought to have some dignity.

"Well," she said, "I guess I never really saw one."

Sometimes she roasted a few of her precious potatoes in the coals of the bonfire, and they tasted wonderful with a little of the butter that she kept in a mason jar down in the edge of the spring.

Most of the potatoes were destined for planting, and, as soon as there was a stump-free patch between the cabin and the barn, Meggie began to dig and plant.

The men kept leaving their work on the barn to help her dig. "This here ain't no work for a lady, Ma'am."

"It don't look like a person can be a lady and make a homestead at the same time," Meggie said. "Besides I can't afford to pay you for work like this, because I haven't got enough money."

"This is extra," Spike said, grinning.

"One on the house," said Rudy.

"No, no. You go back to the barn," Meggie insisted. She felt them watching her from the rafters of the roofless barn, as she worked. It made her a little uncomfortable. Still she was very happy digging, and pulling and shaking the fine roots out of the loose soil that seemed to be nothing but rotted leaves and sand. I wonder if it will grow things? she thought. Will I be here long enough to see a real good garden? Isn't it silly to go through all these motions if one really doesn't plan to stay? And to cut all these beautiful big trees that took so long to grow? Isn't it a shame really? But then they will all be cut someday—only I won't be here to see it.

It was curious how one did not think much at a dance or at the family dinner table, or even in one's own room at home with its white lace curtains and its pretty wallpaper printed in a lattice-work with blue morning glories all over it. Yet, digging in leafy mold in a small clearing among trees, or even riding horseback on a mountainside, all sorts of unaccustomed thoughts came to one.

Sometimes she thought of Bundy Jones as she worked, and she thought what a funny name Bundy was and also that being a botanist was a funny occupation for a man. At the same time she liked both name and profession. She saw herself time and again, objectively, as a small figure in a panic being swept downstream, and she saw Bundy coming after her to rescue her. This was the sort of thing a girl's Prince Charming would do for her, she thought shyly and wistfully. Not that she had a Prince Charming yet, but most of the books she read encouraged her to be on the lookout for one. She felt Bundy's firm hands guiding hers on the reins. "Let them pass through your fingers in this way," he had said. "You've got to hold onto a horse as if you mean it. You'll learn. You're doing fine." It pleased her in a very special way to have him praise her and put the reins the right way through her fingers.

Yet she knew instinctively that his eyes had been on Lorena even when he spoke to her. It wasn't fair, when Lorena was married to a wonderful person like Jeff, that she still got all the attention. Naturally Lorena couldn't help it and there was no use blaming her. To be beautiful was a wonderful thing. A beautiful person couldn't help it that all the heads turned her way. It was the way fate dealt things out, and Lorena was good and kind and deserved to be beautiful and turn so many heads.

As she worked Meggie wondered sometimes if Bundy Jones would keep his promise and stop for dinner with her someday. He had said he would bring trout, and she planned how she would cook it, and what she would have to go with it. She thought that it would be fun to show him all the improvements she had made, and how much of a home she had already established.

Besides her potatoes, Meggie planted radishes and lettuce because they were quick, and she was dying for something fresh to eat. Dehydrated soups were rather watery and weedy tasting unless one added the precious potatoes, and her pack-horse mixture of split peas, lentils and rice was monotonous. Something fresh out of a garden, she thought, would really be a triumph.

The timber willies were skeptical about her garden.

"You got to make one, sure, to prove you got a home here. But there's a lot of shade falls on your clearing morning and evening, and the nights is chilly. Maybe you work damned hard for nothing."

"Oh, I hope not," Meggie said.

Sometimes she wondered, in her new-found liberty, if Jeff had really been wise to stake so much on this homesteading venture. They had made a nice profit on their stone and timber claims the year before, but that had been very easy. They had come out to Bolster and stayed at the hotel which was run by English people and was quite luxurious for the frontier. A timber locator had taken them out one by one and shown them some corner stakes set in snowy ground under pine trees. Later, when they compared notes, they suspected that they had all seen the same corner stakes. Anyway it had not seemed to make much difference for, whatever they actually saw, they all acquired land, and Uncle Ralph's company took it off their hands almost immediately, without any further effort on their part.

But this was different. Here they were in forest reserve and they were sinking all they had made on the stone and timber claims into establishing homes which could only be, after all, a kind of pretense. As Uncle Ralph pointed out, of course, this land was worth a much greater risk than the land around Bolster because the timber was so much finer. In the long run, if they succeeded in proving up on the land, they would get back all of the original investment and a great deal more.

Meggie knew that Jeff was already making money as a timber locator. He charged a hundred dollars to locate a homesteader on a claim, and Meggie suspected, although Jeff never told her, that there was a bonus from Uncle Ralph for every homesteader he located on a claim in this valley. Many of the homesteaders were unable to pay the hundred dollars, but Jeff was willing to take the equivalent in other forms. Meggie had seen two diamond rings among the loose change in his wallet, and, in a country where people were eager to gamble on timberland, she knew what these meant.

Jeff, with his own horse, came and went a good deal that summer. He met the pack trains of new settlers and took them into other parts of the valley. When he expected to be gone for a few days, he rode down the trail to Meggie's place and asked her to stay with Lorena.

Meggie reflected without rancor that no one thought very much about her staying alone, but for Lorena it was impossible. This was acceptable to Meggie, and she packed up her nightdress and tooth brush and comb in the case with her mandolin and walked up the trail at her leisure after Jeff had ridden away.

She hated to leave Spike and Rudy alone, because she suspected that they did not work very hard when she was gone, and probably the bottle came out of its hiding place in the barn. But she wanted to please Jeff and keep Lorena from getting lonely, and for herself she looked forward to company and talk and gaiety.

Charlie Duporte was still there to play her mandolin in a way Meggie herself could never play it. In the evenings he sang to the two girls and kept them gay and laughing. He was in and out of the house at all hours like one of the family at Jeff's place. Spike and Rudy came in at mealtime to Meggie's table, but in the evening they ventured no farther than her porch steps. Meggie was glad that they seemed to know instinctively how far a workman could presume on the hospitality of the employer. In town such things were simple and easy to regulate; but here in the wilderness one did not always know where the lines of social distinction could be drawn.

Charlie, of course, was a homesteader himself. He had paid Jeff his location fee, and he had gone to see his own place and cut a little brush there. In the fall he meant to build his cabin, and spend the winter trapping and clearing at his leisure.

"I got plenty time," he said. "This summer I have some fun, earn some money. Then in winter, when you all gone, I sit in here alone and get my belly full of silence, eh?"

On some days when Lorena was very tired of cooking on a smoky stove and washing clothes in a tub of sun-warmed spring water and trying to create something out of nothing, Charlie was the only one who could make her laugh. On such days, she could scarcely bear the sight of Jeff; and Meggie was equally irritating to her.

But Charlie knew how to compliment her when her ego needed bolstering; he knew how to sing something sentimental when she was tired or annoyed. Just the sight of his flashing white teeth in his dark face, his eyes sparkling and eager, coaxing her to mirth, was infectious, and before she knew it she was smiling. She had no great opinion of him, but in a situation that bored her and tried her very cruelly, she found him diverting. Sometimes she, too, thought of Bundy Jones and wondered where he was. Lorena was likely to remember people who looked at her with admiration, and the admiration in Bundy's eyes had been unmistakable.

2.

One day Meggie heard a shot up trail, and she ran out of the cabin to see who was coming. The two lumberjacks left the shakes which they were splitting for the barn roof and came down to join her.

"Don't sound like McSweeney's gun," Spike said.

"Maybe Mr. Bundy Jones," said Meggie breathlessly.

"Him!" scoffed Rudy. "He wouldn't know enough to warn he was coming. Bet he ain't even got a gun to shoot."

"Oh, I bet he has!" said Meggie.

But the visitor who presently emerged from among the trees was Eye MacGillicuddy.

He sat his horse negligently, his hat pushed to the back of his head, his jaws busy with a quid of tobacco. Behind him followed his pack horse and three dogs. Jessie was unchanged, but the nuzzling, blind puppies had become gamboling creatures with large paws and flopping ears. There were only two of the puppies, however.

"I brung you your dog, lassie," the ranger said.

"Oh, you did!" cried Meggie. "You really did! I hardly dared expect you'd remember. Oh, you are simply wonderful, Mr. MacGillicuddy. Which one is mine?"

"Can you no tell?"

"Oh, yes," said Meggie, "he's still got the white tip on the end of his tail. Oh, he's simply beautiful. I love him already. Oh, what fun!"

She sat down on the pine needles and held out her hand. The three dogs came wagging and sniffing around her, scenting good will and unaffected welcome.

"But there were three puppies," said Meggie. "Where's the other one?"

"I give him away already, Ma'am," Eye said.

"Oh, did you?" Meggie said. "To whom?"

"Give him to that fellow collecting plants and such, that Bundy Jones."

"You found him?" Meggie asked, "Mr. Jones, I mean? Has he got a camp? How far away?"

"Oh, he's up yon mountain, and full of questions as a dog of fleas. 'How do you do this, Ranger?' s' he. 'How you do that?' A very inquisitive fella. But no one pumps me, if I dinna wish to be pumped. Up yon he's got him a pup tent under a big tree, but like as not he's away again tomorrow. I trailed him quite awhile before I overhauled him. He doesna bide long in a place, seems, but he eats well. He's no fool in the woods. We'd a bonnie meal off the country, trout and mushrooms, and cow parsnip cooked up like asparagras, and bannock and huckleberries like a shortcake for an after. Makes my mouth water now to remember, on a day like this when I've no fared so well."

"Dear me!" said Meggie remembering her duties as a hostess. "Stake out your horses and come right in. I'll feed you as quick as I can. And I'm a real homesteader with a sourdough bucket now, Mr. MacGillicuddy. Aren't I, Spike and Rudy?"

"You sure are, Ma'am," they cried loyally.

Meggie ran into the cabin and began to bustle. This was her first guest beside Jeff and Lorena and the two regular boarders. She had beans already cooking and sauce made from dried apples, but in addition she opened one of her precious tins of corned beef, and put a pan of muffins into the oven. As she worked she kept thinking about Bundy Jones in his pup tent on the mountain cooking his wild foods over his campfire. If he'd only come by here, she thought, I'd show what *I* can do.

She let the young dog with the white tip on his tail come into the cabin with her. He sniffed about uncertainly, suffering his first pangs of claustrophobia. But Meggie cajoled him with sweet words and let him lick out the empty beef tin. She passed him bits of this and that as she worked, and talked to him affectionately.

By the time the men came in to dinner he was curled beside the stove, banging his tail on the floor in blissful domesticity. Jessie and the other pup looked in at him from the other side of the door sill but he was already smug in the knowledge that he had found his human.

"What should I call him?" Meggie asked.

"I never give the pups no names," the old man said. " '*Hey, you*,' is good enough to keep them following along. Let their new masters name 'em. However, you could call yon fellow Tippy, if you've no better thought for him."

"But I have," Meggie said. "Would you mind very much if I called him MacGillicuddy? I could call him Gilly or Cuddy for short. I'd like that, if you didn't mind, Mr. MacGillicuddy."

Eye nodded and grinned.

"It's a good name," he said, "an' sons I have none to bear it, nor lassies neither for the matter of that. I'm a lone man with a dog. Have as much sport wi' my name as you see fit."

"But it's not sport," Meggie said. "It just seemed a good way to keep me remembering how I came by him. And who's to get the last pup? Miss O'Rourke?"

"Aye. She's a sour an' havering Irishwoman, but she'll no mistreat an animal. I'll push on down trail to her place tomorrow, if you'll let me sleep wi' the men in your barn the night."

"Of course, you must stay here the night," Meggie said, "and I'll tell you what I'll do. Tomorrow I'll go with you to see Nan O'Rourke. Will you let me do that? Will you let me ride your horse part of the way? I've never seen her place."

"Aye, lass, you can ride the whole way, but I canna bring ye back. I'm headin' on for the river."

"I can walk back alone in a day, I'm sure," said Meggie.

She was delighted at the chance. In town she scarcely knew Nan O'Rourke to speak to on the street. She had gone into Nan's millinery shop for hats with the easy condescension of the privileged person to the tradesman. But now they were suddenly on an equal footing, and the journey over the mountain had given them a common bond. Meggie was willing to overlook differences in social station, age and experience to find out how Miss O'Rourke was making out in the wilderness. She yearned for some sort of feminine contact in a country that was predominantly male. Of course, there was Lorena who was so very dear to her, almost the sister she had never had. Yet, much as she loved Lorena, there were reserves between them that were hard to explain. She welcomed the openness, even the crudeness that she knew she would get from Nan O'Rourke.

It was like taking a holiday to mount Eye's horse the next day and ride down the trail to visit a neighbor. Eye walked beside her, and pack horse and dogs followed behind. There was a fair blue sky far above, and filtered and sifted sunshine fell in shifting patterns on the trail.

Meggie and Eye chattered and gossiped all the way, the one as pleased to have company as the other. They talked about dogs and horses and the people of Cold Spring, and the rocks and flowers along the wayside; about the fire watching in summer and the game Eye trapped in winter and how much he got for his pelts.

"Do you know?" Meggie said, "I haven't seen anything bigger than a squirrel in these woods. Folks talk about game and wild things. Goodness gracious! I haven't seen a thing."

"Ah, lassie," said Eye, "ye're too much of a chatterbox to see the wild things. They hear or they smell you long afore you see them and they're away to another place. Happen you'll see the wild things, if you're all alone sometime and no one to talk to."

"Well, that's something to look forward to anyway," Meggie said. "I'll be alone soon. The men are nearly done working on my place."

"And how does your brother feel about you livin' all alone down there? A nice young lady like you? Is he no a bit scared for ye?"

"No," Meggie said. "It's lonely, but I don't know what could happen to me."

"Maybe—maybe," Eye said. "Still ye're a wee bit of a lassie to be homesteadin' all by yoursel'."

"I'm not afraid," Meggie said, "at least not very much. And we need the money."

"Aye, ye're town folks," Eye said. "Money's the thing with you town folks. If ye'd live in the woods as long as I have, ye'd not bother yourselves about money. All a man needs to be content is a couple of horses and a dog, some beans and flour and a bedroll."

"Then you've got everything you need for contentment, haven't you, Mr. MacGillicuddy?" Meggie said admiringly. "Life is very simple, when you look at it that way, isn't it? I don't think I ever knew anyone before who could be happy like that with just what he had."

"Ah, weel," Eye admitted, "I ain't saying I didna learn my contentment the hard way, lassie. I used to have wants that God himsel' couldna satisfy. But in the long run I simmered down to enjoyin' what I could get. It's easier so."

Nan O'Rourke responded to the shot Eye fired with a yell that shook the forest. Whether her outcry was prompted by joyous welcome or raw-edged nerves, Meggie could not tell, but at least she folded Meggie to her bosom like a long-lost relative. Meggie returned her embrace with warmth.

Nan appeared leaner and stringier than she had at the beginning of the season. She was sunburned and dirty, and her black hair streaked with gray fell untidily down her back. She had been working in her garden, and Meggie could see that between the stumps she already had some neat rows of sprouting vegetables. The older woman began coiling up her hair and apologizing for her appearance.

"I haven't got a soul to dress up for," she said, "and between me and myself there's no pride at all to speak of."

"Well, you look just fine to me," Meggie said, "and are you really all alone? Where's your timber willie?"

"I packed him off a couple of weeks ago," Nan said. "I worked right with him like a man and drove him pretty hard. He was glad enough to get away. But I didn't have either money or time to squander on him. We worked like the devil and it's little enough to show, yet I'm proud of it."

"You got a pretty good cabin, Ma'am," Eye said, "but where's your barn?"

"If your aristocratic government horses got to have a barn, MacGillicuddy," Nan said, "there's a bough shelter up there at the edge of the clearing, but I'll be doggoned if I'm going to build a log barn just for an old ranger that drifts in once a summer. How far does a poor woman have to go to convince the government of her good intentions? The barn will come later, MacGillicuddy. The barn will come later. Just keep your britches on."

"Look here," Eye said. "I come here in amity to bring you a dog. Don't bite my head off. Do I have to carry a white flag to get a meal off a you, Ma'am?"

"No," Nan said. "I'm mighty pleased to see you both. I've pretty near forgot how to welcome folks, I guess, not seeing anybody for so long. Come in and see what I've done to my cabin."

The log cabin was small with only one window at the back and no porch or steps or rocking chairs. But, when Nan opened the door, Meggie gasped with astonishment, for inside it was a bower of pink roses.

"Whatever in the world!" cried Meggie. "How beautiful! Are they real? Where'd you get them?"

"I made them," Nan said proudly. "It wasn't much trouble to bring in a couple of rolls of pink and green crepe paper, and look what a spread it makes. I fashion them in the evenings when I'm here alone. It's something to do to keep from going crazy. You ever read what Mark Twain said about someplace that was so quiet you could hear your microbes gnaw? He was talking about this place for sure."

There were bouquets and garlands and wreaths of artificial roses as natural as life all over the small cabin. The effect was gay and stimulating.

"It keeps me in mind of the millinery shop at home," Nan said, wistfully. "I'm pretty near as proud of my roses as I am of helping hoist up these logs to make four walls. I tell you I worked right along on this place as good as any man, and I've put me in a darned good garden. That's the tough part of me. But in the evenings when there's nothing to do, the female in me comes up, and I make roses."

"Oh, I think it's perfectly lovely!" Meggie cried. "Will you teach me how to make them? But I haven't any tissue paper, and I'm not very clever with my hands."

"Darling," said Nan, "I'll give you a nice big bunch to take home with you. They'll brighten up your house like anything."

"My God!" said Eye, "the woods is full of flowers, real ones
with roots that suck the earth." But the two women only laughed at
him.

"Men!" said Nan, wrinkling her nose in disgust. "They understand nothing, poor brutes."

Meggie had brought a small knapsack on her back with her
nightdress in it, and a gift of coffee and raisins from her precious
stock of supplies.

There was a good smell of cooking meat in Nan's cabin.
"What is it?" Meggie asked, sniffing the air. "I know salt pork back-
wards and forwards. It isn't that."

"Rabbit," said Eye. "The woman's been chasing rabbits as well
as making paper posies."

"It's the truth," Nan said. "I remembered a snare we used to set
when I was a kid. It took me a time to rig it so's it would work,
but, by thunder, one day I caught me a bunny, and I've kept the pot
boiling ever since."

"It smells awfully good," said Meggie, round-eyed, "but how
in the world do you get up the gumption to kill the poor little
thing once you've caught it?"

"I take a stone," said Nan, "and biff it once or twice over the
head. It gives a twitch and that's the end."

"Oh, horrors!" Meggie said. "I never could do that—not if I
was starving."

"Then I skin it," continued Nan, evidently relishing the grue-
some details, "and I rub salt on the hide and stretch it on the back
of the cabin. I can't decide whether to make me a coverlet of the
hides or tote them back to town for trimming winter hats."

"Summer hides are no much good," Eye said. "You spend a
winter in here some time with a good trap or two, and you'll get
you some hides that will be worth money. I'd rather live on hides
mysel' than on cut timber."

"But animals are alive," Meggie said. "You cut a tree, it doesn't
hurt and bleed."

"It's the same thing," the old man said. "Only yon trees been
living here a hundred years maybe, sheltering the animals. The hares
live but a season or two, and without the trees they've no shelter
at all, and they'll soon disappear."

Meggie thought that she would never be able to swallow a mouthful of the stewed rabbit, but she had had a long ride, and her appetite was naturally healthy. When it came right down to it, she made a hearty meal and enjoyed it very much. But she was careful not to remember the stone and the biff on the head and the last twitch, while she was eating.

She found that she and Nan had a hundred things to talk about, all the way from cooking and planting to the townspeople of Opportunity. Here their observation points had been so different, that it was quite fascinating to Meggie to get Nan's point of view; to learn, for instance, that the judge's wife who always dressed so conservatively invariably tried on red hats with feathers before she selected the usual plain black. And Nan knew the fast women who lived near the railroad tracks and who really wore the red hats with the feathers. She could tell what kind of lace-bedecked chemises they wore and what kind of musk perfume they used.

"But they're no good," said Nan, "for all they smell nice. It's not alone the immorality of them, darling, but they're cold at heart and they'll cheat a poor milliner as easy as a minister's wife will, and for less cause, because they've more money to spend than she has."

Eye MacGillicuddy sat outside with his back against a stump and smoked a pipe while the ladies talked. "Havers an' clavers!" he said disdainfully, and all three dogs, who lay about him in various attitudes of relaxation, thumped their tails at the sound of his voice.

In the evening Eye sat with the ladies inside the cabin, and put in his good word for the men, himself in particular. Both Meggie and Nan found that they had a greater toleration for his long yarns than they had had on the trail. At that time they had been exhausted from a day of hardship, and there were other men about who made Eye appear old and garrulous. It was surprising what a few weeks of isolation in the woods could do to make any man at all appear entertaining.

Meggie thoroughly enjoyed herself, and she felt tempted to accept Nan's invitation to stay several days. But she knew she must get back to her own place. Rudy and Spike, if they kept on working after she was gone, would be almost through with her job.

She would have to be there to give them their last week's pay, and to see that everything was done up properly.

"Then I'm going to be terribly lonely," she said to Nan. "Will you come up and see me then?"

"Maybe I will," Nan said, "but I'm not much of a walker and there's an awful lot to do when you're alone on a place. You'll find that too—just splitting firewood and carrying water and keeping a pot boiling, it's enough to tie you down."

In the morning, when she came to the point of starting the long walk up the trail alone, Meggie felt rather appalled at her temerity in coming so far from her own place.

Eye was departing in the direction of the river. He tied short ropes around the necks of the two young dogs.

"They'll want to follow the horses," he said. "O'Rourke can tie hers to the table leg until I'm out of sight, and, Miss Meggie, you'd best lead your dog the whole way if you want to keep him."

Nan tucked a bunch of artificial roses under the flap of Meggie's packsack, and she insisted on sticking one in the band of Eye's dilapidated hat beside his assortment of trout flies and hooks.

"Woman," Eye said, "you're fair daft, tryin' to compete with nature on her own stampin' ground."

"Come off your high horse, MacGillicuddy," Nan replied. "You need a flower in your bonnet if ever I saw an old geezer that did. Stop grumbling now."

3.

Meggie had a little trouble with her dog at first. She had made considerable progress in his good graces, but at the same time he was reluctant to see his mother and Eye and the two horses departing in another direction. He yelped and cavorted and dangled at the end of his rope while Meggie hung sturdily to the other end of it.

"Honey, you'll choke yourself," Meggie cried. "Stop it, MacGillicuddy. Come along now, Cuddy. Now, Gilly. Now, Cuddy. Now, Mac. Come along now, Mac. My goodness, it'll have to be Mac. I'm never going to be able to call 'Here, MacGillicuddy,' all through the woods when you're out chasing rabbits."

So she talked to the dog as she dragged him along after her, and finally he gave up his hopes of regaining the adventurous life he knew, and resigned himself to trotting beside her. The horse smell faded from his nostrils, together with the agreeable smell of the ranger's unwashed overalls.

For some time Meggie chatted amiably with the dog, then she fell silent. The trail was a gradual upgrade all the way, and the day was warm. When she stopped talking, she was oppressed by a great silence. Now and again a bird broke it with a trickle of song, and sometimes there were mysterious rustlings in the brush beyond the trail. A thought occurred to Meggie: If I were to step a few paces off the trail, I might be lost, really lost, forever, to starve and die. The trees beyond the trail are all alike, all alike. For a moment the thought frightened her.

It was like the feeling she had had one summer night, when she was nearly twelve, and she and Papa had stepped onto the terrace before she went to bed. Papa was fond of the stars and he knew a lot about them. That night he had tried to give her some idea of their magnitude and how they were really other worlds and hung spinning in a terribly infinite space, billions of miles away. Before that the stars had been a close, familiar canopy to her, and just beyond them lived God in His shining Heaven. She had even fancied that the stars were little windows through which the glory of Heaven shone. But now suddenly Papa had given her this vision of limitless space, and it had so terrified her that she could scarcely get to sleep afterward. Today it was so with the forest. It seemed to be limitless and so impersonal that she felt it was hostile to her. This thread of a path that man had made was all that saved her from it.

"Oh, God," she prayed, "don't ever let me lose the trail." But ever since she had been deprived of the cosy vision of God's Heaven just beyond the stars, she had found it more difficult to pray to Him. Where was He? In which direction did one look, if not upward to the stars? And was He here in this forest where her voice would reach Him?

The dog was going forward now, not hanging back. He sniffed the ground, and pricked his ears to listen. His tongue hung lolling from his mouth. She was glad to have him with her.

When she thought it must be noon, Meggie stopped and took

out the bannock and cold-rabbit sandwiches that Nan had made for her. She sat on the carpet of pine needles beside the trail and ate, tossing bits to the dog who watched her avidly, intent on missing nothing. Nan had even put in a bit of cold huckleberry pudding cut in a slice like cake. It was delicious, and Meggie thought, I must learn to live off the country, like Nan and Bundy Jones. It's so much better than eating out of cans or on salt pork and beans. Yesterday she had helped Nan look over the huckleberries to make the pudding. Nan had picked them at the edge of her own clearing.

"The woods are full of them now," Nan said. "Just keep your eyes open, you'll see them."

When she continued on after lunch, Meggie began to look for huckleberries. It took the curse of vastness from the forest, she found if she noticed the little things along the way. Here a delicate fern, like green lace; there a bit of rock shining with mica; and in a damp and sheltered place, a single lady's-slipper, small and succulent and delicately lavender with spotted throat. Oh, that was lovely! Meggie thought, too lovely to pick; a thing to leave in its perfection, but always to remember.

She began to enjoy herself again, and when she saw huckle-berries hanging thick on a bush just off the trail, she stopped to pick. She tied the dog's leash to her wrist, for she didn't yet quite trust him, and she used the crown of her hat as a receptacle to hold her berries.

There was an open space here where sunshine reached the forest floor and Meggie saw that the berry bushes went on for a long distance beyond the trail. But she was careful to keep the trail in sight. That was the one thing she would always remember in the woods.

The huckleberries were a dark, purplish red, and each one had a little ring or depression at the blossom end. They had a silvery bloom that easily bruised, and the smell of them was wild and strong. I'll just get enough for a pie, Meggie thought, and won't Spike and Rudy be surprised?

She was wholly preoccupied and happy when suddenly Mac began to growl and she saw that the hair along his mongrel back had risen in a standing ridge. At the same moment she heard a movement in the brush nearby, and, looking up, she saw that she was neighbor to a bear. The dog lunged forward toward the bear, dragging Meggie with him; and the bear reared on its haunches and seemed to be towering toward them.

Meggie uttered such a scream as she had never in her life let out before. The sound of it frightened her almost as much as the sight of the bear. Even the dog and the bear were affected by it, and seemed to be frozen for an instant where they stood. Meggie screamed again and again. She couldn't stop screaming. She saw the bear let himself down on his forefeet, and she was sure that he was coming at her.

She dropped her hat and berries and began to run, dragging the young dog behind her. The dog had suddenly lost his will to resist, and he galloped along beside her, in a puzzled confusion of fear and playfulness.

Meggie got the trail under her feet and continued to run along it screaming as she went. Soon she could scream no more, because she needed all her breath for running. Her side began to ache, and every breath she drew was like a knife driven into her lungs. Still she ran on, and never dared look back.

But now she looked ahead with terribly intent eyes, for the forest seemed full of life and sinister movement. The trees flicked by her; the bushes rustled; behind every rock some hidden danger lurked.

Then, on the trail ahead of her she saw the snake. She saw it very clearly, lying there, right in her path, only a few steps ahead.

Meggie stopped running and stood still in a terrible silence. The screams that had risen so easily to her lips at sight of the bear were all gone. The puppy was silent too. He drew back from the snake uneasily, his lips lifted from his teeth as in disgust. A little drip of frothy saliva drooled from the corners of his mouth. The snake continued to lie in the path but it raised its head and hissed at them; a tiny darting tongue flickered and shimmered in anger and menace.

Meggie knew nothing of snakes except that they inspired her with horror. She did not know whether this one was harmless or armed with some lethal venom. She stood in a terrible silent quandary—whether to run back into the arms of the bear or to go forward into the toils of the serpent. Behind her were Nan and

Eye, but ahead of her was—home. Yes, it was her own place, *home,* the first time she had ever uttered the word seriously in her own thoughts.

The snake was coiling slowly with a sinewy movement that filled her with unreasoning terror. The pattern on its back was beautiful—a cold geometry, a kind of classical poetry in pattern and movement. But it had no legs. It must have been that which filled her so completely with disgust. It crawled on its belly, but so adroitly, so smoothly, with such deliberate purpose. She could not bear to look at it, yet neither could she bear to look away. A kind of desperation seized her—to get away, to get away. Yes, to get *home.* Yet she dared not step over it. What could she do? She plucked up her courage and seized a rock.

Almost coolly now she freed her wrist from the leash of the dog and took aim. Made skillful and strong by terror, her aim was better than she could ever have imagined. The rock hit the snake in the midsection and pinned it to the trail. The head and the tail writhed and twisted in horrible contortions. Meggie picked up another stone and flung it, and then another and another. The head of the snake became a bloody pulp and the little tongue no longer wagged. The tail continued to writhe and twist, but now Meggie went in closer and beat the tail into immobility.

And now she saw that it had really not been a large snake at all, and she remembered that Charlie Duporte had once told her he had never seen anything but garter snakes in these woods. She stepped around the bloody rocks in the trail and started home.

She had forgotten the dog and his rope, but he followed along docilely behind her, the rope trailing.

She walked more slowly now trying painfully to control her wild, uneven breathing. The tears began to run down her cheeks, and sobs complicated the painful, panting breaths she drew. At first she cried for herself, alone in this unfriendly place, and then suddenly she was crying for the snake, the loathsome thing that she had killed. But it had been small, really, and fearful as herself. It had been innocent and unknowing, and she had killed it. Now it was herself that she found loathsome. So she wept uncontrollably as she climbed the gentle rise in the trail toward Bide a Wee. She never knew how far she walked on crying, but it was a long time.

At last she heard the sound of the little stream that ran on the other side of the trail from her cabin. Around the next bend she would see the clearing, she would hear the axes of the men; she could go into the house and shut the door and begin to get supper.

She sat down beside the stream and took the light packsack off her back. She began to wash her swollen face in the clear cold water. She took off the heavy shoes and bathed her feet.

The young dog came up beside her and licked her cheek. She patted his head and said, "Good boy!" Her breathing grew gradually more normal and her heart no longer pounded. She looked around her at the mossy rocks and up at the high trees. The feathery tips of the pines were soft against a far blue sky. Beside her there were some very pale pink flowers growing together on the mossy bank. She noticed how the delicate, hairlike stems rose out of the ground and at a certain height each stem branched and bore two single flowers. They were so delicate that one would scarcely notice them in passing by, yet there were a great many of them and each was fashioned with the utmost elegance.

Her glance returned to her packsack and she saw the tissue paper roses sticking out of it. She had arranged them very carefully on the top of the pack so that they would not be crushed. Now she was angry with them because they were too pink, too large, and too unreal. She took them out of the pack and dropped them one by one on the surface of the stream. Away they went, gay and incongruous, into the dark, the unknowing forest. One of them was caught in a little eddy of backwater, and she saw how it slowly disintegrated. The gaudy pink color faded first and the tissue paper grew white. It continued to eddy very slowly in the clear water, and then it gradually sank and lay like an alien ghost on the mottled pebbles of the small dark pool.

Meggie gave a long sigh and rose up to go on. She did not know why she had thrown away Nan's artificial flowers, unless to expiate her own crime against nature. The dog jumped up too, and gamboled joyously around her. She went on quietly, and presently she saw where the last trees of the clearing had been cut, and then she saw the cabin, and how much nicer than Nan's it was, with the porch and the boxes of ferns and the two windows. She sighed again with relief and with gladness. Her volatile spirits had begun to rise.

4.

The men were nowhere in sight when she came into the clearing. There was no sound of ax or hammer. She called, but there was no answer. She went into the cabin, and she saw that they had left it in disorder after getting their breakfast. The dishes had not been washed and the coffeepot full of grounds stood on the cold stove.

Mechanically Meggie began to pick up the cluttered dishes, and to put kindling into the stove for heating water. She hated to see things left untidy after a meal; still she felt that the cleaning up should come later, and that her first concern must be with the whereabouts of the men. But she could not make up her mind what she should do about them. She felt tired out with her day's adventures and unable to cope with anything further at the moment.

Whatever am I doing in this place? she thought. Yet only a couple of hours ago the cabin had seemed to her like home. If I didn't have to face it all alone, she thought—if Jeff or Papa or Mama or *someone* were only here to help me! She considered putting her packsack on her back again and pushing on up the trail to Jeff's place. But she was too weary for that, and besides she had a certain streak of stubbornness that bade her stay where she was and face her own problems.

When she had the fire going and the kettle on, she left the cabin and went up to the barn. She saw that the men had finished shingling the roof, and that the barn door stood ajar. She called the names of both men again as she went along.

The dog came with her, casually good-natured, but a molehill in her newly-made garden interested him more than any man scent.

Meggie went to the barn door and pulled it all the way open. She had not looked in there since the men had begun to sleep in it. They had made bough beds and spread their blankets on them. An unlighted lantern sat on a rough table made of split logs. The place was in disorder and she could smell whiskey and a sour reek of perspiration and uncleanliness.

Spike was sprawled on his blankets, sleeping heavily, but Rudy had struggled up and was coming toward her. His black hair stood up wildly on his head, and his eyes were bloodshot. To Meggie's frightened eyes he loomed larger than the bear, but he smiled at her foolishly and tenderly.

"You sure got back here quick," he said in a thick voice. "Never thought you come so soon, Meggie. We finished barn roof, got to take a little rest. You see that, Meggie?"

He had never called her by her first name before and Meggie was annoyed at the impertinence.

"You've been drinking!" she said angrily. "How dare you do that on my place? How dare you call me by my first name like that?"

He kept coming toward her unsteadily and smiling at her. "Don't be so mad," he said. "We ain't done nothing to you, a nice little girl like you. Ain't the barn done good? Ain't we treated you all right?"

"Yes," Meggie said, "you have. But I don't like your drinking on the job. You ought to know that. I've started the fire now, I'll make you some coffee. When you feel like sobering up, you come down and get some. But you've got to behave yourself, do you hear?"

Meggie was surprised at the spunky sound of her own voice. She wouldn't have dared talk up to Rudy like that, except that this was just the last straw after a frightful day, and she'd got beyond mincing words. He kept coming toward her smiling that fatuous smile.

"My God, you got a pretty little look to you, Meggie!" he said thickly. "You got a sweet, kind heart, ain't you? Sweet and kind. I don't care how damned tough you try to talk."

Meggie turned and ran again. She heard him trip on the door-sill and fall behind her. The half-grown dog, delighted to see her run, left the molehole and gamboled beside her. She let him into the cabin with her and shut and barred the door.

"You fool!" she said to him. "A lot of good you've been to me today." She sat down on the edge of her bed and began to shake all over. But the water was steaming in the kettle, and presently she stood up and made herself a cup of strong tea. The warmth went through her, and the shaking stopped.

I'm the fool, she thought reproachfully. Whatever made me think I had the nerve to be a homesteader? If I get out of here alive, I'll never come back.

She washed up the breakfast mess and began to cook supper. She made a pot of coffee, but neither of the men came down to get it. It began to grow dark and she wouldn't have ventured to take the coffee up to them if her life depended upon it.

Well, let them live on their horrible bottles, she said to herself, and I'm thankful I've got a bar on my door on the inside. I never did a smarter thing than that.

She got down the cumbersome old pistol that had caused her such amusement in Cold Spring, and laboriously she loaded it. The very look of it now filled her with alarm, but she felt it was her duty to put it in shape for defending herself if the need arose. She could not imagine where she would find the courage to shoot it, but surprising things in herself kept emerging. Maybe if she had to—

After she had eaten a lonely supper and tidied everything up, she found that she was unable to keep her eyes open. She felt as if she had been hit on the head or drugged. She struggled against the feeling as long as she could; then she undressed and went to bed. The bunk was hard, in spite of the leaf and dried fern mattress she had made, but she fell asleep like a child with a great sigh of relaxation.

Some time later she woke up. It was still dark and she could barely make out treetops against a starry sky through the cabin window. At first she thought it was the dog that had awakened her. While she slept he had established himself on the foot of her bed, and now he was moving uneasily against her feet and growling deep in his throat.

What now? Meggie thought in alarm. She knew that she ought to throw the dog out of her bed and teach him right at the start not to take liberties. "Mac! Get down," she said. His growling made her uneasy, however, and she raised herself on one elbow to listen.

Then she began to hear the men shouting at each other up at the barn. They were arguing in loud voices, and they sounded angry. In a moment she was sure that they were fighting. She crept out of bed and went to the back window. The dog's feet thudded on the floor after hers, and she heard him whining to get out.

"No you don't," Meggie said to him fiercely. "You've got to guard and protect me and do your duty by me, if it kills you, you fool."

From the window she could see a faint light glowing from the barn door.

"They've got the lantern lit," she whispered. "Oh, dear God Almighty, don't let them set the barn afire."

The sounds came to her more clearly as she knelt at the window. They were swearing at each other, and she could hear the thud and crack of blows.

"If one of them kills the other, what'll I do?" Meggie whispered. "What'll I do? What'll I do?" She even saw herself single-handedly having to bury a corpse.

She wondered if she ought to go up there with her pistol and intervene—but not in her nightdress—heavens no! She couldn't do that. And the very thought of dressing and cocking the pistol and going out into the darkness to separate two fighting men made her feel weak and limp.

Gradually her bare feet on the split log floor grew cold as ice. The men were still at it, hot and heavy in the barn, but, when she faced up to it, there wasn't a thing she could do. Bewildered and dismayed, she crawled back under the blankets. In a moment she felt the dog leaping up again on the foot of the bed. He curled himself reassuringly against her legs, and drew a long sigh of contentment. She certainly should have booted him out, but his warmth and weight against her feet and legs were infinitely comforting.

The sound of fighting went on for some time. Then abruptly it ceased. Everything was very, very quiet. There was always a gentle sighing sound in the tops of the pines, and now that was all, absolutely all. Meggie lay for a long time shivering, and then she went to sleep again.

5.

There was a shower in the very early morning, but by daylight the sky was crystal clear and everything bright and newly cleansed. Drops of water sparkled on every frond and needle, and the varying shades of green were brilliant and intense. A smell, almost a perfume, of damp earth filled the air. It was a glorious morning.

Meggie got up and stretched her aching muscles. Yesterday and last night seemed to her a nightmare from which she was mercifully awakening. It had all been fantasy and surely she had taken it too seriously. She dressed hurriedly and lighted the fire.

Then she went down to the stream to wash her face in cold water and fill her bucket. As she went she sang "Jesus, Lover of My Soul" in a firm voice. Hers was not a very tuneful voice, for she did not have Jeff's true ear or range and quality in singing. But the bravado of singing hymns before breakfast gave her a comforting feeling that "God's in his heaven, all's right with the world." Certainly the hillside was "dew-pearled" this morning and something was "on the wing," for bird songs came trickling down to her from all sides.

She went on getting breakfast for three as usual, and she did not allow herself to speculate or wonder. When the meal was ready, she went to the door and called, "Come and get it," as the lumberjacks had taught her to do.

She stood in the doorway waiting, and she couldn't control the accelerated beating of her heart. Her mind said that the fight she thought she had heard could not have been real, yet her heart seemed to know that it had been.

Presently she heard steps at the side of the house, and she saw that Spike was coming in alone.

"Where's Rudy?" she asked in a small voice.

"He's gone," Spike said. He looked pale, but perfectly sober this morning. There was a dark bruise on his right cheek under the eye, but he looked clean and his hair was slicked up wetly above his parti-colored forehead.

"Where has he gone?" asked Meggie.

"He didn't say," Spike said.

"Well, *why* then?" Meggie persisted.

"We had a argument," Spike said. "We beat hell outa each other, but I won. That's all you got to know, I guess. He lit out and hit the trail before it turned light."

"But I didn't pay him for the last week," Meggie said. "I owe him money."

"That don't matter. We had a good summer. We didn't aim to ask you no pay this last week. It ain't your fault he didn't stop by to collect."

"Well, come in to breakfast," Meggie said. "But it isn't right, you know. People shouldn't fight, not for anything. Don't you know that?"

"You tell that to the birds," Spike said laconically.

"And drinking," Meggie said, "that's awfully foolish too. Where does it get you?"

"Don't start preachin' at me," Spike said. "This morning I ain't in no mood for preaching."

"So I see," said Meggie.

They ate in silence. Spike made a good meal after his fast, but Meggie's throat seemed suddenly constricted and the sight of food disgusted her. When she rose to get the coffeepot from the stove, Spike put out a hand and pushed her back into her seat.

"I'll wait on you this morning," he said. "You been waitin' on us all summer, a real nice little girl like you, waitin' on us."

"Don't be silly," Meggie said, but something different in his manner frightened her. She let him get the coffeepot and pour his own coffee.

"What's the matter?" he said. "You ain't eating nothing yourself."

"I'm not very hungry," Meggie said.

As soon as breakfast was over, Meggie said, "I'll write you a check now. You'll want to hit the trail, too, I expect, as soon as you can."

"No," he said, "I'm in no hurry. I could go on helping you here for nothing for a while if you was to say the word."

"Oh, I don't want that," Meggie said. "The barn is finished. I want you to go now, right away this morning."

He laughed at her, a short laugh like a bark. Then he began to range around the cabin, looking at all her things, in a way he'd never done before.

Meggie put his money on the table.

"There it is," she said. "You're all paid up now."

"It's funny you should be payin' me," he said. "I ought to pay you for a real nice summer."

Meggie thought that she would have run out the door and left him then if she could, but he was between her and the door. Mac, the dog, was lying out on the porch in the sunshine scratching his ear. He seemed to have no sense for danger, and the lumberjack had the familiar scent of all the men he'd ever wagged at.

Spike saw the pistol lying on the shelf beside her bed.

"What you doing with this?" he asked, laughing his short laugh. He took the pistol in his big hands and looked at it. "It's loaded too, by God! I bet you couldn't shoot it though. But you don't need to be scared of me, girlie. I plan to treat you gentle, if you don't fight back."

"Oh, go! Please go," Meggie begged.

"That's not a way to talk, after you been so sweet and friendly all summer. You never let on which one you liked best, but we let the fight decide it. I won you twice, sure 'nough. First it was poker, but Rudy wouldn't swallow that, and I had to beat him black and blue to put it over. Now he's gone, and you and me's alone here."

He kept moving slowly toward her, and Meggie recognized the heavy look of tenderness he bent upon her although she had never before seen it in a man's face. She felt weak with pity as well as fear. She kept moving backward away from him as he moved toward her. And he had taken her pistol and put it out of her reach. He had taken her only weapon. She felt that she was utterly defenseless and that this was the culmination of the nightmare.

"Don't. Please don't," she said. The edge of the table shelf by the rear window pushed against her back. She had gone as far away from him as she could, and he was still coming toward her, taking his time, enjoying himself in his own way.

"You been so easy all summer," he said. "What makes you want to fight back now? You're real pretty when you're mad."

"Listen, Spike," she said. "You're all wrong. I guess I know the kind of woman you must think I am, but really I'm not. I'm not."

"All women are alike," Spike said, "the same as all men are. They only want one thing." His face was dark and uglier now, and Meggie's feelings were no longer complicated by pity. She said coldly: "But maybe they want that thing in some particular way. Maybe they want it the way they plan it."

"Nobody never taught you very much, did they, little girl? And your brother now, what does he do to keep you safe and taken care of? You're all alone here. And I aim to let you in on some of the things you've missed."

He was coming quite close now, and Meggie could not take her eyes away from him. But her hand was groping behind her on the window shelf. She didn't have the pistol but anything, anything, would do. She was a fighter too, she knew it now. If he hadn't said that about her brother, about her being alone— Suddenly her groping fingers found the neck of her mandolin. She remembered that she had left it there carelessly instead of putting it back in the case. She brought it up and down with all her strength and crashed it in splinters around the lumberjack's ears. He drew back in astonishment, a little trickle of blood running down beside his eye. Uncertainty was mingled with the surprise that spread across his face.

Meggie felt suddenly released from her paralysis. She felt capable and strong. "Now you get out of here," she cried. "You get, and don't you ever come back, because I'll—I'll blast you to blazes if you do."

For an instant Spike hesitated, then he turned and went out of the cabin. The dog, aroused at last from his sunny comfort, barked him off the porch. Meggie flung his check after him and closed and barred the door.

Then she sat down and looked at the wreck of her mandolin. I always hated it, she said to herself. I hated to practice, I hated to take lessons. But I couldn't sing well or do water colors or embroider like other girls, and I was trying to get some ladylike accomplishment to please Papa and Mama. If I had practiced a hundred years, I couldn't have played it as well as Charlie Duporte can play without ever having taken a lesson. Well, there goes nothing!

Coffee was still in the pot, and she put it back on the stove to warm it up. Now she was ready for her breakfast. She ate a stack of sourdough pancakes and drank two cups of coffee, and then she crawled into her bunk between the blankets and slept until noon.

IV

THE MIRROR

1.

Jeff Carney went back and forth on the trail restlessly, meeting homesteaders and staking claims. Between these trips he found it hard to settle down to the work of his own homestead. Lorena was silent and withdrawn, and the work itself was distasteful to him. He was better off on the trail.

But unfortunately even there he carried his discontent and resentment along with him. It was not dispelled by the sunshine and bracing air of mountain trails nor diminished by starlight. He brought it back to the cabin and laid it at Lorena's feet as a tribute to her reproachful beauty.

When his wound seemed to be healing, he tore it open again so that he might suffer. It was true that his hopes had been dealt a cruel blow, but his trouble seemed to go deeper than this into a basic insecurity. As Papa had tried to make a darling little lady of Meggie, he had also tried to build a tough and successful young male of Jeff, and the blows of the hammer and chisel were still visible on a soul which had never been a block of granite. Jeff had grown tired of trying to be what Papa expected him to be, but at the same time he felt that he had had a right to expect the best of what his father could leave him.

His insecurity arose from the knowledge that he had never measured up to the senator's expectations of him. He saw himself through his father's eyes and later through his own as a lesser man than the old man had been. With Uncle Ralph it was even worse, for the charm and ruthless self-confidence that were in his father were multiplied over and over in Ralph. And he knew with envy that Lorena admired Ralph. No, he could never get out from under the long dark shadows that the older men cast, standing tall and invulnerable behind him.

One day he happened on Bundy Jones's camp in the woods, and Jones seemed glad to see him. Bundy asked him to share a meal, and he ended by spending the night there.

Bundy served up a really delicious mess of food, something that smelled good and almost made a man think he was eating meat.

"What is it?" Jeff asked.

"Morchella," Bundy said.

"Well, again, what's that?" Jeff asked, laughing. He felt relaxed in Bundy's company. Away from Lorena, the dislike he had felt for Bundy on the trail faded away. Bundy seemed to take life very easily, and the ease was infectious.

"Mushrooms," Bundy said.

"My God! do you dare eat them?"

"Not all kinds of them," Bundy said. "But this kind you can't mistake. There's no poison one like it. It looks like a little wrinkled cone, dull colored and not pretty, but you'll find plenty in the burned-over places, and you can't beat them for food."

"How do you know all this?"

"Well, it's my job to know," Bundy said, "and I probably spend too much time feeding myself. I'd get fat if I didn't walk it off, hunting up stuff. I kind of pride myself on living off the country. There's a certain satisfaction in it."

"You haven't a worry in the world, have you?" Jeff asked enviously.

"Oh, gosh, yes!" said Bundy eagerly. "I have a lot of them. More than you would suppose." He rolled and lit a cigarette. Then he said, "How are the homesteads going?"

"Oh, fine," said Jeff, "just fine. Got our houses up and gardens in. You should come down and see."

"I've thought of that," Bundy said. "Maybe I will. And Mrs. Carney? Is she—liking it?"

"She's doing very well," Jeff said. "Very well, I think."

"She isn't bored?"

"No," Jeff said. For a moment he was tempted to share his

anxieties and insecurities with Bundy, but he did not do so. It was pleasanter to lay them aside for the time being, and listen to Bundy talking of trees and plants. One thing this summer in the woods was teaching Jeff, and that was to keep his own council. Everyone had complaints out here. They did not listen to the complaints of other people. It was no use asking for sympathy or understanding among people who had none to spare. It was only to Lorena that he still brought his troubles. He had a constant compulsion to make her see him as a man wronged and not responsible for the meagerness of what he had to offer her. This was a thing beyond his reason or his power of control.

So they sat by the campfire and Bundy talked about trees and plants as living beings. He sat there absorbed, scratching his dog behind the ear, and seemed to proclaim that he and the dog and the trees and the little gray and orange lichens on the log behind his back were all one and a part of the same thing.

Jeff moved uncomfortably and restlessly, because he dimly remembered that once he had had a similar vision. But now he was an adult and it was gone, and lichens to him were part of the earth he walked on, and trees were so many board feet of lumber. Yet the memories plagued him when he was with Bundy.

Jeff remembered the first summer when he had come in here. He was fourteen, and somehow young for his age although he was tall and well grown. Everything had been wonderful to him then. The size of the trees had astounded him; the color of a moccasin flower had given him pleasure; he had felt a fury of love for the stocky little horse that carried him. But now when he tried to recapture this sense of pleasure, it had become only a memory and it defied recapture.

He thought that it was no wonder adolescence was painful to many people as it had been to him; for it was a combination of death and birth, and both of these experiences were couched in human agony. Adolescence was the death of wonder and fancy and trust in things outside yourself, he thought. It was the death of clear, uncolored vision and of innocence; the death of safety and of the sensation of being cherished; the death of a belief that anything wonderful can happen.

And while many things struggled in death agony, many others

were born. Some of them came slowly and painfully; others were snatched and flung out into the living turmoil with ruthless anguish. The bewildering new sense of sex was born, and all the dark, mysterious impulses; the feeling that now it is up to you, and that for what your life becomes only you are now responsible. To Jeff, along with the tremendous new feelings, came loneliness and defeat, and the shame that he was not one of the minor deities as he once thought he was. There was unnamed regret, too, for the losses he had suffered. Without knowing where he had lost them, he missed the wonder, the fancy, the trust in other people. He was confused by the fact that he no longer saw clearly, in bright, primary colors; for every image now was surrounded by a nimbus of new meaning, and all the simple landmarks were shrouded in fog.

Yes, Jeff thought, he had suffered; his world had narrowed. Where there had seemed to be many opportunities open to him, now there seemed only one and he was dissatisfied with that. He thought, if a man could only bring his childhood along with him, complete with wonder, trust and clear vision, he might be a happy adult. But suddenly, from the belief that anything wonderful could happen, he had awakened to the realization that probably very little would, and that the very little was drab and disappointing.

Looking at Bundy Jones's face, ruddy and contented in the firelight, Jeff thought that some of the child in Bundy had probably survived. There was a certain naïve simplicity in the fellow that was out of keeping with his age. He still seemed to look at things as if he were seeing them for the first time. He still wore a bloom of innocence and well-being that irritated Jeff as much as it fascinated him.

No, he would never again rattle off his woes to Bundy as he had done that first night in Cold Spring. They kept gnawing at his vital parts, but more and more Jeff was learning to suffer his anguish in silence.

Yet something in Bundy reassured him. Coming back from his own far thoughts, Jeff began to listen again. Bundy was saying, "These trees are going to be more valuable if they are left uncut. You don't believe that maybe. But they'll do more people more good right here than they will if they are sawed into lumber and shipped away."

"You believe that, don't you?" Jeff said slowly.

"Yes, I believe it," Bundy said. "When the Forest Service is a little stronger, it will put men in here to make this forest produce. They'll cut with wisdom what's right for cutting, and they'll replant and work it like a farm."

"And you and I'll be dead then," Jeff said.

"Maybe not. Anyway, can't you see beyond yourself?" Bundy asked. "Can't you get a vision of a better future? Is money so important?"

"I need money here and now," Jeff said. "I've always had it. I can't survive without it."

"I'm sorry for you," Bundy said. He said it sincerely, and Jeff did not take offense.

Before he left him the next morning, Jeff found himself urging Bundy to visit the homestead.

"All right," Bundy said. "I'll come down soon."

2.

When Jeff reached the homestead Lorena was standing before the shelf on which her hand mirror was propped. She was brushing her long dark hair. She looked around at him.

"Hello," she said. Then she looked back at the mirror and began to coil her hair. It was as if he had just stepped out into the clearing and then returned. Actually he had been gone three days.

What did he want? Some foolish demonstration? Yes, he wanted her to run to him crying, "Dearest, I thought the time would never end!" or "Darling, I have been so lonely!"

He stood in the doorway and watched her coil her hair. He knew every quick and expert movement of the slender wrists and clever fingers, and how the dark hair shone from brushing. It was a beautiful ritual to watch. But he knew that she did it for herself and not for him. Sometimes he was as jealous of her mirror as he was of other men.

There were the full-length mirrors on the closet doors in the big house at home. They had always been there, and as a little boy he remembered his mother standing before the one in the master bedroom looking at the hem of her skirt as a dressmaker knelt beside her and pinned it into place.

In his mother's day the mirrors had been connected with dressmakers and occasional balls or receptions. They had been inanimate things. But after Lorena and he were married, the mirrors became a part of their daily living. When he would have liked to have her look at him, it seemed to Jeff that she was always looking in a mirror. She would be twitching a waistband, adjusting a sleeve, coiling her beautiful hair. Her eyes searched and questioned the eyes of the woman in the mirror. She stepped close to the mirror and examined her skin for tiny flaws or imperfections; she stepped back and lifted her lovely chin to get the complete effect.

At first, during their courtship, he had been jealous of his Uncle Ralph who had been her employer. But, although he knew that she admired Ralph's qualities as a businessman, he felt now that he had been foolish to allow himself to feel jealousy. It was only because he loved Lorena so much; and, in spite of all that life had given him in the way of security, he never really felt secure. But as soon as he overcame his jealousy of Ralph, there had come this mad and senseless resentment of the mirrors. He might have laughed at himself for entertaining it, except that he took himself and his feelings seriously and he had no great sense of humor.

If we had children, he thought, it wouldn't be like this. She would grow warm with love for children. Yet wouldn't he be jealous of *them?* He wondered. He thought not. He thought that he could have loved his children very much. Together he and Lorena could have met and grown close in their love for their children. And why did he use the hopeless words "could have"? Surely there was time yet for children, and one need never give up hope. Yet it was odd that there had been none. In his troubled searching of soul, he sometimes asked himself was it his fault or hers? And why did they not have children? But he did not speak of it to her. He knew that she disliked responsibilities. She was happier, or thought she was, without them.

Watching her again absorbed in her mirror, he thought that here in the woods, away from the tall beveled glasses on the closet doors, away from everything effete and shiny, he should have been spared his resentment of mirrors. But she had brought one with her. It was only a small one to reflect her face, but, like a familiar idol, it had been the first thing placed in the new cabin. Smelling the raw fresh smell of split pine indoors and the smell of burning slashings in the clearing, even before the mud chinking was in place, he had seen her propping her mirror on the crude shelf.

Charlie Duporte, looking in the doorway at her, had said, "Now you're home, Mis' Carney. A lady puts her mirror up, she's home. Ain't it so?"

Lorena had turned to him and smiled her slow, wonderful smile.

"Where a man hangs his hat," she said, "and a woman hangs her mirror. It'll pass for home, I guess. Where else?"

They had laughed as if they shared some joke that Jeff could not see. There was always this feeling he had of being left out of things which he did not understand. Sometimes it made him hard to get along with.

"Well," she said, now, still with her back to him, still pinning her hair, "aren't you going to say 'hello'?"

"Hello," he said mechanically. "Hello, Lorena, hello. I'm back again. Aren't you surprised? Aren't you pleased?"

"You said you'd be back today," Lorena said. "Why should I be surprised? And of course I'm pleased. It's so devilishly quiet here."

He went into the cabin and turned her around to face him. She smiled at him and kissed him, but he felt the perfunctory nature of the kiss. He always wanted so much more than he was given. He held her with his hands around her two arms above the elbows. The upper arms were warm and soft, and slender enough for his hands to hold them firmly.

"Oh, Lorena," he said, "love me! love me! You do, don't you? A little bit?"

"Of course I do, Jeff," she said. "How can you be so stupid about things? Would I be here, in this awful place, if I didn't love you? What do you think?"

"Oh, Rena," he said. "I meant everything to be better for you. You know that."

"Yes, I know," she said. Impatiently she disengaged herself and moved away from him.

"It isn't right," he said to her for the thousandth time. "I was brought up to expect something better, for myself, for you."

Lorena leaned back against the table in a posture of utter relaxation. She looked at him with a smile of tolerant amusement, tinged with scorn, as one would smile at an angry child who beats its head against the wall to no purpose.

If he could have convinced her that he had been wronged; if he could have felt her for a moment on his side, looking at his position from his point of view, he might have regained his perspective. But he must always be on the defensive, because she was so beautifully and becomingly amused by his futile antics. He yearned to convince her. He wanted to exact her loyalty and wifely support. That he could not do so became a further grievance to him.

To be tied by a hopeless agony of love to someone who pitied and scorned you—that was the last indignity.

"Don't keep harping on the past, Jeff," she said. "You're too young for that."

"But I feel unhappy for *you*, Lorena."

"I never asked you to."

"I know. You don't ask me for anything. But I can't help feeling that you are disappointed."

"You see!" she said. "You're utterly hopeless. I just got through telling you that I loved you enough to stay even here, in a place like this, for you. But are you happy? No, nothing pleases you. Nothing suits you. If you would just relax, and make the best of what comes, make the best, I say. Pull yourself up by your own bootstraps."

"That's one of Ralph's expressions," he said irritably.

"Well, why shouldn't I use Ralph's expressions?" she asked. "I heard them every day for a long time. They may have lacked originality, but they were full of vigor. They were picturesque, and he backed them up with action. He was a man."

"I know," he said, "and I'm not. Isn't that it?"

"Oh, stop it. Let's not quarrel. Quarreling is almost as tedious as doing nothing. It bores me terribly."

"I don't want to quarrel, Lorena. I love you. You know that, don't you?"

"The gramophone is stuck," Lorena said. "The disc is going

round and round in the same place. Of course, you love me, darling. Of course, I love you. Let's not worry it."

In town these recurring domestic interludes with Jeff got on Lorena's nerves. But out here it was doubly trying, when there was nothing to distract one from the sighing of the pine trees and the senseless twittering of the birds. When there was nothing—nothing. Yet, as she said, quarreling with Jeff bored her more than the silence of the wilderness. She wanted desperately to be amused, to have things turn out happily.

She ended by kissing him again and making peace. She began to ask him about his trip, and it was somewhat diverting to her to hear that he had seen Bundy Jones and had invited him to visit them.

3.

All summer, for some reason that was obscure to him, Bundy had put off visiting the homesteaders. They were his first responsibility this summer, yet his feelings about them had become unreasonably complicated since he had met them. It was all very well to have cut-and-dried feelings about homesteaders when they existed only on paper in a Department of Agriculture office; but when one knew them as individuals it became harder to spy on and intrigue against them. That, of course, was putting it much too strongly. He meant them no personal harm, and his loyalty to the Forest Service was as stanch as ever.

He decided that his delay in going to see them stemmed from his desire to be perfectly fair to them, to give them every opportunity to prove that they could make homes here and live in them. He was sure that they could not, but he was willing to give them the benefit of the doubt.

Jeff's invitation, however, stirred up his resolution to go. Once he had made up his mind, he was amazed to find how eager he was. He packed his horse and left a clean campsite, and as he rode down the trail he whistled a tune he had heard in a vaudeville theater in Washington last winter. Much as he loved solitude, he was looking forward to the prospect of company.

He went the rounds of the homesteads slowly, stopping at each place he came to, and giving each owner time to show him the new log walls, the reluctant garden struggling among the stumps, the proud gropings toward civilization.

"You'll never make it," he told them. "You know this is a forest reserve. It isn't meadowland."

"But they tell you, if you can make a home, you get it. Who's to say we ain't making a home? By God, we're here, on the spot. We've built and broken ground. Pinchot's in Washington making his big stink. How does he know what we've got here? Eye MacGilli-cuddy hasn't raised no row."

Bundy traveled slowly, taking time and making a pretense of leisure which deceived himself and gave him a feeling of virtue. Yet always at the back of his mind there was a sense of going toward one place. The one place toward which he traveled was built around and lighted by a woman's smile. In spite of the glimpse of her inner self which he had caught on the trail, he still imagined Lorena Carney to be serene and fortunate and as happily married as most women are. She was unattainable, as are so many of the dreams of young and naïve men. Nevertheless her face continued to shine in his camp-fire in the lonely evenings, and the sight of it was the chief objective of his pilgrimage.

When he arrived he brought a creel full of fresh trout wrapped in green leaves and a hatful of huckleberries. He had washed in a stream and freshly combed his hair. He looked a proper gentleman, as well as healthy, young and eager.

Lorena was alone in the cabin when he arrived, and she came toward him without haste, smiling the smile he remembered and holding out both hands.

"Oh, I'm so glad you've come," she said. "I expected you a long time ago. I was sure you had forgotten me."

"No," he said gravely, "I never did. Never at all."

"I don't believe that," Lorena said, pressing his hands a little before she let them go. "But I'm glad you're here. Jeff and Charlie (you remember Charlie Duporte?), they're working up in the clear-ing. Shall I call them?"

"There's no hurry," Bundy said. "I figured on staying the night, if you'd let me pitch tent in the clearing."

"That would be wonderful," she said. "I get terribly lonely. I'm crazy to see someone with a fresh viewpoint. I want you to tell me things to amuse me. I want to hear everything about you and what you've done, since that day you rode off and left us."

"That's a big order," he said, "and the things I've done aren't spectacular. You wouldn't really be amused."

"Yes, I would," Lorena said. "Just the sound of your voice amuses and pleases me. Sit down. Our chairs are horrors of discomfort, but you'll make me forget them by telling me everything. Please."

Ordinarily Bundy wasn't a talker, but, under her friendly prodding and probing he found himself doing all he could to satisfy her eager curiosity. He told her about his various campsites and how he kept going higher to keep the horses in fresh grazing, and about the lookout point he had discovered near the top of Freezeout.

"There were miles and miles of timber country spread out below me there," he said. "Miles and miles of virgin forest, and not a thread of smoke, not a visible habitation. It gives you a feeling— I can't tell you."

"You love it, don't you?"

"Yes," he said. "Yes, somehow I do."

He told her about the big cougar tracks he had seen in the marshy ground by the spring, and about the twin fawns.

"I came on them suddenly in the deep woods," he said. "They were lying together in a shady place. One of them pulled itself up on its wobbly legs and looked at me, kind of scared and curious. The other lay still, and it knew by instinct or some way its mother had informed it that immobility is its best protection. That was a sight worth seeing. There was a green bank beside them covered with hundreds of tiny pink twin flowers. Twin fawns, twin flowers— Funny. I get a lot of pleasure out of things like that."

She sighed, and he thought he had run on too long. But she kept asking him more questions, and he told her about the new mosses and lichens he had found, some that he had never seen classified in a book. .

"There should be a better book on Western plants. Too little has been done. Someday perhaps I'll do a book—just about Western mosses and lichens."

"But they are so small," she protested.

"That's part of the fascination," cried Bundy eagerly, "so small, and yet there're perfect. Like the larger plants, the mosses have their own minute flowers and fruits. The lichens are even more wonderful—not a single plant but a combination of algae and fungi growing together."

"But all so small," she said again.

"You must imagine yourself an ant," said Bundy seriously. "To an ant, the mosses and the lichens are a forest."

Lorena burst out laughing at that.

"I've had enough forest. I won't imagine myself an ant just to be able to live in a forest within a forest. I've seen too many trees."

Bundy laughed too.

"I'm slightly crazy, you know," he said. "You'll have to forgive me. I've been alone all summer with my slightly crazy thoughts."

"Alone all summer!" Lorena said. "Don't I know how awful that can be!"

"But I have a kind of theory," Bundy said. "I think a man alone in nature either loses or finds himself. If he gets lost easily, maybe the loss isn't very great. But, if he learns to understand and live with himself alone, then—then I think he ought to be complete and ready to face things as they come."

Lorena's smile blessed what he said, and he didn't feel as much a fool as he might have felt in turning himself inside out. To have been able to speak so freely to her gave him a strong sense of happiness and well-being.

Jeff and Charlie came in then, and Lorena cried out in dismay that she had forgotten to prepare any luncheon for them. Charlie laughed and began to get out the flour and bacon as if he were accustomed to this. Bundy hurriedly cleaned his fish, and Jeff set the table. In the end Lorena was guest at a very good meal and did not have to lift a finger.

4.

After a week of solitude Meggie was desperate for company. Her own thoughts which had grown stale with repetition disgusted her. She felt that she did not know herself at all, and that she was living with a violent and ruthless stranger instead of the old Margaret Carney. She needed a confessional and she decided to unburden herself to Lorena. The need was so strong one morning that she packed her knapsack and braved the unknown terrors of the trail and the as yet unexplored dreariness of returning later to an empty cabin, in order to walk up the trail to Jeff's place.

As soon as she was on the trail she felt better, and she thought that neither a bear nor a snake would intimidate her today. The dog was delighted to see a little action at last. He yelped with pleasure and ran around her in circles. "He's the worst fool dog I ever saw," Meggie said to herself, "but I'd die alone here if I didn't have him, bless his faint heart!"

She threw back her shoulders and breathed deeply as she walked. She let her hands swing rhythmically with her stride. She felt strong and confident, and better pleased with herself than she had been in her cabin. She knew she had sins to confess, but for the moment she forgot what they were.

When Meggie reached Jeff's clearing she was surprised to see horses, hobbled and grazing. She stopped and looked at them, and it came to her with a shock that they were Bundy Jones's horses. He promised to come to see me, she thought. She almost turned around to go back to her empty cabin. He came to Lorena's first! But as she stood in the trail, ready to turn back, she thought, how childish of me! Yes, I really am a child. It's certainly time I grew up. All this violence and now this silly jealousy. What in the world is this place doing to me? And, of course, he'd come to Jeff's place first—it's the first one of our homesteads on the trail down from the mountain. What could be more natural?

Still she went on slowly, having lost the bright edge of her sense of well-being.

They were all at lunch when she went in and they made her sit down, and Charlie brought her a plate and cup. She saw that they were enjoying the fresh trout that Bundy had promised to bring to her. But she resolved to be big about this. The thing she wanted first and foremost was to unburden her mind and conscience. Everything would straighten itself out after she had done that.

"Well, how goes it, Meggie?" someone asked.

"Why, all right, I guess," Meggie said. "A few things have happened to me. I met a bear and killed a snake and—"

"You killed a bear?" cried Lorena laughing.

"No, no," Meggie said. "I ran away from the bear, but I killed the snake."

"What kind of a snake?" they asked.

"I don't know," Meggie said. She had a fleeting temptation to tell them it was a rattler, but she added, "I've a notion now it was only a garter snake. That makes it all the worse that I killed it. Something came over me. There's a streak of violence in me that I don't understand or like at all." She looked rather comically troubled, and they all began laughing at her and teasing her.

"*You* violent? That's a joke!"

"She'll be felling trees and beating up lumberjacks next."

"But you don't understand," Meggie said. "I did, I have. It's on my conscience."

"Out here one shouldn't have a conscience, should one, Mr. Jones?" Lorena asked lightly. "I put mine in moth balls and left it behind me in town along with my fur cape."

Bundy had been smiling at Meggie, but now he turned to Lorena, and his look changed. It seemed to grow deeper and more intense. To Meggie it seemed a parched and hungry smile, and, in the midst of her preoccupation with herself, she thought, he has been lonely too.

But Bundy's voice was easy and natural when he said, "You don't need a conscience, Mrs. Carney. You're pretty enough without one."

"Now that's lovely, Mr. Jones," Lorena said. "I really didn't think you knew how to make complimentary speeches. I thought you were the strong and silent type who wouldn't know the way to please a lady. Aren't you surprised at him, Jeff?"

"Nothing surprises me," said Jeff shortly.

There was a fleeting pause, and then Charlie Duporte said, "That's what the skunk said when the lady called it a pussy cat." The remark was pointless but they all laughed and went on to something else.

Only Meggie sat silent, thinking to herself, I almost told them. If I had told them, they would have laughed. It would have been another joke to them. No, I will never tell it now, because it is not a joke to me. It is not a joke that I broke my mandolin over the head of a man I had been leading along all summer. For that's what I did. I see it now, although I never thought what I was doing at the time. I'm a depraved and violent woman on the inside, but there's no use trying to make anyone else see it. I'm through being laughed at for my pleasant little follies. I'll just have to learn to live with myself and keep my mouth shut, I guess.

"Can't we play cards?" Lorena was saying. "When do we ever get so many people together at one time in this place? Let's make a holiday for once. What's the matter, Meggie? You're quiet as a mouse."

"A penny for your thoughts, Meggie," said Jeff, as he used to say when any unaccustomed silence fell on her. At this invitation, she usually started to chatter again and tell him everything that she had been thinking.

But this time she smiled at him, gently because she loved him, and she said, "My thoughts aren't worth a penny. Let's have some cards. I'm ready. Shall it be whist?"

"But there are five of us," Lorena said.

This was the moment when Charlie should have found some pressing occupation awaiting him in the clearing, but apparently he had no intention of missing the conviviality.

"Then we play poker," he said. "Five is the best for poker."

"My goodness!" Meggie said, "I don't know anything about poker. Is it a lady's game?"

"Ladies? Are there any here?" Lorena asked, "in this place?"

"Maybe not," said Meggie. "No, I guess there aren't."

"But poker's a good game," Lorena said. "I learned to play it from the best poker player in Idaho."

"Who was that?" Bundy asked.

"I don't think you know him," said Lorena, smiling a secret smile.

"She means my Uncle Ralph," said Jeff crossly.

"So he plays cards too?" said Bundy. "I know he gambles in fortunes and forests and large glittering things. I didn't s'pose he had time for cards."

"On a winter evening he can be very cosy and amusing with a deck of cards," Lorena said.

"None of us has money to lose," Jeff objected, "at least the Carneys haven't. Maybe Jones is better fixed."

"No," Bundy said, "my wealth is all in trout and huckleberries."

"Then let's not ruin ourselves any further on poker."

"We play whiskey poker," Charlie said, "nobody bets in that. We leave out money. You got chips?"

"No," Lorena said, "but matchsticks will do. The winner shall have the right to ask a favor of each of the four losers."

"Like forfeits?" Meggie asked.

"Something like forfeits. The winner shall be the one with the most matchsticks when we've played as long as we want to play."

"Then someone will have to teach me how," Meggie said.

They played all afternoon. The sun moved across the floor from the small paned window. The cards slapped onto the rough table with a small, crisp sound. Meggie and Jeff played perfunctorily and often Meggie yawned, for, although they had the family name, they had missed the contentious Carney spirit. Neither of them had the family passion to win for the sake of winning.

But Lorena was happy for once. Her eyes sparkled and her cheeks were red. She loved the uncertainty of chance, and the opportunity to pit her skill against the cold relentlessness of probability. She played eagerly and with inspiration. Bundy and Charlie also played with conviction as if their lives depended on it. Hand followed hand, and most of the matchsticks were heaped up before the three who played to win. After the matchbox was empty Meggie soon lost her last sticks.

"Well, I'm glad it isn't money," she said. "I'm going out to see my dog and get a breath of air. May I stay here tonight or must I go home?"

"You can stay," Lorena said, but she did not look up from the hand she was cherishing.

Jeff was soon finished, too, but he sat beside the table watching the others, feeling the old resentment at being a loser, without asking himself why it should always be so.

Meggie went out into the clearing and looked up at the tops of the trees. The light still shone brightly there, although the clearing was in shadow. Mac and Bundy's dog, reunited in brotherhood, had been enjoying a lazy afternoon. Now they rose and stretched and wagged around her.

The cards had depressed Meggie. She saw no sense in them. But the light on the trees, the friendly dogs, the sight of horses peacefully standing head to tail switching flies off each other's noses, all this reassured her and put her back in a good humor. She sat on a stump with the dogs lolling around her, and fell to musing. Forgetting for the moment that she was a violent woman, Meggie thought of a ball she had attended, and of a little white hat with blue cornflowers that Nan O'Rourke had once trimmed for her, and then she planned how she could turn her tan flannel suit and get another winter's good of it. Before the sun left the treetops, the mosquitoes began to bother her, and she went into the cabin.

Lorena sat flushed and triumphant with all of the matchsticks piled before her.

"Is it over?" Meggie asked.

"Yes," Bundy said. "She has won everything. She's supreme and superb."

"I had good cards," Lorena said, her eyes sparkling.

"And knew to play them," Charlie added. Lorena basked in their admiration.

"Are you going to punish us for losing?" asked Bundy. He wants her to punish him, Meggie thought.

"Yes," Lorena said. "Now comes the day of reckoning. I'm going to punish all of you."

"All right," Meggie said. "You want me to get supper, I expect."

"Yes," Lorena said, "you shall get supper. Jeff will build the fire and set the table. Charlie must split the wood for morning and see that the horses are fed."

"And what do I do then?" asked Bundy Jones.

"You take the buckets and fill me a washtub of water from the spring."

"But I don't know where the spring is."

"I will show you," Lorena said. She sprang up laughing and put the bails of the empty buckets in Bundy's hands. Then she ran out of the cabin, still laughing, and leading the way.

It was almost dark beyond the clearing under the big trees.

Lorena went ahead quickly, her feet sure on the narrow path. Bundy stumbled behind her, feeling acutely each stone and broken root under his feet. The fern fronds swept sensuously against his legs. Excitement and anticipation mounted unreasonably in his calm blood.

When they came to the spring it had a silver gleam on its surface in the dark wood. A poorwill had begun its monotonous chant away through the trees.

"Fill up your buckets," Lorena commanded.

Bundy knelt and filled the buckets with the brisk water. When he straightened himself, a heavy bucket in each hand, Lorena stood on tiptoe and kissed him lightly on the mouth. He had an overwhelming urge to put his arms about her, but before he could rid himself of the buckets, she had laughed and gone, running ahead of him back to the clearing.

As he returned to the cabin, the poorwill kept calling somewhere in the forest. The call started slowly and mournfully, and then it accelerated until it reached a painful climax of apprehensive emotion. Then the voice fell silent.

Bundy was a slow thinker, and he was inexperienced with women. When he was near Lorena he felt on the verge of some great discovery or experience. His intentions toward her were innocent and blameless, but at the same time she seemed to promise something mysterious which he desired without calling it by name. Other men, more experienced, would have had a name for it.

Now he waited for an opportunity when, unencumbered by pails of water, he might find her alone. But there was no such opportunity. She looked at him and laughed, but there were always other people with them.

In the end there was nothing he could think of to do, except leave the next day as he had planned.

While he was packing his horse the next morning, Charlie stood looking on, a grin of amusement or possibly of malice on his mobile face.

"I bet she kiss you down dere by the spring?" he said in a low voice.

Bundy felt himself reddening, and anger got the better of him. "It's none of your damned business," he said.

"I know," Charlie said, quietly, still grinning, "but t'ings like that interest me. She a very nice girl. I ain't got not'ing to say against her. You lucky fella, don't you know?"

"Shut up!" Bundy said. He was ashamed of the falsetto note of desperation that slipped into his utterance of the two words. He tightened the pack straps savagely.

It had been arranged that Meggie was to ride his horse as far as her cabin, and that he would have lunch there before he went on down the trail to Nan's.

Charlie disappeared into the edge of the clearing to work, but Lorena and Jeff stood by to see them off.

Lorena linked her arm in Jeff's and together they presented a picture of serene domesticity. Bundy was baffled, as well as annoyed with himself for being too susceptible. Yet his eyes searched Lorena's wistfully, looking for a sign. There was no sign at all, except, perhaps, in her last words.

"Come again, Mr. Bundy Jones, *Bundy*," she said. "Next time *you'll* win, and you can call a forfeit on me."

"I'll remember that," Bundy said.

Meggie sat in his saddle and he walked beside her through the morning woods. They went in silence except for the pack bell and the snorting and blowing of the horses. Silence never troubled Bundy, and it didn't occur to him to wonder why the volatile Miss Carney had nothing to say on such a bright green and gold morning.

5.

When they reached Meggie's place, she said, "Come in and I'll get you some food." She got out the coffeepot, put some salt pork into the pan, and stirred soda into the sourdough for pancakes. This was not the banquet she had planned for Bundy Jones, but the trout had been yesterday, the banquet at Lorena's.

"May I look around your place?" Bundy asked.

"Yes, do," Meggie said. "I'm kind of proud of it."

When he came in to eat he had shaken off some of his abstraction. "You've done a good job here," he said. "There's only one thing that gives you away."

"What's that?" she asked. "What do you mean 'gives me away'?"

"It's the sign over the door," Bundy said. " 'Bide a Wee.' Why did you call it that?"

"I don't know," Meggie said. "I liked it. One time I saw a cottage by the sea named that. Why not a cabin in the pines? You want me to call it 'Journey's End'?"

"If you're not planning to stay long, why do you call it anything?" he asked. "Why do you name it?"

"I like to give things names," Meggie said. "Don't you? Haven't you named your horses and your dog?"

"Sure," Bundy said laughing. "Do you know what I named my dog? Macgillicuddy!"

"And you call him Mac!"

"How did you know?"

"Because it's the only possible solution. I call mine Mac too." They laughed, and Meggie added, "I'm working on a name for you. Mr. Jones sounds very formal in the woods."

"You might call me Bundy," he said. "It's a crazy name but people seem to remember it better than John or Henry."

"I'll let Lorena call you Bundy," said Meggie. "When I've figured you out, I'll have my own name for you."

"Figured me out?" he echoed.

"Yes," Meggie said. "There's something odd about you. You aren't all plants and lichens. I think you're very interested in what we're doing here. You don't want us to stay. And that's in spite of liking to play cards with us. You admire pretty homesteaders, but you don't really wish us well."

Bundy was surprised, and he was also tired of being probed by discerning commentators.

"Look," he said, "do I have to apologize to you for admiring pretty homesteaders? You're one yourself, I s'pose you know."

"I didn't mean me, and I don't want any apologies."

"That's fine, because you're not getting one. I hope that's clear."

"Yes, it's clear."

"And as to the other, I *do* wish you well," Bundy said. "I've only tried to warn you to save you trouble later on."

"Well, we're in it now," Meggie said. "We've got to go on and do the best we can."

"Then change the name of your place to 'Journey's End,'" he said, trying to make his tone sound light.

"I'll think it over," Meggie said, "but I'm beginning to enjoy doing things my own way. I never had a chance before this summer. I was anybody's little butterfly at home, but now I'm discovering how tough I can be. And I'm stubborn, too. I've named my place. I think I'll keep it my way."

"Well," Bundy said, "I've got a name for *you*. I'm going to call you Miss Sourdough. These are real good pancakes, Miss Sourdough of Bide a Wee."

"Yes, they *are* good," Meggie said. "I'm proud of my sourdough bucket, and my porch boxes and my rocking chairs."

"You must have had good help. I never knew a lumberjack to make a rocking chair. Or did you make them yourself?"

"No, I had good help," Meggie said.

As he was eating Bundy looked around the room and saw her smashed mandolin hanging by its ribbons from a nail on the wall.

"What happened to your mandolin?" he asked.

"It had a little accident," Meggie said.

"I see that. But it looks beyond repair. Why do you keep it hanging there? A souvenir?"

"Yes, a souvenir," Meggie said. "I keep it hanging there for several reasons. One is, it reminds me not to be scared in an emergency; and another is, if I haven't got a pistol handy, it makes a pretty good weapon."

Bundy looked at her curiously.

"Miss Sourdough of Bide a Wee," he said laughing.

Presently he got on his horse and rode away down the trail toward Nan's. The pack horse and his dog followed him. For quite a while Meggie could hear the sound of the bell on his pack horse, before the silence of the pines closed in again.

Meggie sat on the porch for some time. Then she shook her shoulders impatiently and got up.

"I'll make a pie," she said to the dog, "and then I'll weed and cut brush until I've got appetite to eat it. Lord knows there's plenty to do."

6.

Sometimes the other homesteaders up and down the valley came borrowing or visiting, and Meggie welcomed them. Company broke the still monotony. Once the Kleins came by with their boy Jimmy, and Mrs. Klein and the boy stayed overnight with Meggie while the husband went on to the river to fish.

"We figured to stay at your brother's place," Mrs. Klein said. "I'm scared to stay alone with mister gone. But we never got the invite there, and so we come on here."

"I'm sure Lorena would have liked to have you," Meggie said. "Maybe she didn't think."

"I don't know," Mrs. Klein said. "She's real pretty, but I guess she's proud. She's right cordial to Mister Klein, but it looks like I'm not good enough for her. Maybe no woman is ever good enough for her. It's just the men she's got eyes for."

"Oh, really, Lorena isn't like that," Meggie said. "You must have caught her on a bad day or something."

"Well, she's too much the grand lady for me anyway. I feel easier with you. You're just plain folks, and I don't have to assume no airs with you."

Meggie was making a windmill for Jimmy with a pin, a twig, and a small square of her precious writing paper. She cut the four slits in the corners of the paper thoughtfully. She could imagine how Mrs. Klein's assumed airs would greatly annoy Lorena, but somehow she felt no annoyance herself.

"We all get lonely out here," Meggie said, and this seemed to her to explain everything. The loneliness made her ready to accept strangers because she was naturally gregarious. But she sensed that Lorena would react differently. Yes, Lorena was proud and easily annoyed. Lorena had shaken the plebeian earth off her feet, at least as far as women were concerned, and she wouldn't want to slip back into the mire again. She would hold herself aloof, and enjoy being haughty with women like Mrs. Klein.

But Meggie relished the sight of a ragged little boy running joyously in her clearing; and she was glad to trade recipes with his mother. She learned how to make bread from Mrs. Klein.

"I thought maybe you didn't know how," Mrs. Klein said, "so I brung some dry yeast with me. Sourdough can get mighty tiresome."

The finished loaves were coarse-grained, but they tasted delicious to Meggie.

"I never noticed how bread really tasted before," marveled Meggie. "In town it's just bread, but here it's something special."

"Doing without things has its merits," Mrs. Klein said. "It sharps up your appetite. Next time the packer comes by, you ask him to bring you some yeast from Cold Spring."

"I will," Meggie said.

When Mr. Klein came back from the river they had a trout dinner.

"Could I go fishing sometime too?" Meggie asked. "Do you think an inexperienced person like me could catch a fish?"

Mr. Klein guffawed. "Miss, you bend a pin and put a worm on it, you got you a pretty trout in these here streams."

"A pin?" marveled Meggie.

"Well, maybe not a pin. But a right small hook. It's the trout that's inexperienced out this part of the country."

"Listen," cried Meggie excitedly. "Take us with you sometime, Mr. Klein. Take your wife and Jimmy and me."

"I don't know if I could stand it," Mrs. Klein said.

"Oh, Ma, come on. Please," Jimmy said.

"We'll take it under consideration, Miss Carney," said Klein.

One evening Jeff came down to see Meggie. Her heart leaped with pleasure at the sight of him and doubly so because he was alone. She and Jeff had been very close as children, and it was like old times to have him to herself. He seldom had the time or inclination to come down to her this summer. It had taken her some time to adjust to the idea that Jeff meant her to stand on her own feet and earn her homestead by herself.

"Are you all right here, Margaret?" he asked. "Sometimes I worry about you."

"You needn't," Meggie said. "I seem to be weathering it."

"You look well," he said. "I like to think you're well. You aren't too lonesome?"

"No. I can stand it."

"It won't be long, you know. At least I hope it won't be long."

"You haven't heard me complain."

"No, no. You haven't complained."

The evening was sharp and Meggie lit the kindling she had laid in the stove for morning, and got out the coffeepot.

"Have you had supper, Jeff?"

"Oh, yes," he said. "Yes, I had all I needed."

Some lack of enthusiasm in his reply made her produce what food she had on hand and spread the table for him. He ate well, talking casually, and afterward he sat quiet, looking at the fire which flickered behind the damper of the stove. His hands hung idly between his knees. They were well shaped hands, rather small for a man of his size. Meggie noticed regretfully that the slim, tapering fingers had grown rough this summer, and that the nails were broken and stained.

From Jeff's hands her eyes went to his face, and in it she saw new lines of uncertainty and anxiety. It was as if she had lived too close to him at home to get perspective. She had leaned on him and felt the physical strength of his shoulders. The moral strength she had never questioned.

But now that she was learning, little by little, to stand alone, a distance had separated them, and, shocked by her own temerity, she recognized the lines of weakness and uncertainty in his face. Her old blind admiration for him was suddenly confused and overwhelmed by pity.

"What's the matter, Jeff?" she asked. "Anything special?"

"Oh," he said, "sometimes Lorena and I can't bear to be under the same roof together out here. It wasn't so in town. I came down here to get a breath of fresh air. Where else could I go?"

"Why, here, of course," Meggie said.

"She gets bored easily. I don't suppose I blame her. A place like this might drive a woman crazy."

"It might," said Meggie quietly. "It very well might."

He lifted his head and looked at her curiously, as if he had been momentarily jarred out of his own small round of thoughts to observe her for the first time.

"You, too?" he asked.

"Oh, I never said so," Meggie replied. "It's just that when I'm alone here, there's only the sound of the wind in the pines. Lorena's got you."

"I'm a dull fellow," Jeff said, "no better than the wind in the pines."

"I never thought so," Meggie said. "We used to have a lot of fun together at home. You used to be very gay. You used to sing."

"I can't sing any more. What voice I had is gone. I won't ruin it completely by using it here in this raw air. I'll leave the singing to Charlie. He's probably serenading her now, while I'm gone. He waits for me to go."

"Why doesn't Charlie leave now?" Meggie asked. "He hasn't cleared or built on his own place yet. Aren't you through needing him?"

"Lorena likes to have him. He amuses her. It would make her angry if I sent him away."

"I think you might stand up to her a little more, Jeff. You're too considerate. Maybe she'd be more contented if you told her what she had to do." Meggie was surprised to hear herself saying this, and Jeff looked at her in surprise too.

"That's funny coming from you, Meggie. I thought you girls would always stick together."

"It isn't a question of sticking together. I think maybe women are like children. They feel more safe somehow if there's authority to turn to."

"No, I don't think so," Jeff said, "not with Lorena. She would be angry with me if I took a high hand. I can't risk that because I love her."

"Well, Jeff, it's you in the long run, you who will always matter most. If there are others, they are just passing fancies."

"Still it's a bit tedious," Jeff said, "and slightly ludicrous. I stand off and look at it, and laugh to myself. Yet it hits the heart too. Well, I should have done better by her altogether. She was meant for town and the good kind of life there."

"In a year or so we'll have it," Meggie said. "You always tell me that."

"Sure," Jeff said. "I know. Still there are times I wonder. Even if we get these places, how much will we make out of them?"

"Heavens, Jeff," Meggie said, "look at the white pine we've got —these vast, incredible trees. They ought to make us rich."

"They'll make somebody rich," Jeff said. "Ralph and the lumber company most likely. But do you want to see them cut, Meggie?"

Meggie was open-mouthed for an instant.

"Well, Jeff," she said, "you *are* low tonight, aren't you? I hate to see your spirits low. It dampens mine."

"I always took it out on you, didn't I, little kid? I s'pose that's why I'm here tonight, although I never thought of it that way when I came down. —Just that you do me good."

"If I do, that's enough."

"There's nothing wrong really, except my own black moods— and Lorena's. It's just that this life bores her. The more there is to do, the less she wants to undertake it—and there are too many men in here and no women. How about you? Haven't the men bothered you, little sis?"

Meggie thought swiftly of the fight in the barn and the broken mandolin, but she said, "I'm not the type, Jeff. You ought to know by now. I guess I'm safe."

"It's funny," he said, taking her word for it. "You're a pretty kid, but I guess both of us lack the roving eye, the something that attracts the opposite sex. Perfect ladies and gentlemen, the Carneys —meant for better things."

He laughed now, but his laugh hurt Meggie more than his silence.

I shouldn't care for him so much, she thought. Maybe that's part of our dilemma. —A couple of Carneys, like a very small island, with the ocean of the world around us.

"Well, say something, Meggie," he said roughly.

"I was just thinking. And on second thought, there isn't much to say."

"Then I'm going back up the trail," he said. "You all right here, Meg? I do worry about you."

"Of course, I'm all right. I'm getting so I like it."

"I'm going hunting soon," Jeff said. "I'll bring you some venison or birds. It'll be a change from salt pork."

"I won't put the pot on until I see the game," Meggie said.

"You can count on it," Jeff said.

He lighted his lantern and opened the door, leaving it open after he had gone out. Meggie followed him and looked out into the darkness. The hot close air of the room flowed away into the night. Between the high still plumes of the trees, the stars were bright and clear, and there was a frosty edge to the air.

"We'll be going home soon, Jeff," Meggie said. "A few months in town will do us all good."

"Town seems a long ways off," Jeff said, turning to look back at her across the lantern light. "The two places are so wide apart. Can we ever get them back together again?"

"A day in town," she said, "and we'll never know we've been away."

"Sure," he said. "Goodnight."

"Goodnight, Jeff." He mounted his horse and she saw his lantern bob along to the turn of the trail. Then for a moment longer it twinkled among the trees. When it had passed the big cedar it became invisible, and the lonely night closed in again, dark and still except for the whispering of the pines. Meggie stood looking into the darkness for a moment, wondering if all this solitude were giving her a new ability to stand aside and appraise. That was a thing she had never done before this summer. Soon she went into the cabin and closed the door. Before she went to bed, she wound the clock. This had become a sacred ritual. It seemed to Meggie, if the clock ran down, she would indeed be lost.

7.

Meggie's sturdy solidity, a quality he had seldom remarked in her before, gave Jeff a personal illusion of courage.

When he reached his cabin it was late, but the lamp was still lighted. Lorena had not gone to bed. She waited up for me, he thought, and his spirits rose perceptibly. But when he entered the

cabin, he saw that she and Charlie were playing cards and had not
given a thought to the time.

They sat on opposite sides of the table and smacked down the
cards with crisp good cheer. Lorena had a pile of matchsticks in
front of her and she was in excellent spirits. She had been moody
and angry when he left her earlier in the evening.

Jeff longed for her happiness, yet was miserable to see that
someone beside himself had created it.

"All right," he said. "Do you know what time it is? You'd
better break it up."

"I'm winning," Lorena said. "I'm having a good time."

"I let her win," said Charlie laughing. "I give her real good
time."

"He's just bragging," said Lorena. "He doesn't have a ghost of
a chance when he plays with me."

"That so!" Charlie said with high good humor. "I play with
her, I sure am beat. Ain't got a chance to win no way at all."

Suddenly Jeff felt the mingled apprehension and relief of having
made a decision.

"Charlie," he said, "I'm going to pay you off tomorrow. The
work's almost done here. I can take care of the rest. You've got your
own place to build."

Charlie's face fell.

"Ain't no hurry," he said. "I be in here all winter. I fix my
place then. One fella works alone, he handle logs best when he got
some snow to slide 'em on."

"We appreciate what you've done here," Jeff said formally,
"but now we don't need you any more."

"Who says we don't?" cried Lorena passionately. "When did
you decide all this?"

"Anyone can see it," Jeff said. "The place is in good shape for
a first year. The two of us can manage for the rest of the season."

"And half the time you're gone! How am I to get on alone?"

"My sister does," Jeff said. "You and she can stay together
when I have to leave. You shouldn't have to sit here playing poker
with a—a hired man."

"You don't like the company I keep?" Lorena said angrily.
"Well, just produce a couple of duchesses then, why don't you?

Besides, Charlie's no hired man. You ought to be ashamed to say so after all he's done for us this summer."

Charlie stood by grinning with perfect equanimity. His eyes sparkled. He enjoyed a spirited scene of any kind, and the more so if he were the subject of discussion.

"Never mind now," Charlie said. "Tomorrow I go. But I come back some time; we finish our poker game one day some other time, Mis' Carney. So everyt'ing be all right, eh?"

To Jeff's surprise Charlie did pack up and leave the next day. After screwing himself to the pitch of sending Charlie away, Jeff veered back in the other direction, and was filled with remorse. He even tried to dissuade Charlie from leaving and offered a last-moment apology. Lorena remained in the cabin and had nothing to say, and this disturbed Jeff more than anything she might have done.

Charlie was perfectly cheerful and friendly, but resolute.

"You was God-damn right, Jeff," he said genially. "I sure as hell better get me started build my house."

"I'll come down and help you," offered Jeff impulsively. Charlie laughed with pleasure.

"No," he said. "You got a pretty missus here. You stay. Give her a fine good time. I don't need no help."

After he was gone, the days seemed long, even to Jeff. Lorena made a perfunctory effort to bestir herself around the homestead, but she could not conquer her feeling of resentment against Jeff. In town it had never amused her to make Jeff squirm. She had looked away in distaste when she saw him squirming under other people's blows. But suddenly here, so far away from other distractions, she found a fascination in tormenting him. It was something to do, and it gave her a perverse satisfaction.

Small favors, that she might have bestowed on him in the natural course of things, she withheld, and watched with sharp attention how the disappointment blossomed on his sensitive face. She thought up trifling cruelties and inflicted them artfully, knowing in advance how he would react. She enjoyed the power she had for making him jealous of other men.

For all of this she despised herself, yet found in it the only outlet and diversion for her thwarted ambitions and emotions.

Lorena had one anxiety that summer, and it was that she might lose her beauty here in the woods where no one would know or see. What is not seen ceases to exist. Was that a superstition or a fact? She did not know; but her yearning for admiration, not one man's admiration but the admiration of many, betrayed her into anxiety.

She avoided the strong sunlight and wind as much as she could. She had not brought lotions or creams with her because all the pack-horse space had been needed for provisions. She could brush her hair and keep it silky, even in spite of the hard spring water in which she had to wash it. But her complexion was another matter. She fancied that it would coarsen from exposure, as her hands coarsened and reddened from rough work.

Now that Jeff's financial expectations had come to nothing, she felt more keenly than she had ever felt before that she must rely on her beauty. As a young girl she had known this, but then there had been time. Now the time was going by, inexorably, and she could not hold it back.

When Charlie was there, she read her reassurance in his eyes. She read it in the eyes of Bundy Jones. But after they had gone only her mirror could be relied upon to give her reassurance.

Jeff's admiration no longer stimulated her, at least she no longer trusted it to give her the information she desired. She had a feeling that Jeff would go on loving her blindly even if she were old and ugly. Instead of pleasing her, this thought depressed her. It made her beauty seem valueless. So she clung to the testimony of her mirror as the last consolation of a desperate summer.

One day she was looking into her mirror when Jeff came in. She was examining her face minutely for roughnesses or imperfections, for the dreadful blackhead or the beginning wrinkle. When she heard the door close, her eyes flicked toward it in the mirror. The sound of the door always stirred a hope in her, but, when she saw that it was only Jeff, she went on preening herself without paying any attention to him.

Jeff stood behind her waiting, and querulous anger began to replace his hope and his anxiety.

"Well," he asked, "who are you making yourself beautiful for now?"

"For myself," she answered coldly. "Is there anyone else?"

"I guess not," he said. "I used to think there was. I used to think you might want to make yourself pretty and sweet for me."

"Pretty and *sweet!*" Lorena said. "Those are such feeble words."

"How do you want to be called then?"

"Once someone called me magnificent," Lorena said. "I rather liked that. It's not a feeble word."

"So Ralph called you magnificent, did he?" said Jeff.

"I didn't say so."

"I know the tone of voice you use when it's a question of Ralph. He called you magnificent and you'll always remember that. But what else did he ever do for you? Isn't it Ralph who put you here, on a homestead in the woods? Where you hate to be?"

"He was trying to give you a chance. If you didn't like his way, you might have thought of something better yourself."

She continued to look in the mirror as she spoke; and now she propped the mirror on the shelf and took up a tiny tweezer to pluck an offending hair from an eyebrow.

Jeff came up behind her angrily and took the little mirror from the shelf. Lorena turned on him fiercely and they struggled for possession of her treasure. Angrily, despairingly, they fought each other. But Jeff had a man's strength, and he threw her back against the bed and dashed the mirror to the floor. It broke into a great many small pieces.

Then he went out of the cabin and slammed the door behind him.

Lorena sat on the edge of the bed, quietly, without tears. But her face was white with self-pity and despair. And only one thought kept turning around and around in her mind. I can't get away. There's no place to go. I can't get away. There's no place to go.

8.

Late in August the Kleins came by for Meggie and took her to the north fork of the Clearwater River to fish. They passed Nan O'Rourke's place on the way, and she left her work and joined them.

"I never fished with no passel of women before," said Mr. Klein. "Don't you gals go falling in the water and looking out to be rescued by me, because I ain't that kind of man. You got to fend for yourselves like."

The ladies made no objection to these arrangements. They were all in high good humor, and competing to top each other's jokes.

There was a deserted cabin by the river where fishermen usually spent the night. Part of the roof had been broken in by bears the previous winter, and no one had bothered to repair it. If anyone expected to be plagued by mosquitoes, he brought his own piece of cotton netting and draped it over his face while he slept. A few supplies had been left on the shelves the year before, and Meggie was fascinated to see a can of sweet cocoa which had baffled one of the bears. It bore the marks of large, strong teeth, but the bear had eventually given it up as an insoluble problem without being able to extract the cocoa.

There was always a great sound of rushing water at this place, and general conversation had to be shouted to be heard.

Mr. Klein dug worms and distributed hooks and small sections of line which the women tied to sticks. Klein himself had a bamboo pole and a small selection of flies, but nobody questioned his right to these perquisites of the expert.

"Now you can wade or set on a log or a boulder as you see fit," he said, "but don't crowd each other and don't visit. This ain't no sewing society. There's plenty of trout, but you got to tinker with 'em a little. You can't just haul 'em out the first try. Look for a quiet pool, and maybe you'll see one of them fellers waitin' there to catch a-holt. Good luck to you, an', for God's sake, don't tail me too close." He went downstream, and the three women and Jimmy started fishing near the cabin.

Gradually Meggie moved upstream from rock to rock. The water was very cold and it rushed impetuously and noisily around the many objects that tried to impede its progress. There were boulders and fallen trees, and in the cool damp river bottom heavy moss decorated everything with a green cushion from which sprang little ferns and other minute growths unfamiliar to Meggie. Overhead arched the great trees, making this a tunnel of green and brown darkness filled with furious sound. It was like an underground river. The ferns and plants along the bank were shaken by the draft of the moving water as by a little wind, yet the tops of the trees were still. She had a sensation that she herself was moving, floating, falling with the rushing water. In a panic she sat herself firmly on top of a boulder, resolved to stay there until her senses grew accustomed to this new environment. Below the boulder was a quiet pool. Its surface rotated very slowly, carrying a small yellow leaf gently around and around. It was impossible to estimate the depth of the pool, but the bottom of it, brown and mottled with leaf and pebble, was clearly seen.

Meggie dropped her line into the water of the pool, and saw the worm-wound hook duck below the surface, and float luminously toward the pull of the current. She watched dreamily, expecting nothing. Then suddenly it seemed to her that a segment of the mottled bottom of the pool detached itself and took on a life of its own. It moved very swiftly with waving fins and a wide eye, and it struck with a hungry mouth at the worm on the hook.

In mingled horror and triumph Meggie caught her first fish. She jerked it out of the water, and pursued and battled it over the mossy rock, until it lay panting and inert, completely hers. Then she sat looking at it, trembling all over with a chill excitement.

"Oh, heavens!" she kept saying to herself in a small voice. "Oh, my heavens!"

Finally she took courage to bait her hook again and drop the line into the pool. But this time nothing happened.

She could see Nan some yards below her on the bank of the stream. She tried to call to Nan to show her the fish she had caught. But Nan could not hear her voice over the tumult of the water. Meggie thought of going back, but the untried water upstream intrigued her. She wrapped her fish in leaves and ferns and, for lack of a creel, put it in her packsack. Slowly she pushed upstream, climbing and slipping over rocks and logs. She fished a little here and there, but not very purposefully. She had caught her fish. My heavens! She had caught her fish! Another one would have been an anticlimax. There was a dim, mysterious something in this place that gave her pleasure enough, without the wild uncertainty of catching trout.

When she had gone some distance upstream she saw a little clearing in the density of woods along the bank. Through the trees there was a soft blue haze of smoke, and a clean smell of burning twigs. She stopped, frightened. She was a long way from friends, and men, she was now aware, could be as terrifying as bears or snakes. But curiosity wouldn't allow her to go back without some cautious investigation. The noise of the stream covered any sounds she might make. She began a slow advance, peering around trees until she could obtain a clear view.

Finally she saw the two horses standing head to tail switching flies, and a little stab of elation pierced her. Now she moved more confidently, and she was not surprised when she discovered Bundy Jones leaning over a pan of soapy water on a rock near his fire. He was gravely absorbed in the homely occupation of washing his socks.

Meggie had the advantage of him because he was deep in his solitary thoughts and did not see her. She paused to put back the locks of hair that had been unsettled by twigs and brambles, and she took her fish, now starkly dead, out of her knapsack. Laughter bubbled up like a fountain inside her.

So she appeared in the range of Bundy's vision with the disconcerting suddenness of an apparition. She held out the fish to him, and said, with a great attempt at gravity, "I brought a trout for your dinner, Dr. Livingstone."

"Good God!" said Bundy, straightening himself in astonishment. "It's little Sourdough! Where did you come from?"

"'Out of the everywhere into the here,'" said Meggie good-naturedly. "I'm as surprised as you are. You certainly hide yourself in the oddest places."

"Not at all," he said. "There's a perfectly good trail in here. Didn't you see it?"

"No, I came up the stream, but I'd be glad to take the trail back. We're staying overnight at the old cabin on the main trail."

"We?" Bundy queried.

"I came with the Kleins and Nan O'Rourke."

"Well, fine!" Bundy said. "There's no one I enjoy more than Nan O'Rourke. I just thought maybe your brother—"

"No," Meggie said. "It wouldn't be much use trying to interest Lorena in fishing. This is the first time for me too. But look what

I got. I caught it all myself and I'm proud. You really ought to be good enough to look at it."

"Why, that's fine," Bundy said. "A regular beauty. It's a speckled trout, and I'll bet it gave you a battle."

"Oh, goodness, yes!" said Meggie. "I chased it all over the boulder. I didn't know whether he'd get me into the water, or I'd get him onto land. You never saw such a fight."

Bundy took a coiled metal tape line out of his pocket, and gravely measured Meggie's fish. He didn't tell her that he threw them back at that size.

"I'll clean it and fry it for you," he offered.

"No thank you," Meggie said, "I've got to go back. They'll think I'm lost. It *is* an odd sensation, though, when you think you're all alone in a wild place, to come on another human being."

"*I* knew *I* was here all the time," Bundy said, laughing. "The astonishing thing was seeing you materialize. I'm not sure yet that you're real."

"Yes, I'm real," Meggie said. "I feel more real every day. The girl I was in town—she's the ghost. I don't know if she'll fit me any more when I go back."

"That's an odd thought," Bundy said. "Maybe you don't have to fit into the old skin when you go back. I'd hate to try fitting into some of my castoff skins."

"Well, you encourage me," Meggie said. "Maybe you'd better show me the trail back now."

"I'll go along with you," Bundy said. "Do you want to ride a horse?"

"Is it far?"

"No, it's not far."

"Then let's walk."

"I'll make the fire safe first."

"Do you always do that?"

"Yes," Bundy said. "Have you ever seen any kind of forest fire?"

"No."

"I've seen enough to know it's hell on earth. When the trees are so close, fire leaps from tree to tree, roaring like a speeding train, and afterward it smolders for days in dead logs and moss, waiting for another breeze to fan it up again. All this timber you folks are so keen for—you let a spark get loose in it, and maybe you won't have a stick left standing."

"How awful!" Meggie said. "But I'm always careful, and everything's green and damp."

"It's been a wet year," Bundy said. "Wet years are the ones to pray for in timber country."

Bundy could be entertaining on a forest trail, if one were interested in his particular world. Meggie asked him if he knew the name of a minute white flower that covered the forest floor like lace in areas beside the trail. Instead of one name she loosed a torrent, foamflower, *Tiarella trifoliate,* Nancy-over-the-ground, saxifrage family, together with a great deal of information, about panicles, threadlike petals not to be mistaken for antherless stamens, and trifoliate leaves.

"If you're interested in flowers," Bundy said, "I'll show you something pretty. It's just a few steps off the trail."

Meggie followed him through the trees until they reached a marshy spot which was covered in a deep cushion of pine needles. They walked across it as on deep carpeting, their feet sinking a little with each step. Up through the reddish brown of the needles pushed an interesting assortment of mushrooms and toadstools, some of them fantastically colored orange and yellow and red. But Bundy pushed on farther. They were far enough from the stream to have lost its steady clamor, and their feet made no noise on the deep needles.

Suddenly Bundy took her hand and drew her up beside him. The action was totally unconscious, Meggie saw from a swift glance at his face. He was looking at something on the ground ahead and his eyes were gravely happy.

"*Monotropa uniflora,*" Bundy said. "It's a saprophyte."

Meggie saw that here in this silent world, pushing up the brown needles, were dozens of white flowers with drooping heads, heavy as if molded from white wax.

"Indian pipe," she murmured.

"Ghost flowers, too, they call them," Bundy said. "Do you see why?"

"Yes. They're more like ghosts than pipes, standing white like that, against the dark needles."

"Well, I just wanted you to see," Bundy said, dropping her hand and turning back. "I never found so many together in a single place before."

"I'm glad you showed me," Meggie said.

When they reached the old cabin, the others had not yet returned. They sat down on a fallen log from which a pine seedling had begun to grow among mosses and ferns.

"Look," Meggie said, "A tree growing on a tree."

Bundy began to tell her about the cycles of forest growth, how nothing is lost in nature, and how death and decay feed the new life. He told her how lichens begin to break down rocks, and prepare the way for mosses, and later ferns; how the roots break the rock further and water seeps in, and eventually soil is formed. He described the cycle of the forest trees, how open places are first populated by red alders and the sun-loving Douglas fir, and gradually by the white pine and western red cedar, and last of all by the Western hemlock which is a rapid grower and does not mind deep shade.

Under the dark shade of the hemlock, the other seedlings cannot live, and so eventually the hemlock forms the climax growth until fire or wind destroys it, and the cycle begins again.

"All of this looks unchanging," Bundy said, lifting his hand to the trees arching over them. "It's slow, but actually it's always changing, moving, living, going on its way. A tree has a life like a man, but maybe its life is measured in hundreds of years instead of in decades. I look at one of these big trees and I get a feeling of— well, it's respect, maybe a kind of awe."

Meggie was moved by his gravity, his eagerness, his contentment with nature. They fell silent, sitting, thoughtful, on a decaying log with a seedling tree growing up between them. At home there had been a flower garden, but no one had ever told her how to look at growing things before.

9.

It seemed a long time before Charlie came by, and Lorena reproached him.

"I thought you cared what became of me," she said. "I thought you were a kind-hearted fellow."

"My golly!" Charlie cried, "There ain't no kinder-hearted fella anywhere around than me. Don't you know dat?"

"But you deserted me. You went and left me here."

"You know what I t'ink of you?" Charlie said. "You one spoiled little lady. Dat's what I t'ink." Charlie flashed his winsome smile at her, and she was pleased. If anyone had told her seriously that she was spoiled, Lorena would have been angry; but she took it as a compliment when it was offered on the silver platter of an admiring smile.

Early that Monday morning Jeff had ridden away to Cold Spring to meet his last group of homesteaders. With the August trails open and dry, he expected to cover the distance in one day.

Lorena had begged to go with him, but, even if she rode the one horse and he walked, the trip to Cold Spring would have taken a half day longer.

"No," Jeff had said, "you've got to stick it out until fall. Only a few weeks more. That isn't asking too much, is it?" Lorena thought it was, but she did not say so. Jeff had made her promise to walk to Meggie's that morning and stay there until he returned at the end of the week. She had dawdled over her breakfast and her packing, already weary with boredom and discontent. The sight of Charlie's cheerful face, appearing unexpectedly from the lonely forest, put a different aspect on the day. The emptiness vanished; Lorena was no longer weary.

Charlie ranged around the cabin, looking at everything. He had missed this place as much as he had been missed, but he was careful to keep his tone light and his smile carefree. He noted that her mirror was gone from its shelf, but he did not mention it.

"I'm go to town," he said, "get me a grub stake. You like I get you anyt'ing?"

"Jeff has just gone in," she said. "He'll get supplies." But she was thinking of something she had wanted to do, something that she had not cared to confide to Jeff. She paused, and then she added casually, "But you could carry a letter for me."

"Sure," he said. "You want to write a letter?"

"Yes. Can you wait a minute?"

"For you, I always got plenty time. Go ahead. I wait."

Lorena had been thinking of writing a letter for weeks, but, not having an opportunity to send it by anyone but Jeff, she had postponed facing the final decision of whether or not she really wished to write it. Now she made the decision, and sat down at the table to write. Jeff was gone and Charlie had come opportunely. With everything appropriately arranged for her, it would have seemed like flying in the face of providence to fail to write the letter.

Lorena did not write fluently or with pleasure, and furthermore she knew the hazards of putting things down on paper. Ralph had always said, "Never put it down in black and white, if you can arrange it with a smile over a glass of wine. Letters pop up again at awkward times and places."

Ralph would remember saying this to her when he read her letter. Ralph remembered everything, coolly and clearly, and few things had the power to move him. Yet she had seen him moved, and herein lay her desperate hope.

Jeff had brought her some attractive note paper on one of his returns from town. It was very delicately pink and it had gilt edges. "A valentine," she had called it disparagingly, but at the moment it seemed to her appropriate to the message she had in mind. She took pen and ink and wrote *Dear Ralph* at the top of one of the sheets. After that she sat still with her pen poised over the paper, trying to think how best to word her appeal.

Several times she had urged Jeff to write, but he had always refused. Jeff had little pride, but what he had seemed to be concentrated in his attitude toward Ralph. He resented and hated Ralph for not being more generous with him, and his resentment had crystallized into a stubborn determination never again to ask for favors.

She kept turning her intention over in her mind, and presently she crumpled the paper on which she had committed the indiscretion of writing a name, and began again.

Dearest, she wrote rapidly. *Help us. Help me. You don't know how hard this is to bear. I can't go on here in this place. You could do something for me if you cared a little bit. You are the only one who could. Yours, Rena.*

Charlie sat in a chair in the shadowed corner of the room and watched her writing. He saw her concentration and anxiety, and how gracefully her head bent forward on her supple neck. He saw how the shadow of dark hair brushed her cheek, and how her eyes were lowered and veiled like those of a woman asleep. The light-hearted smile that he put between himself and the world left his face.

When Lorena looked up at him, she was surprised for an instant by the intensity in his eyes, but her own problem was more important to her than his, and she said to him urgently: "Don't ever tell Jeff I sent a letter, Charlie, will you? You may see him in town. Don't tell him that you have the letter."

"Who you writing to?" he asked. He got up from the chair and came near the table.

"You'll have to see the address," she said. "I'm writing to his Uncle Ralph. But Jeff wouldn't like it. He would be angry with me. Promise you'll never tell him, Charlie."

"So I promise, what do I get?" Charlie asked.

"You get my thanks," Lorena said.

"I t'ink you give that Jones fella a little more than thanks," he said, "and what's he ever done for you more than Charlie do?"

Lorena began to laugh. She folded her letter quickly so that he could not see what she had written. Then she sealed it in an envelope. She hesitated before writing the address. On second thought, she decided to leave the envelope blank and write the address on a separate slip of paper.

When she had done this, she jumped up and came close to Charlie. She put the unaddressed envelope in one of the pockets of his Hudson's Bay jacket, and the slip of paper in the other.

"Take it like this," she said, "and address it just before you mail it. Do you understand?"

"You don't take chance, do you?" Charlie said. "Only on me you take chance. How you know you can take chance on me?"

"I know you'd do whatever I asked you. It's true, isn't it?"

"How you know?" Charlie repeated, looking at her seriously, without his careless smile.

Standing close to him, Lorena considered. Then she said, "Charlie you're wonderful. There's nobody anywhere like you. Put your hands behind your back and I'll give you a kiss, and then you go quick and mail my letter. And don't ever tell a soul. Do you promise?"

"Sure. You mean it, then I promise."

Lorena took his face in her hands and kissed him. "Go along now," she said, "and be a good boy. I pretty near could fall in love with you, if you stayed around here too much. Do you know that? Jeff's perfectly right to tell you to keep away."

10.

Charlie did not press his advantage. He adjusted his packsack on his shoulders and prepared to depart. He had a day and a half of brisk walking ahead of him, but that fact in itself would not have hastened his departure. His instinct for dealing with women told him that Lorena would think about him more if he left her wondering.

She stood in the cabin door and watched him go, wistfully, because she wanted to be going too. To be going somewhere, anywhere, that was her deepest wish. Any kind of trail would have been welcome so long as it led to people, to life, to excitement. But here she stood in the doorway of a solitary cabin in a vastness of forest, and the best she could do was to walk down to Meggie's and smother in Meggie's witless optimism.

Where the path from the cabin joined the main trail, Charlie turned and waved and grinned at her.

"Au revoir, ma belle, ma petite," he called. "Au revoir, mon âme!"

He whistled and sang as he walked out of the valley and up the trail toward the mountain. And yet one thing bothered him. The letter in his pocket seemed to be hot to his touch. He felt it, like a live coal, burning a hole in his pocket. He didn't know what he should do about it.

When he sat down to rest as the trail started uphill, he first rolled himself a cigarette, then he took the slip of paper out of his pocket and read the address. It was a detailed address with city, street, office building and number. If he should lose it, he would never be able to remember it.

He knew that Lorena had been Ralph Carney's secretary, and his quick intuition told him that Jeff could not forget or forgive that. He knew that in some way Ralph's shadow stood between Jeff and

Lorena. There were other things that stood between them too. He was quick to see that, and, whatever the rift, his sympathies were all with Lorena. He had a low opinion of Jeff as a man in a world of struggle. A timber locator, *sapristi!* He thought of what he, Charlie Duporte, might have done with himself had he been born in Jefferson Carney's shoes. He could see himself, well born, smooth speaking, taking advantage of every opportunity. He spat contemptuously into the path at the thought of Jeff's inadequacy.

One did not spit in contempt at the name of Ralph Carney, however. It carried weight and influence in this part of the country; it was blazed on every tree. Yet Charlie did not like it.

Having smoked his cigarette, Charlie got up and put the slip of paper back in his pocket. He walked quickly up the trail, making good time. He had a great store of nervous energy, but it did not prey upon him or sap his strength, because, when he rested, he could relax completely, as a dog relaxes, unworried about the next period of activity.

As he walked, he kept remembering the one time he had encountered Ralph Carney. It was a little incident, but, partly because Ralph was a big man, it had made a big impression on Charlie.

Ralph had got off the train, up in one of the mining towns where Charlie had been last winter. Ralph was expensively and elegantly dressed, which fact alone made him stand out among men who wore Mackinaws and high boots. Everyone knew who he was, and they all ranged themselves around the station platform watching him with curiosity and respect. There was a small deputation to meet him, and he walked down the platform between two lumber foremen who talked to him gravely and eagerly. Just before the three men left the platform to get into a hack, an old, half-drunken panhandler stumbled into Ralph's way, holding out his cap.

"Down on my luck, Mr. Carney," he whined. "Got me a bad back workin' for you. You give me somepin for a cup of coffee?"

"Coffee?" Ralph said impatiently. "You've had too much of something, but I'll be damned if it's coffee." People who heard him laughed. He pushed the old panhandler aside, got into the hack, and drove away.

Everyone knew the lumberjack was worthless and deserved nothing, yet the frontier country was openhanded and free with its purse strings, and common men particularly admired large gestures in their public characters. Something of Ralph's elegance and lack of generosity still rankled in Charlie's mind. It was the only time he had seen Ralph Carney, and he had no wish to see him again.

In Cold Spring Charlie washed up at the hotel, and received news of the outside world with mild curiosity. It mattered very little to him if earthquake, flood or tornado had plagued some portions of the earth. Murder, rape or suicide did not stir his fancy unless it occurred within his range of experience. Charlie's world was in the woods or the mines, and did not extend far beyond Cold Spring or Bolster. He had never acquired the townsman's nervous dependence on a daily newspaper.

Charlie was not a drinker in the lumberjack's sense of the word, but he enjoyed a glass in the society of the Pontarliers. When he came to Cold Spring, he went first to the hotel, then to the saloon. After he had had a couple of drinks with Pontarlier in the front part of the saloon, he went around to the back door and had a glass of wine with Madame Pontarlier.

Today, when he pushed open the swinging doors of the saloon, he saw that Jeff Carney was there, leaning against the bar, his face flushed and a glass in his hand. A little liquor gave Jeff a rosy outlook, and there were many times now when he needed the contrast of a rosy outlook to his usual hopeless state.

"I thought you was out settling homesteaders," Charlie said.

"They haven't got here yet," Jeff said. "Looks like they've been delayed."

Charlie felt the letter again, hot in his pocket. "Promise you won't tell Jeff," she had said to him. Intrigue always tempted Charlie, and it would be easy now to make a little trouble between them, to widen the rift that he had already noted. His fingers fondled the letter as he waited for his drink.

But he was genuinely loyal to Lorena, and the temptation to betray her passed. He had a light conscience, but strong loyalties. He did not necessarily mean to do what Lorena wished with the letter, but whatever he did would be, in his estimation, what was best for her, first for Lorena, and then for Charlie. There are many ways to skin a cat.

"Did you see Lorena when you came by my place?" Jeff asked.

"Yes, I see her. She was packin' to go to Meggie's place. Was fine," said Charlie smiling.

"Damn these folks for not coming in on time," Jeff said, "not when they said they would. I don't like to leave Lorena alone."

Charlie finished his glass and spoke to Pontarlier who had greeted him warmly.

"Madame Pontarlier at home?"

"Mais, oui. She will be looking for you."

"I go then," Charlie said.

Madame Pontarlier was sitting as usual in her majestic calm with her dog on her knee. Leisure and timelessness seemed to surround her, along with her crimson bows and white ruffles. Charlie liked to come here. To speak in Franch gave him a feeling of dignity, which his lack of fluent English often denied him. They spoke volubly and warmly, with gestures and easy laughter. Nothing hurried them. They were like a mother and son meeting after a long absence, content in each other's society, only a little moved, but with many common trivialities for discussion.

At last Charlie said, "Madame, vous connaissez Ralph Carney, n'est-ce pas?"

"Oui," Madame replied. "Je le connais."

"What kind of man is this fellow then? Tell me, Madame."

"Ah," said Madame Pontarlier smiling. "There is a man that I admire. There is a man of which every woman dreams. He is a man who knows what he wants and goes to get it, who takes and leaves as he chooses. And little people, little things, they do not stop him, because to himself he is all that matters. Isn't it so with all of us? Yet we are afraid, the rest of us, to go against society to get what we want. Ralph, he is not afraid."

"And you would trust him with your heart, Madame?"

"Why do you ask that?" Madame said. "Do you speak of me or of someone else? It was a long time ago when I would have given my heart to him. But I am a Frenchwoman. I have never trusted blindly. I have tried to understand, not trust."

"Then you would not trust him."

"My God, no! I would not trust," Madame replied. "But why do you ask this?"

"I have a letter for Ralph Carney, but I think it is better not to mail."

"Ah," said Madame. "So! And you are asking my advice? Is that it?"

"No," Charlie said. "I wish to know what kind of man this is. I do not ask advice. I act my own way and no one else is blamed."

"Very well," Madame said. "To keep your own council is a good thing. But I will tell you this: one does not trifle with Monsieur Carney. He is a big man and he strikes hard."

"It is not Monsieur Carney that I fear to displease," Charlie said. "If he does not get the letter, how will he know that it was written?"

"Ah," replied Madame. "So."

Charlie went to the store to purchase his supplies. He had to buy carefully, both because he lacked money and because he intended to carry everything he purchased back across the mountain in his packsack. He bought brandy and tobacco, tea and sugar, small sacks of flour and beans, salt pork and lard. This was as much as most men cared to tote on a two-day journey, but Charlie had one more thing in mind, and he wanted to get it before Jeff Carney did. He spent time selecting it, because he wanted it to be exactly right.

The thing he finally chose was bulky for a packsack that was already well filled, but Charlie had it wrapped very carefully in several layers of newspaper. He placed it at the inner side of the pack, so that it rested flat against his back when he took the sack onto his shoulders. The hard, square surface of his purchase, resting on the fluent muscles of his back, gave him pleasure.

He ate enormously at Mrs. Pulver's bounteous table. He was still there, his hunger nearly appeased, when Jeff Carney came in after the dinner bell had rung the second time and sat beside him. Jeff ate little. He did not have a strong stomach for liquor and in trying to pass the time without thinking, he had consumed too much of it that afternoon.

"When are you going back?" he asked Charlie.

"Tomorrow morning I go back. You want me do you any jobs?"

"Yes," Jeff said. "Stop by Meggie's and tell Lorena that I've had to change my plans. These folks are coming in tomorrow. They'll still have to get outfitted. Tell her it'll be five or six days before I can get back to the homestead. Tell her to stay at Meggie's till I come to get her."

"You write it all down in a letter, maybe?" Charlie said. "You put in love and kisses—make her feel good, eh? I t'ink she like get letter."

Jeff paused, pushing the food distastefully around his plate with his fork. He fumbled in his pocket for a pencil.

"No," he said, "I haven't any paper to write on. My hand isn't very steady—too much riding yesterday, I guess. No, I won't write. You tell her, Charlie."

"Sure," Charlie said, "you trust me tell her my own way, eh?"

"When'll you get there?"

"Thursday noon, I have good luck."

"Well, tell her to expect me Sunday then, or Monday at the latest. Tell her I had to change my plans. You do that, Charlie?"

"Sure, I tell her," Charlie said.

"Thanks," Jeff said. "She won't like it."

"I try make her like it, Jeff," said Charlie, smiling.

"Come back to Pontarlier's, I'll give you a drink," offered Jeff.

"No, I go to bed now," Charlie said. "Get me early start to-morrow. Thank you the same."

As he had said, Charlie went up to bed in good time, and slept well. Very early the next morning he started back toward Freezeout and the Floodwood Valley. He walked alertly, and whistled as he went. He still had the unaddressed letter in one of his pockets, but somewhere along the way he had lost the complicated address that should have been written on it.

It was late summer; the streams were low and easily crossed; there was no snow left on the mountain. The trail had been well worn by many feet that year, and it seemed to Charlie that the going had never been pleasanter.

He was dog-tired when he reached the halfway cabin beyond the pass. But he felt content with himself and the world. In the dusk he entered the cabin and made a fire on the hearth. After he had cooked some bannock and made tea, he sat before the fire and rolled and smoked several cigarettes. He was fond of society of any sort, but loneliness did not embarrass him. Tonight he savored it as if it had been a velvet-thick liqueur on his tongue.

He thought of the night in June when they had all passed through here before, and when he had cooked for her. He saw her dark head outlined against the stars as some of them had stood in the clearing before bedtime. He had complimented her and she had moved away from Bundy Jones and put her hand on his arm. They had slept in the same room, but widely apart. The earth turned, time changed, and strange things came to pass. The trick was to be able to wait with patience, and not to be dismayed by delays.

The next morning Charlie was completely rested. He ate sparingly, shouldered his pack, and began to descend to the valley. On this part of the trail, the bank next to the mountainside glistened with mica and bits of brightly-colored rock. Charlie was fond of things that glittered and were brightly colored. He picked up small bright stones as he went along, and put them in his pocket. When he came down to the valley floor among the great trees, he pulled strings of ground pine and twisted them into a kind of garland or wreath.

He went steadily down the valley past Klein's and Taggart's and Smith's with only a hail and a wave of the hand in greeting. He did not want to spare the time for casual visiting along the way. At Jeff's place he stopped, but he did not try the door to see if it was locked. On the doorstep he laid his evergreen garland, and then he took some time and care to arrange his pretty stones inside it so that they formed the letters RENA. He was satisfied with his handiwork. He shouldered his pack again and continued along the trail to Meggie's place.

11.

The two girls were at work in Meggie's garden. Meggie had coaxed a little leaf lettuce and some pithy and bitter radishes into being, and she was very proud. The other vegetables looked hopelessly anemic, but Meggie still struggled against the brakes and weeds that kept trying to return to the natural habitat from which she had evicted them. Meggie worked energetically, laughing and chattering as she hacked and pulled at the stubborn brakes, happy to have Lorena's company.

Lorena worked sporadically, now pausing to look with regret at her stained hands, now gazing with dreaming eyes into the mysterious green depths of the forest that edged the clearing. It was agreeable to her to let Meggie's chatter flow over her, knowing that she could listen or not as she chose. Her discontent drew off a little, but it never quite let go. Without realizing that she was following Jeff's moral pattern, she had begun to take a certain settled comfort in her discontent, to accept it as her inevitable and melancholy fate. She saw herself as someone to be pitied. Yet the fact that she had sent the letter stimulated her hopes, and colored her thoughts.

Charlie's arrival gave both girls a lift of pleasure. He looked gay and handsome in his red and white jacket. His eyes were dark and bright, and his teeth flashed white in the deeply tanned face. He had washed in the stream before he came into the clearing, and his long walk sat lightly on him.

The two girls ran to him, and Lorena held out her hands. "Oh, Charlie! Charlie! How did you get back so soon?"

"Me, I flew like birdies all the way," said Charlie laughing. He flapped his arms in imitation of wings.

"Take off your pack and stay for lunch," said Meggie.

"I do that," Charlie said. "I got one pretty good big appetite, by gar!"

Meggie disappeared into the cabin to prepare the food, and Lorena went close to him and said: "Did you mail my letter, Charlie?"

"What you t'ink?" he asked, smiling at her.

"I think you did," Lorena said.

At luncheon Charlie said, "Too bad you girls ain't got a longer time to visit, eh?"

"What do you mean? Did you see Jeff?"

"Sure, I see Jeff. He says to tell you that he change his plans."

"How are his plans changed?" Lorena asked.

"Dem people he expect, they don't show up. Too bad, I guess, eh?"

"He's coming home sooner?" Rena asked.

"How can he keep away?" cried Charlie, laughing. "He got a pretty wife to home, he cut his journey short, by gar."

"You mean he isn't going to wait in Cold Spring?"

"Why wait? Them people didn't come."

"Well, when does he get home? Why didn't he come along with you?"

"He had a little business settle up."

"In the saloon?" asked Lorena coldly.

"That where I seen him. But I t'ink he come by night tonight."

"Surely he wouldn't make it from Cold Spring in a day," Meggie said.

"He got a horse, ain't he?" Charlie said. "He do it if he really want to. Them trails is pretty good now all the snow gone out."

"Well, Lorena, you can wait until he comes here anyway," Meggie said, hating to lose her company.

"It's sure he couldn't make it on here in a day," objected Lorena. "Maybe to our place, but not here."

"Too bad he find an empty cabin up there when he come," Charlie said, "an' got to cook his own supper. Maybe I go back and get some coffee and some bannock ready for him, eh?"

"I'll go," Lorena said. "I'll start right after lunch. Will you walk me back, Charlie? I hate these woods alone."

"I could go," Meggie said.

"Then you'd have to make the return here alone. Charlie won't mind walking me back, will you, Charlie?"

"No," Charlie said. "I got a lot of time. I walk you back, Mis' Carney."

Lorena gave herself up to the pleasure of walking through the sun-flecked woods with Charlie. His hand touched her elbow sometimes when they came to a hollow in the trail or a fallen log. There was respect in the touch, but also a something daring and sensual. Perhaps it was only her heightened perception that made her feel this. Something was happening to her for a change, and the awful boredom receded and left her intensely aware of herself and Charlie. She was not perfectly sure that he had not lied to her, and that suspicion added to her zestful expectation of adventure. Simply to be leaving Meggie, simply to be returning to Jeff would hardly have put her in this marvelously expectant frame of mind.

She reveled in movement and change, and just to be on the trail with a man, no matter who he was, who loved her, made a golden transition from one dull plateau to another. They looked at one another and smiled, with understanding and appreciation. There was nothing much to say. Charlie hummed a little, and sang, and sometimes spoke to her in French.

"What do you say?" Lorena asked carelessly. She knew by the tone that what he said was meant to please her.

"It is prettier to say in French," said Charlie. "You do not need I say in English? No?"

"No," said Lorena.

When they came to the cabin, Lorena saw her name in colored stones surrounded by a green garland.

"Who did this?" she asked.

"Some chipmunk must have do," said Charlie, laughing.

"Clear it up," she said. "What if Jeff had seen it?"

"Are you afraid of Jeff?"

"Yes—no."

"I t'ink not. What you give me if I clear it up?"

"No. No. Don't be tiresome," said Lorena. "Just because I gave you something for mailing my letter—"

"I didn't mail your letter," Charlie said.

They had entered the cabin, and he was pulling off his packsack. He spoke so casually that at first she scarcely registered his meaning. When she did, she whirled around and faced him with blazing eyes.

"You didn't mail my letter?"

"No."

"Why didn't you? Why didn't you?" she cried.

"You must forgive. I lose the little paper with address."

"Oh, no! Stupid and awkward! How could you do that?"

"It is too bad!"

"Too bad! Too bad!" Lorena cried. "Oh, this was mean and wicked of you, Charlie."

"No," he said. "I done smart thing for you. You write to some man begging him. Maybe he spit on you."

"That was no business of yours. You—you fool! You have no right to decide a thing like that for me. You haven't any right."

"Yes, I have right," he said. "You know what right it is. I love. You know that, Rena."

"You fool—you stupid fool!" Lorena cried. "That doesn't give you any right. You aren't the only man that's ever loved me."

"I am the man that's here," said Charlie gravely.

"Oh, wait till Jeff comes home," she cried. "Just wait."

"I tell you something else," said Charlie smiling. "Jeff ain't come home tonight, Rena. Not until Sunday. Maybe Monday."

"You lied!"

"I t'ink you knew I lied." He said it smiling at her.

Fury gave Lorena a wonderful sense of liberation and joy. She took the first thing she could find at hand to throw. It was a piece of pine wood from the wood box, and it hurtled through the air and struck Charlie on the shoulder. He had expected battle but not so promptly. They both cried out, Lorena with fury and Charlie with surprise.

She seized another piece of wood and lifted it to strike, but Charlie caught her wrist and held it poised in air. He was stronger than any man she had struggled with before. She felt her grip on the stick relaxing and her will melting. The more she felt her will slipping, the more desperately she struggled. She began to shout at him, ugly words that she had thought lost long ago in her unhappy childhood.

He pinned her arms down now from behind, and held her hard against his body. She could hear, she could feel, that he was laughing. There was more pleasure in this than in fighting with Jeff—to fight with laughter! Still she was sure she hated him. She knew she couldn't afford to let him win.

Holding her from behind like this his wrists were vulnerable. She bent her head and bit him on the wrist. Feeling his flesh, his warmth, the salty flavor of his blood in her mouth, she shuddered and cried out again. He turned her around, still holding her hard against him.

"So you drink my blood," he said. "How you find it? Sweet? If a dog do that I put a bullet in his head."

"You're terrible," she cried. "I hate you—don't you know?"

"I know," he said. "Tell me again you hate."

"I hate! I hate!" Lorena cried.

"You look all time so calm," he said, laughing, "but I know! I know! All time a little she-tiger slept. Now I wake her up."

"Let me go, Charlie," she begged. "You're hurting me."

"So you will bite again? No?"

"I'm sorry I bit."

"Oh dieu en ciel! She sorry now she bit. Look, you make me bleed."

"Let me go," Lorena said. "I'll wash it for you. I'll put a clean cloth on it."

"You mean that? Can I trust?"

"Yes," Lorena said. "You lie to me. But I won't lie to you. I never lie to you."

"I lie for you because I love. I lie to get three days with you. You understand? You know now why I lie?"

"Be still," Lorena said. "Didn't I just tell you how I hate you?"

"And never would you lie to me!" he said laughing. "Get me some water for my hurt." Suddenly he let her go, and offered his wrist for her inspection. Lorena saw with remorse how her teeth had marked him.

"Oh, Charlie!" she said.

"It not so much," he said. "Maybe I don't need no cloth on it."

"Yes," Lorena said. "I'll fix it right for you. I hurt you with the stick, too, didn't I?"

"Why do we hurt each other, Rena?" he asked. He asked it simply and without laughter.

"I don't know," Lorena said. She went to get a solution of carbolic acid that Jeff kept in an emergency box with bandages.

When she returned, Charlie was standing by her dressing shelf, looking at himself in a handsome new mirror. The mirror was twice as large as the old one, of a clear, beveled glass and set in a neat frame.

His eyes, reflected in the mirror looked into hers. They were crinkled with tenderness and laughter.

"I see some damn fool fella got you a new mirror, Mis' Carney," he said.

Lorena set the bottle and the roll of bandage down on the table. She moved slowly because everything was turning upside down inside her. She felt the tears starting and running down her cheeks.

"Oh, Charlie!" she said. "Charlie! Charlie!"

V

SNOW

1.

For several days Eye MacGillicuddy had been worried about his little bitch. From the mountainside he saw the blue thread of smoke from the Marble Creek Valley, but it bothered him less than Jessie's state of health. The woods were not dry this year as they had been some seasons, and, if lightning struck a tree and set it blazing, there was slight danger that the fire would get out of control. Time enough to worry about the fire if the wind came up, but today was as still as you'd ever be likely to see it. The thread of smoke went straight up and it did not seem to be enlarging.

Jessie's need, however, was immediate and pressing, and Eye did not know what to do about it.

Nearly a week before they had met a badger on the trail, and Jessie had gone after it. Usually badgers waddled away from Jessie's shrill attack, and in a few moments she gave up the pursuit and came wagging along behind Eye's horse, pleased with herself for having cleared the trail. But this time the badger stood his ground to do battle.

The animal was large of its kind, but Eye was willing to bet on Jessie's superior skill and intelligence. He sat his horse to watch the encounter with every confidence that it would be a brief one.

The two creatures were well matched in weight and energy. The bitch was built high and slender, while the badger was low and broad. Yet the badger was quick, in spite of short legs and broad back, and his strategy was always to keep his head toward the bitch so that she could not take him from behind. Jessie danced back and

161

forth, barking, and seeking an opportunity to close in from behind. So they sparred for a few moments, each watching for a chance to rush in and seize the other in a vulnerable place. The badger fought silently and for its life. Jessie had begun in sport and with a bravado of barking; but, as she tired and became aware of the grimness of the battle, she too fought silently.

They circled and darted at each other for some time, then the badger made a quick lunge and caught the bitch by the upper flesh of one of her hind legs.

Jessie yelped with pain and swung around, striking out with both front legs. Her sudden reversal shook the badger loose and momentarily confused him. Instantly she closed in from behind and caught him by the back of the neck. Her teeth sank in deep and she shook and tore him until she had killed him.

When the badger was dead, the bitch dropped him beside the trail, her lips curled away from her teeth in disgust. She limped away through the woods to a stream that ran nearby, and waded into it, first to stand panting, and then to drink, as if she wished to purify herself.

Eye called her and looked at her wound. It did not seem serious to him, and he took her up behind the saddle and continued along the trail.

The wound that the badger's teeth had made on the bitch's leg was in an awkward spot for her tongue to reach. The next day Eye noticed that her limp had grown worse instead of better. When they stopped to make camp that night, she did not care to eat, but lay, trying to lick her wound, and growled or whined when he attempted to probe the hurt.

The only medication Eye carried around with him was a small flask of whiskey. He poured some of the whiskey into the wound, and later tried packs of mud from the edge of the stream. The day he noticed the thread of smoke from the Marble Creek Valley, was the day on which he decided that Jessie could not travel any farther, even on the back of his horse.

Eye had weathered various illnesses himself. One spring he had somehow survived an attack of pneumonia alone in a camp on the mountainside—alone, that is, except for his bitch. Another time an ax had slipped and cut his foot, and, with only Jessie for company, he had managed to endure until the wound was sufficiently healed to let him get on horseback and ride into Cold Spring. He felt confidence in his tough hide and his ability to recover from the illnesses that afflict the human being.

Where his bitch was concerned, it was another matter. She had become child, wife and home to him, and anything that threatened her frightened and confused him. Now he saw, with increasing alarm, how her whole leg became swollen and throbbing. The infection was spreading rapidly and he did not know how to stop it.

She lay on one of his saddle blankets, panting and inert. She would still wag her tail, feebly, for him, but her eyes were dull and glazed, and she would not touch food. The wound seemed to have closed but the leg stuck out stiff and helpless, and the skin was taut over the swelling. It was hot to his touch.

"Eh, Jessie, lass," he coaxed, "this ain't no way to do. You canna lay down an' die on me. No, that ain't right, lassie! Do ye no ken, I'd be lost without ye? I'd be a lone old man without no dog, Jessie. Come now, lass, there ain't no badger worth a fuss like this."

The little animal made an attempt to thump her tail in friendship, but Eye could see that she herself had given up the struggle. Only a desperate remedy could save her now, he felt.

He built up a strong fire and sharpened his hunting knife. He did not know if he could save her, but he meant to try. When everything was ready, he strapped her to a log and cut off her leg and cauterized it with a brand from the fire. Then he laid her down gently in a sheltered place and sat beside her to watch. Gently, he dribbled water onto her dry lips, and saw how her dull eyes gazed at him with affection even after he had done this fearful thing to her.

When the ordeal was over, he found that he was shaking, and now and again a tear ran out of the corner of his eye and down his nose or across the rough, gray furrows of his cheek. He continued to talk to Jessie as he sat beside her, telling her that she was good and brave and calling himself an old fool for caring so much what became of her.

Toward evening he thought that she was cooler and that her eyes were brighter. She lifted her head and lapped a little water from a bowl which he held for her. Neither one of them had slept much the night before, but now they both slept quietly in the tent on the mountainside. The horses munched and pulled at the grass outside the tent. The night was overcast and dark, but the air was still.

Bundy Jones came by very early in the morning. In the late afternoon of the previous day he had seen the smoke on Marble Creek from one of the lookout points. He did not know if the ranger had seen it, but he felt it his duty to ride posthaste to put it out, on the chance that he was the only one who knew about it.

Bundy was surprised to find the ranger encamped halfway down the mountain.

"Man," he said, "don't you know there's a fire started in the valley?"

Eye MacGillicuddy had come out of his tent, eyes bleared with sleep.

"Aye. I knew there was a fire," the ranger said.

"But you didn't go," said Bundy.

"Happen 'twas a small one," Eye replied, "without wind, 'twill burn itself out."

"But can you take that risk? What if the wind had come up while you slept?"

"My little bitch was sick," Eye said. He stood there helpless in the morning light. The cool glare of it lit his thin, gray face and his untidy clothes. All too plainly they had been slept in for many days.

Bundy had a reasonable tolerance for a man's devotion to his dog. He was already fond of the awkward puppy who gamboled beside his horse and shared his solitary campfire. But he thought that no such bonds should go beyond the boundaries of common sense, or endanger the safety of the forest.

Looking at the ranger now, he felt that he was learning what he had wished to know.

"And so you mean to say you'll let a fire get out of hand because your dog is sick?" Bundy felt his anger rising as he spoke.

"Who says 'tis out of hand?" Eye asked.

"Perhaps not," Bundy said, "but who knows how soon it will be? Get your things and come along. We'll see to it."

The ranger hesitated. "You go on down there, if you want to. Jessie's not fit to travel yet. I canna take her, and I canna leave her."

"For God's sake, man!" Bundy cried angrily, "What kind of forest ranger are you?"

"Not bad," said Eye mildly. "Yon fire will be out before you get there. Take my word for it."

"And you're the only ranger here to see to all these woods!" cried Bundy. "Don't you have any feeling of responsibility?"

"My bitch is sick," the old man answered stubbornly.

Bundy rode posthaste down into the valley to put out the fire. He was hot with anger all the way. It was all very well for a lonely old man to cherish his pet, but a ranger's first duty was to look after the forest. His personal life or inclination should never be allowed to stand in the way. Bundy felt that now he knew all he wanted to know about Eye MacGillicuddy.

When he reached the valley he found the fire out. But his opinion of Eye MacGillicuddy as a responsible person remained unchanged. His report in Washington would be simple and concise.

2.

Before snow fell on Freezeout Mountain, the homesteaders had deserted the Floodwood Valley. Only Charlie Duporte remained to do his belated building, and Eye MacGillicuddy, with his little three-legged bitch at his heels, remained to do his winter trapping. The garrulous old man talked more to himself this winter, or was it to his dog and horses that he talked? He was glad on the whole to have the forest to himself again.

Charlie worked hard, straining to raise log walls before winter closed in, and often he sang as he worked, because there was nothing that could quench his exuberant spirits. But this winter for the first time he was sometimes lonely in the wilderness. Game was abundant, and eating was good for a man alone who was handy with gun or trap. When the cold weather came he could freeze a deer carcass and keep it for weeks, provided he could also hang it out of reach of wolves and cougars.

Among the pines winter gave little warning until the first snow fell. No premonitory blaze of color, as among deciduous trees, pointed the season. The brakes turned rusty brown, and here and there a mountain ash or shrub turned yellow; but the pines made no concession to the time of year, except to drop their cones. Chipmunks and red squirrels soon took care of those.

Before snow fell there was a great silence in the forest, for the birds knew what was coming and they flew away. Only the trees continued to make a quiet sound of sighing as the wind passed through their branches.

Charlie had his cabin tight and secure before the deep snow made outdoor work impossible. It was a small cabin, but Charlie's wants, although they were intense, were few in number. He had packed in a stove and supplies, and he quickly made what crude and simple furniture he needed. As much time as possible he spent out of doors, even after the snow came.

Once, when a blizzard kept him indoors for three long days and he had cleaned and oiled his guns, slept his fill, and grown bored with solitaire, Charlie took out of his pocket Lorena's unmailed letter. He looked at it for some time, turning it over and over; then he opened it and read it. He read it several times, and, reading, he was able to see Lorena clearly. He saw her flashing with anger and melting with tenderness. He saw her cruel and he saw her kind.

That the letter had been intended for another man, did not dismay him. It served only to remind him of an agreeable summer, the best he had ever had. Now that the winds howled around his lonely cabin, he was glad to have a souvenir of happier days.

No woman had ever written him a letter starting "Dearest." He did not intend to make ill use of this one, but, as a memento of Lorena, he thought that he would keep it. He tossed the envelope away, but the folded letter he kept in the inner breast pocket of his Hudson's Bay jacket. Once the touch of Lorena's letter had seemed to burn him; now it became for him a sentimental token. The creases of the pink note paper grew worn with the pressure of his fingers. The gilt edges gradually became tarnished.

3.

Back in Opportunity, the homesteaders found life unchanged. While they had been away, some of the outlying streets had been paved, a new grain warehouse had been built near the railway station, and a revered pioneer citizen had died. Yet these changes were scarcely noticed on the surface of the town life.

Nan O'Rourke went back into the millinery store and relieved her sister who had kept shop for her while she was gone. Summer was a dull season in the millinery business. The great rush came at Eastertime, when the women stampeded for new spring hats; but in summer they went bareheaded or wore sunbonnets when they hung out clothing in the hot back yards. In summer the milliner began to stitch velvet and felt and beaver fur onto the big buckram and wire frames in preparation for the fall trade.

Nan's sister, Delia, was well intentioned, but she lacked Nan's touch. She had a family at home to be fed and her imagination was most deeply involved with them. She kept the shop open, but the work did not move forward as Nan would have it.

So, fresh in from the woods with hands roughened by coarse work, Nan found the autumn season upon her and nothing provocative to display on her shelves. It was the first season that the work had seemed tedious to her.

"Sew! Sew! Sew!" she grumbled. "Well, if I get my homestead and make a pile of money, maybe I can lay off a little, hire a girl, or give up the shop altogether and take a vacation." She didn't say "get married," because she had long ago relinquished that idea.

Meggie Carney came in to see her soon after their return. Meggie had brought her dog into town with her, and he sat beside Nan's dog outside the shop, snapping at flies, in sociable contentment. Neither of Jessie's puppies seemed to amount to much, but at least they were good-tempered and enjoyed comfort, and were now swallowing civilization whole like any other unexpected tidbit.

"Well, darling, is it a hat you want now?" asked Nan. "I've

a beauty in blue velvet with a small ostrich plume that I must have made express for you."

"I can't afford a hat, Nan," Meggie said, "and furthermore I don't want one. Is it wrong to come in your shop and waste time, if I don't buy?"

"Come into the back room whilst I sew," said Nan. "You won't waste my time and I'll give you a cup of tea, nice and strong. Is something troubling you, darling?"

"Yes," Meggie said. "I think I'm going crazy, Nan. I was busy all summer and I had a good time. Now I'm home and there's nothing to do. We're too poor this year to live the life we used to with parties and everything expensive and gay. I know I get on Lorena's nerves, and after all it's her house now, not mine, really. I have to talk to someone, Nan, and who do I know well enough to talk to like this? I thought I had a hundred friends in town, but when it boils down to telling troubles and asking advice, I can't think of one I want to go to without sacrificing my pride."

"Pride!" Nan said. "That's the trouble with a swell upbringing. The most they hammer in your head is pride. Why don't you scrap pride, and get yourself a job?"

"That's what I'm thinking of," said Meggie. "That's what I want your advice about."

"Go ahead," Nan said. "The town will talk no doubt, but do you care?"

"I don't think so," Meggie said. "The only thing is, it will hurt Jeff, I'm afraid. But in the woods this summer, I got to thinking, Nan. I thought, 'I am myself, I can make my own decisions.' Maybe you don't know what a step that was for me. I've always before been someone else's little girl. Is it wrong, Nan, to step out and be myself—even if it hurts someone else?"

"No, 'tis not," said Nan. "If you ask me, a person's not whole nor alive until he learns the wonderful fact that he can stand up alone and make his own decisions. Maybe it's lonely and maybe it's a punch on the nose he'll be getting for his impudence, but it's a wonderful thing to be self-reliant."

"But my trouble is," said Meggie. "I really don't know how to do anything that's worth paying for."

"I'd give you a job here," Nan said, "but it wouldn't pay much, and you'd be meeting all your society friends at their very snootiest."

"Well, I could take that, I guess," Meggie said, "but I'm all thumbs when it comes to sewing or trimming. I'd ruin your business for you. If I dared to ask for it, I'd be better off in an office or the library or the courthouse. I just haven't yet got up my steam to go around asking, and saying 'No. No experience,' and having them turn me down—people I know, maybe. And they'll go home and tell their wives 'You know who asked me for a job today? Margaret Carney! I pitied her, but what can I do? She doesn't know anything.' "

"Listen here," said Nan, "you're beat before you start if you talk like that. I'll give you a couple of strong cups of tea, and then you go out and down the street, and you smile and hold your head up and put on a good bluff, and you go into every office and shop along the block until somebody hires you. You hear that?"

"All right," Meggie said, "I will. And, if nobody will have me, I tell you what, I'll come back here and trim your hats and ruin your business for you for nothing."

They laughed together and drank off a quantity of tea, and then Meggie set timorously forth. That she finally landed a small job in the office of a lumberyard amazed not only the town and her family but Meggie herself. She was jubilant and humble by turns. She had a feeling that, single-handed, she was conquering the world. Her pay check for the first week was fifteen dollars, and she felt she was a millionaire.

On damp days the smell of raw lumber that surrounded the office was like a bracing perfume. It was an extension of the fresh, sweet smell of her cabin in the forest. She liked the sound of men's voices and the backing of drays in the muddy yard. She heard lumber being piled or clattering down and horses whinnying, and in the distance the nasal snarl of a planing mill. "These were trees," she said to herself, walking between the house-high piles of fragrant boards. Her thoughts went no further than that, and she was content.

4.

Lorena was also strangely content this winter. The comfort of town, even without the luxury of ready money, was like a silken cushion about her. She could appreciate it as she had never done before. The long mirrors reflected her in the beautiful silk tea gowns and negligees that she had bought in the first year of her marriage before the flow of money stopped.

Meggie got up early, with the most disgusting energy, and started breakfast, and Jeff brought coffee to Lorena on a bed tray. He raised the blinds and fixed the pillows at her back and kissed her, and Lorena smiled at him kindly and affectionately. Later she rose and bathed at leisure and stepped warily through the long day, savoring it. She did not mind the added housework that she had to do after Meggie surprised everyone by getting a job. The housework was not difficult with good stoves, good furniture, a boy to deliver groceries, water running in a porcelain sink at the turn of a faucet, a modern toilet that flushed at the pull of a chain. The doctor said that exercise was good for her, and that she might do anything about the house except lift heavy loads.

Lorena's body had always been her dowry, and she had taken a serene interest in it. Now mystery and expectation were added to its beauty and importance. For, after several years of unfruitful matrimony, Lorena and Jeff were going to have a baby. Suddenly the shared hope seemed to have straightened out everything between them.

Jeff was filled with tenderness, with confidence and ambition. He was busy this winter putting his father's papers into shape and jotting notes for the senator's biography, which he had been asked to write. This was not work for which he had predilection or training, but it was a dignified occupation. It did not set people to gossiping as Meggie's crazy job in a lumberyard did, and it would leave him free to make the six-month journey into the homestead which was required to establish residence.

He worked in his father's old law office in the Carney Building. The Carney Building had long since been sold to pay his father's debts, but the senator had retained a long-time lease on the small office on the second floor, and his papers and books were all there. Many people had advised Jeff to sell the big house and relinquish the office. In time he meant to do so. The family finances would have benefited greatly by a trimming down and clearing up old obligations and entanglements.

But Jeff's inclination was always to hold on to the secure

past, to keep up the old appearances. If the homesteads could be made to pay handsomely, perhaps the position of the Carneys could be saved.

He wanted more than ever to save the past for the future, now that he was to have a child.

Warmed by Lorena's parting smile and kiss, Jeff went to the office, with its musty smell of past activity, in a happy frame of mind. He could almost date the beginning of his present happiness. He had returned to the homestead after the last summer trip with settlers, and had found Lorena waiting for him. The house was in order, the hot food ready, and Lorena's attitude toward him suddenly changed from indifference to kindness. Sometimes he asked himself why she had changed, but the change was on the whole so welcome and so badly needed that he did not probe far. To have her again, as in the first days of their marriage, kind if not passionate, that was enough to satisfy him, and he asked no questions. And out of this new warmth and kindness had come the miracle for which they had been vainly waiting.

Ralph came to town briefly that winter, and Jeff in his new-found confidence would have asked him to the house for dinner. But Lorena did not care to see him.

"No," she said. "Let him take you out for lunch. But I'm not up to getting dinner for Ralph just now. He'd miss the service your mother used to have. I don't want him to see us like this."

She did not know why it was that she preferred not to see Ralph. Was it because he would find her less beautiful than she had been? Or was it because she had been on her knees to him, even if he did not know it?

She was grateful to Charlie now for withholding her letter. "You beg—he might spit on you," Charlie said. No, she was through with Ralph Carney now, and wholly preoccupied with the changing chemistry of her body. She wanted to be left alone in a kind of drifting peace.

5.

Bundy Jones left his horses and dog with McSweeney, put on city clothes, and went back to Washington. His attitude had changed this year. He could not put his finger on the difference, yet he knew it was there. The public monuments, the circles, the celebrities no longer moved him with naïve elation. They had lost their novelty and he had lost his youthful capacity for admiration and wonder. He was involved in a job which was very likely to have distasteful aspects. He meant to do it competently, but he had lost his zestful feeling toward it.

He reported fully to Pinchot on the wonderful white pine country of the Idaho Panhandle, and G.P.'s praise could still move and inspire him. When it came to a question of what to do about Eye MacGillicuddy, Bundy had only to relate the incident of the fire in the valley and the sick bitch on the mountainside, to give G.P. a comprehensive picture of the ranger.

"How about sending Matt Hinson out there next year?" said G.P. He was thinking aloud rather than asking advice. "Matt is a wonderful organizer. He needs a move. We will give him help, and he can put the Forestry Service on a respectable basis in there."

Bundy was pleased to think of having Matt nearby again. Matt Hinson would be the best possible man for the place. He avoided thinking about Eye MacGillicuddy and what was to become of him. The old man was more of a trapper than a ranger anyway.

"What about the homesteaders?" G.P. asked. "You haven't reported on them."

Something tightened in Bundy when it came to the homesteaders. They were not so easy to describe as were the ranger and the superb and lofty trees. How could he really know their motives? Yet he did know. Putting aside a reluctance to report about them, he told G.P. everything: how the timber was filling up with townspeople who could not possibly expect to make permanent homes there without cutting down vast areas of forest; how the lumber companies were backing the settlers in every way, urging them to expect easy money and a quick sale.

"Can you prove this?" G.P. asked.

"I'm not sure," Bundy said.

"Unfortunately," G.P. said, "I've discovered that everything has to be proved by law. You can see a moral right, but if the other side can twist a shred of law around to defeat it, they will cheerfully do so, and you haven't a leg to stand on."

"I know," Bundy said, "but I think this can be proved eventually." Into his mind flashed a single image. On a handsplit shingle, lettered in ink, was the name of a homestead, "Bide a Wee." But he dismissed it with impatience, saying, "They'll make mistakes and we must watch for them. But it won't be easy. We're going to have to fight for this."

"We'll fight," Pinchot said. "This will be one of our test cases. We're fighting on more fronts than one these days. We're fighting for coal rights and water power and care of the soil, as well as for ranger stations and proper use of Indian lands. Under T.R. it's been a good fight. With Taft coming in, I don't know, but I hope that we'll continue to have the President's backing. I'm sure of one thing—we can never consider the forest as a detached unit. It's all tied up with these other issues."

The last year of Roosevelt's administration was a particularly good one for the conservationists. In the spring of 1908 T.R. had called the governors of all the states to Washington for a conference on conservation. It was the first time that the movement, which had originated and centered in Washington, was called to the attention of the individual states, and there had been a hearty response to the President's enthusiasm. This had been followed by the creation of a national Conservation Commission to consider water, forest, land and mineral resources. By December the Commission had completed its report and met in Washington; and its findings constituted the first inventory of natural resources ever made by any nation, an inventory of three million square miles of the richest continent on earth.

Bundy shared the excitement and sense of achievement that pervaded the department that winter. In February the President called another conference with even wider scope. The North American Conservation Conference included representatives from Canada and Mexico, and its discussions included the natural resources of a continent. Both Roosevelt and Pinchot felt that conservation might form a basis for world peace, if it could be practiced on a world-wide scale; and so, as a result of the successful North American Conference, invitations were sent to fifty-eight nations to meet at the Peace Palace in The Hague in September, 1909, for a World Conservation Congress.

When Taft succeeded Roosevelt on March 4, thirty nations had already accepted the invitation to the World Congress, but under Taft the plan was somehow shelved, and the World Congress was never held. Whether it might have helped to hold back the rising tides of war and depression and hatred among nations, there is no way of knowing.

Taft was genial, law-respecting, and, unlike his predecessor, he did not go out of his way to look for trouble. He regarded Pinchot, from the start, as the moderate man often regards the fanatic. He wrote to his brother Horace that he considered "Gifford as a good deal of a radical and a good deal of a crank." The new President had other friends and other fish to fry. When he formed his first cabinet, his appointment of Ballinger as Secretary of the Interior was a red flag to the conservationists. They had tangled before. This time Ballinger came fresh from his law office in Seattle where he had been attorney for the Cunningham coal claimants in Alaska and for several Alaskan coal companies whose chief hope was to obtain government lands for private use.

Bundy was acquainted with a government investigator by the name of Glavis who had been on the trail of the Cunningham claims for some time. Glavis said he could prove that most of the claims were fraudulent, and that the whole Alaskan coal region was being readied for sale to the monopoly which was already in possession of much of the new Alaskan land and enterprise.

So the winter passed from elation and high hopes in the Forestry Office to disappointment and a knowledge that a struggle was inevitable.

On the social side Bundy was gayer than he had ever before been. The Roosevelt administration went out in a blaze of easy money and splendid frivolity. Washington waltzed and two-stepped merrily. Military bands and orchestras played, heavy dinners were served in many courses by skillful servants on hand-painted china. The ladies were magnificent in tiaras and egrets and monumental hats.

Good-looking young bachelors were always in demand, and gradually Bundy began to develop the social confidence which he had failed to learn in the West. Still he was never quite at ease in

a ballroom, and he was grateful for her help when Iris Cavanaugh
began to take him in hand.

The arrangement was good for both of them, because, while
she had the social poise which Bundy lacked, Iris was a quiet girl
and not greatly sought after by the gay young men. They became
acquainted casually at a party where many young people were having a hilarious time. Bundy and Iris found themselves on the side-
lines, looking on rather than participating. They smiled at each
other with humor and friendliness, and it was easy to go on from
there.

When he found that she was the only daughter of an important
Washington lawyer, Bundy was impressed but not deterred. There
was nothing about Iris Cavanaugh to make him ill at ease. She was
nice and fresh-looking, pretty if you happened to think so, and she
was understanding and had a sense of humor. Her father's volubility
had made her a good listener, and she flattered Bundy by giving her
undivided attention to his pet enthusiasms. She already knew the
ins and outs of the political situation and was sympathetic to the
conservation ideals.

If she knew very little about botany and forestry and Western
white pine before Bundy came into her life, she soon acquired a
detailed working knowledge of these things. She never let him see
it if she felt bored.

Bundy guessed that she was older than he was, but he recognized that she was a wonderful girl, the kind of girl who would
make some man a wonderful wife. The thought of a wife for himself
had always been a long way in the future as far as Bundy was concerned. He had no money and he wanted his fill of footloose freedom in the wilderness before he established a home. With Iris he
had the comfortable feeling that she would wait. Attractive as she
was, still she was the kind of girl about whom a man need not feel
rushed. So he saw a good deal of her and thought of her with the
deepest friendliness and gratitude.

Toward the end of the winter, Bundy even began to think that
someday he would make a declaration of his intentions and ask
her patience with a long engagement.

But one night as they sat at a quiet table in a restaurant, she said to him out of a clear sky, "You have a girl in the West, haven't you?" Bundy looked at her in surprise. He had been talking about the mountain pine bark beetle and how to combat it and this brought him up short. The sudden turn of conversation to the personal confused him.

"Why, no," he said. "Certainly not. No, I have no girl in the West."

She smiled at him very kindly. "I think you have," she said, "whether you know it or not. You wouldn't love the trees so much if there wasn't a woman sitting under them."

From surprise and confusion, Bundy slipped into annoyance. He began to argue that the very fact of his being so interested in the forest meant there was no woman involved. But Iris only looked at him and kept on smiling.

"I think there's some reason why you can't have her," she said. "And so you won't admit she's there."

They went to the theater after that and saw an amusing play. But all through the evening Bundy kept seeing Lorena's face as he had seen it in the smoke of his campfires during the summer.

It was odd that a girl who had never heard of Lorena Carney should have been the one to tell him that he loved her.

When they went back to Iris' home that night, Bundy stood a moment on the doorstep, his hat in his hand.

"Iris," he said, "she's married to someone else, married before I met her."

"I'm awfully sorry, Bundy," Iris said. "I shouldn't have brought it up. Only I had to know."

"I was going to ask you to marry me sometime, you know."

"You're sweet, Bundy," she said. "I saw it coming, and I had to find out about the other first."

"But it needn't make any difference?" Bundy said, half-heartedly. "I've never touched her. I never can."

"Maybe it shouldn't make a difference, but it does. I wouldn't want to marry unless I have—everything— It's small of me, I guess, but I'd rather be single."

They continued to be friends, although as the winter waned they saw less and less of one another. One of Bundy's associates took up where he had faltered, and found Iris amazingly understanding because she already knew all about the pine bark beetle and the problems of reforestation, and could ask the most intelligent of questions.

Bundy was adrift again, but not without self-knowledge. Now he went back over the summer with open eyes and saw where and when great things had overtaken him. Remembering Lorena's kiss by the spring in the woods, he blamed himself for his slow reactions. He saw no logical future for himself and Lorena. Yet now that his eyes were open he could never put her out of his mind. All his dreams were bent toward seeing her again. He remembered the forest, the sound of wind among pine needles, the lichens and mosses on the rocks, and loveliest of all a woman with red lips on a twilit trail.

Bundy had a surprised conscience and he suffered; yet his first realization of love transported him to unsuspected regions of pleasure. He had the rest of the winter to get used to the idea that he loved Lorena Carney, and to come to terms with himself as to what, if anything, he could do about it.

6.

The thing that Ralph had particularly come to Opportunity to say to Jeff was that the homesteaders must fulfill their six-month residential obligations. There was other business, of course, but this was his main theme. Homesteaders in the past had not bothered much about the letter of the law, but now things were tightening up in Washington. Anyone could see that there was going to be a fight for this white pine, the finest stand left in the West. It must not be lost to government reserve through the homesteaders' lack of compliance with the regulations.

"Sometimes I wonder," Jeff said, "who will know whether we go in there this winter or not?"

"They'll know in Cold Spring. Besides you'll have to swear to it," Ralph said. "Do you want to perjure yourself?"

"But isn't the whole thing—" Jeff began.

Ralph cut him short. "Don't say it," he said. "You're in there to make a home. They'll ask you why you didn't stay in there all winter. You can tell them, you have to wait for better roads before you can spend the whole winter there, but you have complied with the regulations. You haven't let six months elapse between your visits. It's your home. You understand that, don't you?"

"Yes, of course," Jeff said. "Still it's an awful journey in the winter, particularly for the women. I can't take Lorena. I won't. It's out of the question this year."

"If *you* go, they'll overlook Lorena's absence, I suspect. But Margaret will have to go—any of the women who are taking homesteads in their own right. They'll have to go."

Meggie had never been on snowshoes in her life, but she was beginning to welcome the adventurous unknown. She worried about leaving her job which she had come to like, but February was a slack season in the yard, and she did not expect to be gone more than a week or ten days. The manager, not unmindful that this willing little secretary was, surprisingly, the niece of Ralph Carney, agreed to let her go and to keep her job open for her.

"Shall I take my dog?" she asked Jeff.

"Lord, no!" Jeff said. "What would you do with your dog? We'll have enough trouble getting ourselves in there."

"Well, I just asked," Meggie said. "He was good company last summer, and I hope he's a protection."

"I'll protect you," Jeff said irritably. "Leave your dog with Lorena." The whole affair made him irritable. To go into the forest country in winter, and especially with women, was a difficult project. The taking up of a homestead had seemed so simple at the outset, an easy solution to the money problem. Was there any way to easy money? he wondered.

Jeff had acquired a nervous habit this year of smoking cigarettes. He rolled his own as Charlie and the timber willies did, curving the little brown paper between his fingers and tilting the tobacco into it from the small drawstring pouch. But his hands were not always as steady as Charlie's, and sometimes the tobacco spilled on the front of his shirt or onto his knees. When he had rolled the slender brown cylinder and sealed the edge of the paper with his tongue, he twisted the two ends and struck the match with his thumbnail. That, too, was a trick he had learned from Charlie. He drew deeply on the cigarette, half closing his eyes, as if the smoke which he had so laboriously prepared was distasteful to him.

February seemed the best month for the journey in to the homesteads. By that time it was probable (although one never knew) that the worst of the storms would be over. The snow would be settled and hard packed. The treacherous thawing would not yet have begun.

February was best for Nan too. She had her spring hats pretty well in hand, and the women wouldn't clamor for them until the week before Easter.

"Do you think we can stand it?" she asked Meggie. "We'll have to walk all the way. They don't ride horses in winter. It's too tough on the horses."

"I know," Meggie said. "But what else can we do? Now we're in this thing, and we've put our money into cabins and all that."

"Your sister-in-law is lucky," Nan said. "What I wouldn't give for a man to fight my battles for me!"

"Well, Nan, you and I haven't got 'em," Meggie said cheerfully.

"You will have," Nan said, "and my advice to you is: grab a man soon. A girl can very easy get left, and then she's got to do everything herself, as I've found to my everlasting edification."

"No candidates in sight," Meggie said. Nan considered.

"I thought maybe Bundy Jones was just a little sweet on you last summer, Meggie. A botanist might be quite useful as a homesteader's husband."

Meggie found herself blushing as well as laughing. "Oh, don't be silly," she said to Nan. "If I get a hundred and sixty acres of good timberland, I won't need a man."

Nan snorted. "There's one thing that's better for a woman than a hundred and sixty acres of good timberland. And you don't know what it is, do you, you little goose?"

Meggie did not answer, but Nan went on, "It's a husband, that's what it is. And don't let your opportunities slip by without grabbing one."

"Well," Meggie said mildly, "so far I haven't had to stand my suitors in line and pass out numbers. Let's forget about husbands and concentrate on how many pairs of woolen underdrawers we've got to wear to keep from freezing."

"Lord! Lord!" said Nan, "I thought I was the realist. Maybe you'll make a better old maid than I do, after all."

7.

Other homesteaders had made the trek before them. There was a fair trail out of Cold Spring on the hard-packed snow. Klein and Taggart joined them in the little town and McSweeney went with them as guide. The familiar landscape had taken a fantastic turn that would have been confusing without a local guide. The trees were hung with festoons of snow and filigrees of frost; drifts changed the pattern of mountains; and rivers lay silently buried under ice and snow. One located rivers and streams by the absence of trees, looking upward rather than downward to trace their courses. There was a great silence over the white landscape except for the thin, lonely whining of the wind. The sky was clear and blue and the short-lived sun shone without warmth.

Everyone carried snowshoes and a pack. Even the two women had small packs because they would have to eat during the few days they were gone, and one could not depend upon this wild white land to nourish and sustain. No one wished to waste time in stalking and hunting on a journey such as this. Actually they saw no sign of life in the woods, except for the carcass of a deer which lay in a bloodied and trampled spot some distance out of Cold Spring.

"How horrid and untidy!" Meggie said. "What did that?"

"Some careless hunter, I guess," McSweeney said. He saw no reason to make these women hysterical by mentioning cougars or wolves. Either word would be likely to set the damn-fool females to screaming and lamenting, he felt sure. Women on the trail at any time were bad business, in winter worst of all. Still he was beginning to have some admiration for their pluck. There had been others that winter—a new breed as far as McSweeney was concerned. Some of them had outlasted the men. It was a strange phenomenon. It used to be only men, McSweeney thought, who were willing to risk their lives in the gamble for a little money. Now there were women, too. Maybe he was old-fashioned, but he didn't like it, and the worst of it was, he thought, that they didn't really understand the dangers.

Afoot on a well-packed trail one made better time than with a pack train. Meggie missed the bells, but she walked briskly with her mind set well ahead. She had learned during the summer that she had more endurance if she fixed her mind on the farthest limit of the day rather than if she walked bit by bit without visualizing her destination.

At noon they stopped briefly to build a fire and make hot coffee. Walking in woolen clothing, they had kept reasonably warm, but the fire felt good to their hands and faces. They were tempted to linger, but McSweeney was firm. "We stop now, we begin to stiffen up. We got to keep going. Dark comes early."

They had not been obliged to use the snowshoes yet, but now Freezeout loomed ahead of them, white as a wedding cake, decorated with the froth of blowing snow. Behind it, clouds were forming, low and soft and heavy. Gradually the clouds climbed up the sky behind the mountain and spread gently and steadily over the whole sky, eliminating the bright blue and the chilly sunshine. As they went higher, the cold became more intense and the wind dashed sharp ice crystals into their faces.

Something else was beginning to trouble Meggie, but she knew that there was no use mentioning it to anyone. She had to go on now, and there was no remedy as far as she could see. Her summer boots had seemed perfectly adequate in town, and she hadn't wanted to spend needed money on larger ones. But the extra pair of heavy woolen socks had made the boots fit snugly, and now, with much walking, her feet began to swell. The boots seemed tighter and tighter with every step she took.

"Are your feet hurting you?" she asked Nan.

"Sure," Nan said, "they feel like bricks. But I got my brother-in-law's boots. Lord knows they're big enough, if only I don't fall over them. How about yours?"

"Oh, they'll do," Meggie said. She was determined not to cause trouble on this trip. She had outgrown the helpless girl of last summer.

So they toiled up the mountain, sliding and stumbling, wading through drifts, thinking with longing of the halfway cabin. Meggie could see in her mind the firelight dancing on the walls; she could

smell bacon and coffee. At the cabin she would be able to take off
her shoes. To divert herself she tried to remember the odd things
travelers had written or carved on the cabin walls.

> *Ada, for you I pine*
> *for you I balsam.*
> *Billy B. '03.*

Where was Billy now? Where was Ada? Had they married?
That was six years ago. Perhaps they had six children. If twins ran
in either family, there might be twelve by now. Oh, really, what
nonsense! But, when she reached the cabin, she would be able to
take off her shoes.

> *A fool there was.*
> *Here his name, Chuck Harger*
> *Lewiston, Ida., '01.*

Oh, Chuck, you aren't the only one! Who let me get into a
place like this? She looked ahead at Jeff, bent forward into the
wind, walking with his head down. Once she had trusted Jeff so
completely. But ever since this homestead venture, her trust had
been waning. Every day she saw more clearly that one could not
lean on other people or trust one's life to other people's judgment.

If she had never tried to homestead, but had only gone out
independently and got herself a job like any common girl from the
other side of the tracks, everything would have been easier. She
was happy enough with the little job in the lumberyard, but, if she
had learned something practical instead of going to that empty-
headed finishing school, she might be doing useful, lucrative work
by now, in a warm bright office with a comfortable chair and comfortable shoes. The homestead was to be so quick and easy, like the
stone and timber claim.

She brought her mind back resolutely to the halfway cabin.
She could take off her shoes there. The firelight would dance on
the rough walls; she would read the familiar, funny signatures.

> *God helps them that helps thereselves*
> *but only old Devil on this here Mt.*
> *O. D. D., '06*

It was three years ago that O. D. D. had left his bitter wisdom on the cabin wall. And he had scrawled it after a day like this, no doubt; a day like this, and he had taken off his shoes and stretched his feet to the fire and drunk hot coffee.

Out of the heavy clouds the snow began to fall. It came down lazily at first, one large flake after another, drifting on the wind in sullen beauty. McSweeney, who was ahead, quickened his pace. He knew all kinds of weather, and this was a kind he did not like. If they could beat the storm to the summit and get over the little pass, they would be sheltered by the trees and could find their way to the halfway cabin. He did not know how much extra speed and exertion the two women could make. He thought, By God! I'm a softie. I ought to set my foot down and refuse to take these blasted females. Having them along could kill a man's chances.

The snow fell faster and faster, shutting out the mountain on the left and the deep valley that dropped away to the right. The six people kept going upward in a twilight of snow, plodding and struggling, shielding their faces from the stifling gusts of stinging crystals.

It was not until the falling snow began to darken that Mc-Sweeney was certain he had lost the trail. They should have reached the hump by now, and be going down the other side to the cabin. Instead they were still climbing. He paused, uncertain, and the others came up around him. They were grotesque figures, plastered with the wet snow, almost unrecognizable.

"I think we missed it," he said. "There should have been a boulder on the right and a spur of mountain running down gradual to the valley. We turn there and start down between the boulder and the mountainside on the left."

"Ya, I know the boulder," Klein said, "but how you gonna see it in a blizzard?"

"We'll find it," McSweeney said, "but we got to go back a ways, I think."

They turned back with reluctance. For a while they could see their tracks and it was a change to be going downhill.

"We must have veered left too soon," McSweeney said. "We'll try it farther on."

The wind was blowing furiously now and carrying a heavy load of snow that it winnowed up into drifts. Sometimes the drifts were waist high, sometimes the mountainside was swept bare. The snowshoes were of no help in this loose and shifting snow. They had to struggle through the drifts as best they could. Three of the men went ahead, breaking the trail, one of them came behind, and Nan and Meggie stumbled between them. Meggie's feet had ceased to pain her. They felt numb and dead, two loads to be lifted and set down, lifted and set down.

At one of the bare-swept spots, McSweeney gave a shout. He had found the trail again. He seemed to know where he was, and he pushed forward with more speed and confidence. But it was almost dark before they reached the boulder. The snow, blowing over the top of it like a white fringe, outlined it in the dusk. The narrow passage between boulder and mountainside was filled with drifts, but the men were jubilant now and ready to meet new difficulties. Meggie saw by their sudden high spirits how desperately lost they had been.

On the other side of the pass the darkness was complete. McSweeney took a lantern out of his pack and they stood around him to protect him from the wind while he lighted it. Now the lantern went before them, a small glimmer in hostile immensity. The wind was less violent here, but drifts were deep. They floundered downward, and at last they were among trees. But the halfway cabin was nowhere visible. They could not find it, and, when they came back on their own tracks, they knew that they were wandering in circles.

McSweeney stopped. "We'll build a fire here," he said. "Two of you men can stay here with the women. One of you can come with me to look for the cabin."

"Build a fire!" Jeff said. "How can you do that? here? in this snow?"

"We've got to try," McSweeney said. "Break branches and pile them up here, dig out some kind of shelter. If you've got anything dry that will burn, bring it out; we'll use it to get the wood started."

Nan helped to collect wood, but Meggie stood waiting in a blind daze. Thoughts drifted through her mind like the drifting snow, but fear, even the instinct for self-preservation, was absorbed in the cotton wool of inertia and weariness.

When the fire was blazing, they melted snow and made coffee, and ate the remnants of the bread and cheese they had brought for lunch. If they could have reached the cabin there would have been a feast of bacon and bannock. But here it was difficult enough to make something warm to drink without trying to cook solid food. The green pine sputtered and crackled, but there was enough pitch in it to burn in spite of the falling snow. As it burned the fire melted down through the drifts, so that walls of snow rose slowly around them. These helped to shut the cruel wind away, but the melting snow continually threatened the fire and soaked their clothing.

McSweeney and Klein took the lantern and went looking for the cabin. Jeff and Taggart had their hands full to keep the fire going and a supply of branches shaken free of snow and piled ready. Meggie and Nan sat in the melting snow, dozing and tending fire. Somewhere below them in the valley they could hear wolves howling.

About midnight the storm ceased. The clouds were drawn back across the sky, as they had been drawn across it in the early afternoon, by an unseen hand. The wind died. It was very cold and still, and in a deep blue sky millions of stars glittered above the treetops. McSweeney and Klein returned, weary and disgusted. They had not found the cabin.

"Snow must have drifted over it," McSweeney said. "Damned if I can find it." As soon as it began to grow light, they made more coffee, and prepared to go on.

"I hope you've got your tree blazes and corner markings high enough to show," McSweeney said. "Your cabins are likely to be covered."

"Maybe we ought to go back," Taggart said, "and try some other time."

"God, no!" Jeff said. "We've made it this far. It's easier to go on now. It's not far now, and we can rest and cook before we start back."

"Maybe you'd ought to ask the women what they want to do," Klein said.

Jeff looked at Meggie. He had scarcely looked at her all night. Sometimes it is easier not to look at the person one loves, if one is plagued by guilt. She looked small and pinched in the cold light. Her feet were stretched out before her as if she disclaimed them.

"Well, Meggie?" Jeff asked.

"If I can go on anywhere," Meggie said, "it better be to the homestead."

8.

As McSweeney had predicted most of the cabins were buried in snow, but the blazes on the trees had been made in winter and they were easy to follow.

Klein and Taggart dropped off at their places, but the others went on beyond Jeff's to Meggie's place. Meggie dared not stop until she got there. Once stopped, she felt she could not start again.

At Meggie's place McSweeney stubbed a toe on the gable of her roof, and so they found the cabin, The two men dug a tunnel down to the door, and there it was, with "Bide a Wee" printed over the door in smiling letters. Meggie looked at the sign without smiling. For a number of miles she had struggled on automatically because there was no alternative except to die alone in the snow. Now that she was here, she was scarcely capable of feeling relief.

Jeff helped her into the cabin, and there was a good supply of dry wood there for starting a fire. Someone had to clear the chimney first, and they dug out one of the windows, so that daylight entered. Soon there was warmth and Nan, who was still chipper, put on the coffeepot. Meggie lay on the bed and Jeff took off her shoes.

"I think they're frozen," Meggie said. "I don't feel them any more. It's like I didn't have any feet."

"Get in a pan of snow," McSweeney said. "She's frosted her feet for sure. We've got to do what we can to bring them back."

"Maybe hot water—" Meggie said.

"Hell, no!" McSweeney said. "We start with snow and try to rub the circulation back into them."

Nan and McSweeney had intended to go on to Nan's place that afternoon, but instead they spent the night at Meggie's. As the cabin grew warm Meggie began to burn with fever. She dozed and started up again and babbled incoherently. Jeff was grateful that Nan had offered to stay.

McSweeney ranged the cabin looking for food, but Meggie had

thriftily carried whatever supplies she had left back to town with her the previous summer.

"You folks got a lot to learn," McSweeney said. "Homesteaders shouldn't never strip their cabins bare of supplies. Even if they don't use things themselves, some poor devil is likely to come by during the winter and save himself from starvation with your extra flour and beans."

"I left some stuff at my place," Nan said, "providing the bears and lumberjacks haven't toted it away."

"The bears, smart souls, have gone to bed," McSweeney said. "But till we see what you've got, we better eat light of what's in our packs. We'll be a day later than we calculated to get back to Cold Spring."

The next morning Meggie was herself again. The shifting dreams of the night before, the dreams of walking on hot coals, of adding long and baffling sums of figures in the stuffy office of the lumberyard, of sitting with Bundy Jones on a log in a forest of endless trees, of killing snakes that writhed about her ankles, of having knives and needles thrust into her feet, her feet, her feet—the dreams had mercifully gone.

She sat up on the side of her bunk and smiled wanly at them.

"Top of the morning to you, darling," Nan said. "Will you have a thick beefsteak or a couple of pork chops for breakfast?"

But there was only oatmeal porridge and that exceedingly thin, and, at McSweeney's suggestion, Nan had made the coffee weak.

It was clear and cold and Nan and McSweeney started early. "We'll try to be back by night," McSweeney said, "and get started back to Cold Spring early tomorrow morning."

"And if anybody asks you did I spend the night at my homestead," Nan said, "you'd better all swear that I did."

"Oh, Nan, we will!" Meggie said.

After they had gone, Meggie tried to put on her boots.

"Jeff, I can't," she said. "My feet are swollen too much. Oh, Jeff, how can I walk back tomorrow? I can hardly bear my weight, and I can't get my shoes on."

Jeff looked at her anxiously, but he did not know what to say to her. Finally he said, "You'll be all right by tomorrow. You'll have to be. Keep your feet up as much as you can. You'll be all right. I'll have to go back and see my place today. I'll be here again in a few hours."

Meggie lay in her bunk in the silent cabin with her feet propped up on a box. She read Myrtle Reed's *Lavender and Old Lace* and *The Trail of the Lonesome Pine* to keep her mind off the situation. They were not as interesting as she remembered them. When the fire burned low, she hobbled to replenish it. It was easy to skip lunch because she was not very hungry.

Sometimes she slept, and when she awakened she saw with pleasure the rough-hewn walls, the warm stove, the homemade cupboards and bookshelf. She saw with pride that the cabin was sturdy and tight. The mud chinking which she had helped to put in last summer was firm against drafts. She thought about Spike and Rudy with gratitude and a kind of disillusioned affection. They had built well, and, in a way which was unfamiliar to her, they had meant well. She saw again that somehow it was she who had been at fault in her dealings with them. Yes, surely, the fault had been hers.

Before dark the other three returned. Jeff brought a little flour that Lorena had left in the bottom of a can. Nan had found a small supply of flour and dry beans—not as much as she remembered. She put the beans to soak in melted snow water. "Maybe we can have them ready to eat for breakfast before we hit the trail out of here," she said cheerfully.

"I don't know if I can go tomorrow," Meggie said, "I can't get on my boots."

They stood looking at her, and no one said anything. At last Nan stirred and said: "If we could make a little sled or something, maybe we could pull her."

"Over the mountain?" snorted McSweeney. "And just suppose we could, she'd freeze harder than she froze in them boots, if she was to sit still on a sled all day."

"She'll be all right by tomorrow," Jeff said. He had a feeling that saying made it so, and at least one avoided a little longer the painful necessity of facing reality.

But by the following morning the reality had to be faced. Meggie could not possibly undertake the trip back in her present condition. Klein and Taggart came up to the cabin to see why the others had not come by for them on the return trip.

"God! don't you know we ain't got enough food to monkey around here sittin' by the fire? Why ain't we on the trail?"

"There's only one thing to do," McSweeney said. "We leave her alone here with all the food we can spare, and we go in to Cold Spring for supplies. Jeff and I'll come back out as fast as we can with food, and by that time she'll be ready to travel."

"I'll stay with her," said Nan.

McSweeney looked at them. "No," he said, "we can spare one person enough food for four, five days or a week, but not two. Now before we get out of here, we've got to rustle enough wood to keep her stove going. We've got to do that now, and fast. If we make it up to the halfway cabin before dark, I think we'll find it, now that the weather's cleared."

"There's a good big woodpile right behind the cabin," Meggie said, "if you can dig down to it."

She saw them carrying in the armloads of snowy wood with a sinking heart.

"Try your shoes again, honey," Nan urged. Meggie tried, but, even if a larger pair of boots had been forthcoming, Meggie knew that her feet were still too swollen and painful to bear walking on.

"It isn't right to leave her here," Nan said to Jeff.

"I know," Jeff said. "But what can we do? You heard McSweeney. When we're on the trail, he's the boss."

"I'll be fine," Meggie said. "I really will. Only come back. Don't, for Heaven's sake, forget about me."

"There's only one other possibility," McSweeney said, "Eye MacGillicuddy and Charlie Duporte are both in here somewhere. We might try to locate one of them. But the chances are they won't have much to eat either, and I honestly think our best chance is to head back to town."

"It's all right," Meggie said. "Go on, get started, so you'll find the cabin before dark. I'll be all right. Go on."

It was only the silence that bothered Meggie after they left. The summer silence had been full of bird song and insect voices in the grass and the continual sighing and whispering of the pines. If there were any sound in the forest outside now, it was filtered away by the snow and the heavy log walls of the cabin. She heard each rustle of the fire in the stove and each charred twig that fell. She had kept up a brave show of courage before they left, but, after they were gone, her courage dwindled.

One thing, intended as a reassurance, kept troubling her. Jeff had kissed her goodbye. Much as they loved one another, he hadn't touched or kissed her for years. But before they left he had kissed her. It had seemed sweet to her for the first few hours of silence. Jeff had kissed her! But then the silence was so deep, it was almost as if she were already in her grave, and she began to wonder: Was it, in fact, goodbye? Was it her final contact with humanity?

She hobbled up at that, replenished the fire, got a bucket of snow from the white wall outside the door and put it on the stove to melt.

"Anyway I won't die of thirst," she said aloud. The sound of her voice frightened her. I mustn't start talking to myself, she thought. Crazy people do that.

She found the tattered copies of *The Wide World Magazine* that Rudy had left for her, and she went through them slowly, reading the sensational adventures with thoroughness and attention. People were always in hazardous positions in these stories. Her situation was nothing compared to the situation of the mountaineer marooned on a crag in the Himalayas or to that of the hunter lost in the steaming jungle in the Belgian Congo. And they had lived to tell their tales. Or had these cheap adventures been dreamed up by hack writers in boardinghouse bedrooms? At any rate she derived little comfort from these stories.

Suddenly she wished she had a Bible. It was really fantastic that she hadn't thought to bring one. The Bible and Shakespeare, weren't those the two books people chose to take with them to the desert island? That's what she had told Rudy. And what had she brought here? *Lavender and Old Lace* and *The Trail of the Lonesome Pine!*

Lying in her bunk in the quiet night, she tried to recall passages from the Bible, but she found that she really knew very little, word for word. She knew the Lord's Prayer and the Twenty-third Psalm and the Ten Commandments and the Golden Rule. After those, all she could remember was *Jesus wept*. She remembered that, because someone had once told her it was the shortest sentence in the Bible. But surely there were many others elsewhere just as short. You could say a great deal in two words: *I came. I went. I froze my feet.* No, that was four words—see how many two word sentences there were. *I slept. I ate. I starved. I died.* And there was another —it consisted of a single word: *Alone.*

She thought, in a panic, how the others might be lost on the mountain going back, and, if they died, the knowledge of her plight would die with them. But they would be together. She was all alone.

She thought that if they did arrive at Cold Spring safely, they might feel it beyond their strength to return for her; or storms might intervene and their return would be delayed until it was too late. At this point she went back to the Twenty-third Psalm and the Lord's Prayer. And then it was time to stoke the fire again, and dole herself a small amount of food.

Several times during the night Meggie wound and set her alarm clock, so that the fire would not go out while she slept. She dreaded the awful ringing of the alarm in the silent cabin; yet she dreaded more awakening to find the cabin cold and the fire completely dead. She had matches, in case the fire did go out, but somehow to keep the fire burning seemed to her essential. The fire symbolized continuity, it was life and hope.

Last summer's calendar hung on the wall above the bookshelf, and she tore off the pages from September through December. The last page contained a miniature calendar of the new year. Meggie was grateful for this. What if time had ended here last December? Now she checked off the days in February as they passed, so that she would know where she was in time and how long the ordeal lasted.

The time went slowly. The clock ticked the minutes. The hours were gradually amassed and noted and left behind. Evening came and she wound the clock and made a check mark on the calendar. The small amount of food dwindled.

Three days went by. Meggie began to think: Tomorrow, if everything goes perfectly and there are no delays, tomorrow night they might come. I won't expect them, but it is barely possible.

The pain and the swelling were receding in her feet. She could not yet put on her shoes, but in her woolen socks she walked up and down the cabin, testing her endurance. She wondered, if they failed to come, could she find her way back alone?

But why did she keep thinking that they might not return? Why had she lost the old faith that everything would come out all right? She could remember not long ago, when life had been handed to her on a silver platter, and she had expected the best. Now, suddenly, she expected nothing and trusted no one but herself. It was a lonely feeling, yet there was something good in it, a certain robustness which she had never known before. If she could get rid of fear— She did not want to die yet—not with this new flavor of self-reliance sweet on her lips.

She had eaten so sparingly that she was possibly a trifle light-headed on the third night. She wound the clock but forgot to set the alarm. She kept thinking about her life, how futile and unplanned it had been thus far. Now that she might be on the point of losing it, it seemed a shame that it had floated rudderless so long. She thought of the many things to see, to taste, to smell, to hear, to touch. She felt that she had been walking in a vacuum all this time, in a bubble of self that excluded the precious world beyond. It was odd to become aware of the world and all its limitless, sensuous beauty for the first time here in a snow-buried cabin where the only sounds were ticking clock and rustling fire, and the supply of food almost gone. If I live through this, I will notice everything, she vowed. I will see and hear and feel. I will try to understand.

She slept a long time, and when she awoke the cabin was cold. Something had startled her, some alien sound or presence. It was not the clock alarm, or any of the things she was accustomed to in the cabin. There was some strangeness in the air. Was it the cold? She realized that she had let the fire go out. Frightened, she groped for the candle and matches. Her hand was half extended toward the shelf beside her bed, when there came a sound that she had never heard before. It was a terrible cry, a shriek, almost a woman's voice screaming in extremity. It seemed to Meggie that the cry was in the cabin with her. It was loud and close, full of a wild, suspenseful grieving.

Meggie drew back her hand and lay tense and listening. Horror surged over her in waves of hot and cold and left her trembling and sweating. There was a moment of silence that pulsed and beat with waiting, and then far up the valley came an answering cry.

Through a timeless period Meggie lay still and waited. Then

the near voice cried again. But now it was not quite so close; for the first time she was certain that it was outside and not in the cabin with her. She drew an easier breath, but still she lay trembling.

It was as if an angel of death had come for her, and at the moment when he screamed his triumph, some other tortured angel had called him away. Come, come, give her another day. Let her suffer as we have suffered. Give her another day.

When the silence had grown heavy and peaceful with passing time, Meggie got up and lit the stub of candle. She split kindling and made a new fire. The cabin seemed beautiful to her, thick-walled and secure. She took the last coffee she had and made herself a potful. She drank a cup of it slowly, holding her hands around the cup to get all the warmth and comfort it had to give. She would keep the rest for later in the day, and she would re-use the grounds until no more flavor came out of them. She was determined to live.

When it grew light, she opened the door and looked out. A scattering of new snow had fallen in the night, and on it were fresh tracks. They were like the tracks of a cat, only very large. They had come to the door and to the window. In her new awareness Meggie could fancy that it was the sniffing at her door and window that had awakened her. She thought, Dear God, I heard a cougar cry. I heard its mate answer it. But they were not alone. There were two of them.

9.

When Meggie got back to town, she kept telling Lorena that she had been reborn. Lorena was horrified by the whole experience that they had undergone. She made them tell it over and over: how they were lost in the snowstorm, how Meggie froze her feet and stayed alone in the cabin, how it was seven days before Jeff and the packer could get back to her through the unseasonable storms, how they had all been hungry and exhausted before they were finally safe in Cold Spring. She made Meggie describe the yell of the cougar and how it had filled her with terror in the lonely night.

Lorena seemed to get a kind of morbid pleasure out of hearing these details. It almost seemed that her vicarious experience was more terrible than their actual experience had been.

"What do you mean 'reborn'?" she demanded irritably. "How could an awful experience like that do anything but terrify you?"

Meggie did not know. It was a thing she could not explain to Lorena, if Lorena would not see it for herself. Words could not describe the thin, clear sense of self-realization which had come to her in the hungry days when she lived with herself alone and faced death as a familiar possibility. She knew it was useless, yet some compulsion made her go around telling everyone that she had been reborn. Her friends in Cold Spring smiled to her face and chuckled behind her back. Poor little Meggie, she had had an awful experience. But she had come out of it unchanged. She was, indeed, a card!

Only Nan O'Rourke really believed her, and that was because Nan, too, had been lost on the mountain in the snow, and could go on to imagine what might happen to a woman's mind in a solitary cabin buried in drifting snow.

"I was afraid your hair would be white when we saw you again, Meg," she said. "I heard of a woman once whose hair turned white overnight. What happened to her? My gosh, I don't remember. I only remember that her hair turned white."

"Nothing changed my looks," Meggie said, "but what happened to me happened inside. I can't tell it. It's something I feel—in here," she added, putting her hand on her breast with the direct and unaffected gesture of a child.

VI

OLLIE

1.

In spite of her winter experience, Meggie was eager to go back to the homestead. She found herself planning ahead and collecting the things she would need for a summer in the woods. There was no more caviar and tinned meat. She knew what she needed for subsistence, and she wanted to keep it simple, simple but adequate—never again to be afraid of hunger. She was determined to have a better garden this year, and she asked all the gardeners she knew how to make the most of the short, intense growing season, what to do about too much shade, how to get rid of roots and stumps. The answers she got were varied and contradictory. She sorted them over in her mind, using her own judgment as well as she could. But she thought hopefully, I'll ask Bundy Jones, when I see him, and he will know. To think of Bundy Jones gave her a lift of pleasure.

She was obliged to remind herself (as she always did in thinking of men they both knew) that he preferred Lorena, otherwise her anticipation might have gone out of bounds. She often grew tired of playing second fiddle to Lorena, but there seemed no help for it. Perhaps after Lorena's baby came—

Lorena's peaceful winter was followed by a restless spring. Her interest in her role as creator of a new life began to wane when she looked in the long mirror. At first the unexpected excitement of pregnancy had given her richer coloring, brighter eyes, a more tranquil spirit. But now her beautiful body was distorted and heavy; her face lost color and her eyes luster. She did not like the sudden sensation of an alien creature, however small and defenseless, moving and turning in her womb. She began to think again of all the material goods that she wanted of life, and undoubtedly the baby would be another obstacle to her getting them. Any fool can have a baby, she thought, the ugliest, the most stupid female can produce a kid. I'll be just like all the rest of the women—no richer, no more beautiful. She was angry that she had allowed this thing to happen to her. Her mind closed against those fleet, ecstatic memories which had sometimes warmed her during the winter. Now they seemed only part of a great human folly. I was going to be so smart, she thought, and now look at me!

The warm weather came very early that year. The streams were full of mountain snows in April, and by the end of May it seemed perfectly feasible to return to the homesteads.

"The earlier we go, the better it will look," Jeff said. "Meg and I will go now, put in gardens, clean the places up, and be back in town with you before July."

July was the time Lorena had set for her confinement. The doctor had suggested June, but Lorena had said positively, "No, it couldn't be June." They all felt that Lorena should know.

Suddenly Lorena wanted to go with them. She was in a panic at the thought of being left alone in town. Looking as she did, what would she do with herself? What *could* she do in her present state? Lie on a chaise longue? Fan herself in the unseasonable heat? Die of boredom among solicitous old neighbor women?

"I'll go with you," Lorena said. "Jeff, let me go with you."

Jeff was touched. He felt very tender toward Lorena now, but he also felt strong with a new masculinity and responsibility.

"No, darling," he said, "you couldn't make that trip. We wouldn't let you now."

"If Meggie can face it again after the time she had last winter, I ought to be able to do it. We need this homestead more than ever."

"But you hated it so last summer," Jeff said.

"I hate it here," Lorena answered, "looking the way I do. I'm better hidden in the woods."

"Nonsense," Jeff said. He did not pretend to understand Lorena. The best he had ever done was to try to placate her and make her happy.

"I'm healthy," Lorena continued. "I'm not the first female who's ever had a baby."

But the prospect of being a father gave Jeff a new reservoir of determination, even toward Lorena.

"No," he said. "You stay in town. I'll be back before July. That's final, darling."

Lorena made a little face. She was not really certain that she wanted to go into the woods rather than relax in the comfort of town; yet she hated to see anyone going anywhere when she was left behind. It gave her a terribly blank feeling of unfulfillment. She wanted her own way, and she hated to be balked and thwarted. Most of all she hated to have to obey Jeff.

"My Lord! Our grandmothers had babies in the wilderness!" she said.

Still there was nothing to do at the moment but pretend conformity. *After they are gone,* she said to herself, *I'll do exactly as I please about everything.*

2.

To their surprise Meggie and Nan found themselves celebrities in Cold Spring.

"You're the gals got friz up on the mountain, ain't you? S'prised you come back after that. Don't they learn you nothin' in town?" But in spite of the joshing, there was a note of admiration and approval in the voices.

Mrs. Pulver even gave a coffee party in their honor to which came Mrs. McSweeney and Madame Pontarlier. It was something rare to see Madame Pontarlier leave her salon and move, full-breasted and majestic in her white dress, like a sailing ship in a breeze, across the grassy meadow between the saloon and the hotel.

She patted Meggie's hand.

"You have grown, my little one," she said approvingly.

"My husband never thought you'd come again another year," the packer's wife said. "He was plumb taken back to hear you was in town."

"Well," Meggie said, "*I* never thought about *not* coming back."

"Maybe we should of," said Nan, "but we're not as bright as we might be."

One topic of conversation had the Cold Spring tongues wagging. News had come from Washington that there was to be a new ranger. It had come in a letter to Eye MacGillicuddy, and he had thrown the letter on the hotel table in disgust and let everyone who could read it. He was asked to be a deputy and help the new ranger get started with his duties. A ranger's cabin was to be built and lookout posts established.

"Lookouts?" Eye cried. "I got my lookouts. I never had no need of a cabin. Jessie an' me we got our tent, we can move quick."

"You ain't been hard enough on the homesteaders, Eye," Sam Carlson said. "Likely that's what they want in Washington, they want some fella they've trained up smart to crack the whip on the folks with timber claims."

"Well, you ain't through yet, Eye," someone else said. "They giving you this deputy job."

"That's a lean bone to an ol' dog," Eye said. "They couldna weel do less."

The next morning he fitted himself out with supplies and packed his horse. He took Jessie up behind his saddle and started for the woods.

"Ain't you going to wait for the new ranger, Eye?" they called. "Ain't you going to be his deputy?"

"Let him whistle for a deputy," Eye said. "If airy body doesna come, let him whistle again. Let him howl like a wolf, and happen the wolves will come and give him a hand. Let the new ranger whistle."

By the time the Carneys and Nan O'Rourke arrived, the story had become a saga. Everyone told it with modifications and embellishments. The townspeople were all agog to see the new ranger who had not yet put in his appearance.

"The poor old coot," Nan said. "Gee whiz! I'm sorry for the poor old coot." She referred to the former ranger, not the new one.

Jeff was concerned. "We'll have to watch out for this new man. Eye was a reasonable fellow, but one of these smart chaps from Washington—you can't tell what they're up to."

"Well, we need better fire protection," Mrs. Pulver said. "Eye can't do everything alone. It's high time, liking Eye as well as I do and all, still it's high time that we had a change."

This year the trip into the homestead was easy and smiling all the way. Riding along a dry, well broken trail behind Nan O'Rourke, Meggie could not help feeling that all her troubles were over. Although it was earlier in the season than their first trip last year, the river was easy to ford without swimming the horses, and the only snow lay in the high northern creases of the mountain where the sun did not penetrate. The air was glorious.

On the mountain McSweeney pointed out the spot where they had missed the trail in the snowstorm and wandered farther up the mountain instead of into the pass. The spot was bland and peaceful now in heavy sunshine. Later they saw the charred remains of the fire they had built. It was scarcely a hundred feet from the halfway cabin which they had been unable to find.

"This is an ornery country in winter," McSweeney said, "especially for ladies." But he was more friendly to the two women on this trip. Perhaps his wife had said a good word for them, perhaps it was only because Miss Carney had bounced back from her grueling experience with such remarkable aplomb. Here she was, beaming happily at everything, apparently as childlike and gullible as ever. Either she was a fool or a brave woman, he did not know which, but he began to suspect that she must have a vein of toughness somewhere in her make-up.

Meggie saw her cabin with delight. She unpacked her food supply and put everything neatly into cans and on shelves. She wound her clock and hung a new calendar over the old one that had marked the dreadful February days. On her bookshelf, she put her mother's Bible and a copy of Shakespeare. She did not know if she would find much time to read them, but having them there seemed to guarantee her desert island against further disaster. She had a dictionary, too, and a copy of Palgrave's *Golden Treasury*. I really thought about it this time, she told herself proudly, I'm starting to plan my life a little bit.

The woods were full of trilliums and the uncurling fiddleheads of ferns. The birds were bubbling over with courting music, and the sun shone.

Meggie dug her garden until she was tired, and then she rested

by burning brush. Many stumps of the trees which had furnished
the logs for her cabin walls still stood in the way of her gardening.
She built her brush fires around them; but they were stubborn
and hard to destroy. When she finally got a stump to burn, it
smoldered for many days, going underground to follow the course
of the roots. Meggie remembered Bundy Jones's warning about fire,
and she was as careful as she could be.

Charlie Duporte came by to see her a day or two after her
arrival, and she asked him about Bundy Jones.

"I ain't seen him," Charlie said, "but I hear he's coming back.
Dat feller comes from government, I t'ink. You better look out what
you say to him. Maybe he yap on you to old man Pinchot."

"Oh, I don't think so," Meggie said. "He's really very nice."
Still she had sometimes wondered about this herself.

She found that she was very glad to see Charlie. His smile was
so gay and infectious. He had purchased a mail-order guitar over the
winter, and he could play and sing a whole evening away without
ever repeating a song. The homesteaders liked to see him come by
with his guitar sticking out of the pack on his back. It was well
worth a few meals of their precious food to have Charlie lighten the
lonely evenings with his songs.

Somehow when he was at Meggie's the talk was always of
Lorena. At first Meggie made up various excuses to explain why
Lorena had not come with them, because to speak of a woman's
pregnancy to a man outside the family seemed to her quite indelicate.
Still frankness was in her nature, and they were all so proud that
Jeff and Lorena would soon be parents, she herself an aunt, that
presently the truth came out.

Charlie looked at her oddly, and she thought that really she
should remember that she had been reared a lady even if she was
now acquiring the manners of a homesteader.

"I shouldn't be so outspoken, I guess," she said, blushing.
"Still we've all thought a baby would be wonderful for them. And,
after a baby comes, I've noticed, no one is ever embarrassed to speak
of it. It's only beforehand that there's all the mystery and hush-
hush."

Charlie said, "And Missus Carney's well? She gets along all
right?"

"Oh, yes," Meggie said. "She was determined to come with us, only Jeff wouldn't let her. He'll go back in town, of course, before it happens."

Charlie began to strum his guitar. He sang something softly in French, and then he laughed. The odd look was gone.

3.

Jeff worked furiously on his homestead, in a way that he had never worked before. He did not enjoy work which grimed his hands and broke his nails, and he saw no future in it except to pull the wool over the eyes of some government inspector who might be asked to decide whether this was a home or a speculation. He had never been very happy, and he had no inkling of the fact that unhappiness is often inherent in deceit. The positive satisfactions of integrity were not as clear to him as the more illusory satisfaction of money and superficial success. So he worked silently and grimly, and, putting in a garden, he experienced no lift of anticipation for the harvest, nor relished the sensation of clear air and sunshine on his back. He had no feeling of accomplishment or pride, only an anxiety to be done and get back to Lorena.

Charlie came on from Meggie's place, rested his packsack and his guitar against the side of Jeff's cabin, and went to work beside him.

"I'm short of money, Charlie," Jeff said. "I can't pay you anything this year."

"By gar, don't speak of money," Charlie said. He laughed richly and warmly and spat with satisfaction on the earth he had turned. "I work all spring on my place. Ever't'ing grows like crazy up dere. I ain't got nothing left to do now, only see my friends. I work here for the fun of it."

Charlie could get through twice the amount of work that Jeff could do in a day. He had been cutting and clearing all winter, digging and planting all spring. He was used to hard work and seemed to enjoy it. Jeff, painfully sunburned and lame in all his muscles, watched with a combination of relief and envy as Charlie's tough brown arms dug into the reluctant soil. Roots and stumps that seemed to Jeff impossible to dislodge alone, came out of the earth with comparative ease when Charlie's back was in it.

"Well, I'll tell you, Charlie," Jeff said. "When I clean up a fortune on this white pine, I'll pay you back then."

Charlie grinned. "We all be rich then, Jeff," he said. "You don't owe me not'ing."

All of the irritation, which Jeff felt with Charlie when Lorena was around, vanished. Charlie was a good cook and kept a neat cabin. For a couple of weeks they were like brothers, and Jeff saw the work dissolve before their combined attack. He would get back to town and Lorena much sooner than he had dared to hope. He had his good friend Charlie Duporte to thank for this.

It was a very good growing season. Even under the heavy shadow of the forest, the hot sun filtered and glowed. In the clearings it beat down intensively, and the homesteaders often had to carry buckets of water from stream and spring to refresh their thirsty plants. Even the nights were hot and dry, which was unusual here at any time, and particularly so in May and June.

"Bet it's hot in town," Jeff said. "Poor Lorena!" He thought of her constantly with great tenderness. He was sorry that he had had to forbid her coming with him. He knew how she hated the physical discomfort of her condition, and he knew her loneliness. She had never had the knack of making women friends. She was too far above them both in beauty and intelligence, he thought. Even with Meggie, there had always seemed some sort of barrier to complete understanding, and Meg was such a simple little soul, too.

When he was finally on the trail for Cold Spring, leaving Charlie behind him to keep the place going, Jeff felt triumphant and as nearly elated as he ever allowed himself to become.

Cold Spring was unusually active and alive this year. There had been several minor forest fires in the region and small work crews had been brought in to get them under control. The Clearwater Association which had been formed by the lumber companies, aided by contributions of individual homesteaders, had done a certain amount of fire fighting in the past. Now, with the new ranger in control, the government was taking a more active part in the policing of the forest than it had ever done under Eye MacGillicuddy. The new ranger seemed eager to work with the lumber interests where it was a question of saving timber. How much he would oppose them in other matters was anybody's guess.

"You want my opinion," Sam Carlson said, "this here ranger is more to spy on homesteaders than to look for fires. We always got fires here in summer. Sure, they started earlier this year, but what the hell? We got so much timber in here, a few patches catch fire, burn a spell, and go out, what difference does it make?"

"It makes a lot of difference," Mrs. Pulver said, "as you well know. I'm thankful we got a smart new ranger in charge. He's bringing in a nice bit of business too." She surveyed her second table with satisfaction. Fire was bad, but fire crews were good. Her kitchen hummed with activity.

Matt Hinson, the new ranger, did not look like a tenderfoot. He was as hard-bitten and stringy, in his way, as Eye MacGillicuddy, and a lot more energetic. He was building a ranger station and lookout on one of the mountains, and he came and went with pack trains of material. He had his own pack mules and did not do much business with McSweeney. But in other ways he brought business to the town. The storekeeper, the blacksmith, the saloons, along with Mrs. Pulver, felt the effects of the men and activity he brought along with him.

As for Eye MacGillicuddy, no one had seen him since the change had been announced. He seemed to have disappeared in the forest. But that was not unusual. He was often gone for weeks at a time, whether on government business or business of his own, no one knew or cared. Hinson had never made a point of asking for him, and was doubtless relieved on the whole to find that he did not have the old man on his hands as hindrance or reproach.

Before the stage for Bolster left town, Jeff met Bundy Jones on the street. Bundy had come in the day before, and was stocking up with supplies. The two men stopped to shake hands.

"Well, so you're back again, Bundy?" Jeff said. "I figured you'd have all the mosses and lichens you could carry off in your little box last summer."

"You'd be surprised," Bundy said, "how many there are. I'm trying to get them all. It's never been done in this region before."

"You're looking fit."

"I had a good winter. And you? How's the homestead going?"

"Fine," Jeff said, "I've got a good garden started. Now I'm going in town for a day or two to see Lorena."

"She isn't with you?" Bundy said. "She didn't come?"

"She'll come later in the summer, I expect," Jeff said. "Her health—important matters, they're keeping her in Opportunity for the first part. I'll give her your regards, shall I?"

"Yes, do," Bundy said. His fair skin colored up like a boy's. "Yes, give her my regards."

All of his winter's self-discovery, indecision and emotion stirred through Bundy's blood. He said to himself with a mixture of relief and despair, she isn't here. She didn't come. If he asked himself what could be the matter with her health, his habitual reticence kept him from asking Jeff. Jeff himself looked unusually fit to Bundy. He seemed to have more purpose and confidence. He was going home with eagerness to see his wife.

Bundy watched him board the stage with envious speculation. I don't know very much about them—not even about Lorena, Bundy thought. I've let this idea carry me away. I've got to forget the whole thing. If I can.

4.

When Lorena was on the train, she felt happy. Well, I'm going someplace, she said to herself. I'm moving. I'm not bored. The thought of the pack-horse trip over the mountain that lay ahead of her—nothing dismayed her. I'd rather be going to New York or Chicago in a Pullman car, but, if I can't do that, oh Lord, at least I'm moving! For the moment I'm not bored.

Everyone was kind to her in the station, on the train, and when she changed to the stage at Bolster. Yet she was irked to see that the kindness emanated from sympathy with her condition rather than from gallantry. Old ladies who would have looked down their noses at her a few months before were solicitous for her. Fatherly men were helpful to her; the more dashing young men gave her a wide berth.

Well, it will soon be over, Lorena thought. I'll work hard to get my figure back and be good looking once again. I've heard people say having a baby ripens a woman, makes her more beautiful, more mature. But I must be careful never to let it happen again.

They were surprised to see her in Cold Spring. Even Mrs. Pulver dropped her air of nonchalance.

"Why, my dear, your husband has just gone into town after you. Didn't you know he was coming? It couldn't have been more than yesterday he left."

"Jeff? Gone into town?" Lorena burst out laughing. "What a farce!" she said. "*I* didn't let him know I was coming. *He* didn't let me know."

Somehow her heart was lightened by the thought that Jeff would not be there to meet her. He would not be standing in the cabin door looking at her with reproach and adoration, with possessiveness and pride and humility and frustration, all mingled and warring on his face, and reproach finally gaining the upper hand. "Lorena!" he might have said, "you have endangered the life of our child!" It was true, she thought, that the unborn child was becoming even more important to him than she was. Well, when it came, he could have it then. It could be his, entirely, and for that she would ask back her own life, and have it to herself again without his ineffectual tyranny. Let him fret and worry and grumble over the child as much as he liked; she would be free.

She also had an impish child's delight in tormenting Jeff. When he reached Opportunity and found her gone, he would rush in a frenzy about the neighborhood asking for news of her. He might even suspect that she had left him, gone away with Ralph, perhaps, or a tall, dark stranger. When the woman next door, where she had left the key, told him that Lorena had gone to the homestead, he would rush back, sweating and fretting all the way. He wouldn't have a night's rest, but arrive breathless and anguished at the homestead, and then Lorena saw herself standing calmly in the doorway smiling at him. "Well, what's all the fuss about? Was it so strange? I came to join you. I'm healthy. It's all very simple, and look how you've worked yourself up for nothing."

Lorena went to McSweeney to hire horses for the trail, but McSweeney was stubborn.

"You better wait at the hotel, Mis' Carney, until your husband gets back. There's no pack train spoke for right now. I wouldn't like to make a special trip in for one lady."

"You mean you don't want to be responsible for me, isn't that it?" Lorena said. She gave him her most enchanting smile, but McSweeney was not a susceptible man. He was a devoted husband and a believer that wives should stay at home.

"Put it bluntly, ya!" McSweeney said.

"Then I'll hire a couple of horses and go alone," Lorena said, still smiling sweetly at him, although her nerves were beginning to twitch. "You wouldn't refuse to rent me a couple of horses, would you?"

"Your husband's got his own two horses pastured out behind the hotel. I don't usually let mine out without I go along and take a train," McSweeney said stubbornly.

Lorena considered. It might be even more of a joke on Jeff to take his horses, and let *him* make the negotiations with McSweeney when he arrived. She was getting a certain malicious pleasure out of all this, and she did not intend to sit around the hotel waiting for Jeff while everybody looked at her and talked her over, the men joking about her in the saloon, the women clacking about her in the Pontarlier's parlor. She refused to be coddled by Mrs. Pulver. The thing now was to find someone who was willing to help her with Jeff's horses—even if she had to ride one horse alone and leave the things she had brought with her to be packed in later.

As Lorena stood in a quandary, she saw Bundy Jones coming up the Cold Spring street. She saw his sturdy innocence, fresh as the summer dew, and even a block away it had a great attraction for her. She stood and waited for him with her slow, intimate smile. She saw how he started at the sight of her and reddened. She saw, too, that her condition was a shock and an embarrassment to him. But she held out her hands to him, and said, "Bundy, will you help me?" She knew in advance that he would.

5.

They rode slowly on the dusty trails in a close companionship and trust. Once Bundy had accepted Lorena's condition, he was filled with solicitude and eagerness to help her. Somehow it made everything easier for him. It put her beyond his reach, wrote finis to any wild hopes he may have entertained. Yet it gave him the happiness of being near her, of cherishing her without the entanglement of his own inexpert emotions. Sometimes he trembled with happiness at being near her, but, feeling a new maturity of renunciation and moral strength, he no longer blushed like a school-boy when she looked at him. The ache was pleasurable; the suffering a kind of delight.

Lorena, too, rode the trail in unaccustomed peace. She was often in physical discomfort, but her mind was at rest. She did not look backward or forward. The one thought that enveloped her in peace was that Bundy had taken charge of her and would do the best he could for her without asking anything in return. She could not remember that anyone had ever given her love without asking a return. She was distrustful of renunciation, yet at the moment she accepted it with gratitude.

Bundy brought her water from the springs they passed. He lifted her down from the horse at noon and spread a blanket for her to lie on while he prepared her lunch. He brought one of the saddles for her to use as a pillow. Lorena watched him curiously, still caught in an abeyance of malice and boredom and frustration.

"I feel so peaceful," she said. "You are taking better care of me than the packer would, or Jeff either. Jeff fusses and fumes and never gets anything done. In the end I fuss and fume, too, and take pleasure in defeating him. What makes me so peaceful with you, Bundy?"

He smiled at her over the smoke of the campfire, wanting to say, "Because I love you," but refraining for fear the words would make an unnecessary complication in the open sunshine of the moment. It was always easier for Bundy to be silent than to speak. So he was silent now.

After lunch Lorena slept, her head resting against the saddle. When she awoke, feeling cool and refreshed, she found that Bundy had resaddled his own horses, and got everything ready for departure. He rested on the other side of the dead fire watching her and waiting for her.

She sat up hastily and pushed at her hair. For a moment she was annoyed that he had seen her sleeping, abandoned to the ugliness of her condition, a pregnant woman lying awkwardly on the ground.

"Don't look at me," she cried.

"I'm sorry," Bundy said. "I've thought of you all winter

and seen your face in my mind. I couldn't help watching you, now that you're here."

Lorena was mollified. She drew a long breath.

"I think you're sentimental, Bundy."

"The proper phrase is 'a sentimental fool,' isn't it?" Bundy said.

"A certain kind of fool appeals to me very much," Lorena said. "I'm one myself, but not sentimental. No, something about my life has made me a hard fool. You know that, don't you, Bundy? I'm hard and mercenary."

"I don't believe it," Bundy said.

"I s'pose a sentimental fool wouldn't," Lorena said. "But it's so. I don't exactly know why, but it's so. Well, I can go on now. Saddle my horse and help me on, will you, Bundy?"

They rode along the trail in silence for a time, Bundy's dog and the pack horses following. But out of the peaceful vacuum of her mind, the question she had raised drew restless thoughts of a past she had tried to suppress.

"I don't know why I'm hard and mercenary," Lorena repeated, "unless it's that I have a memory of hard and mercenary people. I have a long memory of trouble that I can't live down."

"A memory of trouble?" Bundy echoed.

"Yes, a memory of trouble that goes way back in my childhood so far—so far I can't tell at all how old I was. But I can still hear people crying shame and blame, and I can feel loss and sorrow and something threatening hanging over me. And I see myself a little child standing alone in the midst of troubles I can't understand, alone and friendless and perhaps doomed. You'll laugh at me, but it's a mental picture that somehow colors my life. It sets the tone."

"This is stupid," Bundy said seriously. "Surely you can set the tone of your life to suit yourself. A childhood memory shouldn't daunt you. Throw it out, blot it out, make up your mind to forget it."

"No," she said, "because it has some value for me. It has some meaning that—someday, maybe—I'll understand. I don't want to throw it out. I can't. It's too much a part of me now."

They rode in silence, but Lorena felt his sympathy like something tangible, and she was content to have it so.

At the halfway cabin, Bundy surrounded her with care, and Lorena accepted whatever he offered with simple gratitude. It was a kind of idyl, like something she had read in a romance. She thought it unnecessary for him to leave the cabin to her and sleep outside under the trees, but it was all part of the strange, peaceful dream in which they were moving. Life would begin again with violence and annoyance, with emotion and frustration, when she had reached the homestead. But now in the high altitude on the side of the mountain, she still felt suspended in a kind of peaceful innocence that gave her a glimmer of what her childhood might have been under better circumstances.

When Bundy came in the cabin in the morning to cook her breakfast, he said: "How beautiful you are, Lorena."

"No! No!" Lorena said. "Not now. Please don't say so now."

"Yes, even now," Bundy said. "I've never seen anyone more beautiful." Lorena was coiling her dark hair again, and he remembered the other time when he had first seen her do it.

"You don't have a pocket mirror, do you, Bundy?"

"No," he said laughing. "I shave by feel, by guess or by gosh, as the saying goes."

"Bundy," Lorena said, "you know I might have loved you last summer. But you were too slow. I've done things quickly all my life. I couldn't wait for you."

"You kissed me last summer," Bundy said. "Yes, I was slow. I wasn't sure until in the winter a girl told me I was in love. I was trying to fall in love with her, but she knew— She said 'You've got someone out West.' At first I denied it. I said, 'No, of course not.' But then finally I understood, and I knew it was you."

"Maybe after this business of mine is over, Bundy— There ought to be a future for everything, and you're the kind of man I need, I think. You know I could have had anybody—anybody, Bundy, if I'd been smart and not had to hurry. When I took Jeff Carney I thought I was getting everything a girl could want." Bitterness twisted Lorena's lips for a moment, but Bundy only saw that there was pain in her beautiful dark eyes.

He said to her, "Never mind now. I'll make the fire. We both need some coffee to get us started. You'll be home today."

"Home?" she said, laughing. "Home? In that place?"

"Still you are here," he said. "Why did you come at a time like this, if it is not your home?"

"I don't know," she said. "Really I don't know. Some devil of restlessness gets his fork into me, and I have to move. I couldn't bear it alone in town. No, I don't know why I came. Maybe it was only out of spite or meanness. I don't know."

"Don't speak badly of yourself," Bundy said. "I know better."

Lorena laughed again, but she might as well have shed tears as laughed. She was in a mood between the two.

6.

Riding uphill had not bothered Lorena, but the long slow descent to the valley was unexpectedly difficult. The heat mounted with the day. The trail was thick with dust that kept the horses sneezing and hung a golden curtain of haze among the trailside trees. The plants along the way, that had been green and moist last year at this time, were shriveled and dry and shadowed with dust. Downhill was harder for the horses, too. The uphill going strained all their muscles, but it was a positive, forward-moving effort. On the downgrade they had to oppose gravity by setting their muscles into a pattern of resistance instead of striving. Lorena had never noticed this change of pace before. She had ridden effortlessly and carelessly last year. Now, as the horse picked his way down the hill, she felt herself thrown forward against the pommel of the saddle and rocked awkwardly from side to side.

Bundy rode ahead, but he kept looking back at her. "Are you all right, Lorena? How is it going?"

"All right," Lorena said. But she did not smile at him and her lips were pale. It seemed a long time before they reached the valley floor. It was close and hot under the great trees, but at least there was shade and level going.

Bundy kept looking around at her anxiously. I must look frightful, Lorena thought, but for once she did not care.

"When we get to the Kleins'," Bundy said, "we had better stop, Lorena. Mrs. Klein will be there and she can look after you. You can rest and go on to your place later."

"No!" Lorena said. "No, I can't stand that Klein woman, Bundy. I'll keep going till I get to the homestead."

"Please," Bundy said. "It will be better for you."

"No, really," Lorena said irritably. "They're dirty and cheap. I've never had a thing to do with them, and I don't want to now."

So they rode past the Kleins' and Taggarts' and Smiths'; and Lorena's angry determination was all that kept her going.

She thought of the empty cabin that she had hated so much last year, and, too late, she wondered, in a haze of annoyance and discomfort, why she had indulged herself in this final folly. What had made her come? Was it only to thwart and annoy Jeff? If so, the effort had boomeranged to smite her as well as him. Some glimmer of understanding penetrated the agony she was beginning to suffer, and she saw that mischief bred mischief, that ill will often came home to roost. Yet she knew that she would forget the troublesome moral of this reflection as soon as she was well and beautiful again.

"Meggie's in here," she said to Bundy. "After you get me to my place, you better go for her."

"Yes, I will," Bundy said. He looked frightened now, painfully conscious that nothing in his training as botanist, forester, lover of nature, had prepared him to take over the care of a human being in complicated human distress.

They both expected the cabin to be empty, but, when at last they rode into the clearing, they saw that the door was open, and a thread of blue smoke coiled upward from the chimney.

Bundy let out a yell, and jumped off his horse, dropping the reins over its head so it would stand. He went to Lorena and held up his arms to lift her from the saddle. But she was looking at the doorway of the cabin.

"Charlie!" she said, almost in a whisper. "Oh, Charlie, for God's sake, help me."

It was Charlie who lifted her down and carried her into the cabin. He laid her gently in the bunk and poured her a cup of hot coffee from the pot on the stove.

"Where's Jeff?" he asked roughly. "Why you come, you little fool?"

"I don't know now," Lorena said. "Only I'm here. And you are here, Charlie. Hold onto my hand. I need someone to hold me."

Bundy stood in the doorway, frightened and helpless; and the grave and lofty enchantment of his recent hours with Lorena gradually diminished in brilliance.

"Shall I go and get Miss Carney?" he asked.

"Yes," Charlie said. "Missus Carney going to be all right now, I t'ink, but you go get her sister anyway."

Meggie could not believe that Lorena was at the homestead. "But my brother told her not to come!" she cried. "He was on his way to see her. She—she's going to have a baby before long."

"I know," Bundy said miserably. "No one in Cold Spring would help her with her horses. But she asked me, and I did. It's my fault, if anything—if it was too hard on her. I don't know all these things.'"

"Neither do I," Meggie said. "But whatever happens, you're not to blame. Lorena's willful. She would have found somebody else, if it hadn't been you."

Her words gave Bundy a pang—*somebody else, if it hadn't been you*. He had been so sure that fate ordained him as Lorena's knight. Too slow—too late, she had said.

He waited outside the cabin, rolling and smoking a cigarette while Meggie hastily packed together some things and came to join him.

Bundy had brought Lorena's horse on a leading rope, and now Meggie mounted and rode after him. They rode silently as they had ridden that other day when he had been filled with the speculative wonder of Lorena's kiss. Now he felt dread and an aching premonition of disaster.

7.

When they reached the cabin Lorena still lay in her bunk, moving restlessly, her hair spread in disorder. Her eyes were bright, too wide and bright perhaps.

"It's nothing," she said to Meggie. "I got a little tired, that's all. How are you? You're brown. You look like a little witch. You're thin, too. Haven't you been eating?"

"Yes," Meggie said, "but I've been working hard. My place looks fine. You ought to see it. Oh, Lorena, why didn't you wait for Jeff? He'll be very upset."

"He's so often upset," Lorena said with a sigh. "What difference does it make? I wanted to come. I've forgotten the reason why now. But I wanted to come." She turned her face to the wall as if she were tired.

Charlie stood aside when they came in, but Bundy felt that he was somehow in charge, watchful and alert. The afternoon dragged on and sometimes Lorena slept, sometimes woke with a cry of pain.

"Shouldn't Bundy or Charlie go for someone, for Mrs. Klein or Nan, or even back to Cold Spring for a doctor?" Meggie asked.

"No doctor in Cold Spring," Charlie said. "You go so far as Bolster, you find old sawbones Snope, but he be drunk as hell, I t'ink."

"I don't want anyone," Lorena said. "Just leave me. I'll be better."

But evening came and Lorena was no better.

Bundy moved restlessly about the clearing. Absently he noted the struggling garden among the stumps. He heard the pulling and munching sound of the horses, grazing among rough grasses at the edge of the clearing. He made several trips to the spring for water, because Meggie was heating a tubful of it, with the idea that hot water is a panacea for any ill. And every time that he straightened his back and turned toward the cabin with a heavy bucket in each hand, under the dark trees, a phantom stood on tiptoe and put a light kiss on his lips.

Coming back from the spring for the third time, he heard Lorena scream. The sound rose shrill and anguished and seemed to hover trembling for an instant in the evening hush of the woods. Bundy stopped as if an arrow had struck through him. For an instant he was back in Madame Pontarlier's black and white and crimson cabin, and they were all light-heartedly discussing Lorena's inability to scream. "No, I've never heard Lorena scream. Never," Jeff had said, and Charlie had laughed. "What kind of husband is it who has never heard his wife scream?" And Lorena had looked at Bundy with a conspiratorial glance which seemed to ask him to think kindly of her no matter how heartlessly the rest of them discussed her.

And now he heard her scream, abandoning herself to pain and anguish, and the sound went out and out through the silent forest, and was lost among the trees and in the wild, vast twilight of the wilderness.

Bundy moved again, hurrying toward the cabin, and the sweat came prickling out all over his body. Terror, horror, all the suffering of the world seemed to engulf him at the sound of Lorena's voice.

He put the pails of water down just outside the cabin door, and stood on the threshold looking in. Lorena was quiet for the moment, lying still, her face almost unrecognizably strained and white. She is dead! he thought, calm with despair, but then she began to toss and moan again, throwing herself restlessly back and forth on the narrow bed.

Meggie looked at him with a white face, and Bundy saw that she was frightened too. Only Charlie was calm and in control. He moistened a cloth in water and bathed Lorena's face. His voice was gentle and cajoling. Lorena reached for his hand and held it hard.

"Don't go away. Don't leave me a minute. Keep holding on tight," she said. "The pain's coming again. Oh, God, it's going to kill me."

"No," Charlie said. "Nothing going to kill you. See, I hold you. I help you. Nothing going to kill you. Pretty soon it's all over, and you laugh. Then I sing you a song. You see?"

"What shall I do?" Bundy said to Meggie in a voice that was scarcely audible.

"I don't know," Meggie said. "I wanted to get Mrs. Klein—"

Lorena heard her and said, "No, I won't have Mrs. Klein. I won't have her, even if I die."

"You don't die!" Charlie said. "My gar! Where is your fight, Lorena?"

"Oh, it's gone. It's gone."

"No," Charlie said. "It still there. Stop feeling sorry for yourself. Get mad. You fight it out then. Get it over."

Bundy went out in the clearing again.

"Let me know if I can help," he said to Meggie. He could hear Lorena crying and moaning, and Charlie reassuring her. He felt empty and depressed. The terror had left him, but there was still a conscious ache for the sorrows of the world. He felt his own inadequacy and inexperience. He was hungry, too, for he had not eaten since breakfast; yet he could not bring himself to go into the cabin and prepare food.

Later Meggie called him and gave him a plate of warm food and a cup of coffee.

"How is she? How is Lorena?" he asked.

"I don't know," Meggie said. "About the same, I guess. She's suffering. I hope it won't go on all night."

"Is it always like this?" he asked. "I mean—do they always—" He did not quite know what he meant to say.

Meggie looked at him compassionately. "Don't you suffer, too, Bundy," she said. "Each person has to do his own particular suffering. It's no use feeling other people's pain. Everyone has enough of his own."

She went inside again, a slight, almost childish figure, silhouetted dark for a moment against the lamplight in the doorway.

Bundy sat on a stump and ate and drank what she had given him. He felt chastened, yet somehow comforted.

The night went on very slowly. There was a full moon, but here in the forest, among the tall trees, one never saw the rising or the setting of either moon or sun. Gradually the high sky overhead grew luminous, and, when at last the moon sailed free above the treetops, the clearing below was washed with a mysterious silver light. Dew sparkled on the fronds of fern, and small nocturnal creatures rustled in the grass.

But tonight the moonlit solitude trembled and throbbed with Lorena's anguish. Bundy grew accustomed to the sound of Lorena's screams. He noted how the intervals between them gradually lessened.

There was a faint flush of morning in the sky when Meggie's frantic call brought Bundy into the cabin to assist at the birth of Lorena's child. He had a wild impression of heat, of lamplight, of confusion and pain and blood and fear; and then of climax and relief. And he saw Charlie, who had been calm and resourceful through everything, holding up a small, red creature whose cries had supplanted Lorena's.

"It's a boy," Charlie said, and his white teeth gleamed in a wide smile, as he gave the baby to Meggie for washing.

Bundy had done little except keep up the fire, wring cloths from warm water, and help Meggie lift pans and basins. Now he turned once more to the stove and the coffeepot, and began to prepare breakfast. He found that he was trembling, as if he had been chilled, yet the perspiration still stood on his forehead. He could not look at Lorena, lying still now and relaxed in the rough bunk bed. But Charlie moved around her, caring for her now as a nurse might do, supplanting the midwife he had been a few minutes before. This was a new side of Charlie that Bundy had never suspected, an almost womanish tenderness and resourcefulness.

Meggie washed the tiny baby and wrapped him in a shawl and laid him among pillows on the other bunk. She stood looking down on him with wonder and a kind of maternal solicitude that was new on her unlined face.

Lorena had fallen asleep, and they moved quietly so that they would not disturb her. When Bundy could look at her again, he saw that she was still beautiful, the dark hair wild about the pale face, the eyelids faintly blue and fringed with the long dark lashes that lay like a shadow on her cheeks. His heart seemed to rise in a heavy fluid and beat in his throat and in his temples. A strong sickness went all through his body, and he had an angry feeling that he was going to weep or to be overcome by nausea. He had been stirring oatmeal in a pan, and Charlie came now and took the spoon out of his hand.

"So we eat," Charlie said. "We had a damn tough night."

Charlie was right again, breakfast was the stabilizer they all needed. As he felt the normal flow of his blood returning with food and coffee, Bundy looked at Charlie with respect.

"You're quite a man, Charlie," Bundy said. "You can do a little of everything, can't you?" He did not intend to let patronage or envy creep into his voice. He meant only admiration. Yet Charlie was on the defensive.

"In town you spit on me, maybe, eh?" His voice was genial, yet tinged with bravado. "But here, in woods, Charlie Duporte is good as any man. Better, by gar! You fell a tree as quick an' clean as I do? No! You sing? You cook? You bring a baby into world? No! Charlie Duporte can beat you to it. So! Here is a place to test a man, I t'ink."

Neither Meggie nor Bundy contradicted him. He drew a long swig of hot coffee from his cup, swallowed it slowly, and looked from one to the other of them with a gleaming smile. A shaft of sunlight came over the tops of the trees and fell across the table where they sat eating. They sat there wearily, momentarily at peace with one another, having somehow vicariously achieved a vital and satisfying labor.

8.

Before noon Jeff rode into the clearing on one of McSweeney's horses. He was covered with dust and his eyes were wild with anxiety. He had been riding all night in fretful haste, more exhausted by complicated emotions than by the physical effort. He was angry with Lorena for disobeying and tricking him; he was angry with Bundy Jones for helping her; at the same time he was intolerably anxious about Lorena's health and the safety of the baby; and surrounding every other feeling was the ever-present sense of his own inadequacy and rebellion. Why must things have happened so? What had he done to deserve this treatment, this kind of life? Why could it not be better?

Lorena, having slept and eaten a good breakfast, was sitting up in bed looking at her very small red infant with humorous curiosity. She was beginning to feel a surprised and reluctant tenderness for him.

"Isn't he ugly?" she said. "It's good he's a boy. An ugly man can always get along in the world, but an ugly woman hasn't got a chance."

When she heard Jeff in the clearing, she recognized the querulous tone of his voice before she saw him, and her face hardened. She knew the familiar reproaches and anxieties by heart, and she was infinitely bored by them. As soon as he appeared in the doorway, she said to him in a voice which was languid and amused, "Well, Jeff, you missed all the excitement. How we managed without you, I don't know, but somehow we did."

Jeff fell on his knees by the bed, and for a moment his conflicting emotions resolved themselves into a single overwhelming sense of grateful relief.

"Lorena! Lorena, darling!" he said.

Meggie took the baby and laid it gently in Jeff's arms, and he held it quietly, in awe and wonder, with tears running down his cheeks. Bundy turned and went quickly out of the cabin, but Charlie stood where he was, unobtrusive, but watchful and smiling.

Now that it was all over and Jeff was here to take charge, Meggie could think of nothing but getting back to Bide a Wee. She had left the house in disorder, and another dry day would mean that she must carry water to her garden. Besides this, she felt worn out. The solitude of her own place seemed imperative.

"Go along, Meggie," Charlie said to her. (Somewhere in the dreadful night, he had discarded the "Miss Carney.") "You get some rest now. I cook for Jeff and help here 'til Lorena's up. I call you if we need."

When she went into the clearing, Meggie saw that Bundy Jones was saddling up his horse.

"I'd appreciate it if you'd take me home, Bundy," she said.

He let her ride his horse as he had done once before. He walked beside her, and the pack horse and the two dogs followed behind. There seemed nothing left for them to say to one another, and they went quietly, wrapped in their own private thoughts.

Through a miasma of doubts, Meggie was struggling to regain her usual conviction that all was right with the world. It was because she was so tired, of course, that things looked dark to her. She kept remembering Lorena's anguish, and how she had clung to Charlie Duporte's hand. Yet Lorena had been cool and amused with Jeff's anxiety, and the kiss she had given him had been a casual kiss. Better not think about it now, until she was rested and could take a cheerful view. Yet her mind kept going on in spite of herself, and she saw that life was really vast and baffling, rather than safe and tidy as she had confidently hoped to find it.

As they neared her homestead, she brought some of her thoughts to the surface, and said to Bundy Jones, "It was something strange for both of us, I guess. A person thinks he knows things, but experience is somehow different, shocking, isn't it?"

"Yes," Bundy said. "Yes, it was terrible in a way."

"Maybe we ought to value life more when we know how hard it comes," Meggie said.

"Yes," Bundy repeated dully. "Yes, you are right, I'm sure."

"Well, it's all over," Meggie said, "and he's a nice baby. We can be thankful he lived. If she can feed him now, and keep him alive, Jeff will be happy."

Bundy said with sudden violence, "Charlie was so calm—not like you and me. He helped her. I didn't think he'd be like that. If only I could have helped her! But it was Charlie she wanted—"

Sitting above him on the horse, Meggie looked down at Bundy Jones and saw the crisp hair at the nape of his tanned neck and the little blond curling hairs on his brown wrist, and she knew that her feeling for Bundy Jones was a part of her sadness at finding the world so vast and callous.

For a moment she rested her hand lightly on his shoulder. "Don't take it hard, Bundy," she said gently. "So many people love Lorena. She attracts love so easily because she is beautiful. But I s'pose that she herself can love only one or two."

"You think she loves Charlie Duporte?" he asked angrily.

"I don't know," Meggie said.

"He helped her some way. He could give her something that we didn't have."

"Don't hurt yourself," Meggie said. "It won't change anything. Just put it by now. It's all over."

"Yes, I know that," he said. "But you can tell yourself things like that—and tell yourself. Still you keep thinking."

"Forget it," Meggie said. "It's the best you can do. We're almost to the clearing now. Will you come in and eat?"

"No," he said, "I've got stuff in my pack. Thank you all the same."

"I should thank *you*," Meggie said, "for letting me ride your horse. I was dead tired. I guess you must be too."

"I hadn't noticed it," he said. "I'm going on to the river before I camp for the night."

"If you go by Nan's, tell her the news."

"I will," Bundy said, but he really did not intend to stop at Nan's or anybody's house. He felt now that he had had his fill of the homesteaders, and that he could concentrate at last on being a good forester and botanist. He could forget the uncomfortable turmoil of his emotions, and think only of saving the forest for the nation. Beyond that there was the peace and oblivion to be found in the miniature forests of the moss and lichens. Now he could put everything else out of his mind.

He whistled to his dog, who was brawling good-naturedly with Meggie's dog at the edge of her clearing. The dog came docilely to heel, and the bell on the pack horse started to ring again as they moved along the trail toward the river.

9.

Meggie's garden began to reward her for her efforts and she was intensely pleased. The potatoes she dug were small, but they were good. She felt that this was like digging for buried treasure. You never knew how many potatoes you would find underground when you dug. The roots went hither and thither in the dark loam, and food clung to them, brown balls of starchy energy that nourished and sustained life.

Growth and birth had joined together in her mind now, and she thought of Lorena's baby as she dug potatoes. She felt his flesh in her hands in the warm water as she had washed him, and saw again how wonderfully his tiny fingers were made and how small but perfect in every way he was. Singing a little off tune, Meggie dug contentedly and never minded how grimy she became.

The dry summer made forage sparse for the deer. Once, while weeding her garden, Meggie saw a doe and fawn looking at her across her rail fence. She saw their great dark eyes, trusting and unafraid. Quietly she squatted on her heels, holding as still as she could, but some flicker of movement betrayed her, and suddenly they galloped away through the woods, their tails like white beacons behind them.

That was all very well, but the next morning she found that several deer had jumped over her fence and enjoyed a fine feed on her cabbages and carrot tops. She could see the sharp little two-pointed tracks all over her neat rows.

It was a big job to raise the height of her fence, but she saw no other solution to the problem. She did not have the skill or strength to cut large trees and split them into rails, but she did the best she could by cutting long, straight saplings and fastening them on extensions above the top rails.

Rudy and Spike should have known enough to make the fence higher, she thought. But then they had never really believed she could make a garden that would be more enticing to deer than the forage of the forest. It took her a week to repair her fence, and in the meantime she saw nothing more of the deer. Toward the end of the week, as she toiled to surround herself with a higher barrier, she began to think she was a fool to work so hard. The deer had been wandering by and were probably ten or twenty miles away by this time. For all she knew they might be feasting on Nan's garden now. Still she went on working until she had finished. She liked to see a job through to the end.

But several days after the fence was done, the deer broke through again, eating and trampling what she had so carefully planted and nurtured. Meggie was angry, but all she could do was repair the fence. It became a continual struggle between her and the deer, until finally the garden was not worth fighting for any longer.

Oh, well, Meggie thought, I'm not dependent on it. If I had to stay here—if I had to depend on a garden to live, that would be different. But I'll be back in town, working in the lumberyard before long. I'll just pull in my belt a little more and wait for the big money.

One day Meggie was surprised to see Eye MacGillicuddy riding into her clearing. Normally she would have felt no surprise, but this summer folks said he had really lit out, dropped off the face of the earth. Some predicted that he would follow the Lolo Trail over into Montana and not return to the shame of seeing another ranger in his place. But here he was, as if nothing had happened.

"Oh, Eye!" Meggie cried. "I'm so glad to see you! How would you like to shoot me some venison? I guarantee it'll be real good. It's vegetable fed."

"They spoiled your garden for you, did they?" Eye chuckled. "An' you gals think you're farmers, don't ye? Yon O'Rourke woman got the same trouble with her garden you have. 'Shoot me a nice vegetable-fed deer,' says she, 'An' show me how to keep the blasted things out of my patch.' Well, I done both for her. I canna play no favorites, I'll do the same for you, lass."

"We've missed you, Eye," Meggie said. "Where have you been? We've all longed to have you back."

"Aye, ye think the new man will be harder on you," Eye said. " 'The old man is a softie,' ye think. Yon Nan as much as said so to me, and 'Poor old coot!' she says, 'I'm sorry for ye.' First time I ever had airybody feel sorry for me. 'Tis almost worth gittin' the sack, to have the women weepin' an' greetin' for me. However, I'll take a good hot meal before a bucket of tears any day of the week includin' the Sabbath."

"I'll feed you like a king, Eye," Meggie said, "only help me do something about the deer, if you please."

"Won't your dog run 'em off?"

"My dog is the best company in the world, and I'd die of loneliness without him, but he's no earthly good for anything else."

"Funny," Eye said, "none of them pups took after Jessie. Their father must have been a good-for-nothing."

"Eye, what are you going to do now?" Meggie asked.

"I'm cogitatin'," Eye said. "Meanwhile these woods is my home. Dinna push me any further, lassie."

So Meggie had fresh venison. There were no game laws in here then and the season was whenever you wanted to shoot. Eye showed her how to hang empty tin cans like cowbells from the rails of her fence.

"I've knowed it to scare the deer away, an' then again I've knowed it not to. Ye can but try." He stayed long enough to cut up the meat for her and show her how to dry what she could not use into pemmican strips. Together they stretched the hide on the back of her cabin.

"Happen you lack shoes, you can sew you some moccasins, lassie," Eye said with a chuckle.

Since Eye was going in that direction, Meggie sent one of the venison haunches to Jeff and Lorena. She had not been there since the birth of the baby, although she had thought of them every day; but, more and more, she was engrossed by the struggle to keep her own place going. She was amazed to realize how the depredations of the deer had occupied her thoughts and energies to the exclusion of everything else.

"Tell Jeff to come and see me," she said to Eye. A few days

later Jeff came. Meggie had not really expected that he would heed her request, and she was pleasantly surprised.

She greeted him with a flood of eager questions, most of them about the baby. "How is he? What have you named him?"

"We gave him the family name," Jeff said, "Oliver Jefferson Carney, Third."

"Ah," Meggie said, "I thought you'd do that."

"Lorena insists on calling him Ollie," Jeff went on, "but I'm going to call him Oliver J. right from the start, just as father always was called. It's a good name, a famous name. Maybe he'll amount to more than I have. Jeff is no kind of name for a man."

"A man makes his own name, Jeff," Meggie said. "It doesn't matter what his parents call him. Either he's got success in him or he hasn't."

"I know you're right," Jeff said. "What is it they say about every other generation going in its shirt sleeves? Well, I'm the shirt-sleeve generation. My kid is going to get back to the cutaway coat and the high silk hat. It's a kind of superstition, I guess, but that's why I call him Oliver J."

"But you haven't told me how he is," Meggie said. Jeff's face clouded with some inner anxiety, and he spoke more reluctantly now.

The baby seemed to be well, Jeff said, although he hadn't grown as they had expected. But none of them knew much about babies and they had no scales to weigh him. Lorena was able to feed him, thank God, but her milk was not very plentiful, and the fact that he cried a great deal made them fear he wasn't getting all he should.

Charlie had taken Jeff's horse into Cold Spring and brought them a load of canned milk, and now they were using that to supplement his food, and they expected he would soon begin to gain.

"The baby should have been born in town," Jeff said. "He should have gone his full time. I blame Lorena for that. But we're doing the best we can. As soon as he's huskier, we'll take him back home to Opportunity. Charlie's helped us all he can. He's been wonderful in all this. Someday I hope I can pay him with good money."

Meggie said nothing to that. She had seen the tenderness in

Charlie's face as he helped Lorena through her anguish, and she thought that money was not important to him, that it might even anger or insult him. But Jeff had not been there to see, and then perhaps he was too wrapped up in himself to read other people's faces.

Jeff was moving restlessly around Meggie's cabin, and now he came to a stop before her shelf of books.

"I see you've got Mother's old Bible here," he said.

"Believe it or not," Meggie said, "I needed it last winter. This year I brought it along to ward off disaster. You see, I'm superstitious too."

"Well, I hope you won't need it," Jeff said shortly. But after a moment he added, "A baby in the family makes one think though. We weren't brought up to any purpose or belief beyond success, Meggie. You know that, don't you?"

"I've begun to understand it. Yes," Meggie said.

"I don't want Oliver J. to be like that, Meg. I want him to have—to have some idealism and ambition beyond easy money and success. Do you see what I mean?"

"Yes," Meggie said. "I do see, Jeff."

"If we can get out of this homestead business—get on our feet again—I know we're in a kind of shifty position, fraudulent, if you like."

Meggie was shocked. "But fraudulent," she said, "what a nasty word, Jeff. We never meant anything like that, surely. Uncle Ralph wouldn't have sent us here."

"*Ralph*," Jeff said. "Do you know he's rotten with greed and selfishness?"

"Jeff!" Meggie said. "Don't talk like that. It frightens me. We have to get these places now, you know we do."

"Yes, I know we do. Only sometimes I get to thinking. You read the papers these days, and it's the young people, the people our age, who are on the side of democratic action against the old monopolies. Maybe it's radical, but young people should be radical, they have all the years ahead to grow conservative in. And you and I, all of us homesteaders, aren't we sheltering under the old monopolies? What are we fighting for besides ourselves? Why, the special interests, the lumber interests. I think we're hanging onto the coat-tails of the selfish past."

"I never heard you talk like this before," Meggie said. "And aren't you still locating homesteaders? Aren't you going right ahead with it?"

"I haven't located a new homesteader this summer," Jeff said, "but it's not because I wouldn't if they offered me money for it. No, it's because people have been scared out by the goings on in Washington, by the new ranger, if you like. They think we'll never get these places, and maybe we won't."

"Well," Meggie said, "I'm not scared out. I'll fight for this place, every inch of the way. If we're wrong, we're wrong. But this is a fine time to discover it."

"Don't get excited," Jeff said. "I'm just talking. Don't you know me well enough to know that I may have noble thoughts, but lack the guts to do anything about them?"

Meggie saw the bitter twist of his mouth. "Oh, stop it, Jeff!" she said. "I don't like that kind of talk. You've always had a gift for torturing yourself."

"And you?" he said, suddenly relenting. "I've always tortured you, too, haven't I?"

"No," Meggie said stoutly. "You've always been a good brother."

"Well, that's something," he said. "I think I've made a poor husband. All I can hope now is that I won't make too bad a father."

"You'll make a good one," Meggie said. "Love him and tell him the better thoughts you have. Maybe he'll act on them. Do you want Mother's Bible? Take it if you want it."

"No," Jeff said. "You keep it for your own emergencies. No, this was all a lot of talk. I didn't mean a thing."

10.

Lorena pretended indifference to Ollie. "What a trouble he is, waking me in the night and howling, so I don't get any rest. By this time he ought to be sleeping through, oughtn't he?" But sometimes she held him fiercely, and said to herself, He's mine. He's part of me. He belongs to me. Sometimes she laughed at him and rocked him back and forth. "What a funny little nose he's got! Oh, you're a clown, Ollie. You're a funny one." His mouth, sucking languidly at her breast, sent a tremor through her.

Scolding, laughing, bathing and fondling him, Lorena did not even notice that she had ceased to be bored.

"What a nuisance a baby is!" she said, but at the same time she could not take her eyes from the thin, weaving arms and legs, the tiny clutching fingers.

Sometimes when the baby cried, she held him up to the mirror, his face reflected beside hers. "Look at the baby!" she cried. "Look at Ollie! Oh, what a silly boy he is!" But he was too young to be diverted. If the mirror had a place in his life, he did not know it.

Lorena, Jeff and Charlie lived together in perfect amity that summer. There was a kind of innocence in their three-cornered relationship which revolved about the thin and listless baby in the cradle.

Charlie had made the cradle. Lorena asked him for a crib, but some submerged instinct or memory of a soothing infancy had put him to the greater effort of producing rockers for the bed, so that Ollie might be gently rocked when he was peevish.

Charlie was a quick worker, and that year he did not spare himself. He took much of the household burden off Lorena's shoulders so that she could devote herself to the baby. He performed cheerful miracles of strength and endurance in clearing stumps, digging, hoeing and building. Because he was ashamed to let Charlie outdo him, Jeff worked twice as hard as he would have alone. The place began to look more civilized than any other homestead in the valley. Jeff and Lorena both began to take a pride in it.

If the baby had been stronger, everything would have gone smoothly for them that summer. But the canned milk did not agree with him, and Lorena found her own supply diminishing from day to day. She tried different proportions of canned milk and water, but the fact was that she did not really have a formula or know at all what she was doing.

From careless ignorance, she fell into alarm. Suddenly she began to insist that they return to Opportunity.

Jeff flared up angrily. He saw only that she was going to be unreasonable again.

"No," he said. "You came out here. You were willing to take all the risks. But somewhere your whims and fancies have got to stop. You aren't going to take a five-week baby over the mountain on a pack horse, and then by stage and train for another couple of days in hot weather. The heat will be much worse in town."

"This time it's not a whim," Lorena said. "The little thing is hungry and I don't know how to feed it. I don't know what to do."

"He'll be stronger. Soon he'll take the canned milk and it'll agree with him. You see if it doesn't. The pioneers had babies, didn't they?"

"Yes, and they lost them too," Lorena said.

"What do you say, Charlie?" Jeff cried. "Is she right or am I?"

Charlie looked at them without smiling, but he said, "You got to decide that yourselves. I don't want no responsibility between you, one way or the other."

"We'll stay," Jeff said.

When he could make a decision without wavering, he felt competent and strong. Lorena's whim had got them into this. He had not been there to override her whim before, but this time he was here. He could prevent a serious mistake. During the week, in spite of her pleading, he kept his resolution.

11.

In August there was a National Irrigation Congress in Spokane, and, because both Pinchot and Ballinger were scheduled to speak, Bundy decided to attend the meeting. If he rode northwest from Cold Spring for ten or twelve miles, he could catch a small steamer on the Sainte Maries River that would take him into the Saint Joe River and through Coeur d'Alene Lake to Coeur d'Alene city. From there it was a short ride by rail to Spokane.

Although he was a botanist and a forester, Bundy saw irrigation as one of the many problems with which conservationists were bound to be involved. This year in particular, with Taft in control and Roosevelt hunting big game in Africa, the conservationists were hotly united in their efforts to put down monopoly wherever they found it.

Floating on the silent river, he felt detached for the moment from controversy, from love and disappointment, from past and future. He saw how the pale green grasses bent and swayed at the margin of the dark water; how, on the glassy surface ahead of the boat, the white clouds made a frosty gleam of reflected light. It was only in the train that he began to be excited by the thought of returning to civilization. The noisy confusion of the railroad station buzzed agreeably in his ears.

The lobby of the Davenport Hotel, incongruously luxurious for a small Western city, was full of incongruously assorted people. There were Reclamation Service men and small farmers interested in the practical application of irrigation to their regions; and there were politicians and lumbermen who knew that if water power slipped from the hands of the privileged few, the forests, the coal mines and the other unexploited resources were likely to follow. There were newspaper men from the local papers and also from the great national dailies. In its wider implications the Congress went beyond the control of water, beyond the quarrel between Pinchot and Ballinger over Alaskan coal, and became another test of the Taft administration.

Mingling with the crowd in the close hot air, Bundy felt the excitement of impending battle. He saw Ballinger, small, neat, and close-lipped, moving confidently among men who believed that there was still some of the national pie to be shared among them. He saw Pinchot, long and thin, the aristocrat who has espoused the cause of the people, indefatigably charming and ready to take infinite pains. On this trip Pinchot had Alaskan coal rights and the saving of water power sites on public lands on his mind, yet he was not too busy to interview individual homesteaders of timberland, when he could reach them, warning them in plain language that he would use all his strength to defeat them. This steam roller of general farsightedness, combined with attention to the most minute details, made the man formidable.

Glavis was there too, and Bundy read a special significance into his presence. It was no secret that Glavis' investigations in Alaska had become an embarrassment to the Taft administration. Only a couple of weeks earlier Ballinger had taken the investigation of the

Cunningham coal claims out of Glavis' hands, and put it into the hands of a third investigator. It seemed likely that both Glavis and his predecessor had been removed as government inspectors because their reports were at variance with the interests of the monopoly.

Aside from the fact that an estimated three hundred million dollars' worth of government land in the new territory was at stake, Bundy had a personal interest in the Alaskan coal case. He felt that, although the values were smaller, it paralleled the situation in the Clearwater forest. The principle of private ownership against the public good remained the same, and the outcome of one situation would undoubtedly affect the other.

Bundy suspected that Glavis was in Spokane now to appeal to Pinchot for help. Because most of the Alaskan coal claims lay within the Chugach National Forest, Pinchot had a technical right to involve himself in the matter. He and Glavis, although of different ages and positions, were much alike in disposition. They were tenacious, idealistic, and on the alert for a brawl. Bundy saw them deep in conversation, and suspected that the conversation would bear fruit.

He saw Ralph Carney there, too, the center of his own group of admirers. Bundy looked at him with curiosity and attention. He saw that the lumberman was handsome and vital, dark but graying about the temples. He was as different from Jeff Carney as could be imagined, and yet there was something similar about the mouth. As the serviceberry, the rose and the silvery cinquefoil seem to the casual observer to be different, yet to the botanist have a family resemblance, so Bundy felt a family resemblance among the dissimilar Carneys.

The convention hall was crowded on the day when the Chief Forester and the Secretary of the Interior were scheduled to speak.

Pinchot took only ten minutes, but he spoke well and packed the essence of his philosophy into a few words. He and Roosevelt had been criticized for straining the law to forward conservation, and now Taft and Ballinger were making a virtue of standing firm on the letter of the law.

"An institution or a law is a means, not an end," Pinchot said, "a means to be used for the public good, to be modified for the public good, and to be interpreted for the public good." He went on to say that "strict construction [of the law] necessarily favors the great interests as against the people" and to charge that "the great oppressive trusts exist because of subservient lawmakers and adroit legal constructions." This was a red flag to lawyers and a gauntlet to Ballinger. Yet there were plenty of people in the audience who applauded.

Bundy heard the familiar credo in Pinchot's final words. "I stand for the Roosevelt policies because they set the common good of all of us above the private gain of some of us; because they recognize the livelihood of the small man as more important to the Nation than the benefit of the big man; because they oppose all useless waste at present at the cost of robbing the future; because they demand the complete, sane, and orderly development of all our natural resources, not forgetting our rivers; because they insist on equality of opportunity and denounce monopoly and special privilege; because discarding false issues, they deal directly with the vital questions that really make a difference with the welfare of all of us—and most of all, because in them the plain American always and everywhere holds the first place. And I propose to stand for them while I have the strength to stand for anything."

Bundy joined in the applause, feeling with pride that the speech was on a high level. There was a tense moment of waiting for Ballinger's reply; but, when it came, it was roundabout and colorless, a careful avoidance of the challenge rather than a reply. There was nothing in it either to commit him to a policy or to give offense. The meeting had not yielded the sensational developments which the reporters had anticipated; yet it made front page news all over the country, and Pinchot's speech was widely quoted.

Bundy had enjoyed the hotel meals, the soft bed, the reunion with civilization, most of all his brief encounter with G.P.; nevertheless he was not sorry to see the last of the hot assembly rooms and the crowds of restless people. In the prow of the small boat, returning up the river, he was content to watch the water, mirrorlike, dark green and undisturbed by ripples, waiting for the prow of the boat to carve a silver furrow in the green reflection. He returned with satisfaction to his dog and his horses, and to the simplicity of the wilderness.

12.

All during the week of Jeff's resistance, Ollie grew feebler. There seemed to be a gradual diminishing of a life flame that had never flickered brightly. It was difficult to tell from one day to the next whether there had been a change, yet they could all sense it. Lorena had stopped begging and protesting, and perhaps that was what finally moved Jeff most.

The day the baby refused food altogether, and lay quiet and listless in the cradle, Jeff saddled his horse and came to the cabin. He was white with anguish and defeat.

"Wrap him up, Lorena," he said. "We'll take him. There's some kind of doctor at Bolster. Maybe he'll know what to do."

"I think it's too late, Jeff," Lorena said. She said it hopelessly, without rancor.

Jeff put Lorena on the horse and laid the baby in her arms. He walked ahead, leading the horse. It was already late in the day, and a haze of golden light illuminated the dusty air behind them.

Charlie stood before the cabin and watched them go. He had said nothing either way all week, because he did not know any more than they did where the best course lay. As he saw them go, he was reminded vaguely of a holy picture he had seen in one of the churches in Quebec when he was a small boy and still susceptible to holy pictures. In the picture an old man with a beard led a donkey on which rode a woman with a babe in her arms. Charlie did not often think of the past, or conjure up artistic images. So he dismissed this one quickly, because this was Lorena and Ollie, and it was Jeff, the blunderer, who led the horse.

They reached the halfway cabin by nightfall, and it was impossible to go on farther that day. The baby lay quiet. He would not eat, but neither did he cry.

"He would cry if he were in pain, wouldn't he?" Jeff said. "I think he's somewhat better, a little bit, don't you?"

"Maybe so," Lorena said, but her tears welled up as she said it. She had never wanted a little, helpless creature hanging upon her for its livelihood. Yet, since Ollie had come, her feelings had subtly changed. Ironically now she longed to feed, to nurture, to cherish this baffling, helpless thing, and yet for some reason she could not. Her tears ran down her cheeks, not in anger, but in sorrow and pity for another life, for something outside herself.

Finally she and Jeff slept, exhausted by the past day, expecting to push forward on the next one.

But in the morning, when they awoke, the baby was dead.

Lorena did not comb and twist her hair that morning. It fell in disorder down her back. Her eyes were swollen and red but she did not weep any more.

"We might as well go back," she said in a dull voice.

"Oh, Lorena," Jeff cried, "I was wrong. Forgive me, Lorena, forgive me." His shoulders shook with helpless sobs.

Lorena put her hand on his shoulder. "Listen, Jeff," she said. "Maybe it would have happened either way. It can't do any good to grieve. I'm afraid of grieving. Listen now, Jeff. We've got to bury him."

"Not here," Jeff said, "not in this lonely place. The snow's so deep here in the winter and the wind blows. I was here last winter and I know."

"We'll take him back to the homestead then," Lorena said. "It snows deep there, too, and the wind blows, but that's where he belongs. He belongs to the homestead, first to last."

She carried him back in her arms, holding him gently and carefully as she had done on the way out. Her dark hair blew untended about her shoulders.

She thought dispassionately. "It's the fourth time he's traveled this trail, poor little Ollie!" and for once she saw life as an odd phenomenon, cruel but completely outside herself—she no longer the hub and center of it as she always had been.

Charlie dug the small grave at the edge of the clearing for them, and put together a sturdy box. Word went up and down the valley and the other homesteaders came, even Nan O'Rourke who lived the farthest down the valley.

Lorena would have preferred to put him away quietly without any fuss of sympathy and curiosity. But she said nothing and even suffered Mrs. Klein to kiss her. Jimmy Klein did not run or shout in the clearing that day, but stood by the grave with awe on his round face. Lorena thought, My God, he was little like Ollie, too, but somehow she fed him. He's never seen death before either, poor little devil.

There was no preacher in the valley, but Meggie brought her Bible and stood up sturdily with a pale face, and read scripture to them before Charlie put the little box down into the grave.

Then shall the dust return to the earth as it was; and the spirit shall return unto God who gave it.

In my Father's house are many mansions: if it were not so, I would have told you. I go to prepare a place for you.

Meggie had heard the words at both her mother's and her father's funerals, but, now, reading them herself under the arching pines, they shook her more profoundly. She saw the words for the first time not only as Christian comfort but as an anchor for man's drifting boat to the security of the past. The many times the words had been spoken deepened their significance and made them holy in a purely human way. In them lay the unshed tears of all bereavement.

When the dirt began to fall on the little box, Jeff burst out crying, and Lorena took his hand and led him back to the cabin.

It was perhaps too much fuss to make for a baby who had existed for only six weeks and had been so feeble from the start that he could scarcely have been said to have lived. Yet it was the first funeral in the valley, and the first time the homesteaders had ever been all together in one gathering before. They were individualists, wanting only to turn a quick dollar and get out of here. Yet for a moment they had come together to see a baby laid away in virgin soil, and in that moment they were temporarily united.

Jeff had never carved wood before, but now he set himself to split and smooth a slab of wood. He worked at it in the evenings by candlelight, and, when it was quite smooth, he cut a small cross on it and the words

Oliver J. Carney III
June–August 1909.

Charlie was more practical. He heaped the little grave with a heavy mound of stones, and, although Lorena never spoke of either man's project, she knew that Jeff was thinking about himself and the deprivation to his family tree, and that Charlie was thinking about a baby alone in a hostile wilderness.

Lorena began to brush and coil her hair again and keep herself neat. But she did not look into the mirror as often as she had. Somehow, when she did, she heard her own voice saying, "Look at the baby! Look at Ollie!" and there was a little, listless head beside her cheek. She heard again and again, when the wind went through the trees at night, his hopeless, seeking cry whose cause she was unable to satisfy.

Charlie sat by the cabin door in the evening and played his guitar and sang. He sang the lighthearted songs rather than the sad ones. Sometimes they played cards together.

Jeff, carving and smoothing his slab of wood, was annoyed by their callousness. He wanted to send Charlie away; and yet the thought of darkness closing down on Lorena and himself alone in this tiny clearing, surrounded by miles and miles of terribly empty forest, frightened him. He could be bitter about the lighthearted singing, but at the same time he could not dispense with it. He had come to rely on Charlie in everything he did.

When Bundy Jones came back from his journey to Spokane, he met Taggart on the trail and asked what was new. Taggart told him the Carneys had lost their baby boy and that the valley people had all gone to the funeral. Bundy sat still on his horse, and a wave of the sickness that had gone over him after the baby's birth shook him again.

At first he thought he would go on up to the lookout point and forget the whole thing. But, whether he wished or not, he was concerned with Lorena and her baby. Nothing could ever blot out the journey he had taken with Lorena, and the way he had been involved with the baby's birth. He wondered—if he had refused her request that day in Cold Spring, if he had been a little wiser— Still how could one know? Meggie had said to him, "She would have found somebody else, if it hadn't been you." That was the thing that rankled, really—it was worse than the sense of guilt. But to forget it all was quite impossible.

He rode down to the homestead, wondering what he could say to Lorena. He did not even know whether she would be grieving or relieved. When he saw her, it was her dullness that shocked him. She was neither angry nor sorrowful nor yet untouched.

She looked at him with level, serious eyes, and she said, "It's better, isn't it? Better to die before you live, so you won't know how bad, how hard, living is? He won't ever know now."

Bundy saw that she was seeking to rationalize some sort of comfort for herself. He did not tell her how much he prized his own life, how he was glad and thankful to live and have all his senses, no matter how cruel and hard the living was. To him life was the one great gift, the only true good, and what one made of it was the supreme test of achievement. But he said to her, "No, he won't know how hard it can be."

She did not seek to detain him. After they had exchanged a few banalities, there seemed no more to be said, and Bundy rode back up trail again the way he had come.

It was at the end of that summer that Bundy lost his dog. He had stopped to make camp for the night in a deeply wooded place, and before he had finished pitching his tent he missed the dog and heard him yapping and howling as if he had treed some game. Bundy took his gun and went in the direction of the sound.

In the silence and loneliness of the summer he had come more and more to depend on the dog's companionship. Now he saw that the dog had a couple of bear cubs treed. Bundy called, but the dog was in a frenzy of excitement and would not mind the summons.

Bundy saw the mother bear, awkward but swift, coming to protect her young. He raised his gun, shooting to frighten rather than to kill because he was reluctant to leave two young things motherless. But before the shot had left the gun, the old bear struck the dog with her paw and sent him spinning against a tree.

He never knew what hit him, Bundy decided later, when the bears had lumbered away and he could retrieve the dog's body.

Bundy took the dog up in his arms, and this seemed the final desolation of a troubled summer. As he held the dead mongrel in a kind of dazed and surprised bereavement, a solitary picture came into his mind. It was of a stubborn old man standing before a tent on a mountainside while a fire burned in the valley below. "My little bitch was sick," the old man said.

VII

OLD LETTER

1.

It was an exciting winter in Washington, and Bundy steeped himself in it. He let the social life flow by him without regret this year. Iris smiled at him across a dance floor at one of the few functions he attended, and he led her out to dance.

"Well, how did it go, Bundy?" she asked.

He wanted to say, "It's all over, Iris. I'm free as the air," but, although he believed this, he could not put it into words. Too much that was sad and dark and incomprehensible surrounded his release, and he could not be lighthearted or brazen about it.

"Things are all right," he said. "I went to Spokane for G.P.'s speech and it was a corker. The Secretary of the Interior didn't have much to say. But things are moving along. You've heard about Glavis' article in *Collier's*, haven't you?"

"Yes, of course," Iris said.

All Washington buzzed and simmered over the Glavis article. Iris wasn't particularly interested in discussing Glavis, for she had heard him discussed pro and con at every meal for several days when her father was at home. But, if that was the way Bundy wanted to turn the conversation, well enough, it was a livelier topic than the pine bark beetle. At the end of the dance another partner claimed her. She was not often a wallflower any more. She thought that probably she could thank Bundy for that. He had rescued her last year and got her started. As she danced away, she watched him a little wistfully over the shoulder of the new partner who was

236

quite willing to be personal and leave Glavis to the politicians. She saw that instead of going toward the line of waiting debutantes or the punch bowl, Bundy was making for the exit.

She sighed briefly, but then she had to laugh at something amusing that her partner said to her.

G.P. was deeply involved in the Ballinger fight this fall, yet he never lost his control of details.

"Bundy," he said, "I'm going to take action against the homesteaders in your valley. We'll put the proof that they can make homes there strictly up to them. I've written Matt to tack up contest notices on every cabin door this winter. If they want to fight, we'll arrange hearings for them. I want you to draw up the case against them. You know it better than anyone."

Bundy sat over his papers at night, and ran his fingers through his hair. Yes, he knew the case against the homesteaders better than anyone. He heard Lorena's laughing voice saying, "Home? In that place?" He saw the crudely lettered sign over Meggie's door with the name of her place "Bide a Wee." Yet he felt uncomfortably that somehow Meggie was really trying. He had seen her garden before the deer trampled it. It was a surprisingly good attempt.

The unalterable fact, however, was that this was not farming land, or homeland. Unless the trees were cut, it would never be anything but deep forest. And, if the trees were cut and trundled away to the sawmill, no one could live here either, at least for a long time. In his mind's eye he saw the terrible devastation that would follow cutting, the stumps and careless piles of slashings, the fireweed and brakes growing rankly under open sky, the rivers and streams shriveling and drying to nothing, the final desolation and loneliness. Even the game would desert the place. Second growth would be a long time starting, and it would be of an inferior quality. The beautiful Western white pine, the best in the world, would be a thing of the past. Yet under intelligent forest management, the forest could be made to yield constantly and moderately. The ripe trees could be cut, leaving more room in which the immature trees could develop. Under proper supervision the forest could go on forever, beautiful and serene, yet productive, a sound and democratic business for a great nation.

Bundy took up his pen again and began to write. He devoted

himself exclusively to forestry that winter. Even the illusive forests of the mosses and lichens did not distract him from the future of the white pine.

The Pinchot-Ballinger feud had been moving forward rapidly during the summer and fall. At Pinchot's suggestion and with a personal letter of introduction from G.P., Glavis had taken his report to President Taft on August 18. Taft was spending his summer at Beverly, Massachusetts, and the threat of a public scandal inside his cabinet must have intruded very irksomely on his vacation. Glavis had come on from the West expressly to see him, and Taft greeted him kindly and then and there skimmed through his report which consisted of about fifty pages, mostly copies of official documents concerning the Cunningham claims. Smiling and kindly as usual, the President told Glavis to go up to Boston and wait until further notice. A few days later Glavis was told that he might as well return to Seattle, as the President would not see him again, and in less than a month he was dismissed from the service of the government "for filing a disingenuous statement, unjustly impeaching the official integrity of his superior officers." At the same time Taft made public a letter completely exonerating Ballinger from any complicity in pressing fraudulent coal claims. This was the famous "Whitewash Letter" which led during the Congressional investigation of the following spring to a number of embarrassing revelations.

Having appealed to the President with no success, Glavis now appealed to the people in the *Collier's Weekly* article which appeared on November 13 under the title of "The Whitewash of Ballinger."

The fight was in the open now, and the newspapers were full of it. The autumn of 1909 seethed with speculation and a lining up of forces on both sides.

Pinchot was often out of the Washington headquarters of the Forestry Service that fall. He had been speaking for conservation throughout the West and had met Taft in Salt Lake City in September when the President was making a western tour. They had seemed to be on the friendliest of terms and to be working together for the public good.

In October Taft made his famous trip down the Mississippi to New Orleans to attend the Lakes-to-the-Gulf Deep Waterway Convention. Ten vessels made the 1,165-mile trip, and the President was accompanied by his Vice-President, twenty-five governors, cabinet officers, congressmen, senators and delegates to the Convention.

It was an imitation of T.R.'s river pilgrimage to Memphis for a similar convention in 1907, but this was on a royal scale, and it was well timed to exhibit the President in a favorable light to those who were growing apprehensive over the disposal of water power rights and other natural resources. Pinchot went with him, as Head of Forestry and one of the speakers at the Convention.

While G.P. was out of the office things ran on as usual under the guidance of Overton Price and Alexander Shaw. Price had helped to organize the Forestry Service in its early days and both men were absolutely devoted to G.P. and enthusiastic in the fight for the public good.

After the President's defense of Ballinger, any further criticism of the Secretary of the Interior from official government sources amounted to treason. Yet, while G.P. was out of the office, Price and Shaw continued to give out to the press statements concerning the illegality of the Alaskan coal claims and the Secretary of the Interior's connection with them. They backed all of Glavis' allegations, and kept the case before the public, where Taft's letter had attempted to silence it.

Although Price and Shaw were obviously doing what Pinchot himself wanted done, they were intensely loyal to him and did not wish him to assume the blame for their actions.

Price went to Secretary of Agriculture Wilson when they seemed to be getting in above their heads in government disapproval, and offered to resign, assuming all the blame for the accusations against the Secretary of the Interior which had come from the Forest Service offices.

Pinchot, brought back to the office by this new emergency, had several discussions with the Secretary of Agriculture, issued an official reprimand of the two men, but would not recommend their dismissal from the department.

The affair reached its climax at the end of December. Bundy was at Pinchot's house for a meeting of instructors of Forestry on December thirtieth, the day of Pinchot's return. Secretary of Agriculture Wilson was to be the speaker. Wilson was a solid, grim, bearded man, who had been Secretary of Agriculture during the administrations of McKinley, Roosevelt and Taft. He had seen the Forestry Service grow from almost nothing, and he had also seen Secretaries of the Interior come and go. Unofficially, at least, his sympathies seemed to be with Price and Shaw, although a public reprimand had been essential.

There was no tension that evening, only the usual sense of good-fellowship and enthusiasm which filled the mansion on Rhode Island Avenue. Bundy always remembered this evening of December thirtieth at the Pinchot's house, because it was the last one he was to spend there. Everyone knew that the political volcano might erupt at any time, yet they had gone on climbing the mountain and so far nothing had happened. Perhaps it might never happen. One thing was certain, Wilson and Pinchot seemed to be in complete accord on this occasion. It was a calm and harmonious evening.

It was only later that Bundy recalled the mention of Senator Dolliver's request for a letter from Pinchot which could be read before Congress. Dolliver thought that it was only fair that the case of Price and Shaw should be presented to Congress at the same time that Attorney General Wickersham presented a defense of Ballinger.

Naturally Pinchot was hot to write the letter. Secretary Wilson, calm and cautious, seemed to be temporizing, shaking his head a little and not really believing that the Chief Forester would let his enthusiasm run away with him to the extent of jeopardizing his position by an open defiance of the President. There was a presidential order forbidding any official to apply to Congress for action of any kind, or to respond to any request for information from any Committee or any member of Congress, "except through, or as authorized by, the head of his department," in this case Secretary of Agriculture Wilson.

Whether Wilson gave specific consent, as Pinchot later said he believed that he had done, or not, the fact remains that Pinchot wrote the Dolliver letter. It was a strong defense of everything that Price and Shaw had done to bring out the facts about the Alaskan coal scandals, and it ended by saying that "without question, they did for the people of this country what the people would have done for themselves had they been in a situation to do it."

Pinchot must have known what the reading of this letter in Congress would mean. Perhaps, with his fanatic perspicacity, he saw that the cause needed a conspicuous martyr at this particular moment.

The letter was read by Dolliver in the Senate on January 6, 1910. After two cabinet meetings on January 7, a messenger from the White House brought a letter to Pinchot at his home.

It was early evening and Pinchot was just going out to dinner. He opened the President's letter and saw that he was dismissed from the government service. His mother was reputed to have cried "Hurrah!" and Pinchot himself, settling his impeccably cut evening cape around his shoulders, shrugged those shoulders lightly, and went out to dinner.

2.

The repercussions over the country were intense. Headlines flashed in all the papers, and cartoonists were busy. Taft's dismissal of Pinchot seemed a strong repudiation of the Roosevelt conservation policy and a return to special privilege. Men like Ralph Carney sat back in their swivel chairs and lit fresh cigars, smiling with satisfaction. "It was bound to come. This god-damned sentiment over the people's rights could go on only so long. Where would the people be without the initiative of Big Business? We're back where we started from now, and everything's going to be all right. That damned crank Pinchot is finally out of the way."

But there were a million little people who had begun to think about the sane use of natural resources for the greatest good of the greatest number, and to them Pinchot's dismissal was a grave defeat.

Jeff Carney came home with the news, and as usual his reactions were complicated by deep-seated personal indecision.

"Pinchot's out," he said to Lorena, hanging his hat carefully on the hall rack as he came in. "It looks like we won't have to fight him over the homesteads any longer."

"You always talk as if Pinchot was our personal enemy, the only one between us and the homesteads," Lorena said. "Can one man be all that?"

"Well, he's always been the monkey wrench in the works," Jeff said. "He's a one-man crusade, if you want to put it that way. Everything should be easier with him out of office."

"I must say, you don't look very jubilant about it," Lorena said. "Aren't you pleased?"

"Of course," Jeff said. "Yet I'm fool enough to admire the man; and I wonder if Taft has done himself any good by slapping him down?"

"Oh, come to supper," Lorena said. "Meggie has been out in the kitchen ever since she came in from the yard. I think she's stirred up something stupendous."

"And you? What have you been doing, darling?"

"I've been sewing," Lorena said. "I'm making a new dress for the Chandlers' party. They won't need to look down their noses at us. They won't know but what a dressmaker did it. I'm taking a lot of pains."

Jeff was glad to see her taking pains with anything again. Since the baby's death she had seemed weighted down with apathy. Sometimes he even yearned for her anger and cruelty, rather than this dreary lack of interest. Now, when she sometimes stood before the long mirrors again, holding up lengths of material, looking at herself with something of the old infatuated scrutiny, he did not have the heart to feel resentful.

"But will it really mean that we'll get our homesteads more easily?" Meggie asked, as they sat down to supper together.

"I think likely," Jeff said. "Who's going to put up a big fight with Pinchot out of the way? And these Cunningham claims they talk so much about. If they go through, no one can say a word against our claims. They parallel each other in a way."

"But that's coal," Meggie said, "that's up in Alaska."

"It's part and parcel of the same," Jeff said.

"Even if Pinchot is gone," Meggie said, "there are still people who will fight us. I think the new ranger will, and maybe men like Bundy Jones."

"Jones is a botanist," Jeff said. "He's a very little cog in the forestry machine, if he's a cog at all. How deeply involved do you think he is?"

"I think he wants to keep the trees," Meggie said, "and I think he'd be pigheaded enough to do what he thought was right."

"Bundy?" Lorena said, bringing her wandering thoughts back to the supper table. "He's sweet, but I think he's very easy. I think any woman could wind him around her little finger."

Meggie's color rose. "That's not fair, Lorena. I think he's got a very strong integrity."

"What good does a very strong integrity do," Lorena asked lazily, "if a man's soft where women are concerned?"

"Just because he was willing to take you into the woods when no one else would—" Meggie began angrily. But she saw the look on both Jeff's and Lorena's faces. They no longer discussed the events of the summer, or who was to blame or why. With quiet determination everyone side-stepped the subject.

Meggie saw that she had almost precipitated a scene and set Lorena back into her despondency. "I'm sorry," she said. "How did we get away from Pinchot? So he's out of the way, and we are going to have less trouble putting our claims through. That calls for some sort of rejoicing, doesn't it?"

"Yes," Jeff said. "I hope so."

"Oh, God!" Lorena said, "to be rid of those homesteads! to be in money again! to have all this nightmare over and done with!"

"Yes," Jeff said again, "and very soon, I hope."

Meggie did not say anything. Sometimes she had an inordinate longing for the solitude of her cabin under the pines. She was even looking forward to the second winter journey which lay ahead of her. She knew now what the worst could be, and she was planning with care and foresight for a better experience this time.

3.

When Bundy reached the Forestry office on January eighth, he found confirmation of the rumor that the chief had been fired. Consternation and speculation ran through the offices of the department. It seemed impossible to think of the Forestry Service without Pinchot, for he had in a way created it from an unpromising beginning, given it life and meaning, and bound every worker to him by personal interest and enthusiasm. Probably no other department of government at that time had such devotion and loyalty from its members. Somehow the head of the Service had made each least important member feel that he had a mission to perform and was personally responsible.

Pinchot came in as usual, neat and freshly shaven, smiling all around at them. First he called some of the top men in to him and spoke to them alone. Then he spoke to all the members of the Service who were in Washington. It was good-bye, but, if it had sentiment in it, the speech was first of all designed to bind them together and prepare them to go on without him.

"I want every man here to stay in the Service," he said. "I do not want any of you to . . . let this Service fall, or even droop, from the high standard that we have built up for it together. That is first. Never forget that the fight in which you are engaged for the safe and decent handling of our timberlands is infinitely larger than any man's personal presence or personal fortunes. . . . Never allow yourselves to forget that you are serving a much greater master than the Department of Agriculture or even the Administration. You are serving the people of the United States. You are engaged in a piece of work that lies at the foundation of the new patriotism of Conservation and equal opportunity. You are creating a point of view that will in the end control this and all other nations.

"The best service you can do me . . . is for you men to stick to this work. I want you men to stay by it with the same point of view, the same spirit, the same energy, the same devotion that have made the Forest Service the best body of men under the Government.

"This is not good-bye, because there isn't going to be any. We are still in the same work—different parts of it, but always the same work. My interest, my loyalty, and my affection belong to it and to you, and they always will. . . . Go ahead with it, exactly as if I were still here."

Bundy felt deeply moved. He saw that, while perhaps he might have faltered when G.P. was still in control, he could not possibly falter now.

The offices of the Forest Service were crowded with people that morning. It was more like a triumphant ovation than a defeat. Telegrams and letters from people all over the country began to pour in and pile up into the thousands. Until this moment the men of the Forest Service had had no way of knowing how many plain people were behind them, hoping for their success. Now at last they knew.

G.P. went to Europe to meet Roosevelt on his return from Africa, but the men he left behind were sworn to carry on his crusade, even in the minute attention to detail to which he had accustomed them.

4.

The summer of 1910 was hot and dry. It followed a mild winter and a previous summer of slight precipitation. As early as May hot winds blew up from the dry plains to the south and west withering the young growth and shrinking the streams. Fire calls began to come in two months earlier than usual, and the fire crews were increased and strengthened. Everyone knew that rain was bound to come before long, but nevertheless there was an uneasy preparation for what might prove to be a difficult summer.

The early warmth was welcomed by the homesteaders. It meant open trails and streams that were easy to ford. They would not have to wait until June to cross the tricky snowdrifts on the side of Freezeout Mountain. They could wade, instead of swim, the ford.

The mild winter had made the six-month winter visit comparatively simple this year. Meggie had made the trip easily and she was proud of the skill she had acquired with snowshoes.

There had been only one terrible incident in the winter's journey, and Meggie tried to put that out of her mind as well as she could. Nan had taken her dog with them this year. "The poor brute misses me when I'm gone," she said. "He howls and drives my sister crazy. It's an open winter. He'll make out as well as I will." Nan had been last in line as they straggled down into the valley, and her dog had been following along behind her. Suddenly three wolves had come out of the snowy brush and set upon the dog, there within sight of all of them. Even Nan's screams had not scared them off. McSweeney had shot two of the wolves and the third one escaped into the brush, but not before the dog was so mangled and torn that McSweeney shot him, too, to end his suffering.

The incident had shaken all of them, and Nan, crying for her dog, had taken a great vow never to be last in line again. To lag behind for a moment seemed to her to be doomed.

"My homestead's last in line down the valley," she cried. "I've always hated that. But I won't be last on the trail again. There's always something following behind. I've felt it even when I haven't seen it. If it's wolves or wildcats or what, there's always something devilish following behind, hidden in the trees, waiting to pounce. No, I'll never be the last in line again."

Meggie had comforted Nan as best she could. "I'll go on down the valley and stay with you this time, the way you stayed with me last year. We'll be together all the way."

Nan had clung to her hand.

"Oh, Meg," she said, "I'm a fool, but honest to God, I do get scared. That dog was all the company I had most of the time these last summers. I was as batty over him as MacGillicuddy is over Jessie. What am I to do now?"

"We've just got to go on, so far as I can see," Meggie said. "Once you get on a trail, there doesn't seem to be a thing to do but follow it."

Yet this third summer Meggie felt strong and resourceful and happier than she had ever been before. She thought to herself that she had formerly taken it for granted that she was happy, simply through an absence of unhappiness. But now a sense of physical well-being gave her a more positive enjoyment of life. The sharp sting of sunshine on her bare arms, the odor of crushed pine needles, the faraway blue of distant wooded hills, each breath she drew gave her a sensation of pleasure and anticipation. She had an excited feeling that just beyond the next turn in the trail something delightful was awaiting her.

Her cries of pleasure and her unfailing optimism irritated and depressed Lorena. Lorena no longer saw the physical aspects of the trail, the trees and flowers and stones, which gave Meggie such addlepated delight. To Lorena the trail had become a long ordeal of effort which was associated with pain and death, with Ollie and Bundy Jones and Charlie Duporte.

In the end it was the thought of Charlie Duporte that brought her the only comfort and anticipation she had. Charlie could make her laugh when no one else could. Charlie had been through it all with her, and somehow he understood her better than anyone else ever had, better than Jeff, better than Ralph, better than Bundy Jones. The others saw only some part of her which gratified themselves, but Charlie saw her whole and accepted her, the ugly with the beautiful.

It was because of Charlie Duporte that she had come back at all this year. She could easily have persuaded Jeff to let her stay in town this summer. But town was empty, too. It seemed to have no particular meaning for her any more.

She hated the homestead, yet it had deprived her of her pleasure in the town. It seemed to her that the trail between the two was all that she had left, that it was a kind of purgatory through which she was condemned to travel, in dust and horse smell and bewildered discontent. If Charlie Duporte were at the end of it to lift her down and laugh at her, perhaps she might feel beautiful again and take some sweet, malicious satisfaction in living.

Jeff rode moodily, slumped forward in the saddle. The trail had memories for him too.

When the homesteaders reached their cabins in the valley that year they found notices tacked on each cabin door. The government was warning them that it would contest their claims. The new ranger had been all through the valley in the early spring and tacked up the notices. The pieces of paper made little fresh white squares on the weathered wood of the doors. They were the first things one noticed on coming into each clearing from the trail.

The instant reaction that the notices evoked was anger.

"We come in here loaded with supplies for the summer. What we going to do now?"

"Why, stay, by God! If they want to fight, we'll fight."

"It should be easy now old Pinchot's out. We knew all along we'd have to fight it."

Meggie was angry too. "Eye MacGillicuddy wouldn't have done a thing like this to us. It's that new ranger."

"Eye was a ranger too, till they booted him out," Nan said. "I guess he'd have done what they told him to do."

"Yes, but he saw our side," Meggie said. "I know now they put a new man here to make it hard for us."

"Hard?" Lorena said. "Could it be harder than it's been? Does this change anything at all?"

Up and down the valley men swore and women scolded and deplored. They talked it out with a certain amount of gusto and satisfaction. The fight was in the open now, and that relieved the feelings at least.

Only Jeff Carney said nothing. Ralph had promised him that this would be quick and easy—a way to make money in a hurry. He knew now that he had really never believed in Ralph's easy solution. He was neither a fighter nor a talker, but to brood was an old preoccupation with him. He thought back now over all the time he had wasted in this venture which was likely to come to nothing. On his conscience, for the first time, pressed the weight of the many trusting people he had located here in the valley for a hundred dollars, or a diamond ring or whatever they could scrape together as a fee. A sudden sense of shame overwhelmed him for the depths to which he had sunk.

He thought with a pang of added anguish, "But Ollie will never know." If it was a consolation, it was also a bitter pain of loss and waste. There was no use talking with Lorena about this. Anger over the contest notices had somewhat revived her flagging spirits. He knew that she would expect him to fight and win. She would have no respect for a man who could allow himself to be defeated, even with everything, *everything* stacked against him.

Charlie Duporte was there with his guitar. He laughed as usual. "Sure, I got notice. Ever'body did. But what it change? So we got to prove we make homes? Sure, we make homes! I live all winter by my place. Got me two fine bearskin rugs on my floor. Very, very homelike. Some day you come and see." He began to tune his guitar, and Lorena laughed too. She sparkled once more with anger and with laughter. She looked in her mirror and coiled her long dark hair.

Jeff felt the jealousy which had lain dormant last summer rising up in him again. He felt that he should make some gesture or plunge himself into some action. Yet he remained silent, waiting for a token, an incident, he scarcely knew what, to light up the way before him and push him into action.

Toward the end of May the unseasonable drought was broken

by a series of scattered showers that brought relief and confidence to the valley. They eased the nervous tension which builds up in dry weather.

Meggie had made an early start with her garden. "Maybe it's for the deer, but I've got to try anyway," she said to herself. She went out and stood in the gentle patter of rain, her face lifted to receive it. There was a delicious odor of wet dust, of freshly washed pine needles. I'm a vegetable myself, she thought, feeling the cool drops running down her face; and she laughed so that her voice resounded in the silent clearing. A bird took fright and went away chattering among the branches.

Meggie's dog, enlivened by the change of weather and his mistress' high spirits, dashed away after the bird, barking hoarsely. Two seasons of homesteading were settling him into a dependable creature with protective instincts. If he sometimes barked at the wrong person, Meggie felt on the whole that he meant well, and was making progress in the right direction. His chief fault was that on coming out of the woods he felt too self-confident, and would cheerfully set upon any other dog he met regardless of size. Meggie had learned from experience that if she didn't plunge into the middle of a dogfight and separate the combatants, nobody else would. Thus she had added, to the many skills and minor braveries which she was acquiring, the art of stopping a dogfight.

"The only thing is not to be afraid," Meggie told Nan, whose philosophy concerning dogfights had been "let 'em kill each other." "Dogs know it right away if you're afraid, and they don't have any respect for you."

"I s'pose a dog's respect is better than nothing," Nan said. "I had it, and I appreciated it, but the wolves made short work of it."

Nan and Meggie often trudged back and forth to see each other that summer. There was a good deal of comfort to be derived from seeing another woman making a courageous stand in a similarly difficult situation. Their winter's journeys together had endeared them to each other. Lorena had never shared their naïve enthusiasms or been obliged to face their lonely responsibilities. She neither understood nor wanted the kind of childlike comradeship they found in sharing their experiences.

"Nan O'Rourke?" she said impatiently. "What can you see in

her, Meg? The old woman's nothing but a fuddy-duddy milliner."

"But out here," Meggie said, "does that make any difference? Out here what we are depends on such a lot of different qualities and circumstances. Town standards seem a little silly here."

"That's the awful thing," Lorena said. "Here we have to compromise, to throw away the things we value in town."

"Yet look what Charlie Duporte has done for you and Jeff," Meggie said, her glance not quite as artless as it might have been. "And what is Charlie? Only a lumberjack?"

"A man is different," Lorena said. "A man can make his own standards."

"A woman can too," said Meggie stoutly. "I'm coming to the conclusion that ladies are human beings. It's a thought I wasn't raised on, but I like it anyway."

5.

When Bundy reached Cold Spring early in June, he found it transformed from its usual peaceful lethargy into a center of activity. All sorts of men were being recruited for fire fighting: transients from the employment agencies in Spokane and Missoula, road crews, men from logging camps, men from ranches and mines. Emergency spending had been sanctioned by Graves, the new chief of the Forest Service, and Matt had his hands full. He was glad to turn some of the organizational work over to Bundy. At first they had avoided being seen together, but now they stopped trying to preserve the fiction of completely separate interests. Bundy found it easy to throw aside his pretense of detachment when every able-bodied man was being recruited to some phase of the forest protection. It was even easy at times for him to forget the case he had drawn up against the homesteaders in the past winter. He could sleep at night after a day of hard, practical work.

This year he did not hunt for botanical specimens or classify and draw them. He did not fish or prepare gourmet meals of Morchella or seasonal berries. He ate pork and beans and bannock, and when he was not recruiting men in town, he helped to dig fire trenches and followed dusty trails from one fire lookout to another.

After the scant May rains no moisture fell, and the hot and parching weather continued steadily through June and July. No one could remember such a dry season in the history of the region. Hot winds from the arid lowland plains blew northward into the forests, drying the marshes and the old lake beds, melting the last snow from the northern creases of the mountains, reducing the rushing streams to thin shallow trickles.

This was only one region in a widespread area in the Bitterroot Mountains of Idaho and Montana. It was estimated that there were about 10,000 fire fighters scattered through the forests that summer. Later several companies of troops from Fort Snelling in Minnesota were moved into the Bitterroots to fight fire. Later still, convicts were released from some of the Montana prisons to help.

There was a general feeling that the emergency situation might end any day with a good soaking rain. And day after day all through June and July great thunderhead clouds would pile up during the afternoon, promising rain, but only a few drops would fall and the wind would blow the clouds away by evening. Often the clouds were full of thunder and lightning play. The lightning struck whimsically here and there among the great trees, and there was not enough moisture to put out the resulting fire.

In other years fires had burned and died away in the forests during July and August, but in 1910 they began in May and there was nothing to stop them but the efforts men could make. To save the forests became a great regional endeavor. When there were no pressing fires to fight, there were trails to be opened into virgin country, and tool and food caches to be placed at strategic points.

Long files of pack horses and mules moved slowly along the trails into the wilderness and oddly assorted men, most of them city-bred and inexperienced in wilderness ways, fanned out into the lonely forest.

Late in June Bundy was bringing a supply train and a few men in to join Matt at a lookout station on Roundtop Mountain. He had been busy with recruiting and outfitting work in Cold Spring for nearly a month, and he was eager to get out into the forest and face the actual difficulties. They followed a new trail and were headed away from the Floodwood Valley where there had as yet been no fire alarms. Bundy thought of the Floodwood Valley wistfully, wondering who was there and if they knew the dangers that surrounded them.

The men expected to camp that night on the upper reaches of the Clearwater River, but when the trail crossed the shrunken river Bundy could not at first believe that he had reached his objective. This seemed a creek rather than a river. Only the width of the stream bed with its exposed boulders and scattered pools told him that this was the Clearwater. The sound of rushing water no longer deadened the senses. This was a gentle murmur, and above and beyond it he could hear the roll of thunder.

Still no rain fell, and in the morning there was a smell of burning in the dry air and a long way off on the mountainside a small and lazy wisp of smoke. It was nothing to cause sincere alarm.

Yet it gave Bundy a purpose. Matt would probably be on his way there now, and Bundy decided to send the pack train on with two of the men, and take the other three men across country in the direction of the fire.

They began to go up the river, working their way toward the mountain by the shortest route. Fitfully on the breeze they smelled the smoke, but the going was difficult and the mountain farther away than Bundy had estimated. All day they struggled toward it through dry, crackling brush and across diminished streams. At night they made camp, and through the darkness they could see the fire like a red winking eye on the side of the mountain.

By noon the next day Bundy came on men digging trenches to halt the fire's spread. He and his men set to work beside the others, digging in the dry earth under a smoky sky. It was hard work but not impossible here, for they were in open country and a fire trench could be useful. In deep woods a trench was often useless because the fire leaped from treetop to treetop, and only a backfire, in itself a hazardous and tricky thing, was of any help.

Bundy saw the creeping red tongues that moved through the grass and brush as a tangible enemy with which he was glad to come to grips.

He and his men were in time to help Matt's crew put an end to the fire. In a haze of smoke Bundy and Matt met and grinned at each other from blackened faces.

"Well, she's under control," Matt said. "You helped speed it up, but we'd have done it without you."

"Sure," Bundy said. "I just wanted a taste of it."

"You'll get a bellyful before the summer's over," Matt said.

There were a great many things Bundy wanted to know and gradually he got around to asking about the Floodwood Valley homesteaders. Had they returned? Were they still there in spite of the fire hazards? What did they think of the contest notices?

"I think they're all in there," Matt said. "Fire hasn't hit down that way. I don't think they know there's any danger unless some of 'em have been in to Cold Spring. It might be you better ride over that way sometime and tell them to get out. They wouldn't welcome me just now. They think I'm hell bent to do them in the eye, since we posted those notices. Well, if all this country burns off, we can give it to the homesteaders. Land will be all cleared for them."

"They won't want it then," Bundy said. "They want the timber, not the land."

"Well, we won't let it burn," Matt said. "Forestry and fraudulent claims can all go hang this year. What we've got to think about from day to day is saving the woods from fire. It's a big job, but we're holding it. We've got to keep right on holding until the rains come. We can think of other things later."

Bundy determined that he would ride over to the Floodwood Valley at his first free time. They must know by now what the situation was, still he felt that he could not leave it to chance that they should be warned of the fire danger. The thought of seeing Lorena, Meggie, all of them again, stirred a tumult of mixed feelings in Bundy. He both dreaded and anticipated going. Perhaps for this reason, the press of work that piled up day after day to prevent his going did not dismay him as much as it should have done.

They must know, he thought. They certainly must know.

The summer slipped by and still it did not rain. Sometimes the mocking play of lightning would set forty or fifty new fires in a single afternoon. Yet by pouring men into the region and keeping on the alert, the Forest Service seemed to be winning the battle with nature.

By early August the fire fighting had settled into a grim routine, and the men in charge felt that, after controlling the scattered fires for two dry months, they would be able to hold them down now until the long-overdue rains came. It could not be much longer. In Washington, they reckoned with pride from the reports that came in that over three thousand small fires had been stopped and nearly a hundred big ones trenched in throughout northern Idaho and Montana. Nothing so vast had ever been accomplished before in this line; but then there had never before been such a summer. It was a challenge that they had met, and all they had to do now was to continue holding and keeping alert control until the autumn rains.

In the Floodwood Valley, Meggie carried water from her diminishing stream to her languid garden. The days were hot and dry but beautiful. When the great clouds built up overhead and darkened the sun for a time, she thought optimistically, *Now*. This is the time. It'll rain sure this afternoon.

Sometimes there was a faint odor of smoke on the morning air, but the valley remained untouched, and the homesteaders knew very little of the activity that surrounded them in other parts of the forest.

Once Klein, after a trip to Cold Spring for supplies, came down the valley to spread the news.

"Say! There's been fires all round us. You know that? They say in Cold Spring there's ten thousand men fighting fires around here and over into Montana. If it ain't hit us here yet, don't mean it won't. I'm thinkin' of takin' the missus an' the boy and gittin' out of here. But first I come all the way down trail to tell you folks. What do you think?"

Most homesteaders were of the opinion that this summer above all they had better stay on their places.

"We run out now, how is it gonna look to them rangers? They're just waitin' for a chance to see our tails hikin' out of here. It's all they need to make 'em think we don't have homes here."

"I guess you're right," Klein said. "We got to stay and protect our homes all right." He liked to visit as well as spread news, so he continued all the way down the valley to Nan's.

Nan slipped her packsack onto her back and returned with him as far as Meggie's. She was unusually timorous and unsure since she had lost her dog.

"What are we going to do, Megeen?" she asked. "Are we going

to stay in here and get roasted alive like a couple of mud hens?"

"Oh, Nan, I don't want to go," Meggie said. "If I leave now, my garden I've worked so hard on is all going to dry up and come to nothing. We haven't been touched here. I don't see why we should be. The rain can come any day."

"That's what I thought, too," Nan said, "only I wanted to hear you say it. I'm all alone down there at the end of the line. I don't mind being alone, if I know there are other people nearby. But if you all skun out and left the valley, I'd never know you'd gone."

"We wouldn't go and leave you, Nan," Meggie reassured her.

"Megeen, is that a promise?" Nan begged. Meggie was surprised at the urgency in Nan's face. The older woman went on earnestly, "You won't ever go and leave me alone in here, will you? Promise me. Ever since the wolves came out and got my dog last winter, I've been scared of being the last in line. I dream about it, Meg. I dream I'm last and everybody going on ahead of me, and they keep right on and don't even know that something has jumped on me. I try to scream but nobody ever hears me. You know they say that wildcats, cougars, lie out on the branches of the trees, hidden by leaves, and after all the pack train's passed along but one, the thing leaps down and breaks the back of the last horse."

"Nan, you've thought too much about it. You've got to forget the wolves."

"I know. It's an obsession, I guess, like some women fear mice or snakes. With me it's the thing behind me that I can't see that I'm afraid of. If only I wasn't living way down on the last homestead in line, Meggie, and all alone without a dog. Promise you'll never go away without letting me know. Promise."

"I promise, Nan. Honest, I do," Meggie said.

After that she made a good strong pot of tea, and they drank themselves into a more cheerful frame of mind.

"So we stick it out then," Nan said.

"Everybody's going to do it," Meggie said. "We've stood up with the best of them so far. Let's keep our flags flying."

"All right," Nan said. "I'm easier now I know you won't go off without me."

6.

But in the hot dry air there was tension that built up with the passing days. The more Jeff brooded upon the situation they were in, the more hopeless he became. Out of his mental anguish, certain positive ideas began to emerge. If all had gone smoothly, he would probably have pushed them aside, but, since the contest notices had been posted, he began to remember some of the errant thoughts he had had in the past.

There was the thought that he was on the wrong side in this fight. That somehow he was on the side of the selfish interests, while the bright young men of his age were fighting, should be fighting, to put monopoly down. He remembered a talk he had had with Bundy Jones in the first year they had come out here. Bundy had given him a fleeting vision of an ordered forest economy, of a forest producing a crop, forever reproducing itself, instead of a great lumbering out that would leave only devastation. He remembered how the forest had first moved and delighted him when he came here as a boy. Yes, I am on the wrong side, he thought. I have sold my soul for a mess of pottage. If my son had lived, he would have been ashamed of me.

He went often to the edge of the clearing and stood looking down at the tiny grave. *Ollie,* he said to himself softly, *little Ollie.* Even in his own mind he never remembered the baby as Oliver J. He was Ollie now, forever remembered and surrounded by sadness and tenderness.

Once, when he had been standing by the grave for a long time, he turned to go back to the cabin and he saw that Lorena and Charlie Duporte were watching him. There was a look on their faces that puzzled and annoyed him. Were they pitying him? or were they amused? He pretended not to see that they were watching him, but somehow for the moment he hated both of them. Charlie— and yes, Lorena, too. Yes, even Lorena. He could hate her too. The revelation came to him like a blow. What had it all amounted to between them? Was it love, this terrible, one-sided burning of infatuation? Had she ever felt a touch of what he felt?

It began to seem to him that there was only one right course left to him. This was to pull out now and leave the forest as they had found it; to make the other people whom he had brought in here see it as he did, so that they would pull out too.

The danger of fire scarcely penetrated his consciousness. He thought only that they had all been wrong to come here in the first place and that they had better get out. Often he thought of calling a meeting of the homesteaders to tell them this. It would be hard to do, especially since it had been he who had located them. But that was all the more reason why it must be done. Yes, it must be done, he thought. He could abase himself. Self-abasement was akin to self-pity. It gave him a certain bitter pleasure.

For a week after this determination came to him, Jeff did nothing. His old indecision and lethargy entangled him, and to do nothing was the easiest way. Yet the idea continued to plague him. It hung like an unanswered challenge in the breathless air. If he was ever to make a noble gesture, this was the time.

He dared not tell Lorena what was in his mind because she would laugh his resolution away with her scorn. If he told Lorena, his efforts at atonement would be scattered and his good intentions come to nothing. He saw, in his reluctance to ask her help in this matter of his conscience, that she had never really done anything for him. Yet what had he done for her? He could not remember now. They had been chained together reluctantly by his frustrated passion. It was her beauty—but what had she given him, except little Ollie, and he so briefly given?

In the dry heat, Jeff could not eat. He pushed aside his plate of coarse food and paced up and down the clearing.

Charlie was teaching Lorena how to play the guitar, and their careless laughter lingered and echoed in his ears. Lorena seemed resigned, almost contented this summer; but now it was Jeff who felt trapped by the monotony and the restricted vision of the homestead. It was the first summer that he had not gone back and forth on the trail, easing his emotions in activity. Now day followed day of heat and tension, and he had only his own bitter thoughts to keep him company.

Lorena and Charlie looked at him curiously, and Lorena's dark eyes seemed to soften for him.

"Jeff," she said, "what's the matter with you? Why don't you eat? What can I make you that you'll like to eat?"

"Nothing," Jeff said. "I'm getting along all right. I don't want anything."

"I tell you," Charlie said, "You and me go hunting, Jeff. We get some partridge, eh? That taste pretty good maybe."

"Well, perhaps," Jeff said. "But aren't the woods too dry for hunting?"

"First day it rains, we go," Charlie said. "I got to clean an' oil my gun some time. Then we be ready when the rain come down."

"All right," Jeff said. "I'll clean mine too. But there's no rain in sight yet. Nothing comes out of these clouds but more heat. I never knew a year like this." He rolled himself a cigarette, his fingers dry and awkward. He brushed the spilled tobacco off his shirt and drew a deep breath of the smoke.

At the end of the first week in August Bundy Jones rode down the trail, and Jeff was glad to see him.

"So you're still here?" Bundy said. "I thought you'd have the women out of here before this. You know that there have been fires all around you, don't you? It's been a hellish summer."

"We've had no fires here," Jeff said, "but it's been hot. Homesteaders haven't wanted to get out because the government's contesting us. You know that, don't you, Bundy?"

"Yes, I know. I'm sorry, and yet it had to come, Jeff."

"Yes, it had to come," Jeff said.

"I meant to ride through here weeks ago," Bundy said. "I wanted to tell you to get the women out, but there was a lot of work to do. I thought you'd all been warned."

"Are the fires so bad?"

"Well, they've been bad. We think we've got them under control now. Still until the rains come, no one knows for sure."

"You're riding around to all the homesteads?" Jeff asked.

"Yes."

"And you're calling everyone together for a meeting?"

"No," Bundy said, "I hadn't thought of that. I'm telling each one separately."

"But there must be a meeting," Jeff said eagerly. "It's not only the fire danger, Bundy. There are other things to discuss. I've thought it over carefully, and I see we're wrong. We've got no case in here. We ought to pull out. I'll talk to them, Bundy, if you'll call them together. And you talk to them too. Give them your vision of an ordered forest."

Bundy looked at Jeff in surprise. He saw how thin and strained the man looked.

"Why now, you're singing another tune," he said. "You mean you're for giving up the homesteads now without fighting the contest? I think you're wise. You'll save a lot of trouble."

"Oh, I've thought it over," Jeff said eagerly. "I see the right thing to do, but it's hard. You must help me, Bundy. There must be a meeting. Everyone must act together."

"Yes," Bundy said, "but can you get people together here?"

"Last year," Jeff said in a choked voice, "they all came, all of them. It was when my little son died. All of the homesteaders came. They came for the funeral. I think they will come again. I have been thinking all week that I would call them. But it is better if you do it, Bundy. Call them as if it were a meeting about the fire. But I will talk to them, I promise you. Will you help me, Bundy?"

"Yes, of course," Bundy said. "You have made a right decision, Jeff. I'm sure of it. Yes, I'll call them together here. When do you want them?"

Jeff paused for a moment, his face contorted with internal anguish.

"Thursday," he said finally. "Tell them to come Thursday."

Bundy rode away thoughtfully. He did not know what upheaval had occurred in Jeff Carney's soul, but he felt with a grave sense of relief that this might be the solution to the homestead problem. If they could be induced to leave voluntarily, if Jeff Carney could persuade them— It seemed too absurdly easy, and yet the Forest Service had nothing to lose by letting Jeff try. Bundy rode up and down the valley asking all the homesteaders to be at Carney's place on Thursday for a meeting on fire protection and matters relating to the contest of their claims.

It was a time of decision for Bundy too. Many people knew that he had been working closely with the ranger this summer. He felt that the time had come to let everyone know that he was a government man. This was as good an opportunity as any. He dreaded the moment. Yet, he thought, if Jeff Carney can face out his admission, I can face out mine. I never thought he had the courage to put himself in an unfavorable position, and I never realized before how much I lack the courage.

7.

Jeff did not tell Lorena that the homesteaders were coming until Wednesday evening. Her anger flared up hotly at the news.

"Here, Jeff? You've asked the valley people here? Whatever for? What made you do it?"

"Bundy Jones wants to talk to them about the fires," Jeff said.

"But why here? All those people. It's like last year."

"Yes, I know," Jeff said. "It's just about a year now. Ollie would have been walking, if he had lived. Maybe he would be starting to talk."

"Oh, don't!" Lorena said. "Can't you leave the past alone? You carry the past around on your shoulders like a packsack. What good does it do?"

"I can't help it," Jeff said. "But I'm going to change. I'm going to be a better man. You'll see, Lorena. I've been drifting long enough. Now I'm going to take my own way, not somebody else's. I'm going to start all fresh, and make something of myself. You'll see, really you will. "

"I've heard you say that before," Lorena said, "but it's always good news. If you remember it this time—"

"I will," Jeff said. "I've made up my mind."

The homesteaders began straggling into the clearing before noon. Their faces looked anxious and worn. The years in the forest had left none of them untouched. They were thinner and harder, and most of them had changed for the worse. They had all come in here hoping for quick money, yet they had invested time and savings to no immediate avail. They were beginning to be bitter and disillusioned. Anger flashed easily near the surface of their minds.

There were a few notable exceptions. Smith had stopped drinking because to keep himself supplied with liquor out here had simply become too difficult. He looked hale and hearty and was making a good stab at clearing and gardening. Meggie Carney seemed to thrive on difficulties and was blooming like a rose. Nan O'Rourke was thin and her nose stuck out like a beak, yet she and the Kleins were relatively unchanged. But time and circumstances had laid a heavy hand on the faces of the others.

Charlie built up a fire in the stove and began to get out pots and pans.

"What are you doing?" Lorena asked him sharply.

"By gar, they got to eat, don't they?" Charlie said. "Jeff ask them here, we better give 'em a good time, eh?"

Lorena sighed. "All right," she said. "Go on and make a party of it, if you want to. We might as well get all we can out of it." She went to the mirror and brushed back her hair. But she didn't look closely any more. She knew the two thin lines that kept forming between her eyes above the nose, two little lines that creased her forehead; and at each corner of her mouth, an area of hardness. At first she had tried to combat these things by lifting her brows and smiling at her image; but something in her thoughts and feelings penciled them in again when she was not looking. It was no use. They were always there when she glanced at herself casually. They became more and more difficult to erase.

Most of the homesteaders had come on foot. The last ones, those who had been on the way since early morning, straggled in after noon.

"What are we here for?" they began to ask. "Who's got anything to say to us?"

They sat on stumps or stood around the clearing waiting for something to begin.

Charlie and Lorena brought around coffee and doughnuts. Although the whole affair annoyed her, Lorena put herself out to be charming to them. Most of the settlers had their own lunches of cold salt pork and sourdough biscuits. Some of them enjoyed the picnic atmosphere in the novelty of human society. Others were moody and eager to have the meeting finished and get started on the long trail back. The sun beat down, and even under the trees it was hot and dry. The stumps oozed pitch, and twigs and pine needles crackled under their feet.

Bundy was one of the last to arrive. He had a feeling that there was nothing he could say to these people beyond the public message which he had formulated in his mind. He would not run the risk of allowing his emotions to become involved again. These were home-steaders settled on fraudulent claims, and he was a government agent. He was fighting for the broader justice to the larger number of people. He had known from the start that these few people would have to be sacrificed. That he had become so deeply involved with them was an unfortunate by-product of his youth and emo-tional immaturity. It was his own fault. Now, in a way, he meant to sacrifice himself as well as them.

Jeff greeted him nervously when he rode up to the clearing. Bundy left his horse tied to the rail fence and walked beside Jeff to the waiting people. He thought that Jeff looked more haggard than when they had made the plans for this meeting, as if he had not eaten well or slept. A fleeting concern for Jeff's sanity crossed his mind. Still, Bundy knew what mental anguish was like, and per-haps Jeff was saner now than he had ever been. If he were really going through with this—

"You speak first," Jeff said. "They've been waiting a long time." He tried to roll a cigarette, but his fingers were trembling and the tobacco kept spilling. "I'm a bit nervous," he said apologeti-cally. "I'll smoke after it's over." Absently he laid the matches, the book of cigarette papers, the leather tobacco pouch on a stump, as if he were through with them forever. "I'll introduce you, Bundy," he said. "When you've said all you want to say, you can turn it over to me."

"That's fine," Bundy said.

Jeff stood in front of the people and held up his hand. They gathered around him expectantly, some of them sitting cross-legged on the ground, others standing in a semicircle behind.

"I don't have to introduce Bundy Jones to you," Jeff said. "You all know him and like him. He's going to speak to you about the fires."

Bundy began to speak easily about the fires. "Because you haven't had any in this valley, don't think you aren't in danger," he said, and he went on to outline the precautions they should take, and what should be done in case fire started. "You ought to be or-ganized to help each other. If fire starts, someone must be delegated to go to the ranger for help. The rest of you must turn out to dig trenches and build backfires. You've been each fellow for himself out here, but in case of fire you've got to pull together."

He saw their faces turned toward him in listening friendliness. He knew so much about each one, more than he wished to know. "I think the women should be got out of here at once," he said, "Let the men stay if they want to, but women and children should be in a safer place."

He saw Lorena, whose eyes had once so moved him, looking at him with thoughtful calculation. He saw Meggie Carney's up-turned face, round and brown, her blond hair burned almost white and pulled back carelessly from her forehead. Her eyes held more than friendliness; they held a kind of hero worship or adoration that Bundy found exceedingly annoying. He had no claim to a look like that; he didn't want it. He rushed on to destroy it.

"Women have no place in here anyway," he said, giving his sudden anger the rein, as he might have given rein to a headstrong horse. "It's no place for a man, far less for a woman. What pig-headed folly makes a woman think that she can tame the wilderness? What slim chance of making money drives her into a place like this?" He took a deep breath and went rushing on.

"The government is fighting hard this summer to save the forest from burning; and I might as well tell you now that I'm with the government all the way. I've been with it from the start, and I don't know if that will come as a surprise to you or not, but I'm with it, heart and soul. And if we save the woods from fire, do you think that we are going to turn around and hand over what we have saved to the lumber companies for lumbering off? No, we aren't. We're trying to save the white pine for the good of the whole nation, not just to help a few of you to turn a quick dollar."

He saw their faces changing from incredulity to anger. He saw Lorena smiling, a hard, bright, knowing smile. He saw the adoration fading out of Meggie's eyes, and something shocked and hurt taking its place. He had not meant to say what he had to say in anger, but that was the way it came out.

"So now you know where I stand," he said. "I'm going to try to see justice done. Justice can't please everyone. Somebody always has to get hurt. It's too bad, but that's how it is. So I'm asking you now, calmly and sensibly, to get out of here before you're burned out; and, if you aren't burned out, go anyway before you've sunk more time and money in a hopeless cause."

Someone shouted, "You was a botanist, eh? Flowers and mosses, was it? Maybe you tacked them contest notices on our doors, Jones?"

"No," Bundy said more quietly, "I didn't tack the notices on your doors, but I believe they are right. I want to see this land go back into the management of the Forest Service."

"So you want to lock it up. Let nobody get no use out of it?"

"No," Bundy said, "I want to see the forest made to produce a good crop for years to come, not lumbered off for the profit of the lumber companies. Look at it this way. You're not going to make a big thing out of this even if you win your titles. But somebody higher up will. You want to sell out the little people of the United States, the people like yourselves, to make the big fellow richer? I don't think you're selfish enough for that."

"You talking as if we didn't intend to make homes here. How do you know what's in our minds?"

"Let me speak," Jeff said. He was trembling all over, and his face was white. Bundy stepped aside.

"Jeff Carney sees it the right way," he said. "Jeff's going to tell you how he sees it."

"Bundy knows what he's talking about," Jeff said in a choking voice. "We have all been in the wrong. I more than anyone. I see that now. I see how hopeless it is, how wrong. There is no use fighting this. It is—it is—stronger than we are."

Jeff had nerved himself for this moment of confession and self-abasement, but now suddenly he felt his own ineptitude weighing him down like a ball and chain. He saw amazement and scorn blazing in Lorena's eyes, and pity in the eyes of his sister. The others looked at him in angry disbelief and he felt his own convictions waver. For years he had been arguing in his own behalf, trying to justify himself and gain other people's sympathy, and the more he talked the less they had listened. Now he argued for a cause outside himself, something positive that he had come to believe in. He felt the affirmative strength of a belief that was beyond selfish ends. Yet his voice still lacked the authority he needed; it lacked the power to persuade. He stood awkwardly before them, and he felt the sweat breaking out on his forehead.

"It's true," he said. "This is truth that I speak now. You must believe me."

They began to roar and shout at him.

"By God! You took our money, brought us in here."

"I'll pay you back," Jeff said. "When I can. Somehow I'll get the money, some other way."

But his voice was lost in the loud and angry talk among the other homesteaders.

Suddenly Lorena stepped forward, calm and beautifully poised.

"This whole meeting has been a surprise to me," she said. "Men we have trusted have betrayed us. But if my husband won't fight for this place, I will. Bundy Jones is right when he says we've got to stick together and depend on ourselves. But he's wrong what he says about women. Who's going to make a home in here, if it isn't the women? Fire isn't going to drive me out of here, a government plaster on my door isn't going to drive me out. Is there any homesteader here who feels different? If there is, let him step over and shake hands with Jeff Carney and Bundy Jones. They've gone right over on the other side and left us holding the bag."

Her voice rang with the authority Jeff's had lacked. Some of the homesteaders raised a cheer for her, and Charlie Duporte cried, "Listen, all! She got the right idea, Mis' Carney has."

The meeting passed into a phase of complete disorder. In vain Bundy tried to pull it together; he had lost the power to command their attention.

Finally it was Klein who created some kind of order, and exhorted the homesteaders to stand together to protect their homes.

"They got no right telling us we can't make homes here. We done it already. Now all we got to do is stick it out and fight. By God, I like to see them prove we ain't made homes here! Maybe Jeff Carney's scared to fight, but none of the rest of us are."

Bundy looked around for Jeff, but he had slipped away somewhere.

Bundy saw with the clarity of hindsight that the meeting had served only one purpose, and that was to weld the scattered and selfish elements into a united battlefront. What it had done personally to Jeff Carney he could not yet imagine. Even if it left him unscathed, he would always now be followed by mistrust and angry looks. His wife had been the first to beat him down.

Bundy went to the fence to get his horse. He saw Lorena coming toward him and he tried to avoid her, but, before he had unhitched the horse, she stood beside him.

"I suspected you all along, Bundy," she said. "So now I'm ready to forgive you."

"Well?" he said, putting his foot in the stirrup.

"And you will forgive me," she said. "Let's us be friendly enemies, Bundy."

"I don't know if that's possible, Lorena."

"Remember, Bundy," she said, "our trip over the mountain. You were so good to me."

"I'll never forget it," Bundy said. "But it was a long time ago, and all of us change."

"Yes," Lorena said. "Things change us, things outside ourselves. Bundy, you won't fight us? We've all been too close, too fond of one another. Isn't it true, Bundy?"

"That's what makes it hard," Bundy said, "but I can't hold out any false hopes to you. I'm involved in something that's bigger and more important than what happens to me personally. If that sounds stuffy, laugh it off. I'm trying to put a lid on my own desires."

"Bundy, I don't hate you. Don't hate me."

"I never have, Lorena."

He turned his horse's head back toward the mountain, but Lorena laid her hand on the bridle.

"Bundy, I may need you to help me someday. If I ask you, will you come?"

"Ask Charlie to help you," Bundy said. "I think you can manage all right by yourself, but if you need anyone, Charlie's a more resourceful fellow than I am. He'll be glad to help you."

She dropped her hand from the bridle.

"Go along," she said. "I thought you were soft, but you're just as hard as I am, aren't you?"

He rode up the trail without looking back.

8.

Jeff wanted to get away from the angry and accusing eyes. He went into the woods, but even there it was stiflingly hot. He wanted to be cool again, rid of the burning dryness of his mouth and the pain in the back of his head.

Once he came back to the clearing, thinking to get his tobacco and cigarette papers. He did not know why he had failed to put them in his pocket where he always kept them. But people were still in the clearing, talking about him, making angry plans.

Some were beginning to go and he could see Lorena, with Charlie beside her, telling them goodbye. She was trying to put a good face on it, as she had done at the meeting. He knew that she had spoken more effectively than he had but he didn't care now. He could no longer remember why he had felt such an alien urge to put himself on the right side. Now he wanted to be refreshed and cleansed.

He thought of the only spot that, all through this desperate summer, had remained cool. It was the spring in the woods behind the clearing. Welling up stubbornly out of an unknowing earth, the water continued to bubble coolly, even after the streams ran thin and dry.

Stumbling along the path under the trees, Jeff went to the spring and drank and bathed his face in the cold water. He was too tired to plan what he should do next.

So he had been a fool, he thought. His testament to right had come at an ill-timed moment, and once again, as so many times before, he had failed.

He sat on the moss beside the spring and put his head in his hands. At first he was too deeply concerned with himself to notice, but later he saw that Charlie's old Hudson's Bay jacket lay on the moss beside him. Charlie must have dropped it there early in the morning when he came to the spring for water.

Jeff remembered that Charlie had been wearing the jacket the first time he ever saw him. It was that day, a long time ago, when Lorena and Meggie had first come to Cold Spring, and they had all begun the homesteading. Charlie had been on the stage that day too, and he had been wearing the jacket. Jeff had noticed it particularly because the jacket was new and a very handsome one. It had sat easily on Charlie's broad shoulders. Now it was old and soiled. It had given Charlie a lot of good wear winter and summer.

As he looked at it Jeff knew that there would be tobacco somewhere in a pocket of the jacket. He longed with renewed intensity for the comfort of a cigarette.

He pulled the jacket toward him and began to go through the pockets. Matches, cigarette papers, dice and fishline, but so far no familiar cotton draw-stringed bag of tobacco.

Now that he had invaded Charlie's pockets, Jeff felt a careless curiosity. What did another man keep in his pockets? The contents of a man's pockets might be an indication of his character. The dice, now, who but Charlie would have had them there beside the cigarette papers?

He found the tobacco in one of the side pockets, but before he rolled the cigarette, some compulsion of curiosity made Jeff go on looking. What was Charlie Duporte really like? What did he carry in his pockets? There was one pocket left, an inner breast pocket. Before he put his hand into it, Jeff could feel the crackle of paper. Was it a section card? A bill? A letter from his mother? A last will and testament?

Idly Jeff pulled the paper out, and he recognized with shock that it was note paper he had bought for Lorena more than a year ago. The folds of the paper were worn and soiled as if it had been long carried in the pocket. With a painfully beating heart Jeff unfolded the paper and saw Lorena's well known writing. At first the words blurred so before his eyes that he could not read them. Then quite suddenly they came clear, clear and black and unmistakable.

Dearest, the words said, *Help us. Help me. You don't know how hard this is to bear. I can't go on here in this place. You could do something for me if you cared a little bit. You are the only one who could. Rena.*

Jeff read the message through three times, trying to understand and bring it into focus. Then he folded it carefully and put it back in the pocket. He tried to roll the cigarette, but once again his hands were trembling so much that he was obliged to give it up.

He did not go into the cabin until evening came. When he saw the lamplight in the window, he went slowly toward the house. He was not trembling now, but he had rehearsed a series of questions to which he knew that he must have the answers. The answers might annihilate him, but he wanted to go beyond the hedges and fences of old pretense and reach the truth that had been hidden from him.

9.

The faces of the homesteaders kept swimming into Bundy's consciousness as he rode up the trail. He saw them all, disbelieving, angry, determined. He saw Lorena's face in its light and shadow, ranging from scorn and defiance to pleading and cajoling. But he found that it no longer had the power to move him deeply.

Another woman's face disturbed him for the first time. He saw again the look of hero worship and adulation on Meggie Carney's face, and how it had changed to surprise and hurt. The unwarranted trust in him had irritated him, but now he understood that, little as he deserved it, it had been a rare thing, and he had wiped it out. There had been pity on her face for her brother too. She had had a hard day with all of her naïve loyalties and admirations pulled apart and dissipated by a few rough words. She was making a good struggle for her homestead; she was little more than a child—or was she? Certainly there had been a kind of maturity in that look of hurt, the look of pity. She always reminded him of his sister Annie, and that had annoyed him too. Annie was a kid sister, but he wouldn't have hurt her for the world. Bundy was deeply troubled.

He wished that he had stopped to say a word of apology to Meggie Carney. She wouldn't have taken it well, he knew, but somehow he felt he owed it to her. He kept thinking of it as he rode along. He should have spoken to her; accepted her reproaches if he had to, but made his position clear to her at any rate. She had a right to know why he had acted as he had. He owed the explanation both to himself and to her. If he explained it all to her, then, he felt, he could be finally quit of the homesteaders. One last loose end to tie, and then sever all the entangling relations that had ensnared him and made his course difficult.

Halfway up the mountain, he turned his horse and started back. It was another foolish gesture but it was a gesture he had to make. He would ride by Jeff Carney's place without stopping and go on to Meggie's for a few brief words.

He could camp in the woods that night and rejoin Matt and the men on the mountain by the following afternoon. The air was hot and still, and there were no new indications of fire. Quiet air was the next best thing to rain where fire was concerned. Bundy rode slowly. If he had ever had a fine and noble image of himself, it deserted him now.

10.

When Jeff came into the cabin, he saw that Lorena and Charlie were at supper. The lamp in the center of the table lit their faces with a warm glow. There were bread and cheese and tea on the table. He could smell the newly made tea like a perfume in the room.

"Well, hero," Lorena said, "have you come in to eat? Your place is set for you."

The lightness of her tone struck him like another blow. He had thought that there was nothing further she could do to him; but now he knew that as long as either of them lived she would be able to hurt him.

He saw that Charlie had been cleaning his gun and preparing it for hunting. It was propped in a corner behind the door, and Jeff thought swiftly that it was probably loaded and ready for use.

The thought gave him a certain bitter comfort. But first he wanted to have his answers to the questions he must ask—if he could remember them. His head ached sharply and insistently. Unconsciously he put up his hand to touch his forehead.

"Come in, Jeff," Charlie said. There was kindness in his voice. "You ain't eat nothing much since breakfast. You sure be hungry now. Too much hot weather we been getting. Maybe it rain tomorrow. Then we go partridge hunting, Jeff."

"I want to know some things," Jeff said in a low, strained voice.

They both looked up at him curiously, and he saw Lorena's lip curl.

"What do you want to know, Jeff?" she asked quietly. "Maybe there are some things we'd like to know too. Why did you go behind my back and not tell me what you were going to do today? Why did you make a fool of yourself in front of everyone?"

"Those things can wait," Jeff said. "Never mind that now. This must be first."

"Well, then, what is it?"

"I want to know," Jeff said, his voice faltering, "I want to know how long you've been carrying on behind my back, you and Charlie? I want to know—"

"Behind your back?" Lorena said. "What do you mean? We've all lived here together. There's nothing you haven't seen."

"I wonder if that's true?" Jeff said. "I think you wouldn't hesitate to lie to me."

"I've never lied to you," Lorena said. "It wasn't worth the trouble."

"No, I suppose not," Jeff said. "No. I was so blind and gullible you didn't need to lie."

"Come on, Jeff," Charlie said. "Eat something. We ain't mad about this afternoon. I tell Lorena, maybe what you said was good. It don't make any difference anyhow."

"This afternoon?" Jeff said. "No that doesn't make any difference. But the letter does. I found the letter. Now I know, only I have to hear it with my ears too."

"What are you talking about?" Lorena asked. "I don't know what you're talking about."

"Don't you remember then?" Jeff asked. "You've written Charlie so many letters, you don't remember which one?"

"I never wrote a letter to Charlie in my life," Lorena said.

"So you don't lie to me, do you?" Jeff said.

"No," Lorena said. Something in his face frightened her. "Jeff, you're losing your mind. Stop all this nonsense."

"I have lost everything—everything else," he said, "but not my mind. My mind keeps right on ticking. It's my mind now that has to have some straight answers. Then I won't bother you any more. I want to know how long. How long have you and Charlie been carrying on together?"

"I tell you *no,* Jeff," Lorena said. "Charlie is good to me. He makes me laugh. That's all there is."

"How long?" Jeff said. "That's the important thing. Don't bother to lie. Only tell me how long."

"But why?" Lorena asked.

"It's because of Ollie," Jeff said. His voice faltered on the name. "I must know that. Was he mine, or was he—"

He saw them look at one another, really frightened at last. He felt a kind of giddy triumph. But Charlie said quickly, "All this silly talk, Jeff. Come, sit down. Eat supper."

"I must know," Jeff said. "This is the time to tell me."

Lorena rose from her chair and turned away from the lamp-light.

"Jeff, I don't know," she said.

"Then you admit that you and Charlie—"

"It was a long time ago," Lorena said in a low voice. "Since then there hasn't been a thing between us but friendship."

"I really don't care about that," Jeff said. "It was only about Ollie that I wanted to know. And you can't tell me?"

"No," Lorena said.

All three were standing now, looking at each other. It was very hot in the room and an insect of some kind bumped and hummed in the rafters.

Finally Jeff stirred. "There has to be an end to everything," he said. He moved quite slowly toward the corner of the room and took up Charlie's gun.

Suddenly Charlie sprang into action.

"No, Jeff," he cried. "No! There ain't no need for trouble. Put the gun down. It's loaded."

"That's what I hoped," Jeff said.

"Don't be dramatic," Lorena cried. "My God, it wasn't anything. If you wanted to be jealous, you might have started long ago with your Uncle Ralph. I loved him once better than any other man."

"I think I knew that too," Jeff said. He felt calm and determined now. His hands did not tremble at all. The smooth metal on the barrel of the gun felt cool to his touch. He heard Charlie crying to Lorena, "Out! Quick! Get out of the cabin. He's going to shoot!"

"Yes," Jeff said. "I'm going to shoot. We've been coming along the trail to this moment ever since we started homesteading. There's no use running. This is the end of it."

But Lorena ran past him, crying, into the clearing, and he had to shoot quickly before he enjoyed the full satisfaction of power and authority that had begun to come to him with this moment. He would have liked to take it slowly, and do it the right way. But Lorena ran past him, and the hurried shot he fired went over her head.

He heard her running toward the trail, screaming, but Charlie Duporte was still there, moving toward him.

"You said I ought to make her scream, Charlie. You said—"

But Charlie was sudden as a cat and stronger than Jeff. He caught the gun and wrenched it from Jeff's hands. In the end it was Jeff who ran into the clearing and felt the sharp sting of a bullet in his back.

Bundy Jones heard the two shots as he rode down the trail. His first thought was for the safety of the tinder-dry woods.

This summer everyone had abandoned the practice of firing a shot as a warning of approach. To shoot in these woods was a desperate resort. What fool is shooting off his gun tonight? he thought.

Then he heard Lorena screaming. He knew the sound now, knew it intimately and terribly. He put his horse to the trot, and soon he heard her crashing along the trail toward him, panting and crying. He saw her hands and face, white in the starlight, lifted toward him.

"What is it?" he asked. "What has happened?"

"It's Jeff," she sobbed. "He tried to kill me. I think he's killed Charlie."

"Stay here," Bundy said. "I'll go and see." Somehow none of this surprised him.

When he reached the clearing, the lamplight streaming from the open door of the cabin lit up the blades of grass, the pine needles, the stony ground in a luminous trail. Bundy saw that a man was lying in the clearing at the edge of the lamplight and that another man was bending over him.

"Jeff!" he commanded, "Put down your gun! What's the matter here?"

But it was Charlie who looked up at him, his eyes dilated with terror.

"It was an accident," Charlie said. "I been cleaning my gun to go hunting. It went off accidental. Was all an accident."

Bundy knelt hastily beside the man lying on the pine needles, and he saw that Jeff Carney would never tell his side of the story to anyone.

VIII

THE BURNING

1.

Bundy listened to what they were willing to tell him, but he saw that there was only one clear course. They must take Jeff's body to town and turn everything over to the orderly manipulation of law and justice. It is difficult to transport a man's body in the wilderness. In the end they sewed the body into two blankets and laid it across the back of Bundy's pack horse.

"If we could bury him beside Ollie—" Lorena said. She had wept a good deal, and her face was pale and her eyes swollen.

"No," Bundy said. "I'm sorry. It has to be this way."

The hardest thing he had to do was to break the news to Meggie. She took it very quietly, with a surprising courage. Yet he could see that she was all alone in her particular grief. She held herself away from Lorena and Charlie, and from Bundy too. There was nothing they could do to help her because the events of the past days had in various ways made them all strangers to her.

So the four of them started up the trail to the mountain on the eighteenth of August, with Jeff's body like a large, unwieldy bundle bent across the back of a horse. It was past noon before they were ready to go. Jeff and Bundy's saddle horses carried the two women. The men walked beside them.

Lorena kept talking in a shrill, broken voice. "It's this place, this homestead. Everything bad has happened to us here. He was losing his mind—the way he talked yesterday at the meeting! We were all right till we came here. This place made us all cruel and bad. All of us. It's destroyed us. Everything has gone."

275

"Rena," Meggie said in a steady voice, "stop talking now. It can't do any good."

"Meggie's right," Charlie said. "Rena, you got to think it was an accident. We couldn't help. It was too bad. Don't think now, Rena. Let it alone now till we get to Cold Spring. Then someone else decide it for us." But Lorena scarcely heard them.

"I used to tell him," she said, "that he carried the past around on his shoulders like a packsack. Now it's me who's got it. The past is on my back now, and I won't ever lay it down. It will be there—always—always—"

"Keep still, Lorena!" Bundy said sharply. "It's too soon yet to begin feeling sorry for yourself. Keep thinking of Jeff a little longer."

"Oh, you're cruel!" she cried. "I'm thinking of Jeff now more than I ever have before in my life, and I hate myself for what I've done to him." She began to sob.

They climbed up out of the valley in light dry heat that did not lessen as they reached higher altitudes. The horses strained upward, their hides streaked and darkened with sweat. Nothing moved in the forest. The air hung motionless. Even as darkness fell, the heat continued.

At the halfway cabin the two men lifted Jeff's body from the horse's back. It was necessary to let the animal rest and graze during the night.

"We'll have to keep watch beside it, Charlie," Bundy said. "It isn't safe here unless we do. We'll let the women have the cabin."

"Sure thing," Charlie said. "We do the best we can."

Lorena was exhausted by emotion. She lay down on one of the bunks and fell asleep.

Meggie began to make preparations for supper and the night. The men would be hungry. Life kept going on. It had to go on.

Once she paused and looked at Lorena, lying awkwardly relaxed across the bunk. The dark hair was loose behind the head, the lashes lay like a deeper shadow on the blue shadows under the eyes. Lorena looked older than when she had first come here, yet she was still very beautiful.

It's hard to realize, Meggie thought, that beauty and virtue are not entirely the same thing, that where the one exists the other does not necessarily follow. But I'm trying to judge. I have no business to judge, Meggie thought. Even now, after Jeff's death, however it had come about, Meggie felt moved by Lorena's defenseless beauty. She saw the twitching of a nervous muscle in the cheek, heard the half-uttered moaning cry, and she was sorry for Lorena. Angry with her, yet sorry. Sometimes Meggie had envied Lorena, but that feeling, at least, she knew would never come again.

When Meggie lay down on her bunk, her dog jumped up beside her. She did not tell him to get down. He's about all I've got left, she thought dully.

In the night Meggie awoke to a new sound and feeling in the air. There was a gentle sound of rustling in the treetops. At first she thought it was rain, and a kind of happy relief seized her. They had been hoping for rain so long—it was the wish on everybody's tongue.

But then she felt that there was some mysterious and forgotten trouble in her mind which even rain would not cure. Somehow she had no right to be happy. She struggled wider awake, and then she remembered that Jeff had been shot. How or why, she did not quite understand. Charlie kept saying it was an accident. Lorena had said that Jeff had tried first to kill them. Yes, the pain and the trouble were real, and even rain would not wash them away.

Now she lay listening with all of her faculties awakened. She had grown very well acquainted with the sounds and moods of weather in the forest. She knew now that there was no rain, no moisture in the air. It was as dry as ever, but a breeze had begun to blow. It sighed and muttered through the tops of the trees. Somewhere a door on a loose hinge slammed and rattled. Presently she heard Bundy Jones calling to them, and the note of anxiety in his voice was as apparent as the note of menace in the wind.

"Yes," Meggie said. "I'm awake. What is it?"

"What is it? What is it?" echoed Lorena, sitting up in terror.

"The wind is coming up," Bundy said. "I think we had better get started. I don't know what this is going to do to the fires. We've got to get to Cold Spring."

They arose in windy darkness, hurrying blindly. They did not wait to prepare food. The heavy burden of Jeff's body was loaded again onto the pack horse.

When they came over the pass and out onto the bare side of the mountain, it was beginning to grow light. But smoke hung in a heavy cloud below them and here and there bright patches of flame flickered and glimmered through the murk.

"It look bad," Charlie said.

"They're old fires," Bundy said, "fires that have been trenched in and banked. But if the wind gets worse, all hell's liable to break loose."

Suddenly Meggie said, "Nan O'Rourke is alone in the valley. She's the last one down the trail. I promised her I wouldn't go out of the valley without her."

They gazed at her incredulously.

"You can't go back now," Bundy said. "It's too late. All of them in the valley were warned. The cabins we passed yesterday were deserted. Taggart's, Smith's and Klein's. After the meeting I think they all pulled out."

"But Nan didn't," Meggie said. "She went back down the valley. She made me promise. I said I wouldn't go without her."

"How could you remember?" Lorena said. "Everything has changed since you promised. She has two legs like the rest of us." Lorena had regained some of her composure today. She was pale, but she had slept heavily, and she no longer wept.

"But you don't understand," Meggie said. "It's something special with Nan, ever since the wolves last winter. She won't go without me, because I gave my word to let her know."

"You had your brother to think of," Bundy said. "We must think of him now."

"But my brother—we can't help him any more," said Meggie in a choked voice. "Nan is alive."

For a moment Bundy did not know what to do or where his duty lay. Nan, alone at the end of the valley, might not be aware that a southwest wind was raising havoc on this side of the mountain, possibly cutting off escape.

Yet it was imperative to get Jeff Carney's body quickly into Cold Spring, to let Lorena and Charlie tell their story to someone in authority before the outlines of the episode had lost their clarity.

In spite of what had happened, Bundy still had confidence in

Lorena's and Charlie's good intentions. On the strength of this, he made a quick decision.

"I will go back to the valley with Meggie," he said. "You two must go ahead to Cold Spring, as fast as you can."

"You take the three horses," Meggie said. "You'll get to town faster that way. I'm as good a walker now as a man."

"Yes, it's the only way," Bundy said. "When you get to Cold Spring, Charlie, send horses back for us. Send one for Nan and any others they can spare. There will be more fire crews coming out here with this wind blowing. Tell them to look for us. We'll join you in town tomorrow or the next day at the latest."

"I do that," Charlie said. "I come myself, Bundy, if they let me."

"All right," Bundy said. "It's all agreed. If everything works out—"

Meggie walked ahead of him quickly, but with a steady and relaxed stride that indicated endurance. Bundy was deeply troubled. He did not like this digression, yet he admired Meggie's courage and resolution in insisting on it.

They had made other silent excursions together when Bundy's thoughts had been elsewhere. Now he felt an uneasy preoccupation with the small, purposeful figure ahead of him. He had never found the opportunity to say to her what he had turned back to say before death intervened. He wanted to speak to her now, if only to express the most perfunctory sympathy, or share the anxiety he felt. But somehow the straightness of her back forbade it. After all, what could really be said? And she seemed composed and competent in spite of everything.

Finally it was Meggie who spoke first.

"It doesn't sound like the way Jeff would act," she said. "I can't—I can't see why."

"All I know for sure," said Bundy, "is that Lorena's innocent. She was running up the trail crying when I heard the second shot. She said that Jeff had tried to kill her and she thought that he had killed Charlie."

"He had been pushed around for a long time," she said. "But say Lorena didn't do it—don't say she's innocent. That's a big word, somehow."

"I'm not surprised you're bitter," Bundy said.

"No, I'm not bitter," Meggie said. "I've just been standing by watching. I can't help that." Her face looked drawn and pale as she turned it toward him.

Before they were halfway down the mountain to the valley, Bundy stopped.

"I hear a pack bell," he said. "Someone is on the trail below."

There was a sound of climbing horses and creaking saddle leather, and a nasal voice floating up from a switchback on the lower trail.

"—got all these crews in here. It ought to be easy. I done my fire fighting alone. Got a pick and shovel. No one ever give me a crew to do my digging for me."

"It's Eye MacGillicuddy," Meggie said.

"Well, you never had a summer like this, did you?" replied a sharp voice. "Maybe you never asked them for a crew of men."

"And there's your friend," said Bundy. "We won't have to go all the way down the valley after all."

The ears and mane of Eye's saddle horse appeared bobbing and straining upward through the screen of bushes. A dog began to bark, and Meggie's dog answered it.

The powerful wall of fortitude that Meggie had built up and somehow maintained through the past hours suddenly began to crumble. She ran toward them blindly, crying out, "Nan! Nan!"

They came around the bend of the trail before she reached them, Eye MacGillicuddy ahead riding his horse, and behind him on his pack horse, Nan O'Rourke.

"Well, Meg!" cried Nan reproachfully, "you never told me you were going after all. If MacGillicuddy hadn't happened by, I might have burned to a crisp, and no one been the wiser."

"We were coming back for you," Meggie cried, and suddenly she burst into tears.

"Oh, Nan!" she sobbed, "an awful thing has happened! An awful thing!"

She stood in the trail holding up her hands to the older woman in a flood of unrestrained grief.

"Now, now," said Nan soothingly. "What's the matter, Meg? What is it, Megeen?"

Nan got off her horse and put comforting arms around the girl's shoulders. Meggie's wild sobbing shook Bundy unaccountably. He saw that her courage had been a brittle surface that had protected her among strangers and enemies, but that broke down when she felt herself among friends.

2.

If he had not been involved in the necessity of reporting Jeff Carney's death and setting justice of some sort into motion, Bundy would have turned Meggie Carney over to her friends and gone his own way. To find Matt and his crew, or any crew, and throw himself wholeheartedly into the battle against fire, seemed to him the best thing he could do. But it was not so simple.

The four of them must get to Cold Spring quickly and with what good will they could muster. Nevertheless he felt the chill of their hostility. His part in the meeting at Jeff's place would still rankle in the women's minds, and Eye would know now, having heard it from Nan and perhaps a half dozen others, that Bundy had come from Washington to spy on him as well as on the homesteaders. Eye was sharp enough to realize that if they had trusted him in Washington, Bundy would have been sent to work with him, not against him. Yet the older man said nothing. They walked together up the trail, the two women riding the horses. What talk there was concerned Jeff Carney.

Nan was the only one who brought Bundy's name into it.

"If you hadn't got him into such a situation at that meeting, Mr. Jones," she said formally. "Couldn't you see it wouldn't do any good, and poor Jeff making a target of himself with the lot of us? Anyone in the valley might have felt like shooting him. With all you've done to us, couldn't you have skipped that?"

Bundy said steadily: "Maybe you'll never believe me, but the whole idea of the meeting was Jeff's. He planned and wanted it. He asked me to help him. I was willing to go along with him."

"So now he's dead!" Nan said. Bundy saw no reason to pursue it.

The sun was a round red ball in a smoky sky, but the wind brought no relief from the heat. The horses' hides were streaked with sweat as they climbed, sweat ran down the men's faces staining their shirts, sweat streaked Nan's hair and stood in little beads on Meggie's upper lip.

"If it would only rain!" she said with a long sigh. Her burst of emotion on seeing Nan had spent itself. She was quiet again, her mouth held firm in a line of determination.

Now they were again at the top of the mountain and over the pass. There the hot dry wind swirled up around them, carrying gusts of smoke and a faint roaring sound that suggested the rushing of far-off rivers. That sound, like rushing water, and the sudden movement of air gave a momentary illusion of coolness. Yet, going down the mountain on the other side they continued to sweat.

The horses were restless and nervous.

"Damn fools!" Eye said. "They ought to be used to fire by now. They seen enough of it. But a horse doesna have sense or memory where fire's concerned."

"Do you really think we can get through to Cold Spring, Eye?" Nan inquired.

"Ask the authority here," Eye said mildly, nodding his head toward Bundy. "He ought to know."

"Yes, we'll get through," Bundy said tersely. He refused to entertain the idea that anything could stop them.

The lower they went, the more completely they were enveloped in blowing smoke. But the trail was clear, and the trees along the trail had not yet felt the breath of fire.

"If we can get to the river before dark, we'll be all right," Bundy said, "even if we have to spend the night sitting in the water. The other side of the river ought to be clear enough with all of Cold Spring to fight the local fires."

"You hear him?" Eye said amiably. "You ladies got no cause to worry."

Large and small animals began to run or hop along the trail, too intent upon a clear track to the river to fear the horses and humans who were traveling in the same direction. First there were rabbits and a waddling porcupine; then a deer ran swiftly by, its white tail flashing into the gloom ahead.

This added to the sense of strangeness which the horses felt. They began to shy and rear and to try whirling back on their tracks. Finally the two men were obliged to lead them.

Eye's little three-legged bitch rode behind Meggie in her accustomed perch behind Eye's saddle; and Meggie's Mac followed close to the horses' heels. He, too, was infected with the general apprehension. He whimpered as he trotted along, his tail curled under his body as if to make himself as small as possible.

The heavy smoke caused their eyes to smart and constricted their throats. Eye had water in a small canteen, and now he made them wet handkerchiefs or bandanna neckerchiefs and fasten them over their noses and mouths. It somewhat eased the breathing and cooled their hot faces.

The things that made them most uneasy were the running animals and the roaring sound that grew and grew until it seemed to fill the forest. The sound no longer suggested the cool uproar of a river; now it was dry and hot, a rumbling noise of menace and anger. It seemed to fill the ears and overflow into the pores. It surrounded them like the smoke.

Cinders and sparks had begun to fly on the wind, and suddenly Meggie saw the scarlet and yellow flash of flame in a tree. There was blue in it, too. It spurted up quickly like the striking of a match, blazed hotly a moment in the dry needles, then disappeared.

The horses were wild now, rearing and plunging.

"Holy Mother of God!" Nan cried. "I've tried to lead a good life. Forgive me my sins. But let me off this damned horse. Let me off."

"Keep your prayers to yourself now, woman," shouted Eye. "Save your breath. Happen ye'll need it."

Still the horses grew more and more difficult to manage. When they came upon a bear with its hair half burned away, lumbering along the trail ahead of them, Nan's horse broke away from Eye's guiding hand and bolted back toward the mountain. Eye ran after it, shouting and cursing, but the horse was terrified beyond control.

For a few moments Nan clung to the saddle, and then she gave up and tried to jump free. She fell heavily with one foot still caught in the stirrup. The horse dragged her for several yards before her foot came loose. She lay still beside the trail while the horse galloped away. They could hear its shrill neighing as it ran, like a trumpet of disaster.

Meggie's horse neighed shrilly in reply.

"Let me get off," Meggie said.

"You sit where you are," Bundy answered sharply. "Hold the horse steady. We need the horse and blankets and water he's carrying, and I've got to help Eye with Nan. I'm going to let go the bridle and you've got to manage him. Do you understand?" His voice was harsh.

"Yes," Meggie said. "I can. Let go then, will you?" She was angry, too, angry enough to put all the strength she had into a momentary mastering of the frantic horse.

By the time Bundy and Eye reached her, Nan was sitting up beside the trail, looking about her in a daze. The dogs ran up to her sniffing and crying. Meggie's dog began to howl, Jessie to bark.

Eye MacGillicuddy leaned over Nan and peered incredulously into her white face.

"Ye can't kill her," he said to Bundy. "Look how she's comin' out of it. The old lass is sound as a rock."

"How it is, Nan?" Bundy asked.

"I'm shook up," Nan said. "Oh, Lord Jesus, am I ever shook up!"

"Take your time," Bundy said. "Do you hurt anywhere in particular?"

"It's my back and my arm," Nan said. "I don't know yet, but I think my legs will hold me. Where's the damned horse?"

"He's away up the mountain," said Eye. "You fool woman, why did ye try to jump?"

"I was scared," Nan said simply. "Maybe you never been scared?"

"I'm scared now," Eye replied with equal candor and simplicity.

"And I'm hurt too," Nan sobbed. "Maybe you better go and leave me."

"No," Bundy said. "We went back for you when we shouldn't have. We'll take you with us, no matter what."

"I'll walk and let her ride," offered Meggie.

"The horse can carry double," said Eye. "We'll get on faster that way."

They helped Nan up behind the saddle where Jessie usually perched. Bundy led the horse while Eye went ahead to make sure of the trail. The smoke was like a heavy fog, and it was difficult to keep on the track. All their efforts now were bent upon reaching the river.

Meggie thought of the river as she had thought of the halfway cabin on the February night when she had frosted her feet. It seemed the unattainable sum of all good, the mirage that was never to be captured. Still they kept going down toward it.

Now fire was visible here and there through the smoke. Sometimes it crackled fiercely and went out. Sometimes it gleamed with a sullen, static eye in rotten wood or moss.

Suddenly a half-burned tree came crashing down behind them. It missed the horse's haunches by a few feet, and the terrified animal whinnied sharply, and swung around, jerking Bundy with him.

Then they all saw that the falling tree had caught Meggie's dog squarely across the back and crushed him down to the trail. He uttered a startled yelp of anguish, and then lay still. Jessie danced to and fro before him, barking and howling.

Eye came back and tried to lift the burning trunk, but his efforts were useless.

"We've got to go on," Bundy said.

"Yes," said Meggie, almost in a whisper, as if to herself. "Yes, we've got to go on."

Eye took up Jessie in his arms and strode ahead. Bundy turned the horse's head and led it away.

Looking back, Meggie saw how her dog's eyes were fixed on their retreating figures, first with mute pleading, and then gradually glazed with insensibility.

Nan began to laugh hysterically.

"He was the last one of Jessie's pups," she cried, laughing and sobbing. "Remember how we stood around the cabin and looked at them, blind and squirming, and picked out which we would have? We were so hopeful and gullible. We didn't know at all what was ahead of us any more than they did. We didn't know how terrible and cruel the forest can be. None of us knew we'd better have stayed away."

"There, there, Nan," Meggie said, reaching behind her to touch Nan's hand.

"And it was a tree that killed him," Nan continued, wild with laughter and sobbing. "A tree! A tree! There's a tree in here for every one of us. A tree for each one, to fall and crush out life."

"Oh, Nan," Meggie said, "you've had too much. Try not to care. Think of the river now. It will be cool and safe."

"I'm beat," Nan sobbed. "My arm hurts like the devil. I think I musta broke it."

When they had gone a short distance, Eye returned for a conference with Bundy.

"It's all afire ahead of us," he said. "We canna get through to yon river now, I swear."

"We can't go back now either," Bundy said grimly. "Our best chance is to try to get through."

"There's Wilder's Creek off to the right," Eye said. "Seems like the fire's no so strong yet that side of trail. If we can make it, I ken a deserted mine shaft on Wilder's Creek where we could take shelter. Do ye trust me enough to follow me?"

"Yes," Bundy said, "we trust you, Eye. If you know a place, go ahead and lead us to it."

"Sit tight," Eye said to the women, "we're leavin' trail for rough country. Dinna waste breath in bawlin'."

"Let me have Jessie," Meggie said. "I'll hold her here in front of me. You'll have your hands free then."

They left the trail and turned northward, crashing through underbrush and ferns, over rocks and hollows. Sometimes they dodged trees that seemed to come at them suddenly from the gray fog.

Whether Eye was right or wrong, he had set his mind on some objective and was going for it as directly as he could. At least there was no fire here yet, but with the wind and flying cinders it could not be long in coming.

Bundy scarcely thought how odd it was that he should be following blindly where Eye MacGillicuddy led. They were taking the only chance that now seemed possible. He wondered vainly where Matt was. Where were those thousands of men who had been brought into the woods to hold back the fires? Much as he desired it, their personal safety seemed to Bundy a small thing compared to the burning of the forest. All this that he had been bending his efforts to conserve; all this that Pinchot had left in their keeping; what belonged, as he believed, to the people instead of to the lumber companies; what he loved because it was peaceful and beautiful and silent—it was all blazing now in a terrible inferno. Nature herself had prepared their defeat. It was a gigantic joke on man's feeble efforts to plan with reason and to conserve with sanity.

They began going downward rapidly now. The horse, which had lost its wild resistance for a fatalistic submission, slipped and slid on the mossy rocks. Suddenly they felt an upward surge of fresher air. Cinders and bits of charred wood still fell around them, but the breath was easier in their lungs.

"Here's the water," Eye said hoarsely. "You women get right into it. Bundy, untie my bedroll and get the blankets soaking wet. I'll go along a bit and see if I can find the mine shaft."

Nan needed help to get down from the horse. Her left wrist was badly swollen and she supported the left hand against her breast with her right hand. Meggie helped her to unlace the high boots and pull them off.

"Don't fret about your clothes," she said. "Get in. Get wet."

The water was low and it ran warm and full of floating debris from fires it had passed through. Still it was wet, and a fresher, cooler draught of air moved with it. Eye's little bitch hobbled into the stream and lay down, alternately lapping water and panting. Meggie waited no longer, but plunged her bare feet into it, and felt with rapture how it dragged at her riding skirt and went soaking upward to her knees. She caught up handfuls of water to press to her thirsty mouth and to rub over her smoke-blackened face. She helped Nan to drink and bathe her face and then they sat down in the water and let it run around and over them.

A shape reared up from the smoky bend of the stream beyond them, and it was a deer that had been lying in the water, panting. Now it moved on downstream, confused and frightened.

The horse stepped into the water, too, and drank deeply. His sides were heaving, and he made no effort to run away.

Bundy had unrolled Eye's blankets and was soaking them in the stream. They took the water slowly and reluctantly. He had to douse them up and down, pushing and squeezing them against the stones to make them soak up water. At the same time he was aware of the increasing roar of fire overhead, and he knew that they had reached this place of safety just in time.

In a moment Eye came running back, shouting, "God! She's a comin' over. Git down. Git down. There ain't no time to find the shaft."

They lay in the tepid water with the wet blankets over them, and heard the fury of the fire sweep through the branches overhead. It was a sound like the thundering of a gigantic freight train rushing across a high trestle.

Close at hand Meggie could hear Nan sobbing prayers and invocations out of her childhood. The men's hoarse breathing was also close and reassuring. She thought, at least I'm not alone in this. She thought, Blizzard and fire! If I survive, I've seen everything. Nothing left to be afraid of. And Jeff is gone and probably the homestead. Even the dog. But I can start again, if I live. I want to live.

3.

When the roaring had passed over, it was odd to lift the steaming blankets, and see a new world, black and stark, emerging from the smoke. Gradually they made their way upstream and found the mine shaft. There were two men in it, the only survivors of a crew of six who had been digging a fire trench a mile away. Both men were burned about the hands and face, and had lost food and equipment, everything but life.

Smoke and evening merged quickly into a heavy blackness. The wind still raged, but the fire had rushed on beyond them. Still it was unsafe to walk where the woods had been, because there were beds of hot coals and smoldering logs and moss that would not bear walking on for many days.

Eye was disturbed because he could not find his horse. Jessie was safe, but the horse had disappeared with the fire. He started out to look for the horse, but the smoke and gases were still too strong for his lungs. He came back coughing and gasping, glad to take refuge behind the wet blankets which Bundy had fastened at the entrance to the mine shaft.

Inside the shaft there was space for them to sit or lie, and reasonably untainted air came up to them from the depths of the earth.

Bundy had a little food in the packsack he had been carrying. He doled it out carefully among the six of them, and they disposed themselves as comfortably as they could for the rest that they needed for survival.

Eye kept fretting about his horse. "Poor creature! I wisht I'd put a bullet in his head. I owed him that much, but I didn't take time. Now I lost both my horses as well as my job, that went some time ago. Jessie an' me got only ourselves left."

"I'm sorry about your job, Eye," Bundy said.

"No," Eye said. "You pulled me out of it in time. I dinna envy any ranger this summer. He'll be blamed by all for not doing what no man could do."

They were all exhausted and most of them slept. The two fire fighters alternately cursed and snored; and Nan O'Rourke occasionally woke to groan or pray audibly. Meggie and Eye slept heavily, like tired children.

But the events of the immediate past would not let Bundy go. If he dozed for a moment, he came up sharply, hearing Lorena scream, or hearing fire roar through branches. He had the unreasoned feeling that here, in this deserted mine, he and these others were the last survivors on earth; that the forest was all gone and the world beyond it. Dark feelings took possession of him.

Even the unrealized expectations of the unknown miner, who had dug here for gold or silver only to find that the wilderness was reluctant to give up its wealth, weighed upon Bundy. He was haunted by futility: the futility of trying to save the forest, the futility of trying to homestead, the futility of trying to mine gold, the futility of loving where love could not be returned. He smarted to think that surface beauty could be raw and ugly underneath; that a man who was trying to remedy a past mistake might lose his life for his trouble; that things did not come out with the logical rightness that he had been brought up as a child to expect. Sometimes he wondered if Lorena and Charlie had been able to get through to Cold Spring, but that was a minor strand in the heavy fabric of his weariness and depression.

In fact Bundy was so much involved in disillusionment that, when it came, he did not at first sense the change of weather. Usually he was sensitive to the shifting barometer and knew by feel or smell what moved or threatened in the air above. Here they were as if already buried, and that in itself was part of his feeling of doom.

He heard someone moving in the confined space where they had all crowded for survival. Someone arose slowly and cautiously and groped to the mouth of the mine and drew back the hanging blanket.

Bundy raised his head and looked at the figure outlined against the paler rectangle of the doorway. Now, for the first time, he smelled and heard rain. Cool air rushed in with the lifted blanket, and rain was falling in a straight, gray sheet of water on the charred forest outside the mine.

He lay for a moment, incredulous, yet smelling sharply the bitter odor of wet burned wood, the acid perfume of settled dust, and hearing the rhythmic beat and drum of heavy precipitation.

Then Bundy got up quietly, too, and felt his way to the entrance.

"It's raining," he said in a hushed voice.

"Yes, it's raining," Meggie Carney said. "The fires will go out and things will grow again. We'll all survive."

Sometimes her optimism had made him uneasy; but now it lifted him up out of the darkness where he had spent the night. He saw her standing just outside the doorway with her face turned upward and her hands spread to the rain. Some impulse made him take her shoulders and turn her around to face him. When he kissed her, her face was wet and cool.

4.

It was almost a week before they reached Cold Spring. The rain fell in the valleys and unseasonable snow fell on the mountaintops. Yet fires still smoldered everywhere, and the crews of men that survived were kept busy chopping out underground fires and clearing trails which had been made impassable by falling logs and scattered debris.

The two men who had sheltered in the mine with Bundy and the others led them to the remains of a crew camp farther along the stream. Most of the cache of food was still intact, and the surviving crew members had returned to the base and were putting things in shape for living.

"You won't get through to Cold Spring yet," they said. "Better stay here and help us finish up. We need every man, and the ladies can earn their keep by cooking."

It was more of an order than a proposition, and the men who

issued it were a haggard crew, bearded and ragged, some of them painfully burned, others armed and arrogant.

Yet the thing that more than any other determined their stop at the camp was Nan's condition. Her wrist was broken, and she was hot with fever. Without a horse, even with a clear trail, it would have been out of the question to get her to Cold Spring. The men had bandages, and Eye volunteered to set and splint the wrist for her. It was painful, but he did a competent job and Nan felt easier after the wrist was strapped to a piece of board.

"Where did you learn doctoring, Eye?" Meggie wanted to know.

"Learned it on my dogs and horses," Eye said, regarding Nan humorously with his bright blue glance.

"No wonder it hurt so much," Nan groaned. "The old guy never thinks of anything but dogs and horses. He doesn't care a tinker's damn about a woman's aches and pains."

"Dogs an' horses never talk back," Eye said good-naturedly. "You do 'em a favor, they're plumb grateful and never say a word back."

Bundy and Eye worked with the men at digging out stubborn fires and clearing trail. Meggie took over much of the cooking. The crew cook was burned about the hands and face. She worked under his direction willingly and almost happily. It was an interlude of waiting between past and future. The horror had receded, the next step forward was not immediately visible.

Yet Bundy Jones had kissed her and that was a positive thing. It was associated in her mind with the relief of rain, with coolness, and a hope for the future. Now when he looked at her across the camp stove or the rough plank table, she felt herself coloring against her will. But he did not say anything or touch her again. She knew that he was deeply grieved by the burning of the forest. When he spoke to her it was about the delay, which fretted him, in getting to Cold Spring.

"Do you think that Lorena and Charlie got through?" Meggie asked.

"I think so," he said. "They were some hours ahead of us. I think they must have got through."

After the rain came cool bright weather, and the worst of the fire danger was over. Around them spread a black skeleton forest.

It was silent because the birds had died or flown away, and there were no leaves or needles to rustle and whisper in the breeze.

Now that the danger was past and the pressure of work slackening, the fire fighters began to laugh and joke again. They began to shave and wash their tattered shirts in the stream that still ran muddy and full of floating debris.

Meggie and Nan joined in the laughter and good-natured banter. One night after supper someone began to sing, and others joined in.

> "I bin workin' on the railroad,
> All the live long day,
> I bin workin' on the railroad,
> Just to pass the time away."

Someone said, "We ought to have Charlie Duporte here with his guitar. By golly, that fellow, he plays anything. That fellow's full of music, Charlie is—he was—"

Suddenly the speaker broke off and glanced uneasily at Meggie. No one had mentioned Jeff's death in her hearing, but she saw that they knew about it, and also they knew that Charlie was connected with it. An awkward silence fell. Then Meggie said steadily, "Yes, Charlie is a fine musician. He can play anything, anything you ask him for."

The moment passed, and they went on laughing and joking, but they did not sing again.

Suddenly Meggie felt tired out by the long strain she had been under. She thought, Have I forgotten Jeff? How can a week become an eternity and blot out everything?

Later she said to Bundy, "When can we go?"

"Tomorrow, I think," he said. "If Nan can travel, the trail should be broken through."

5.

In Cold Spring they were still burying unidentified bodies in a hastily contrived cemetery just above the meadow.

Thin-lipped and competent as ever, Mrs. Pulver said quietly, "One time we had six of them at once, canvas-wrapped bodies laid

out along the front porch in a row, and no preacher here to say anything over them neither. Next year we better get a preacher in here."

"Next year?" her brother Sam inquired. For once he was the
realist. "Next year we'll be out of here, my girl. Without the
timber, what'll be the use of the town?"

Gradually statistics began to emerge from the great fire of
August nineteenth, and it was estimated that some eighty people
had been killed, and over three million acres burned, with a loss of
probably eight billion feet of standing timber in the three states of
Idaho, Washington and Montana. Many little settlements at the
edge of the forest had been wiped out, and the sizable town of
Wallace, Idaho, had been partially burned. Cold Spring, because it
lay in an open meadow, had escaped, but, as Sam said, there was
probably no longer any reason for its existence.

Yet after the first bitter estimates had been accepted there
began to be reports that many regions had escaped, that sheltered
valleys here and there had miraculously been passed over by the
erratic fire.

"What timber's left standing and green, that's going to be
damned near worth its weight in gold," Sam said. "The fight for
what's left is going to be tougher than it ever was before."

Stories of endurance and heroism went the rounds. A fire crew
in the Thompson River country had clung to the bald granite face
of a mountain wall while the fire swept over them; many people
sheltered in streams and mines as Bundy's group had done. One
man told how he had lain next to a black bear in a stream, and
didn't know what kind of creature it was until they both came up
for air and looked into each other's eyes.

With a grim face Bundy questioned everyone, trying to sift the
mass of half-hysterical information for news of Lorena and Charlie.
No one in Cold Spring had seen or heard of them.

"They had time. They must have had time," Bundy kept insisting. "They were several hours ahead of us. If they had taken the
trail straight in to Cold Spring—"

Meggie looked at him with thoughtful eyes.

"You think they didn't come straight through," she said. She
felt very tired, and it seemed to her now that she did not care as
much as she should what happened to Lorena and Charlie. Perhaps

it was best to have the whole affair end in clean, consuming flames. To be done with it. If this was an inhuman thought, she could not bring herself to feel ashamed.

But Bundy was wracked by unfinished responsibility. He could not let it go.

"You must go back to your home in Opportunity," he said. "I will keep hunting and inquiring. I will let you know."

"My home?" she said. She wondered where it was. She kept thinking of the Floodwood Valley, and how peaceful and quiet it had been in the undersea light beneath the pines. Was this gone now, too? Did it all stand black and stark and open to the sky?

Mrs. Pulver took charge of her and Nan. Meggie found herself in bed between clean sheets after a warm bath in a galvanized washtub. Mrs. Pulver herself brought up a tray of nourishing food. Outside the window a pale gold light lay on the green meadows where the springs had bubbled up all through the heat and drought. There was even a bird out there on a fence post of the meadow, a yellow-breasted lark that sent an unanswered query musically upward in the evening air.

"We're alive," Nan said from the next bed. The doctor from Bolster, for once completely sober, had been brought to Cold Spring to treat burns and broken bones. He had put a fresh splint and bandage on Nan's arm and given her a swig of brandy. She was feeling better than she had felt for days. "It was his doing, too, the old coot. Maybe he isn't a good ranger from their point of view, but he knew where the stream and the mine was. He didn't forget me down the end of the valley either. You weren't the only one who thought of me."

Bemusedly Meggie thought, It isn't the doctor she's talking about, it's Eye McGillicuddy. But nothing mattered to Meggie now except the clean sheets and the comfortable bed. The light faded on the meadow and the lark's inquiring voice sounded farther and farther away until it was finally gone.

She did not know how many hours she slept, but when she awoke it was well along into the next day. She opened her eyes and saw Mrs. Pulver standing with arms akimbo against the brightness of the window.

"I guess you was tired," Mrs. Pulver said. "Dinner's about

ready and here's a letter for you. Nan's out to inquire when the stage is fixin' to go. She's rarin' to get to Opportunity."

Meggie took the letter and she saw that it bore neither stamp nor postmark.

"Bundy Jones left it," Mrs. Pulver said. But Meggie already knew who must have written it, although she could not remember that she had ever seen his handwriting before. The handwriting was fairly large, but clear and precise. Perhaps her heart leaped up too swiftly. The letter was as clear and precise as the handwriting.

My dear Meggie: I am going up to Wallace and Ste. Maries. Reports have come from both places of women, badly burned, coming out of the woods and being sent to hospital. I have not been able to ascertain names. Go back to Opportunity, and I will write you what I find out. I am sorry that I have been so inept in this as in everything. I can only crave your understanding and forgiveness, and say that I admire your courage.

Sincerely, Bundy Jones.

Meggie dressed slowly, and went down to dinner. She felt a trifle lightheaded and uncertain on her feet, as if she were convalescing from an illness. She kept thinking of Bundy hunting everywhere for Lorena, asking in hospitals, on street corners, in rangers' and sheriffs' offices, asking and asking. And it would be better if he never found out, she thought, but no one would be able to tell him so.

"We can get the stage out of here first thing in the morning, Meggie," Nan said. "We can get out, and nobody's ever going to make us come back, not if we don't want to. Let the money we've sunk go to blazes. We're still alive and kicking. I can still put blue roses and egrets on hats. I remember the first time I saw him that Bundy Jones objected to blue roses. Weren't natural, he said. I'm going to have my roses blue and purple and black now, any color I want. I don't know why I ever set out to homestead for easy money."

"So you girls is clearing out," Sam said. "You know what I heard this morning? I heard the Floodwood Valley ain't been touched."

"Don't tell me," Nan said. "I don't want to know."

"Yep," Sam said. "I heard it ain't been touched. Maybe you'd just have had an easier time if you'd stayed in your cabins."

"I would have stayed there," Meggie said, "only—" Her voice faltered. She found she could not speak of Jeff to anyone outside. Bundy and Nan and Eye had been through enough of it with her to understand, but the burden of explanation and a stranger's startled surmise was more than she had strength for at the moment.

Sam regarded her kindly. "I heard—we all of us heard how your brother was accidentally shot. If you was to ask me, I'd say they all lost life in the fire. You don't get through the woods so easy with a body on a horse."

Meggie said, "I've got to see if the valley's really unburned, Sam. Do you know anyone who's going in now? Will McSweeney be going in?"

"He's been fighting fire along with the rest of them. He won't be fixin' to take in any more homesteaders, is my guess. Reason I wasn't out fightin' fire myself, I got a lame leg. I wouldn't be no use to them."

"Meggie, don't be a little fool," Nan said. "You can't go back now, for heaven's sake!"

"They say MacGillicuddy's goin' back," Sam said. "I don't know why. He ain't got no homestead, he ain't ranger any longer, and he's lost his horses."

"He's crazy enough to do it," Nan said, "but he won't want to take a couple of women back in there. He just brought us out. He'll be fightin' mad if we ask him."

"I'll ask him," Meggie said. "If he won't take us, I expect the two of us could do it alone."

"Good Lord!" Nan said, "I just got through telling you I wasn't—"

It was like a miracle to come through the black devastation, over the mountain and down into the green valley beyond.

Climbing over charred logs that lay across the trail, struggling upward through a forest of blackened poles and stumps, they had not dared to hope that they would find anything. Yet the valley was green and fresh after the heavy rains. The earth smelled sweet and good after the sharp odor of burning that still hung over the devastated region.

They found the horse that had bolted with Nan, peacefully cropping grass halfway down on the valley side. He had stepped on his bridle reins and broken them; the saddle still clung askew to his back.

He came to Eye's hand with a wistful whinny.

"Good lad!" Eye said. "Things ain't all gone to waste. You women did the right thing to come back in here. If you'd gone straight in town, you'd a carried your fright in with you. Maybe you wouldna have come back at all. This is the best way."

Meggie stood once more under the great trees on her homestead, and tears ran unheeded down her cheeks. She opened the cabin door and saw that some passing crew of fire fighters had left the place in a mess. They had used her supplies, but all the familiar things were there: the stove, the blankets, the Bible, the broken mandolin. The mess could easily be cleaned up, the used food replaced.

With an equanimity which almost amounted to relief, Meggie saw Eye and Nan leaving to go on down the valley to Nan's place.

She felt that this was where she wished to be and how she wanted to live. She knew now, in an instant's clarity, that this was what the government meant when it asked one "to make a home." Yet the more genuine her sensation of homecoming was, the more she saw the difficulties of giving proof of good intention. Swearing would do no good. Thus, having consciously come home for the first time, she knew with instinctive fatalism that she was going to have a hard time making anyone believe her.

IX

THE HEARING

1.

Meggie sat in an anteroom in the Opportunity Courthouse waiting for her hearing to begin. The Kleins were in there now, trying to prove their good intentions. Almost a year had passed since the fire; it was the summer of 1911.

The homesteaders had all returned to the valley when they heard that the timber was intact. Doggedly, hopelessly, they were more than ever ready to fight for the contested claims. For some reason which Meggie did not understand, their hearings had been set for different places. Nan's had been set in Lewiston, although she had never lived there. Meggie and the Kleins were being heard before Judge Franklin Swift in Opportunity Courthouse.

"Judge Swift knew your father," Nan said. "What I suspect is that your Uncle Ralph has rigged it for you."

"I'd like to think so," Meggie said. Ralph was really her last hope. He had never done very much for them, but this was a matter which concerned him in a business way. Here was beautiful white pine at a time when white pine was at a premium. Surely, he would try to help the homesteaders, if he could.

She did not believe, however, that Ralph had had a hand in selecting Judge Swift to hear the informal proceedings. It was true that Judge Swift had been a lifelong friend of her father and of Ralph; but he had always been on the other side of the fence politically. He was a conservationist, and he had undoubtedly been picked in Washington because his sympathies were known there.

As she sat waiting, her hands folded tensely around the handbag which contained the notes she had made, she thought of the three letters she had written to Ralph about her homestead.

The first one he had answered, very kindly, in the tone of a father. The second which had been to reply to questions of his, and the third, which had been only to let him know the time and place of the hearing, he had not answered.

Seeking some clue to his intention, she went back over the one letter he had written her. There was reassurance in it. *Go ahead,* he had written, *and I will do anything I can to help. You must understand, of course, that I may not be able to do much. Washington has made an obsession of this distrust of the lumber interests. They suspect us of selfish interference before we ever make a move. Our hands are pretty well tied. But if at any time you need financial aid, be sure to let me know. My brother's child need never want while I have anything to give.*

Yes, he had offered financial help (offered, not given), but had he also known, as she well knew, that she would never ask for it? During the past year she had sold the family home and moved into a small apartment near the lumberyard where she still worked when she was not on the homestead. Debts of Jeff's had turned up unexpectedly on all sides. But now those were settled and her head was still above water. She could survive; and, if she could get the homestead, she could live in reasonable comfort as well as on a survival basis. No, she would not ask Ralph for money, but she felt no shame in asking for help in getting the homestead. It was Ralph who had started them on this long trail, and if it were possible to give it, he owed them help.

The rest of his letter had been concerned with Jeff and Lorena. He had asked questions which surprised her.

How was it with them? Were they happy together? You are sure it was an accident, are you not? And sure that they were all lost in the fire? So many people lost in the fire and never since accounted for! Lorena was a very beautiful woman. A loss! A great loss! Once I was fond of her. You know she was my secretary before she met Jeff.

Meggie had answered him cautiously. Hope came easily to her; caution was a trait which had been painfully acquired. But at last she had it. She wrote Ralph that Jeff and Lorena had been happy. To say anything else now seemed to her disloyal. She said the shooting was undoubtedly a most unfortunate accident. In her opinion, she said, Lorena and Charlie Duporte, unable to reach civilization with Jeff's body, had lost their lives in the fire.

She knew that Bundy Jones was not convinced of this. She had not seen Bundy since the day they returned to Cold Spring after the fire, but she had had letters. The forthright handwriting was familiar to her now, and she knew how he had gone on hunting for some trace of Charlie and Lorena, long after everyone else had given them up. What made him so sure that they had escaped the fire? she wondered. Was it only the time probability? Or was it a thwarted conscience, an unfulfilled sense of duty? Or a subconscious doubt of their innocence? Or a hope—a hope that Lorena's beauty was not blotted out? She thought about it a good deal, but she did not know the answer. Perhaps Bundy himself did not know.

Bundy had not come into the woods at all this final summer. She did not know what he was doing, because, even in the letters she had received, he had been entirely impersonal. In the past months she had been able to convince herself that she did not care where he was or what he was doing. Whether they had realized it or not, she knew now that he had always been on the opposite side of the fence from the homesteaders. She also knew that if he was in town now, as she had heard he was going to be, it would be to testify against her. Integrity, loyalty to an abstract principle, these could become disturbing and unnatural qualities among friends, Meggie thought. Yet at least you could trust a man with the trait of honesty. If he were against you he would not waver. You could count on that.

She had seen him waver only once, she thought, and that, as people liked to say, was probably the exception that proved the rule. Why should an exception prove a rule? She did not know. The logic seemed at fault. Still she sometimes dwelt in revery on his vulnerable moment. He had awakened to rain in the night after drought and fire, and he had found her standing in a doorway. Some impulse beyond will and reason had surprised him into kissing her. She wondered if he had since willed the incident out of his memory, or if he, too, sometimes remembered, perhaps cursing himself for a fool. It did not seem likely that he kissed easily, as some men did, without taking thought for the consequences.

2.

Mr. Halpert, Meggie's employer at the lumberyard, came in before the Kleins were through with their hearing. He had offered to be a character witness for Meggie, and she had gratefully accepted his offer.

"Aren't they through with these other homesteaders yet?" he asked. "It's getting late. Maybe they'll put you off until tomorrow."

"Oh, I hope not," Meggie said. "I want to get it over with. I don't know how I'd live through another night of uncertainty. I really don't."

"I think you'll win," Mr. Halpert said confidently. "You've put a lot of time and money in there."

When the Kleins finally came out of the small courtroom at the end of the upper corridor, they were tired and confused.

"How was it? How did you come out?" asked Meggie eagerly.

"They're going to let us know tomorrow, send us a notice or something," Klein said.

"They asked us a lot of questions," Mrs. Klein complained. "Trying to mix us up, I think. It didn't look so good to me."

"You know who's in there?" Klein asked. "Funny thing—old Eye MacGillicuddy turned up to say a good word for us. All cleaned up fit to kill, he was. And who was on the other side? You've guessed it. Bundy Jones. He was a slick one, foolin' us all the time, him an' Jeff Carney—"

"Shut up, Klein," Mrs. Klein said. "You've shot your big mouth off too much a'ready today, haven't you?"

"I didn't think," Klein said. "Excuse me, Miss Carney. Seems you've always been one of us. Them others—"

Meggie passed on into the room at the end of the corridor. It smelled of dust and varnish and old books and human anxiety and fear. Her heart was beating rapidly, but she held her head high and walked in with all the poise and calm that she could muster.

She caught a sharp, blue glance from Eye MacGillicuddy's

weathered face. He was, indeed, dressed "fit to kill"—at least he was clipped and shaved, dressed in a clean shirt and a necktie (probably the first he had ever worn) of a shade of blue to match his eyes. This was Nan's doing, Meggie thought. Lately when she had passed the millinery shop, a little three-legged bitch was often sitting outside, and the sound of voices, bandying insults and tall tales, came cheerfully from the rear room.

Nan would have sent Eye here today, she thought, and she was grateful, yet at the same time a little dubious. Would an ex-ranger, discredited, so they said in Cold Spring, because he was more devoted to a pet than to the forest, be able to do anything to help her? In fact, that Eye in all good nature and good faith was there, frightened her.

And Ralph? Was there anyone he could have sent who might have been less compromising? She could think of no one.

Beyond Eye, across the narrow room, she caught Bundy Jones's glance, somber and introspective. She found that she was able to nod to him civilly without reddening.

She sat in the chair Judge Swift indicated to her. The men had risen when she entered, and she saw that Matt Hinson was there too. They have gone all out to prove me wrong, she thought.

Judge Swift began by asking her a few simple questions: her name, her occupation, the description of the piece of land she wished to make hers. There was a stenographer who recorded her testimony, a clerk who made her swear to tell the truth. Her hand rested briefly on the Bible. Whenever she saw a Bible now, the log walls of the cabin rose around her. She had never needed a Bible in church, only in the forest with miles of snowy solitude around her and a cougar's yell outside, or beside an infant's grave, or on a peaceful summer night when nothing threatened her but loneliness.

"Yes, I will tell the truth," she said.

Matt Hinson began to outline the government's complaint, and she could see that he was here to take the burden of the opposition from Bundy's shoulders. The land was not fit for agriculture, he said. It was forest land and should be kept as such. The homesteaders had cleared small plots and built cabins, and a few years ago that might have been enough. But this was forest reserve, and it must be proved indisputably that the land was agricultural and not forest land before it could be given away to private ownership. What had the clearings and cabins and the sickly gardens really proved? Nothing at all, he said.

"I had a very good garden," Meggie cried. "Mr. Hinson never really saw it. Mr. Jones could tell you if he would. Mr. MacGillicuddy knows."

"Just a moment, Miss Meggie," said Judge Swift. "I'm going to give you every opportunity to tell your side of it. Suppose you begin now by giving us the date on which you started homesteading. Who was it located you on the place?"

"It was June 20, 1908," Meggie said. "I went with my brother, Jefferson Carney, and his wife, Lorena." Her voice faltered on the names, but she took pains to steady it for the next question. This was the duel now, the time when she must step quickly and surely as well as use a steady blade. To try to tell the truth and yet to win her case. Was it impossible? She did not know.

Judge Swift's questions came gently at first, but soon he fired them at her with acceleration of speed and intent. Matt joined him in the questioning. Meggie could feel the concentration of their eyes and their attention on her—Bundy, too, saying nothing, but watching, waiting for her to make a mistake.

Patiently Meggie described the improvements she had made on her homestead and how much they had cost her. She had the cost of everything in black and white. Judge Swift accepted her notes and glanced them over as he asked his questions. "Fifty dollars for a log barn. You needed the barn, I suppose, for your horses and cows, Miss Meggie?"

"Well," she said, "my brother had horses. Sometimes I used his or I hired horses from Mr. McSweeney of Cold Spring. You see, staying in there all summer, I needed horses only to come and go. Later I found that I could walk the trail."

"But the cows? The other farm animals?"

"I hoped to get a cow. I never did. Canned milk is easy to take in."

"Perhaps you will get a cow next year?" Judge Swift said.

"Perhaps I will," Meggie answered hesitantly, then added quickly, "Yes, certainly I will. I've tried to make a home there. Honestly I've tried."

With a quick shift of emphasis, Judge Swift called on Eye MacGillicuddy to testify.

"Miss Meggie, she's been in there every summer, and along every winter too," Eye said. "She started out a wee bit of a lass that every misfortune happened to, but she's toughened up now. I seen her grow up, as you might say, on that homestead. Now if she don't have a horse, like she says, she walks trail the way a man does. Oh, she canna tote so much gear on her back, but she's a sturdy walker all the same. She's got her a sourdough bucket and she rustles her own wood. One winter they was lost in the snow, trying to get in there. She froze her feet and had to stay alone in her cabin whilst the cougars yelled outside. Nearly a week it was, I guess, till Jeff and McSweeney was able to come back for her. But that didn't scare her out, nor fire neither. She lost her brother in there, too. What's she got left? Seems like she's earned her right to that homestead if any woman has."

"Mr. MacGillicuddy, you have always been a friend of the homesteaders, haven't you?"

"I never held them no grudge," Eye said.

"Isn't it true that you were more interested in helping them defraud the government than in defending the forest as you were sworn to do? Isn't that why you lost your job to Mr. Hinson here?"

"No," Eye said, "that isna true. I'd like to see the woods left as they stand. I don't want fire nor lumber companies, neither one, to lay waste. If you ask why I lost my job, Mr. Jones can likely tell you. I had a little bitch I owed a lot to. She needed help an' I give it, at a time when Mr. Jones thought I'd oughta been going after a fire. It was a wet summer, nothing much would a come of a couple hours' delay. It wasn't like last summer when hell-fire raged. Still it made a good excuse to put me down. Maybe I'm a sentimental feller, I don't know. Maybe I value people an' dogs an' horses over and above trees. I guess that's a crime in a forest ranger. I took the ranger job in the days when forests was under the Department of the Interior, when things was easy and friendly-like, before the conservationists got fighting mad about keeping the trees. I notice they havena done so well themselves the past year. But now I'm out of it, and when I see folk making a good fair fight to prove up on homesteads, I ain't afraid to say so. Not being inside their minds, I canna tell you what their intentions might be. But I know they've played square and gone through a lot. If they didna ken what they was gettin' into, they ken it now. I'd like to see 'em get what they have comin' to 'em."

"Well, thank you, Mr. MacGillicuddy," Judge Swift said. "That's all you need to say, I think. Now, Mr. Halpert, did you have some testimony for Miss Carney?"

Mr. Halpert testified as to the times that Meggie had been absent from her work at the lumberyard in order to live on her homestead.

"How could you get much good out of a secretary who resided a three or four days' journey into the wilderness away from her work, Mr. Halpert?" asked Judge Swift.

"Why, she wasn't the only girl I had working," Mr. Halpert said. "She worked when she was in town. I knew when I hired her that she would have to come and go, but we were short of help."

"You know, too, do you not, that she is Ralph Carney's niece?" asked Matt. "You're all in the lumber business together, are you not, Mr. Halpert?"

"No," Mr. Halpert said. "I never saw Ralph Carney in my life. He didn't have a hand in this at all. She came and asked me for a job, and I needed help. I didn't see any reason why I shouldn't hire her. She's been reared up and educated to be a lady, but I'll say Miss Carney took to business very smartly. She's a nice, smart girl, and what I'm here to do is to give her a good character. She's honest and fair, a young lady with a real good character."

"Yes, Mr. Halpert," Judge Swift said. "We all know that Miss Margaret has a good character. But she was very young when she went into this venture. Is it not possible that she was misled into believing that this was a quick way of making money? Isn't it true that the Carneys needed quick money about the time they went into this homestead business?"

"About that I can't say, Judge," Mr. Halpert replied. "All I know now is, I'd trust Miss Meggie to handle the money that comes and goes in the yard, and never have a doubt about her."

"Thank you, Mr. Halpert," Judge Swift said. "Now, Mr. Bundy Jones, I'd like to ask you a few questions. I believe you have known this homesteader from the time she went into the Floodwood Valley."

"Yes," Bundy said. "I have known Miss Carney since June, 1908."

"And you can doubtless corroborate her statements concerning the improvements she has made on this piece of forest land."

"Yes," Bundy said. "I believe that she has made a good effort."

He's been indoors this summer, Meggie thought. He's paler and thinner. It gave her a stab of gratification to see that he was not enjoying this. He hadn't wanted to come; he had made Matt take the brunt of it. Still he was here and answering the questions steadily. Surprisingly she found that she could still feel hurt and vulnerable where Bundy was concerned.

For a moment her attention had wavered from the drift of questions which Judge Swift was guiding toward a single end.

Then she heard his voice suave and guileless.

"You would say then, that she has made a home in the forest, Mr. Jones?"

"I believe that she has tried," Bundy said. "But this is not agricultural land. While the trees stand, this could never be a self-supporting home. The place is very difficult to get to. Everything must be packed or carried in across a mountain trail. At times of the year it is inaccessible."

"Is there any way to prove, Mr. Jones, that Miss Margaret did not intend to make a permanent home in the Floodwood Valley?"

Bundy hesitated. "Such things are difficult to prove," he said in a low voice, "what's in a person's mind—I don't know—"

"Do you recall, Mr. Jones, what Miss Carney called her place?"

"What did she call her place?" Bundy repeated. "Why, I—"

"They tell me that she had a sign over her cabin door," Judge Swift said. "Did you never see her sign, Mr. Jones?"

"Yes," Bundy said, "I saw her sign."

"And now, do you recall what it was she called her homestead, Mr. Jones?"

"Yes," Bundy said. "She called it 'Bide a Wee.' "

"But that was only in fun," Meggie cried out. "It was a kind of joke. It wasn't serious."

"In fact," said Judge Swift, "it was only an example of the lack of seriousness of purpose that has been demonstrated by all these homesteaders. A home? No, a place for a brief sojourn until the timber could be cut and turned into money. The name of Miss Carney's place tells us more in a minute than she is willing to admit in an hour of cross-examination. In fact, it is the clue to everything."

Meggie sat very quiet. She knew now what the verdict would be. She knew that the homesteaders had all been defeated before they ever cut a tree or laid up a log wall and chinked the cracks with mud. She also knew that she had understood this for a long time without daring to admit it to herself. But defeat hurt just the same.

3.

Meggie went blindly out of the courthouse, and began to walk toward her apartment. She remembered that Eye and Mr. Halpert had shaken hands with her and tried to say the polite and hopeful thing. After all the verdict had not been announced, they reminded her. Judge Swift would send her a notice of his decision.

"Thank you. Thank you," she said. "You were both so kind."

But all she wanted was to get away and walk in the fresh air, and then to go to the apartment and make herself a cup of tea. But when she reached the apartment she had no key to let herself in. She saw that she must have left her handbag lying in the chair where she had sat in the courtroom.

For a moment she was frightened out of her haze of disappointment into an acute awareness that this was no time to lose her wits. Her wits were what she had left to live by. To lose them now would be the last disaster. Above everything else she needed to keep her head. She needed the key, the small change, all the inexpensive items that were in her handbag.

It had been a cloudy and oppressive day, but, as she reached the courthouse again, the lowering sun broke through the heavy ceiling of clouds and sent long shafts of orange light across the lawn. Each spear of grass looked separate and intensely green. She went up the creaking wooden stairs inside the building and saw how the sudden flood of late sunshine brought out the dust, the stains, the worn grain of the wood that had been invisible earlier in the day.

It was late now and the building was almost deserted. She

could hear voices behind doors along the hall, but the room where her hearing had been conducted was open and empty. Her handbag lay on the chair that she had occupied. She picked it up and stood a moment in the empty room, going over everything again in her mind. Her mind was clear now, and she thought of the unreasoning confidence she had felt in some kind of personal intervention by her Uncle Ralph. Also she wondered if she had ever really believed that Bundy Jones would testify against her?

This room at the end of the corridor had windows only on the east side. It was growing dusky now. She stood still, thinking, remembering phrases. They tell me that she had a sign over her cabin door—and much further back, Miss Sourdough of Bide a Wee— Why don't you call it something else? Trail's End? Anything. But I'm stubborn. That's the name I gave it. I like to do my own way. But did she, really? Did she really want her own way? Or someone to help her find it?

Outside in the corridor, a door opened. It was the door from one of the rooms that faced the west, and a flood of the late sunlight came through it and made a yellow rectangle on the opposite wall of the corridor. From where Meggie stood, holding her handbag, she could not see the open door, but she could see the patch of sunlight on the wall opposite the door. The shadows of two men appeared in the patch of light.

She heard their voices, Judge Swift's and the voice of someone else who was familiar to her. She knew the deep and resonant, the hearty tone. What they were saying came to her sharply.

"—sorry to do it to Meggie, Ralph, but, you know—"

"Yes. I could not expect any more from you, Frank. The fact is, we have lost the round to you fellows. But another time—"

"Well, there's so much burned over, maybe it's not worth your while."

"What's left is more valuable, of course, than it has ever been. Yet this is a small and isolated region, and to lumber it out by itself would be an expensive operation. Better, I guess, to let you fellows think we're beaten here."

"No hard feelings, Ralph?" Judge Swift said.

"No hard feelings, Frank."

She saw the shadows shaking hands. Then one receded as if

returning to the room from which the western light came. The other figure seemed to be moving forward into the corridor, putting on his hat as he came; a large figure, growing larger and larger in the shadow on the wall until the bright spot was almost obliterated.

"—unfortunate for us—another time."

The voice, deep and resonant, diminished; the shadow passed across the rectangle of light; footsteps went purposefully down the hall and retreated on the creaking wooden stairs. The door closed. The rectangle of light disappeared.

For a moment Meggie stood silent, then some impulse sent her into the corridor, calling his name. "Uncle Ralph! Uncle Ralph!" But he had gone too far to hear her. He had been there, in the office of a friendly opponent to observe but not to intervene. He had not told her he was coming, or spoken to her afterward to say that he was sorry. She saw now that he could not have helped her even if he wished to do so, but he might have expressed regret or offered her some other alternative for the future. She had seen his shadow on the wall, and witlessly she had uttered his name. She was glad now that he had gone too far to hear her.

The empty rectangle of light still shone in her mind, like the reiterated image of the sun on which the naked eye should never look. Suddenly she thought that it symbolized her future, a block of light, empty of figures. What she could make of it, she did not know, but she alone was the one who must people it.

4.

Meggie walked slowly away from the courthouse for the second time. When she was within a few blocks of the apartment where she lived, she saw Bundy Jones coming toward her.

No, Meggie thought, this is more than I can take. This is too much. I cannot talk to Bundy Jones today. She thought that she would turn her head away and pass as if she had not seen him.

But he came straight toward her and stood in her way, lifting his hat formally as if he were a stranger. She had not remembered how much larger he was than she. She could not go around him. She stopped before him in despair.

"Excuse me, Meggie," he said. "I had to see you."

"Oh, no. No, please," Meggie said.

"You must listen," he said. "I've been to your place to see you. You didn't go right there."

"No, I forgot my handbag."

"Will you walk a little way with me? This has nothing to do with the hearing. It's something you have to know."

Meggie felt that she must say "no," and push on by him. Yet she made the mistake, for as far as concerned her resolution, of looking up at him. Their eyes met and held, and Meggie saw that he was deeply troubled. Something in the way he looked at her crumbled her resolution.

"Well?" she said.

He stood looking down at her, trying to speak, finding the words hard to come by.

"What is it, Bundy?" she asked finally.

"It's about Lorena," he said. "I must tell you about Lorena."

"But Lorena is dead."

"No," Bundy said, "she is not dead, Meggie. Lorena is not dead."

"Have you seen her?" she asked.

"Yes," Bundy said, "I have seen her. Will you put this afternoon out of your mind for a little and walk with me? I think I can tell it better walking."

"Yes, I will go a little way with you," Meggie said. She was cold with weariness and apprehension. Yet somewhere, far back in her consciousness, a ray of light was rising. Just to be walking along with Bundy again, if only for a passing moment.

"And Charlie, too, Bundy?" she asked.

"Yes, Charlie."

"Tell me," she said.

As they walked he began to find the words to tell it. But his voice was dry and hard, as if he felt nothing. Yet she saw that he had been shaken by some devastating experience.

"I'll make it as brief as I can," he said. "I can see that you are tired. But it will not take long. I haven't done anything about them yet. I must know how you feel before I proceed."

"How I feel," she repeated dully.

He rushed on now, speaking hurriedly. "I never thought they

were dead," he said. "I don't know why. But I couldn't let it go like that. I kept searching. I kept asking. I felt—well, I had let them slip away too easily."

"It was my fault," Meggie said. "Nan would have got out just as well if I hadn't gone back. You needn't keep on blaming yourself."

"Well, I have bungled lots of things. I know that. But last week, I heard that a man and woman were living in a little mining town in the hills. They had been through the fire and she had been very badly burned. The name was Charles, my informant said. The man was a French Canadian working in the mine. The woman had been a long time in a hospital after the fire, but now she was keeping house for the man. I don't know how I had missed them before. I had tried every lead."

"You thought it might be—"

"Well, I went up there to see. I didn't go to the house until evening when the man would be home from the mine. It was getting dusk, about this time of day. They had a lamp lit inside, and Charlie—he came to the door."

"What did he say?" asked Meggie.

"I said, 'Hello, Charlie,' and he said to me, 'Well, Bundy, so you're here?'

" 'Come in,' he said. 'Lorena will want to hear your voice. Lorena,' he said, 'it's Bundy Jones.' I saw her in the lamplight, standing by the table, and, Meggie, she had been terribly burned. She was blind."

"Blind?" Meggie said. "Oh, no! Not that."

"Charlie took me by the arm and he said to me, nodding and smiling, in a gay voice, 'You see her, Bundy. She hasn't changed, has she?' I couldn't speak at first. You see, she was terribly disfigured. 'Charlie Duporte would never have a woman who wasn't beautiful,' he went on in that light voice. 'You know that, don't you, Bundy?' "

"How horrible," Meggie said.

"I thought so too, at first. I thought, he's making ghastly sport of her. But then in a moment I saw he was serious. It was like a part in a play that he was acting, and this was a cue for me to take a speaking part."

"And you said?"

"I said, 'Yes, she has always been beautiful. She always will be.'"

Meggie heard the unsteadiness in Bundy's voice. Her own was low when she spoke.

"Doesn't she know, Bundy?"

"She was quite gay and natural. At first I thought not," Bundy said. "They asked me in and I drank coffee with them. Charlie told me a story, which I don't really doubt, how the fire surrounded them and they had to abandon Jeff's body in order to escape. It was while we were drinking coffee that I noticed first how her hand would steal up to her face and her fingers would follow one of the seams along her cheek. It was a furtive gesture but I think it was habitual. It seemed to me then that she must know, but that she was playing a part, too, for Charlie. It's very strange. She wasn't like the old Lorena. Meggie, I think they've found a kind of happiness together."

"And what did you do?" Meggie asked.

"I came away without doing anything," Bundy said. "I think we can make a case against them. After they left us, they did not come straight out to Cold Spring, but took another trail up toward Ste. Maries. They abandoned Jeff's body, as very likely they were obliged to do by the fire. But, when they came out, in the confusion of the disaster, they failed to report what had happened. They are living under another name. I think we could make a lot of trouble for them."

"A lot of trouble," Meggie said. "Bundy, we have had it, all of us, a lot of trouble."

"I know," he said, "but this is different. This is a special kind of trouble."

"I never really wanted to find them," Meggie said. "It was you who kept hunting and hunting."

"Well, I had to know," Bundy said.

"And now you do know. And you've got another case to fight, after you've defeated the homesteaders."

"This is your case," he said. "I brought it to you to decide. If you want this kind of satisfaction for the death of your brother, I'll help you all I can to get it."

"Nothing we can do will bring Jeff back," Meggie said. "Whether they are guilty or not, they have been punished."

Bundy drew a long breath.

"That was how I saw it," he said.

They continued to walk on without speaking. They had left the main streets of town and come into the residential section. Trees arched over them as trees used to arch in the forest. These were box elder and poplar trees, not Western white pine, still they rustled and were peaceful in the first dusk of evening.

"About this afternoon," Bundy said, clearing his throat. "I expect you wouldn't understand (how could you?) but I had a job to do. I went ahead and did it."

"I think I understand you better than you do me," Meggie said. "There was a time in there, a few peaceful weeks, when I had a home and intended to live in it and keep it. I really meant to make it a home, to stay, to love it, to have my little house under the trees."

"How long would the lumber interests have let you do that?" he asked roughly. "They'd have lumbered out all around you; they'd have made it very uncomfortable for you; they'd have beaten you out just as surely and more slowly and cruelly than we have beaten you."

"Yes, I suppose so," Meggie said, "but I've always enjoyed my dreams, such as they were."

"You see, I had a dream, too," Bundy said. "It was a dream of a planned and harvested forest that would thrive and go on growing for the greatest good of the greatest number of people. I wanted the exploitation to stop. There has to be some time, some place, where exploitation stops. You happened to be caught at the time and in the place."

"But can you ever really stop it? Isn't it something that will always come cropping up?"

"Yes, probably," he said, "but we can't stop fighting it. Don't you see that, if we do, it will overwhelm us?"

Meggie inclined her head. "Well, I gambled," she said. "I didn't know what I was getting into, but I wouldn't change it now. I gambled and I lost. I grew up doing it."

"I saw you grow," Bundy said. "I've grown up out here too,

maybe in a different way, but it's the same process after all, I guess."

"What will you do now?" Meggie asked.

"I'm taking a job in a small school, teaching botany, next year. It's a compromise with myself. I could keep on with the Forest Service, help reforest the burned areas, get a planned economy into operation. But other men will do that. There are plenty of them eager for the chance. But I've had enough now. I fought this through, but I've discovered that I'm not a fighter. To grow up partly means, I suppose, cutting down the dreams to the reality. I hope I'll make a reasonably good teacher."

"You write a good clear hand," Meggie said. Suddenly they both burst out laughing at the absurdity of her remark.

They walked in silence for a few moments after that. Then Bundy said in a low voice. "Someone, a long time ago it seems, once told me that I was too slow, too late. I think it's so. Yet sometimes it has operated for my own good. I'm late now, and slow. I've been about the nation's business and neglecting my own. I wonder, Meggie—"

Suddenly Meggie knew that he was asking her to help him. She had a strong impulse to hold out a hand to him, but another impulse restrained her. She might be going to go on all her life helping him, she thought, but not now. Not at this moment. This he must do by himself.

"Yes?" she said quietly.

"Meggie," he said. "After all that I have done to you, with the little I have to offer, do you think—I wonder—could we ever get together? I think I'm proposing, Meggie."

"You're doing very well, Bundy," she said. "And, yes, I think we could."

He took her hand and pressed it warmly into the crook of his arm. They kept walking toward the edge of town, under the arching trees. Lights were coming on in the houses along the street. They had forgotten that it was time for dinner.